JOHN HALIFAX, GENTLEMAN

MRS CRAIK

JOHN HALIFAX, GENTLEMAN

ALAN SUTTON

First published 1857

First published in this edition in the United Kingdom in 1991
Alan Sutton Publishing Ltd · Phoenix Mill · Far Thrupp · Stroud
Gloucestershire

First published in the United States of America in 1991
Alan Sutton Publishing Inc. · Wolfeboro Falls · NH 03896–0848

British Library Cataloguing in Publication Data

Craik, Mrs *1826–1887*
John Halifax, gentleman
1. Title
823.8

ISBN 0–86299–910–3

Library of Congress Cataloguing in Publication Data applied for

Cover picture: Jealousy and flirtation *by Haynes King (1831–1904). Photograph: courtesy of the Board of the Victoria and Albert Museum/Bridgeman Art Library, London.*

Printed in Great Britain by
The Guernsey Press Company Limited,
Guernsey, Channel Islands.

BIOGRAPHICAL NOTE

MRS CRAIK (1826–1887) was born Dinah Maria Mulock on 20 April 1826 at Stoke-upon-Trent, Staffordshire, the daughter of Thomas and Dinah Mulock. Her father was then minister of a small congregation. Her childhood and youth were much affected by her father's unsettled fortunes; but she obtained a good education from various schools and, feeling conscious of a vocation for authorship, Miss Mulock went to London in about 1846, much at the same time as two friends whose assistance was afterwards of the greatest service to her, Alexander Macmillan and Charles Edward Mudie.

Once there she rapidly made friends, and found great encouragement for the stories for the young which she initially wrote, of which *Cola Monti* (1849) was the best known. Thus began quite a prolific period of writing, for in the same year Miss Mulock produced her first three-volume novel, *The Ogilvies*, which obtained great success and was quickly followed by *Olive* in 1850. The authoress used her own recollections of East Dorset in her next two novels, *The Head of the Family* (1851) and *Agatha's Husband* (1853).

As well as these longer works of fiction, Miss Mulock continued to write short stories during this time; the fairy story *Alice Learmont* was published in 1852, and several short stories were published in periodicals during 1853, under the title of *Avillion and Other Tales*. A second similar collection, *Nothing New*, appeared in 1857.

Now firmly established as a successful authoress, Miss Mulock took a cottage at Wildwood, North End, London and was quickly accepted by and absorbed into London society. Her personal attractions were at this period of her life considerable, and her simple cordiality, staunch friendliness, and thorough goodness of heart perfected the fascination. In 1857 appeared the work by which she will be principally remembered, *John Halifax, Gentleman,* a noble presentation of the highest ideal of English middle-class life. This was followed, in 1859, by *A Life for a Life*, a novel perhaps more widely read at the time than *John Halifax*. Two more novels followed, in 1863 *Mistress and Maid* and in 1865 *Christian's Mistakes*, neither of which received any great acclaim.

The genuine passion which had upborne her early works of fiction had not unnaturally faded out of middle life, and had as naturally been replaced by an excess of the didactic element. Miss Mulock herself seemed aware of this, for several of her later publications were undisguisedly didactic essays, of which *A Woman's Thoughts about Women* and *Sermons out of Church* obtained most notice.

In her later period, however, she returned to the fanciful tale which had so frequently employed her youth, and achieved a great success with *The Little Lame Prince* (1874), a story for the young. She had published some poems in 1852, and in 1881 brought her pieces together under the title of *Poems of Thirty Years, Old and New*. They are a woman's poems, tender, domestic, and sometimes enthusiastic, always genuine song, and the product of real feeling. Several achieved a wide popularity.

In 1864 Miss Mulock married George Lillie Craik, Esq., a partner in the house of Macmillian & Co., and soon afterwards took up residence at Shortlands, near Bromley, where she continued until her death. She had become very intimate with M. Guizot and his family, and translated his *Memoir de Barante* and books by his daughter, Madame De Witt.

In her latter years Mrs Craik made tours of Cornwall and the north of Ireland, accounts of which were published, with copious illustrations, in 1884 and 1887 respectively. She died suddenly on 12 October 1887.

Mrs Craik's memory, both as a woman and as an authoress, will long be preserved by the virtues of which her writings were the expression. She was not a genius, and she does not express the ideals and aspirations of women of exceptional genius; but the tender and philanthropic, and at the same time energetic and practical womanhood of ordinary life has never had a more sufficient representative.

Based on a biographical note by RICHARD GARNETT

JOHN HALIFAX, GENTLEMAN.

CHAPTER I.

"GET out o' Mr. Fletcher's road, ye idle, lounging, little——"

"Vagabond," I think the woman (Sally Watkins, once my nurse) was going to say, but she changed her mind.

My father and I both glanced round, surprised at her unusual reticence of epithets; but when the lad addressed turned, fixed his eyes on each of us for a moment, and made way for us, we ceased to wonder. Ragged, muddy, and miserable as he was, the poor boy looked anything but a "vagabond."

"Thee need not go into the wet, my lad. Keep close to the wall, and there will be shelter enough both for us and thee," said my father, as he pulled my little hand-carriage into the alley, under cover from the pelting rain. The lad, with a grateful look, put out a hand likewise, and pushed me farther in. A strong hand it was—roughened and browned with labour—though he was scarcely as old as I. What would I not have given to have been so stalwart and so tall!

Sally called from her house door, "Wouldn't Master Phineas come in and sit by the fire a bit?" But it was always a trouble to me to move or walk; and I liked staying at the mouth of the alley, watching the autumnal shower come sweeping down the street; besides, I wanted to look again at the stranger lad.

He had scarcely stirred, but remained leaning against the wall—either through weariness, or in order to be out of our way. He took little or no notice of us, but kept his eyes fixed on the pavement—for we actually boasted pavement in the High Street of our town of Norton Bury—watching the eddying raindrops, which, each as it fell, threw up a little mist of spray. It was a serious, haggard face for a boy of only fourteen or so. Let me call it up before me—I can easily, even after more than fifty years.

Brown eyes, deep sunken, with strongly-marked brows, a nose like most other Saxon noses, nothing particular; lips well shaped, lying one upon the other, firm and close; a square, sharply-outlined, resolute chin, of that type which gives character and determination to the whole physiognomy, and without which in the fairest features, as in the best dispositions, one is always conscious of a certain want.

As I have stated, in person the lad was tall and strongly built; and I, poor puny wretch! so reverenced physical strength. Everything in him seemed to indicate that which I had not: his muscular limbs, his square, broad shoulders, his healthy cheek, though it was sharp and thin—even to his crisp curls of bright thick hair.

Thus he stood, principal figure in a picture which is even yet as clear to me as yesterday—the narrow, dirty alley leading out of the High Street, yet showing a glimmer of green field at the farther end; the open house doors on either side, through which came the drowsy burr of many a stocking-loom, the prattle of children paddling in the gutter, and sailing thereon a fleet of potato parings. In front the High Street, with the mayor's house opposite, porticoed and grand; and beyond, just where the rain-clouds were breaking, rose up out of a nest of trees, the square tower of our ancient abbey—Norton Bury's boast and pride. On it, from a break in the clouds, came a sudden stream of light. The stranger lad lifted up his head to look at it.

"The rain will be over soon," I said, but doubted if he heard me. What could he be thinking of so intently? —a poor working lad, whom few would have given credit for thinking at all.

I do not suppose my father cast a second glance of thought on the boy, whom, from a sense of common justice, he had made take shelter beside us. In truth, worthy man, he had no lack of matter to occupy his mind, being sole architect of a long uphill but now thriving trade. I saw, by the hardening of his features, and the restless way in which he poked his stick into the little water-pools, that he was longing to be in his tanyard close by.

He pulled out his great silver watch—the dread of our house, for it was a watch which seemed to imbibe something of its master's character; remorseless as justice or fate, it never erred a moment.

"Twenty-three minutes lost by this shower. Phineas, my son, how am I to get thee safe home? unless thee wilt go with me to the tanyard——"

I shook my head. It was very hard for Abel Fletcher to have for his only child such a sickly creature as I, now, at sixteen, as helpless and useless to him as a baby.

"Well, well, I must find some one to go home with thee." For though my father had got me a sort of carriage, in which, with a little external aid, I could propel myself, so as to be his companion occasionally in his walks between our house, the tanyard, and the Friends' meeting-house—still he never trusted me anywhere alone. "Here, Sally—Sally Watkins! do any o' thy lads want to earn an honest penny?"

Sally was out of earshot; but I noticed that as the lad near us heard my father's words, the colour rushed over his face, and he started forward involuntarily. I had not before perceived how wasted and hungry-looking he was.

"Fathei!" I whispered. But here the boy had mustered up his courage and voice.

"Sir, I want work; may I earn a penny?"

He spoke in tolerably good English—different from

our coarse, broad, G——shire drawl; and taking off his tattered old cap, looked right up into my father's face. The old man scanned him closely.

"What is thy name, lad?"

"John Halifax."

"Where dost thee come from?"

"Cornwall."

"Hast thee any parents living?"

"No."

I wished my father would not question thus; but possibly he had his own motives, which were rarely harsh, though his actions often appeared so.

"How old might thee be, John Halifax?"

"Fourteen, sir."

"Thee art used to work?"

"Yes."

"What sort of work?"

"Anything that I can get to do."

I listened nervously to this catechism, which went on behind my back.

"Well," said my father, after a pause, "thee shall take my son home, and I'll give thee a groat. Let me see;—art thee a lad to be trusted?" And holding him at arm's length, regarding him meanwhile with eyes that were the terror of all the rogues in Norton Bury, Abel Fletcher jingled temptingly the silver money in the pockets of his long-flapped brown waistcoat. "I say, art thee a lad to be trusted?"

John Halifax neither answered nor declined his eyes. He seemed to feel that this was a critical moment, and to have gathered all his mental forces into a serried square, to meet the attack. He met it, and conquered in silence.

"Lad, shall I give thee the groat now?"

"Not till I've earned it, sir."

So, drawing his hand back, my father slipped the money into mine, and left us.

I followed him with my eyes, as he went sturdily plashing down the street; his broad, comfortable back, which owned a coat of true Quaker cut, but spotless, warm, and fine; his ribbed hose and leathern gaiters, and the wide-brimmed hat set over a fringe of gray hairs, that crowned the whole with respectable dignity. He looked precisely what he was—an honest, honourable, prosperous tradesman. I watched him down the street—my good father, whom I respected perhaps even more than I loved him. The Cornish lad watched him likewise.

It still rained slightly, so we remained under cover. John Halifax leaned in his old place, and did not attempt to talk. Once only, when the draught through the alley made me shiver, he pulled my cloak round me carefully.

"You are not very strong, I'm afraid?"

"No."

Then he stood idly looking up at the opposite—the mayor's—house, with its steps and portico, and its fourteen windows, one of which was open, and a cluster of little heads visible there.

The mayor's children—I knew them all by sight, though nothing more; for their father was a lawyer, and mine a tanner; they belonged to Abbey folk and orthodoxy, I to the Society of Friends—the mayor's rosy children seemed greatly amused by watching us shivering shelterers from the rain. Doubtless our position made their own appear all the pleasanter. For myself it mattered little; but for this poor, desolate, homeless, wayfaring lad to stand in sight of their merry nursery window, and hear the clatter of voices, and of not unwelcome dinner sounds—I wondered how he felt it.

Just at this minute another head came to the window, a somewhat older child; I had met her with the rest; she was only a visitor. She looked at us, then disappeared. Soon after, we saw the front door half opened, and an evident struggle taking place behind it; we even heard loud words across the narrow street.

"I will—I say I will."

"You shan't, Miss Ursula."

"But I will!"

And there stood the little girl, with a loaf in one hand

and a carving-knife in the other. She succeeded in cutting off a large slice, and holding it out.

"Take it, poor boy!—you look so hungry. Do take it." But the servant forced her in, and the door was shut upon a sharp cry.

It made John Halifax start, and look up at the nursery window, which was likewise closed. We heard nothing more. After a minute he crossed the street, and picked up the slice of bread. Now in those days bread was precious, exceedingly. The poor folk rarely got it; they lived on rye or meal. John Halifax had probably not tasted wheaten bread like this for months: it appeared not, he eyed it so ravenously;—then, glancing towards the shut door, his mind seemed to change. He was a long time before he ate a morsel; when he did so, it was quietly and slowly, looking very thoughtful all the while.

As soon as the rain ceased, we took our way home, down the High Street, towards the Abbey Church—he guiding my carriage along in silence. I wished he would talk, and let me hear again his pleasant Cornish accent.

"How strong you are!" said I, sighing, when, with a sudden pull, he had saved me from being overturned by a horseman riding past—young Mr. Brithwood of the Mythe House, who never cared where he galloped or whom he hurt—"So tall and so strong."

"Am I? Well, I shall want my strength."

"How?"

"To earn my living."

He drew up his broad shoulders, and planted on the pavement a firmer foot, as if he knew he had the world before him—would meet it single-handed, and without fear.

"What have you worked at lately?"

"Anything I could get, for I have never learned a trade."

"Would you like to learn one?"

He hesitated a minute, as if weighing his speech. "Once I thought I should like to be what my father was."

"What was he?"

"A scholar and a gentleman."

This was news, though it did not much surprise me. My father, tanner as he was, and pertinaciously jealous of the dignity of trade, yet held strongly the common-sense doctrine of the advantages of good descent; at least, in degree. For since it is a law of nature, admitting only rare exceptions, that the qualities of the ancestors should be transmitted to the race, the fact seems patent enough, that even allowing equal advantages, a gentleman's son has more chances of growing up a gentleman than the son of a working man. And though he himself, and his father before him, had both been working men, still, I think, Abel Fletcher never forgot that we originally came of a good stock, and that it pleased him to call me, his only son, after one of our forefathers, not unknown—Phineas Fletcher, who wrote the "Purple Island."

Thus it seemed to me, and I doubted not it would to my father, much more reasonable and natural that a boy like John Halifax—in whom from every word he said I detected a mind and breeding above his outward condition—should come of gentle than of boorish blood.

"Then, perhaps," I said, resuming the conversation, "you would not like to follow a trade?"

"Yes, I should. What would it matter to me? My father was a gentleman."

"And your mother?"

And he turned suddenly round; his cheeks hot, his lips quivering: "She is dead. I do not like to hear strangers speak about my mother."

I asked his pardon. It was plain he had loved and mourned her; and that circumstances had smothered down his quick boyish feelings into a man's tenacity of betraying where he had loved and mourned. I, only a few minutes after, said something about wishing we were not "strangers."

"Do you?" The lad's half-amazed, half-grateful smile went right to my heart.

"Have you been up and down the country much?"

"A great deal—these last three years; doing a hand's

turn as best I could in hop-picking, apple-gathering, harvesting; only this summer I had typhus fever, and could not work."

"What did you do then?"

"I lay in a barn till I got well. I'm quite well now; you need not be afraid."

"No, indeed; I had never thought of that."

We soon became quite sociable together. He guided me carefully out of the town into the Abbey walk, flecked with sunshine through overhanging trees. Once he stopped to pick up for me the large brown fan of a horse-chestnut leaf.

"It's pretty, isn't it?—only it shows that autumn is come."

"And how shall you live in the winter, when there is no out-of-door work to be had?"

"I don't know."

The lad's countenance fell, and that hungry, weary look, which had vanished while we talked, returned more painfully than ever. I reproached myself for having, under the influence of his merry talk, temporarily forgotten it.

"Ah!" I cried eagerly, when we left the shade of the Abbey trees, and crossed the street; "here we are, at home!"

"Are you?" The homeless lad just glanced at it—the flight of spotless stone steps, guarded by ponderous railings, which led to my father's respectable and handsome door. "Good-day, then—which means good-bye."

I started. The word pained me. On my sad, lonely life—brief indeed, though ill-health seemed to have doubled and trebled my sixteen years into a mournful maturity—this lad's face had come like a flash of sunshine; a reflection of the merry boyhood, the youth and strength that never were, never could be, mine. To let it go from me was like going back into the dark.

"Not good-bye just yet!" said I, trying painfully to disengage myself from my little carriage and mount the steps. John Halifax came to my aid.

"Suppose you let me carry you. I could—and—and it would be great fun, you know."

He tried to turn it into a jest, so as not to hurt me; but the tremble in his voice was as tender as any woman's—tenderer than any woman's *I* ever was used to hear. I put my arms round his neck; he lifted me safely and carefully, and set me at my own door. Then with another good-bye he again turned to go.

My heart cried after him with an irrepressible cry. What I said I do not remember, but it caused him to return.

"Is there anything more I can do for you, sir?"

"Don't call me 'sir;' I am only a boy like yourself. I want you; don't go yet. Ah! here comes my father!"

John Halifax stood aside, and touched his cap with a respectful deference as the old man passed.

"So here thee be—hast thou taken care of my son? Did he give thee thy groat, my lad?"

We had neither of us once thought of the money.

When I acknowledged this my father laughed, called John an honest lad, and began searching in his pocket for some larger coin. I ventured to draw his ear down and whisper something—but I got no answer; meanwhile, John Halifax for the third time was going away.

"Stop, lad—I forget thy name—here is thy groat, and a shilling added, for being kind to my son."

"Thank you, but I don't want payment for kindness."

He kept the groat, and put back the shilling into my father's hand.

"Eh!" said the old man, much astonished, "thee'rt an odd lad; but I can't stay talking with thee.—Come in to dinner, Phineas.—I say," turning back to John Halifax with a sudden thougnt, "art thee hungry?"

"Very hungry." Nature gave way at last, and great tears came into the poor lad's eyes. "Nearly starving."

"Bless me! then get in, and have thy dinner. But first"—and my inexorable father held him by the shoulder—"thee art a decent lad, come of decent parents?"

"Yes," almost indignantly.

"Thee works for thy living?"

"I do, whenever I can get it."

"Thee hast never been in jail?"

"No!" thundered out the lad, with a furious look. "I don't want your dinner, sir; I would have stayed, because your son asked me, and he was civil to me, and I liked him. Now I think I had better go. Good-day, sir."

There is a verse in a very old Book—even in its human histories the most pathetic of all books—which runs thus:—

"*And it came to pass when he had made an end of speaking unto Saul, that the soul of Jonathan was knit unto the soul of David; and Jonathan loved him as his own soul.*"

And this day, I, a poorer and more helpless Jonathan, had found my David.

I caught him by the hand, and would not let him go.

"There, get in, lads—make no more ado," said Abel Fletcher sharply, as he disappeared.

So, still holding my David fast, I brought him into my father's house.

CHAPTER II.

DINNER was over; my father and I took ours in the large parlour, where the stiff, high-backed chairs eyed one another in opposite rows across the wide oaken floor, shiny and hard as marble, and slippery as glass. Except the table, the sideboard, and the cuckoo clock, there was no other furniture.

I dared not bring the poor wandering lad into this, my father's especial domain; but as soon as he was away in the tanyard I sent for John.

Jael brought him in; Jael, the only womankind we ever had about us, and who, save to me when I happened to be very ill, certainly gave no indication of her sex in its softness and tenderness. There had evidently been wrath in the kitchen.

"Phineas, the lad ha' got his dinner, and you mustn't

keep 'un long. I bean't going to let you knock yourself up with looking after a beggar boy."

A beggar boy! The idea seemed so ludicrous that I could not help smiling at it as I regarded him. He had washed his face and combed out his fair curls; though his clothes were threadbare, all but ragged, they were not unclean; and there was a rosy, healthy freshness in his tanned skin, which showed he loved and delighted in what poor folk generally abominate—water. And now the sickness of hunger had gone from his face, the lad, if not actually what our scriptural Saxon terms "well-favoured," was certainly "well-liking." A beggar boy, indeed! I hoped he had not heard Jael's remark. But he had.

"Madam," said he, with a bow of perfect good-humour, and even some sly drollery, "you mistake; I never begged in my life: I'm a person of independent property, which consists of my head and my two hands, out of which I hope to realize a large capital some day."

I laughed. Jael retired, abundantly mystified, and rather cross. John Halifax came to my easy-chair, and in an altered tone asked me how I felt, and if he could do anything for me before he went away.

"You'll not go away; not till my father comes home, at least?" For I had been revolving many plans, which had one sole aim and object, to keep near me this lad, whose companionship and help seemed to me, brotherless, sisterless, and friendless as I was, the very thing that would give me an interest in life, or, at least, make it drag on less wearily. To say that what I projected was done out of charity or pity would not be true; it was simple selfishness, if that be selfishness which makes one leap towards, and cling to, a possible strength and good, which I conclude to be the secret of all those sudden likings that spring more from instinct than reason. I do not attempt to account for mine: I know not why "the soul of Jonathan clave to the soul of David." I only know that it was so, and that the first day I beheld the lad John Halifax, I, Phineas Fletcher, "loved him as my own soul."

Thus my entreaty, "you'll not go away?" was so earnest that it apparently touched the friendless boy to the core.

"Thank you," he said in an unsteady voice, as leaning against the fireplace he drew his hand backwards and forwards across his face; "you are very kind; I'll stay an hour or so, if you wish it."

"Then come and sit down here, and let us have a talk."

What this talk was I cannot now recall, save that it ranged over many and wide themes, such as boys delight in—chiefly of life and adventure. He knew nothing of my only world—books.

"Can you read?" he asked me at last suddenly.

"I should rather think so." And I could not help smiling, being somewhat proud of my erudition.

"And write?"

"Oh yes; certainly."

He thought a minute, and then said in a low tone, "I can't write, and I don't know when I shall be able to learn; I wish you would put down something in a book for me."

"That I will."

He took out of his pocket a little case of leather, with an under one of black silk; within this, again, was a book. He would not let it go out of his hands, but held it so that I could see the leaves. It was a Greek Testament.

"Look here."

He pointed to the fly-leaf, and I read,—

"*Guy Halifax, his Book.*

"*Guy Halifax, gentleman, married Muriel Joyce, spinster, May* 17, *in the year of our Lord* 1779.

"*John Halifax, their son, born June* 18, 1780."

There was one more entry, in a feeble, illiterate female hand,—

"*Guy Halifax, died January* 4, 1781."

"What shall I write, John?" said I, after a minute or so of silence.

"I'll tell you presently. Can I get you a pen?"

He leaned on my shoulder with his left hand, but his right never once let go of the precious book.

"Write—'*Muriel Halifax, died January* 1, 1791.'"

"Nothing more?"

"Nothing more."

He looked at the writing for a minute or two, dried it carefully by the fire, replaced the book in its two cases, and put it into his pocket. He said no other word but "Thank you," and I asked him no questions.

This was all I ever heard of the boy's parentage: nor do I believe he knew more himself. He was indebted to no forefathers for a family history: the chronicle commenced with himself, and was altogether his own making. No romantic antecedents ever turned up; his lineage remained uninvestigated, and his pedigree began and ended with his own honest name—John Halifax.

Jael kept coming in and out of the parlour on divers excuses, eyeing very suspiciously John Halifax and me; especially when she heard me laughing—a rare and notable fact—for mirth was not the fashion in our house, nor the tendency of my own nature. Now this young lad, hardly as the world had knocked him about even already, had an overflowing spirit of quiet drollery and healthy humour, which was to me an inexpressible relief. It gave me something I did not possess—something entirely new. I could not look at the dancing brown eyes, at the quaint dimples of lurking fun that played hide-and-seek under the firm-set mouth, without feeling my heart cheered and delighted, like one brought out of a murky chamber into the open day.

But all this was highly objectionable to Jael.

"Phineas!"—and she planted herself before me at the end of the table—"it's a fine, sunshiny day: thee ought to be out."

"I have been out, thank you, Jael." And John and I went on talking.

"Phineas!"—a second and more determined attack—"too much laughing bean't good for thee; and it's time this lad were going about his own business."

"Hush!—nonsense, Jael."

"No—she's right," said John Halifax, rising, while that look of premature gravity, learned doubtless out of hard experience, chased all the boyish fun from his face. "I've had a merry day—thank you kindly for it! and now I'll be gone."

Gone! It was not to be thought of—at least, not till my father came home. For now, more determinedly than ever, the plan which I had just ventured to hint at to my father fixed itself on my mind. Surely he would not refuse me—me, his sickly boy, whose life had in it so little pleasure.

"Why do you want to go? You have no work?"

"No; I wish I had. But I'll get some."

"How?"

"Just by trying everything that comes to hand. That's the only way. I never wanted bread, nor begged it, yet —though I've often been rather hungry. And as for clothes"—he looked down on his own, light and threadbare, here and there almost burst into holes by the stout muscles of the big growing boy—looked rather disconsolately. "I'm afraid *she* would be sorry—that's all! She always kept me so tidy."

By the way he spoke, "*she*" must have meant his mother. There the orphan lad had an advantage over me; alas! I did not remember mine.

"Come," I said, for now I had quite made up my mind to take no denial, and fear no rebuff from my father; "cheer up. Who knows what may turn up?"

"Oh yes, something always does; I'm not afraid!" He tossed back his curls, and looked smiling out through the window at the blue sky; that steady, brave, honest smile, which will meet Fate in every turn, and fairly coax the jade into good humour.

"John, do you know you're uncommonly like a childish hero of mine—Dick Whittington? Did you ever hear of him?"

"No."

"Come into the garden, then"—for I caught another

ominous vision of Jael in the doorway, and I did not want to vex my good old nurse; besides, unlike John, I was anything but brave. "You'll hear the Abbey bells chime presently—not unlike Bow bells, I used to fancy sometimes; and we'll lie on the grass, and I'll tell you the whole true and particular story of Sir Richard Whittington."

I lifted myself, and began looking for my crutches. John found and put them into my hand, with a grave, pitiful look.

"You don't need those sort of things," I said, making pretence to laugh, for I had not grown used to them, and felt often ashamed.

"I hope you will not need them always."

"Perhaps not—Dr. Jessop isn't sure. But it doesn't matter much; most likely I shan't live long." For this was, God forgive me, always the last and greatest comfort I had.

John looked at me—surprised, troubled, compassionate—but he did not say a word. I hobbled past him; he following through the long passage to the garden door. There I paused—tired out. John Halifax took gentle hold of my shoulder.

"I think, if you did not mind, I'm sure I could carry you. I carried a meal sack once, weighing eight stone."

I burst out laughing, which maybe was what he wanted, and forthwith consented to assume the place of the meal sack. He took me on his back—what a strong fellow he was!—and fairly trotted with me down the garden walk. We were both very merry; and though I was his senior I seemed with him, out of my great weakness and infirmity, to feel almost like a child.

"Please to take me to that clematis arbour; it looks over the Avon. Now, how do you like our garden?"

"It's a nice place."

He did not go into ecstasies, as I had half expected, but gazed about him observantly, while a quiet, intense satisfaction grew and diffused itself over his whole countenance.

"It's a *very* nice place."

Certainly it was. A large square, chiefly grass, level as a bowling-green, with borders round. Beyond, divided by a low hedge, was the kitchen and fruit garden—my father's pride, as this old-fashioned pleasaunce was mine. When, years ago, I was too weak to walk, I knew, by crawling, every inch of the soft, green, mossy, daisy-patterned carpet, bounded by its broad gravel walk; and above that, apparently shut in as with an impassable barrier from the outer world, by a three-sided fence, the high wall, the yew hedge, and the river.

John Halifax's comprehensive gaze seemed to take in all.

"Have you lived here long?" he asked me.

"Ever since I was born."

"Ah!—well, it's a nice place," he repeated, somewhat sadly. "This grass plot is very even—thirty yards square, I should guess. I'd get up and pace it, only I'm rather tired."

"Are you? Yet you would carry——"

"Oh—that's nothing. I've often walked farther than to-day. But still it's a good step across the country since morning."

"How far have you come?"

"From the foot of those hills—I forget what they call them—over there. I have seen bigger ones—but they're steep enough—bleak and cold too, especially when one is lying out among the sheep. At a distance they look pleasant. This is a very pretty view."

Ay, so I had always thought it; more so than ever now, when I had some one to say to how "very pretty" it was. Let me describe it—this first landscape, the sole picture of my boyish days, and vivid as all such pictures are.

At the end of the arbour the wall which enclosed us on the riverward side was cut down—my father had done it at my asking—so as to make a seat, something after the fashion of Queen Mary's seat at Stirling, of which I had read. Thence, one could see a goodly sweep of country. First, close below, flowed the Avon—Shakespeare's Avon

—here a narrow, sluggish stream, but capable, as we at Norton Bury sometimes knew to our cost, of being roused into fierceness and foam. Now it slipped on quietly enough, contenting itself with turning a flour-mill hard by, the lazy whir of which made a sleepy, incessant monotone which I was fond of hearing.

From the opposite bank stretched a wide green level called the Ham—dotted with pasturing cattle of all sorts. Beyond it was a second river, forming an arch of a circle round the verdant flat. But the stream itself lay so low as to be invisible from where we sat; you could only trace the line of its course by the small white sails that glided in and out, oddly enough, from behind clumps of trees, and across meadow-lands.

They attracted John's attention. "Those can't be boats, surely. Is there water there?"

"To be sure, or you would not see the sails. It is the Severn, though at this distance you can't perceive it; yet it is deep enough too, as you may see by the boats it carries. You would hardly believe so, to look at it here—but I believe it gets broader and broader, and turns out a noble river by the time it reaches the King's Roads, and forms the Bristol Channel."

"I've seen that!" cried John, with a bright look. "Ah, I like the Severn."

He stood gazing at it a good while, a new expression dawning in his eyes. Eyes in which then, for the first time, I watched a thought grow, and grow, till out of them was shining a beauty absolutely divine.

All of a sudden the Abbey chimes burst out, and made the lad start.

"What's that?"

"Turn again, Whittington, Lord Mayor of London," I sang to the bells; and then it seemed such a commonplace history, and such a very low degree of honour to arrive at, that I was really glad I had forgotten to tell John the story. I merely showed him where, beyond our garden wall, and in the invisible highroad that interposed, rose up the grim old Abbey tower.

"Probably this garden belonged to the Abbey in ancient time—our orchard is so fine. The monks may have planted it; they liked fruit, those old fellows."

"Oh! did they?" He evidently did not quite comprehend, but was trying, without asking, to find out what I referred to. I was almost ashamed, lest he might think I wanted to show off my superior knowledge.

"The monks were parsons, John, you know. Very good men, I dare say, but rather idle."

"Oh, indeed. Do you think they planted that yew hedge?" And he went to examine it.

Now, far and near, our yew hedge was noted. There was not its like in the whole country. It was about fifteen feet high, and as many thick. Century after century of growth, with careful clipping and training, had compacted it into a massive green barrier, as close and impervious as a wall.

John poked in and about it—peering through every interstice—leaning his breast against the solid depth of branches; but their close shield resisted all his strength.

At last he came back to me, his face glowing with the vain efforts he had made.

"What were you about? Did you want to get through?"

"I wanted just to see if it were possible."

I shook my head. "What would you do, John, if you were shut up here, and had to get over the yew hedge? You could not climb it?"

"I know that, and, therefore, should not waste time in trying."

"Would you give up, then?"

He smiled—there was no "giving up" in that smile of his. "I'll tell you what I'd do—I'd begin and break it, twig by twig, till I forced my way through, and got out safe at the other side."

"Well done, lad!—but if it's all the same to thee, I would rather thee did not try that experiment upon *my* hedge at present."

My father had come behind, and overheard us, unobserved. We were both somewhat confounded, though a grim kindliness of aspect showed that he was not displeased—nay, even amused.

"Is that thy usual fashion of getting over a difficulty, friend—what's thy name?"

I supplied the answer. The minute Abel Fletcher appeared, John seemed to lose all his boyish fun, and go back to that premature gravity and hardness of demeanour which I supposed his harsh experience of the world and of men had necessarily taught him, but which was very sad to see in a lad so young.

My father sat down beside me on the bench—pushed aside an intrusive branch of clematis—finally, because it would come back, and tickle his bald pate, broke it off, and threw it into the river; then, leaning on his stick with both hands, eyed John Halifax sharply all over, from top to toe.

"Didn't thee say thee wanted work? It looks rather like it."

His glance upon the shabby clothes made the boy colour violently.

"Oh, thee needst not be ashamed; better men than thee have been in rags. Hast thee any money?"

"The groat you gave, that is, paid me; I never take what I don't earn," said the lad, sticking a hand in either poor empty pocket.

"Don't be afraid—I was not going to give thee anything—except, maybe—— Would thee like some work?"

"O sir!"

"O father!"

I hardly know which was the most grateful cry.

Abel Fletcher looked surprised, but on the whole not ill-pleased. Putting on and pulling down his broad-brimmed hat, he sat meditatively for a minute or so, making circles in the gravel walk with the end of his stick. People said—nay, Jael herself, once, in a passion, had thrown the fact at me—that the wealthy Friend himself had come to Norton Bury without a shilling in his pocket.

"Well, what work canst thee do, lad?"

"Anything," was the eager answer.

"Anything generally means nothing," sharply said my father; "what hast thee been at all this year? The truth, mind!"

John's eyes flashed, but a look from mine seemed to set him right again. He said quietly and respectfully, "Let me think a minute, and I'll tell you. All spring I was at a farmer's, riding the plough-horses, hoeing turnips; then I went up the hills with some sheep; in June I tried haymaking, and caught a fever—you needn't start, sir, I've been well these six weeks, or I wouldn't have come near your son; then——"

"That will do, lad—I'm satisfied."

"Thank you, sir."

"Thee need not say 'sir'—it is folly. I am Abel Fletcher." For my father retained scrupulously the Friends' mode of speech, though he was practically but a lax member of the Society, and had married out of its pale. In this announcement of his plain name appeared, I fancy, more pride than humility.

"Very well, I will remember," answered the boy fearlessly, though with an amused twist of his mouth, speedily restrained. "And now, Abel Fletcher, I shall be willing and thankful for any work you can give me."

"We'll see about it."

I looked gratefully and hopefully at my father—but his next words rather modified my pleasure.

"Phineas, one of my men at the tanyard has gone and listed this day—left an honest livelihood to be a paid cut-throat. Now if I could get a lad—one too young to be caught hold of at every pot-house by that man of blood, the recruiting sergeant—— Dost thee think this lad is fit to take the place?"

"Whose place, father?"

"Bill Watkins'."

I was dumbfoundered! I had occasionally seen the said Bill Watkins, whose business it was to collect the skins which my father had bought from the farmers round about. A distinct vision presented itself to me of Bill and his cart, from which dangled the sanguinary exuviæ of defunct animals—while in front the said Bill sat enthroned, dirty clad, and dirty-handed, with his pipe in his mouth. The idea of John Halifax in such a position was not agreeable.

"But, father——"

He read deprecation in my looks—alas! he knew too well how I disliked the tanyard and all belonging to it. "Thee'rt a fool, and the lad's another. He may go about his business for me."

"But, father—isn't there anything else?"

"I have nothing else, or if I had I wouldn't give it. He that will not work neither shall he eat."

"I will work," said John sturdily—he had listened, scarcely comprehending, to my father and me. "I don't care what it is, if only it's honest work."

Abel Fletcher was mollified. He turned his back on me—but that I little minded—and addressed himself solely to John Halifax.

"Canst thee drive?"

"That I can!" and his eyes brightened with boyish delight.

"Tut! it's only a cart—the cart with the skins. Dost thee know anything of tanning?"

"No, but I can learn."

"Hey, not so fast! Still, better be fast than slow. In the meantime, thee can drive the cart."

"Thank you, sir—Abel Fletcher, I mean—I'll do it well. That is, as well as I can."

"And mind! no stopping on the road. No drinking, to find the king's cursed shilling at the bottom of the glass, like poor Bill, for thy mother to come crying and pestering. Thee hasn't got one, eh? So much the better—all women are born fools, especially mothers."

"Sir!" The lad's face was all crimson and quivering; his voice choked; it was with difficulty he smothered down a burst of tears. Perhaps this self-control was more moving than if he had wept—at least it answered better with my father.

After a few minutes more, during which his stick had made a little grave in the middle of the walk, and buried something there—I think something besides the pebble—Abel Fletcher said, not unkindly,—

"Well, I'll take thee; though it isn't often I take a lad without a character of some sort—I suppose thee hast none."

"None," was the answer, while the straightforward, steady gaze which accompanied it unconsciously contradicted the statement; his own honest face was the lad's best witness—at all events, I thought so.

"'Tis done, then," said my father, concluding the business more quickly than I had ever before known his cautious temper settle even such a seemingly trifling matter. I say *seemingly.* How blindly we talk when we talk of "trifles."

Carelessly rising, he, from some kindly impulse, or else to mark the closing of the bargain, shook the boy's hand, and left in it a shilling.

"What is this for?"

"To show I have hired thee as my servant."

"Servant!" John repeated hastily, and rather proudly. "Oh yes, I understand—well, I will try and serve you well."

My father did not notice that manly, self-dependent smile. He was too busy calculating how many more of those said shillings would be a fair equivalent for such labour as a lad, ever so much the junior of Bill Watkins, could supply. After some cogitation, he hit upon the right sum. I forget how much—be sure it was not overmuch; for money was scarce enough in this war-time; and, besides, there was a belief afloat, so widely that it tainted even my worthy father, that plenty was not good for the working classes: they required to be kept low.

Having settled the question of wages, which John Halifax did not debate at all, my father left us, but turned back when half-way across the green-turfed square.

"Thee said thee had no money; there's a week in advance, my son being witness I pay it thee; and I can pay thee a shilling less every Saturday till we get straight."

"Very well, sir; good-afternoon, and thank you."

John took off his cap as he spoke—Abel Fletcher, involuntarily almost, touched his hat in return of the salutation. Then he walked away, and we had the garden all to ourselves—we, Jonathan and his new-found David.

I did not "fall upon his neck," like the princely Hebrew, to whom I have likened myself, but whom, alas! I resembled in nothing save my loving. But I grasped his hand for the first time, and looking up at him, as he stood thoughtfully by me, whispered, "that I was very glad."

"Thank you—so am I," said he in a low tone. Then all his old manner returned; he threw his battered cap high up in the air, and shouted out, "Hurrah!"—a thorough boy.

And I, in my poor, quavering voice, shouted too.

CHAPTER III.

WHEN I was young, and long after then, at intervals, I had the very useless, sometimes harmful, and invariably foolish habit of keeping a diary. To me, at least, it has been less foolish and harmful than to most; and out of it, together with much drawn out of the stores of a memory, made preternaturally vivid by a long introverted life, which, colourless itself, had nothing to do but to reflect and retain clear images of the lives around it—out of these two sources I have compiled the present history.

Therein, necessarily, many blank epochs occur. These I shall not try to fill up, but merely resume the thread of narration as recollection serves.

Thus, after this first day, many days came and went

before I again saw John Halifax—almost before I again thought of him. For it was one of my seasons of excessive pain; when I found it difficult to think of anything beyond those four gray-painted walls; where morning, noon, and night slipped wearily away, marked by no changes, save from daylight to candlelight, from candlelight to dawn.

Afterwards, as my pain abated, I began to be haunted by occasional memories of something pleasant that had crossed my dreary life; visions of a brave, bright young face, ready alike to battle with and enjoy the world. I could hear the voice that, speaking to me, was always tender with pity—yet not pity enough to wound. I could see the peculiar smile just creeping round his grave mouth—that irrepressible smile, indicating the atmosphere of thorough heart-cheerfulness, which ripens all the fruits of a noble nature, and without which the very noblest has about it something unwholesome, blank, and cold.

I wondered if John had ever asked for me. At length I put the question.

Jael "thought he had—but wasn't sure. Didn't bother her head about such folk."

"If he asked again, might he come upstairs?"

"No."

I was too weak to combat, and Jael was too strong an adversary; so I lay for days and days in my sick-room, often thinking, but never speaking, about the lad. Never once asking for him to come to me; not though it would have been life to me to see his merry face—I longed after him so.

At last I broke the bonds of sickness—which Jael always riveted as long and as tightly as she could—and plunged into the outer world again.

It was one market day—Jael being absent—that I came downstairs. A soft, bright, autumn morning, mild as spring, coaxing a wandering robin to come and sing to me, loud as a choir of birds, out of the thinned trees of the Abbey yard. I opened the window to hear him, though all the while in mortal fear of Jael. I listened, but caught no tone of her sharp voice, which usually came painfully from the back regions of the house; it would ill have harmonized with the sweet autumn day and the robin's song. I sat, idly thinking so, and wondering whether it were a necessary and universal fact that human beings, unlike the year, should become harsh and unlovely as they grow old.

My robin had done singing, and I amused myself with watching a spot of scarlet winding down the rural road, our house being on the verge where Norton Bury melted into "the country." It turned out to be the cloak of a well-to-do young farmer's wife riding to market in her cart beside her jolly-looking spouse. Very spruce and self-satisfied she appeared, and the market people turned to stare after her, for her costume was a novelty then. Doubtless, many thought as I did, how much prettier was scarlet than duffle gray.

Behind the farmer's cart came another, which at first I scarcely noticed, being engrossed by the ruddy face under the red cloak. The farmer himself nodded good-humouredly, but Mrs. Scarlet-cloak turned up her nose. "Oh, pride, pride!" I thought, amused, and watched the two carts, the second of which was with difficulty passing the farmer's, on the opposite side of the narrow road. At last it succeeded in getting in advance, to the young woman's evident annoyance, until the driver, turning, lifted his hat to her with such a merry, frank, pleasant smile.

Surely I knew that smile and the well-set head with its light curly hair. Also, alas! I knew the cart with relics of departed sheep dangling out behind. It was our cart of skins, and John Halifax was driving it.

"John! John!" I called out, but he did not hear, for his horse had taken fright at the red cloak, and required a steady hand. Very steady the boy's hand was, so that the farmer clapped his two great fists, and shouted "Bray-vo!"

But John—my John Halifax—he sat in his cart, and

drove. His appearance was much as when I first saw him—shabbier, perhaps, as if through repeated drenchings; this had been a wet autumn, Jael had told me. Poor John!—well might he look gratefully up at the clear blue sky to-day; ay, and the sky never looked down on a brighter, cheerier face—the same face which, whatever rags it surmounted, would, I believe, have ennobled them all.

I leaned out, watching him approach our house; watching him with so great pleasure that I forgot to wonder whether or no he would notice me. He did not at first, being busy over his horse; until, just as the notion flashed across my mind that he was passing by our house—also, how keenly his doing so would pain me—the lad looked up.

A beaming smile of surprise and pleasure, a friendly nod, then all at once his manner changed; he took off his cap, and bowed ceremoniously to his master's son.

For the moment I was hurt; then I could not but respect the honest pride which thus intimated that he knew his own position, and wished neither to ignore nor to alter it; all advances between us must evidently come from my side. So, having made his salutation, he was driving on, when I called after him,—

"John! John!"

"Yes, sir. I am so glad you're better again."

"Stop one minute till I come out to you." And I crawled on my crutches to the front door, forgetting everything but the pleasure of meeting him—forgetting even my terror of Jael. What could she say? even though she held nominally the Friends' doctrine—obeyed in the letter at least, "Call no man your master"—what would Jael say if she found me, Phineas Fletcher, talking in front of my father's respectable mansion with the vagabond lad who drove my father's cart of skins?

But I braved her, and opened the door. "John, where are you?"

"Here" (he stood at the foot of the steps, with the reins on his arm); "did you want me?"

"Yes. Come up here; never mind the cart."

But that was not John's way. He led the refractory horse, settled him comfortably under a tree, and gave him in charge to a small boy. Then he bounded back across the road, and was up the steps to my side in a single leap.

"I had no notion of seeing you. They said you were in bed yesterday." (Then he *had* been inquiring for me!) "Ought you to be standing at the door this cold day?"

"It's quite warm," I said, looking up at the sunshine, and shivering.

"Please go in."

"If you'll come too."

He nodded, then put his arm round mine, and helped me in, as if he had been a big elder brother and I a little ailing child. Well nursed and carefully guarded as I had always been, it was the first time in my life I ever knew the meaning of that rare thing—tenderness. A quality different from kindliness, affectionateness, or benevolence; a quality which can exist only in strong, deep, and undemonstrative natures, and therefore in its perfection is oftenest found in men. John Halifax had it more than any one, woman or man, that I ever knew.

"I'm glad you're better," he said, and said no more. But one look of his expressed as much as half a dozen sympathetic sentences of other people.

"And how have you been, John? How do you like the tanyard? Tell me frankly."

He pulled a wry face, though comical withal, and said cheerily, "Everybody must like what brings them their daily bread. It's a grand thing for me not to have been hungry for nearly thirty days."

"Poor John!" I put my hand on his wrist—his strong, brawny wrist. Perhaps the contrast involuntarily struck us both with the truth—good for both to learn—that Heaven's ways are not so unequal as we sometimes fancy they seem.

"I have so often wanted to see you, John. Couldn't you come in now?"

He shook his head, and pointed to the cart. That minute, through the open hall door, I perceived Jael sauntering leisurely home from market.

Now, if I was a coward, it was not for myself this time. The avalanche of ill words I knew must fall; but it should not fall on him, if I could help it.

"Jump up on your cart, John. Let me see how well you can drive. There—good-bye, for the present. Are you going to the tanyard?"

"Yes—for the rest of the day." And he made a face as if he did not quite revel in that delightful prospect. No wonder!

"I'll come and see you there this afternoon."

"No?" with a look of delighted surprise. "But you must not—you ought not."

"But *I will!*" And I laughed to hear myself actually using that phrase. What would Jael have said?

What—as she arrived just in time to receive a half-malicious, half-ceremonious bow from John, as he drove off—what that excellent woman did say I have not the slightest recollection. I only remember that it did not frighten and grieve me as such attacks used to do; that, in her own vernacular, it all "went in at one ear and out at t'other;" that I persisted in looking out until the last glimmer of the bright curls had disappeared down the sunshiny road—then shut the front door, and crept in, content.

Between that time and dinner I sat quiet enough even to please Jael. I was thinking over the beautiful old Bible story, which latterly had so vividly impressed itself on my mind; thinking of Jonathan, as he walked "by the stone Ezel," with the shepherd lad, who was to be king of Israel. I wondered whether he would have loved him, and seen the same future perfection in him, had Jonathan, the king's son, met the poor David keeping his sheep among the folds of Bethlehem.

When my father came home, he found me waiting in my place at table. He only said, "Thee art better, then, my son?" But I knew how glad he was to see me.

He gave token of this by being remarkably conversible over our meal—though, as usual, his conversation had a sternly moral tone, adapted to the improvement of what he persisted in considering my "infant" mind. It had reference to an anecdote Dr. Jessop had just been telling him—about a little girl, one of our doctor's patients, who in some passionate struggle had hurt herself very much with a knife.

"Let this be a warning to thee, my son, not to give way to violent passions." (My good father, thought I, there is little fear.) "For this child—I remember her father well, for he lived at Kingswell here; he was violent too, and much given to evil ways before he went abroad—Phineas, this child, this miserable child, will bear the mark of the wound all her life."

"Poor thing!" said I absently.

"No need to pity her; her spirit is not half broken yet. Thomas Jessop said to me, 'That little Ursula——'"

"Is her name Ursula?" And I called to mind the little girl who had tried to give some bread to the hungry John Halifax, and whose cry of pain we heard as the door shut upon her. Poor little lady!—how sorry I was. I knew John would be so infinitely sorry too—and all to no purpose—that I determined not to tell him anything about it. The next time I saw Dr. Jessop I asked him after the child, and learned she had been taken away somewhere—I forget where; and then the whole affair slipped from my memory.

"Father," said I, when he ceased talking—and Jael, who always ate her dinner at the same time and table as ourselves, but "below the salt," had ceased nodding a respectful running comment on all he said—"Father!"

"Well, my son."

"I should like to go with thee to the tanyard this afternoon."

Here Jael, who had been busy pulling back the table, replacing the long row of chairs, and re-sanding the broad centre Sahara of the room to its dreary, pristine aridness, stopped, fairly aghast with amazement.

"Abel—Abel Fletcher! the lad's just out of his bed! He is no more fit to——"

"Pshaw, woman!" was the sharp answer.—"So, Phineas, thee art really strong enough to go out?"

"If thou wilt take me, father."

He looked pleased, as he always did when I used the Friends' mode of phraseology, for I had not been brought up in the Society—this having been the last request of my mother, rigidly observed by her husband. The more so, people said, as while she lived they had not been quite happy together. But whatever he was to her in their brief union, he was a good father to me, and for his sake I have always loved and honoured the Society of Friends.

"Phineas," said he (after having stopped a volley of poor Jael's indignations, beseechings, threats, and prognostications, by a resolute, "Get the lad ready to go"), "Phineas, my son, I rejoice to see thy mind turning towards business. I trust, should better health be vouchsafed thee, that some day soon——"

"Not just yet, father," said I sadly, for I knew what he referred to, and that it would never be. Mentally and physically I alike revolted from my father's trade. I held the tanyard in abhorrence—to enter it made me ill for days; sometimes for months and months I never went near it. That I should ever be what was my poor father's one desire, his assistant and successor in his business, was, I knew, a thing totally impossible.

It hurt me a little that my project of going with him to-day should in any way have deceived him; and rather silently and drearily we set out together; progressing through Norton Bury streets in our old way, my father marching along in his grave fashion, I steering my little carriage, and keeping as close as I could beside him. Many a person looked at us as we passed; almost everybody knew us, but few, even of our own neighbours, saluted us; we were Nonconformists and Quakers.

I had never been in the town since the day I came through it with John Halifax. The season was much later now, but it was quite warm still in the sunshine, and very pleasant looked the streets, even the close, narrow streets of Norton Bury. I beg its pardon; antiquaries hold it a most "interesting and remarkable" place; and I myself have sometimes admired its quaint, overhanging, ornamented house-fronts—blackened, and wonderfully old. But one rarely notices what has been familiar throughout life; and now I was less struck by the beauty of the picturesque old town than by the muddiness of its pathways, and the mingled noises of murmuring looms, scolding women, and squabbling children, that came up from the alleys which lay between the High Street and the Avon. In those alleys were hundreds of our poor folk living, huddled together in misery, rags, and dirt. Was John Halifax living there too?

My father's tanyard was in an alley a little farther on. Already I perceived the familiar odour; sometimes a not unpleasant barky smell; at other times borne in horrible wafts, as if from a lately-forsaken battlefield. I wondered how anybody could endure it—yet some did; and among the workmen, as we entered, I looked round for the lad I knew.

He was sitting in a corner in one of the sheds, helping two or three women to split bark, very busy at work; yet he found time to stop now and then and administer a wisp of sweet hay to the old blind mare as she went slowly round and round, turning the bark-mill. Nobody seemed to notice him, and he did not speak to anybody.

As we passed John did not even see us. I asked my father, in a whisper, how he liked the boy.

"What boy? Eh, him? Oh, well enough—there's no harm in him that I know of. Dost thee want him to wheel thee about the yard? Here, I say, lad—bless me! I've forgot thy name."

John Halifax started up at the sharp tone of command; but when he saw me he smiled. My father walked on to some pits where he told me he was trying an important experiment, how a hide might be tanned completely in five months instead of eight. I stayed behind.

"John, I want you."

John shook himself free of the bark heap, and came rather hesitatingly at first.

"Anything I can do for you, sir?"

"Don't call me 'sir;' if I say 'John,' why don't you say 'Phineas'?"

And I held out my hand—his was all grimed with bark dust.

"Are you not ashamed to shake hands with me?"

"Nonsense, John."

So we settled that point entirely. And though he never failed to maintain externally a certain gentle respectfulness of demeanour towards me, yet it was more the natural deference of the younger to the elder, of the strong to the weak, than the duty paid by a serving-lad to his master's son. And this was how I best liked it to be.

He guided me carefully among the tan pits—those deep fosses of abomination, with a slender network of pathways thrown between—until we reached the lower end of the yard. It was bounded by the Avon only, and by a great heap of refuse bark.

"This is not a bad place to rest in; if you liked to get out of the carriage I'd make you comfortable here in no time."

I was quite willing; so he ran off and fetched an old horse-rug, which he laid upon the soft, dry mass. Then he helped me thither, and covered me with my cloak. Lying thus, with my hat over my eyes, just distinguishing the shiny glimmer of the Avon running below, and beyond that the green, level Ham, dotted with cows, my position was anything but unpleasant. In fact, positively agreeable—ay, even though the tanyard was close behind; but here it would offend none of my senses.

"Are you comfortable, Phineas?"

"Very, if you would come and sit down too."

"That I will."

And we then began to talk. I asked him if he often patronized the bark heap, he seemed so very much at home there.

"So I am," he answered, smiling; "it is my castle—my house."

"And not unpleasant to live at either."

"Except when it rains. Does it always rain at Norton Bury?"

"For shame, John!" and I pointed to the bluest of autumn skies, though in the distance an afternoon mist was slowly creeping on.

"All very fine now, but there's a fog coming over Severn; and it is sure to rain at nightfall. I shall not get my nice little bit of October evening."

"You must spend it within doors, then." John shook his head. "You ought; it must be dreadfully cold on this bark heap after sunset."

"Rather, sometimes. Are you cold now? Shall I fetch—but I haven't anything fit to wrap you in, except this rug."

He muffled it closer round me; infinitely light and tender was his rough-looking boy's hand.

"I never saw anybody so thin as you; thinner much since I saw you. Have you been very, very ill, Phineas? What ailed you?"

His anxiety was so earnest, that I explained to him what I may as well explain here, and dismiss, once for all, the useless topic, that from my birth I had been puny and diseased, that my life had been a succession of sicknesses, and that I could hope for little else until the end.

"But don't think I mind it, John," for I was grieved to see his shocked and troubled look. "I am very content; I have a quiet home, a good father, and now I think and believe I have found the one thing I wanted—a good friend."

He smiled, but only because I did. I saw he did not understand me. In him, as in most strong and self-contained temperaments, was a certain slowness to receive impressions, which, however, being once received, are indelible. Though I, being in so many things his opposite, had none of this peculiarity, but felt at once quickly and keenly, yet I rather liked the contrary in him, as I think we almost always do like in another those peculiarities which are most different from our own. Therefore I was neither vexed nor hurt because the lad was slow to perceive all that he had so soon become, and all that I meant him to become, to me. I knew from every tone of his voice, every chance expression of his honest eyes, that he was one of those characters in which we may be sure that for each feeling they express lies a countless wealth of the same, unexpressed, below; a character the keystone of which was that whereon is built all liking and all love—*dependableness*. He was one whom you may be long in knowing, but whom the more you know the more you trust; and once trusting, you trust for ever.

Perhaps I may be supposed imaginative or at least premature in discovering all these characteristics in a boy of fourteen; and possibly in thus writing of him I may unwittingly be drawing a little from after-experience; however, being the truth, let it stand.

"Come," said I, changing the conversation, "we have had enough of me; how goes the world with you? Have you taken kindly to the tanyard? Answer frankly."

He looked at me hard, put both his hands in his pockets, and began to whistle a tune.

"Don't shirk the question, please, John. I want to know the real truth."

"Well, then, I hate the tanyard."

Having relieved his mind by this ebullition, and by kicking a small heap of tan right down into the river, he became composed.

"But, Phineas, don't imagine I intend to hate it always; I intend to get used to it, as many a better fellow than I has got used to many a worse thing. It's wicked to hate what wins one's bread, and is the only thing one is likely to get on in the world with, merely because it's disagreeable."

"You are a wise lad of your age, John."

"Now don't you be laughing at me." (But I was not; I was in solemn earnest.) "And don't think I'm worse than I am; and especially that I'm not thankful to your good father for giving me a lift in the world—the first I ever really had. If I get one foot on the ladder, perhaps I may climb."

"I should rather believe so," answered I, very confidently. "But you seem to have thought a good deal about these sort of things."

"Oh yes! I have plenty of time for thinking, and one's thoughts travel fast enough lying on this bark heap—faster than indoors. I often wish I could read—that is, read easily. As it is, I have nothing to do but to think, and nothing to think of but myself, and what I should like to be."

"Suppose, after Dick Whittington's fashion, you succeeded to your master's business, should you like to be a tanner?"

He paused—his truthful face betraying him. Then he said resolutely, "I would like to be anything that was honest and honourable. It's a notion of mine, that whatever a man may be, his trade does not make him—he makes his trade. That is—but I know I can't put the subject clear, for I have not got it clear in my own head yet—I'm only a lad. However, it all comes to this—that whether I like it or not, I'll stick to the tanning as long as I can."

"That's right; I'm so glad. Nevertheless," and I watched him as he stood, his foot planted firmly, no easy feat on the shifting bark heap, his head erect, and his mouth close, but smiling—"Nevertheless, John, it's my opinion that you might be anything you liked."

He laughed. "Questionable that—at least at present. Whatever I may be, I am just now the lad that drives your father's cart, and works in your father's tanyard

—John Halifax, and very much at your service, Mr. Phineas Fletcher."

Half in fun, half in earnest, he uncovered his fair locks, with a bow so contradictory to the rest of his appearance, that I involuntarily recalled the Greek Testament and "Guy Halifax, Gentleman." However, that could be no matter to me, or to him either, now. The lad, like many another, owed nothing to his father but his mere existence—Heaven knows whether that gift is oftenest a curse or a boon.

The afternoon had waned during our talk; but I was very loath to part with my friend. Suddenly I thought of asking where his home was.

"How do you mean?"

"Where do you live? Where do you take your meals and sleep?"

"Why, as to that, I have not much time for eating and drinking. Generally, I eat my dinner as I go along the road, where there's lots of blackberries by way of pudding—which is grand! Supper, when I do get it, I like best on this bark heap, after the men are away, and the tanyard's clear. Your father lets me stay."

"And where is your lodging, then? Where do you sleep?"

He hesitated—coloured a little. "To tell the truth—anywhere I can. Generally here."

"What, out of doors?"

"Just so."

I was much shocked. To sleep out of doors seemed to me the very lowest ebb of human misery; so degrading, too—like a common tramp or vagabond, instead of a decent lad.

"John, how can you—why do you—do such a thing?"

"I'll tell you," said he, sitting down beside me in a dogged way, as if he had read my thoughts, guessed at my suspicions, and was determined to show that he feared neither—that he would use his own judgment, and follow his own will, in spite of anybody. "Look here. I get three shillings a week, which is about fivepence a day; out of that I eat threepence—I'm a big, growing lad, and it's hard to be hungry. There's twopence left to pay for lodging. I tried it once—twice—at the decentest place I could find, but—" here an expression of intolerable disgust came over the boy's face—" I don't intend to try that again. I was never used to it. Better keep my own company and the open air. Now you see."

"O John!"

"Nay—there's no need to be sorry. You don't know how comfortable it is to sleep out of doors; and so nice to wake in the middle of the night and see the stars shining over your head."

"But isn't it very cold?"

"No—not often. I scoop out a snug little nest in the bark, and curl up in it like a dormouse, wrapped in this rug, which one of the men gave me. Besides, every morning early I take a plunge and a swim in the stream, and that makes me warm all day."

I shivered—I who feared the touch of cold water. Yet there, with all his hardships, he stood before me, the model of healthy boyhood. Alas! I envied him.

But this trying life, which he made so light of, could not go on. "What shall you do when winter comes?"

John looked grave. "I don't know; I suppose I shall manage somehow—like the sparrows," he answered, perceiving not how apposite his illustration was. For truly he seemed as destitute as the birds of the air, whom ONE feedeth when they cry to Him.

My question had evidently made him thoughtful; he remained silent a good while.

At last I said, "John, do you remember the woman who spoke so sharply to you in the alley that day?"

"Yes. I shall never forget anything which happened that day," he answered softly.

"She was my nurse once. She is not such a bad woman, though trouble has sharpened her temper. Her biggest boy, Bill, who is gone off for a soldier, used to drive your cart, you know."

"Yes?" said John interrogatively, for I was slow in putting forth my plans—that is, as much of them as it was needful he should know.

"Sally is poor—not so very poor, though. Your twopence a night would help her; and I dare say, if you'll let me speak to her, you might have Bill's attic all to yourself. She has but one other lad at home; it's worth trying for."

"It is indeed. You are very kind, Phineas." He said no more words than these—but their tone spoke volumes.

I got into my little carriage again, for I was most anxious not to lose a day in this matter. I persuaded John to go at once with me to Sally Watkins. My father was not to be seen; but I ventured to leave word for him that I was gone home, and had taken John Halifax with me. It was astonishing how bold I felt myself growing, now that there was another beside myself to think and act for.

We reached Widow Watkins' door. It was a poor place—poorer than I had imagined; but I remembered what agonies of cleanliness had been inflicted on me in nursery days, and took hope for John.

Sally sat in her kitchen, tidy and subdued, mending an old jacket that had once been Bill's, until, being supplanted by the grand red coat, it descended upon Jem, the second lad. But Bill still engrossed the poor mother's heart—she could do nothing but weep over him, and curse "Bonyparty." Her mind was so full of this that she apparently failed to recognize in the decent young workman, John Halifax, the half-starved lad she had belaboured with her tongue in the alley. She consented at once to his lodging with her, though she looked up with an odd stare when I said he was "a friend" of mine.

So we settled our business, first all together, then Sally and I alone, while John went up to look at his room. I knew I could trust Sally, whom I was glad enough to help, poor woman! She promised to make him extra comfortable, and keep my secret too. When John came down she was quite civil to him—even friendly.

She said it would really be a comfort to her that another fine, strapping lad should sleep in Bill's bed, and be coming in and out of her house just like her poor dear boy.

I felt rather doubtful of the resemblance, and indeed half angry, but John only smiled.

"And if, maybe, he'd do a hand's turn now and then about the kitchen—I s'pose he bean't above it?"

"Not a bit!" said John Halifax pleasantly.

Before we left I wanted to see his room; he carried me up, and we both sat down on the bed that had been poor Bill's. It was nothing to boast of, being a mere sacking stuffed with hay—a blanket below, and another at top; I had to beg from Jael the only pair of sheets John owned for a long time. The attic was very low and small, hardly big enough "to whip a cat round," or even a kitten—yet John gazed about it with an air of proud possession.

"I declare I shall be as happy as a king. Only look out of the window!"

Ay, the window was the grand advantage; out of it one could crawl on to the roof, and from the roof was the finest view in all Norton Bury. On one side—the town, the Abbey, and beyond it a wide stretch of meadow and woodland as far as you could see; on the other, the broad Ham, the glittering curve of Severn, and the distant country, sloping up into "the blue hills far away." A picture, which in its incessant variety, its quiet beauty, and its inexpressibly soothing charm, was likely to make the simple, every-day act of "looking out o' window" unconsciously influence the mind as much as a world of books.

"Do you like your 'castle,' John?" said I, when I had silently watched his beaming face. "Will it suit you?"

"I rather think it will!" he cried in hearty delight. And my heart likewise was very glad.

Dear little attic room! close against the sky—so close that many a time the rain came pattering in, or the sun beating down upon the roof made it like a furnace, or the snow on the leads drifted so high as to obscure the window—yet how merry, how happy we have been there! How often have we both looked back upon it in after days!

CHAPTER IV.

WINTER came early and sudden that year.

It was to me a long, dreary season, worse even than my winters inevitably were. I never stirred from my room, and never saw anybody but my father, Dr. Jessop, and Jael. At last I took courage to say to the former that I wished he would send John Halifax up some day.

"What does thee want the lad for?"

"Only to see him."

"Pshaw! a lad out o' the tanyard is not fit company for thee. Let him alone; he'll do well enough if thee doesn't try to lift him out of his place."

Lift John Halifax out of his "place"! I agreed with my father that that was impossible; but then we evidently differed widely in our definition of what the "place" might be. So, afraid of doing him harm, and feeling how much his future depended on his favour with his master, I did not discuss the matter. Only at every possible opportunity—and they were rare—I managed to send John a little note, written carefully in printed letters, for I knew he could read that; also a book or two, out of which he might teach himself a little more.

Then I waited, eagerly but patiently, until spring came, when, without making any more fruitless efforts, I should be sure to see him. I knew enough of himself, and was too jealous over his dignity, to wish either to force him by entreaties, or bring him by stratagem, into a house where he was not welcome, even though it were the house of my own father.

One February day, when the frost had at last broken

up, and soft, plentiful rain had half melted the great snowdrifts, which, Jael told me, lay about the country everywhere, I thought I would just put my head out of doors, to see how long the blessed spring would be in coming. So I crawled down into the parlour, and out of the parlour into the garden; Jael scolding, my father roughly encouraging. My poor father! he always had the belief that people need not be ill unless they chose, and that I could do a great deal if I would.

I felt very strong to-day. It was delicious to see again the green grass, which had been hidden for weeks; delicious to walk up and down in the sunshine, under the shelter of the yew hedge. I amused myself by watching a pale line of snowdrops which had come up one by one, like prisoners of war to their execution.

But the next minute I felt ashamed of the heartless simile, for it reminded me of poor Bill Watkins, who, taken after the battle of Mentz, last December, had been shot by the French as a spy. Poor, rosy, burly Bill! Better had he still been ingloriously driving our cart of skins.

"Have you been to see Sally lately?" said I to Jael, who was cutting winter cabbages hard by. "Is she getting over her trouble?"

"She bean't rich, to afford fretting. There's Jem and three little 'uns yet to feed, to say naught of another big lad as lives there, and eats a deal more than he pays, I'm sure."

I took the insinuation quietly, for I knew that my father had lately raised John's wages, and he his rent to Sally. This, together with a few other facts which lay between Sally and me, made me quite easy in the mind as to his being no burthen, but rather a help to the widow—so I let Jael have her say; it did no harm to me nor anybody.

"What bold little things snowdrops are. Stop, Jael, you are setting your foot on them."

But I was too late; she had crushed them under the high-heeled shoe. She was even near pulling me down, as she stepped back in great hurry and consternation.

"Look at that young gentleman coming down the garden; and here I be in my dirty gown, and my apron full o' cabbages."

And she dropped the vegetables all over the path as the "gentleman" came towards us.

I smiled, for, in spite of his transformation, I at least had no difficulty in recognizing John Halifax.

He had on new clothes—let me give the credit due to that wonderful civilizer, the tailor—clothes neat, decent, and plain, such as any 'prentice lad might wear. They fitted well his figure, which had increased both in height, compactness, and grace. Round his neck was a coarse but white shirt frill; and over it fell, carefully arranged, the bright curls of his bonny hair. Easily might Jael or any one else have "mistaken" him, as she cuttingly said, for a young gentleman.

She looked very indignant, though, when she found out the aforesaid "mistake."

"What may be thy business here?" she said roughly.

"Abel Fletcher sent me on a message."

"Out with it, then—don't be stopping with Phineas here. Thee bean't company for him, and his father don't choose it."

"Jael!" I cried indignantly. John never spoke, but his cheek burnt furiously. I took his hand, and told him how glad I was to see him—but, for a minute, I doubt if he heard me.

"Abel Fletcher sent me here," he repeated, in a well-controlled voice, "that I might go out with Phineas; if *he* objects to my company, it's easy to say so."

And he turned to me. I think he must have been satisfied then.

Jael retired discomfited, and in her wrath again dropped half of her cabbages. John picked them up and restored them; but got for thanks only a parting thrust.

"Thee art mighty civil in thy new clothes. Be off,

and be back again sharp; and, I say, don't thee be leaving the cart o' skins again under the parlour windows."

"I don't drive the cart now," was all he replied.

"Not drive the cart?" I asked eagerly, when Jael had disappeared, for I was afraid some ill chance had happened.

"Only, that this winter I've managed to teach myself to read and add up, out of your books, you know; and your father found it out, and he says I shall go round collecting money instead of skins, and it's much better wages, and—I like it better—that's all."

But, little as he said, his whole face beamed with pride and pleasure. It was, in truth, a great step forward.

"He must trust you very much, John," said I at last, knowing how exceedingly particular my father was in his collectors.

"That's it—that's what pleases me so. He is very good to me, Phineas, and he gave me a special holiday that I might go out with you. Isn't that grand?"

"Grand, indeed. What fun we'll have! I almost think I could take a walk myself."

For the lad's company invariably gave me new life, and strength, and hope. The very sight of him was as good as the coming of spring.

"Where shall we go?" said he, when we were fairly off, and he was guiding my carriage down Norton Bury streets.

"I think to the Mythe." The Mythe was a little hill on the outskirts of the town, breezy and fresh, where Squire Brithwood had built himself a fine house ten years ago.

"Ay, that will do; and as we go, you will see the floods out—a wonderful sight, isn't it? The river is rising still, I hear; at the tanyard they are busy making a dam against it. How high are the floods here generally, Phineas?"

"I'm sure I can't remember. But don't look so serious. Let us enjoy ourselves."

And I did enjoy intensely that pleasant stroll. The mere sunshine was delicious; delicious, too, to pause on the bridge at the other end of the town, and feel the breeze brought in by the rising waters, and hear the loud sound of them, as they poured in a cataract over the floodgates hard by.

"Your lazy, muddy Avon looks splendid now. What masses of white foam it makes, and what wreaths of spray; and see! ever so much of the Ham is under water. How it sparkles in the sun!"

"John, you like looking at anything pretty."

"Ah, don't I!" cried he, with his whole heart. My heart leaped too to see him so happy.

"You can't think how fine this is from my window; I have watched it for a week. Every morning the water seems to have made itself a fresh channel. Look at that one by the willow tree—how savagely it pours!"

"Oh, we at Norton Bury are used to floods."

"Are they ever very serious?"

"Have been—but not in my time. Now, John, tell me what you have been doing all winter."

It was a brief and simple chronicle—of hard work, all day over, and from the Monday to the Saturday—too hard work to do anything of nights, save to drop into the sound, dreamless sleep of youth and labour.

"But how did you teach yourself to read and add up, then?"

"Generally at odd minutes going along the road. It's astonishing what a lot of odd minutes one can catch during the day, if one really sets about it. And then I had Sunday afternoons besides. I did not think it wrong——"

"No," said I decisively. "What books have you got through?"

"All you sent—'Pilgrim's Progress,' 'Robinson Crusoe,' and the 'Arabian Nights.' That's fine, isn't it?" and his eyes sparkled.

"Any more?"

"Also the one you gave me at Christmas. I have read it a good deal."

I liked the tone of quiet reverence in which he spoke. I liked to hear him own, nor be ashamed to own—that he read "a good deal" in that rare book for a boy to read—the Bible.

But on this subject I did not ask him any more questions; indeed, it seemed to me, and seems still, that no more were needed.

"And you can read quite easily now, John?"

"Pretty well, considering." Then, turning suddenly to me: "You read a great deal, don't you? I overheard your father say you were very clever. How much do you know?"

"Oh—nonsense!" But he pressed me, and I told him. The list was short enough; I almost wished it were shorter when I saw John's face.

"For me—I can only just read, and I shall be fifteen directly!"

The accent of shame, despondency, even despair, went to my very heart.

"Don't mind," I said, laying my feeble, useless hand upon that which guided me on so steady and so strong; "how could you have had time, working as hard as you do?"

"But I ought to learn; I must learn."

"You shall. It's little I can teach; but, if you like, I'll teach you all I know."

"O Phineas!" One flash of those bright, moist eyes, and he walked hastily across the road. Thence he came back, in a minute or two, armed with the tallest, straightest of brier-rose shoots.

"You like a rose switch, don't you? I do. Nay, stop till I've cut off the thorns." And he walked on beside me, working at it with his knife, in silence.

I was silent too, but I stole a glance at his mouth, as seen in profile. I could almost always guess at his thoughts by that mouth, so flexible, sensitive, and, at times, so infinitely sweet. It wore that expression now. I was satisfied, for I knew the lad was happy.

We reached the Mythe. "David," I said (I had got into a habit of calling him "David;" and now he had read a certain history in that Book I supposed he had guessed why, for he liked the name), "I don't think I can go any farther up the hill."

"Oh, but you shall! I'll push behind; and when we come to the stile I'll carry you. It's lovely on the top of the Mythe—look at the sunset. You cannot have seen a sunset for ever so long."

No—that was true. I let John do as he would with me—he who brought into my pale life the only brightness it had ever known.

Ere long we stood on the top of the steep mound. I know not if it be a natural hill, or one of those old Roman or British remains, plentiful enough hereabouts, but it was always called the Mythe. Close below it, at the foot of a precipitous slope, ran the Severn, there broad and deep enough, gradually growing deeper and broader as it flowed on, through a wide plain of level country, towards the line of hills that bounded the horizon. Severn looked beautiful here; neither grand nor striking, but certainly beautiful; a calm, gracious, generous river, bearing strength in its tide and plenty in its bosom, rolling on through the land slowly and surely, like a good man's life, and fertilizing wherever it flows.

"Do you like Severn still, John?"

"I love it."

I wondered if his thoughts had been anything like mine.

"What is that?" he cried suddenly, pointing to a new sight, which even I had not often seen on our river. It was a mass of water, three or four feet high, which came surging along the mid-stream, upright as a wall.

"It is the *eger;* I've often seen it on Severn, where the swift seaward current meets the spring tide. Look what a crest of foam it has, like a wild boar's mane. We often call it the river-boar."

"But it is only a big wave."

"Big enough to swamp a boat, though."

And while I spoke I saw, to my horror, that there actually was a boat, with two men in it, trying to get out of the way of the eger.

"They never can! They'll assuredly be drowned! O John!"

But he had already slipped from my side, and swung himself by furze bushes and grass down the steep slope to the water's edge.

It was a breathless moment. The eger travelled slowly in its passage, changing the smooth, sparkling river to a whirl of conflicting currents, in which no boat could live—least of all that light pleasure-boat, with its toppling sail. In it was a youth I knew by sight, Mr. Brithwood of the Mythe House, and another gentleman.

They both pulled hard—they got out of the mid-stream, but not close enough to land; and already there was but two oars' length between them and the "boar."

"Swim for it!" I heard one cry to the other; but swimming would not have saved them.

"Hold there!" shouted John at the top of his voice; "throw that rope out and I will pull you in!"

It was a hard tug; I shuddered to see him wade knee-deep in the stream—but he succeeded. Both gentlemen leaped safe on shore. The younger tried desperately to save his boat, but it was too late. Already the "water-boar" had clutched it—the rope broke like a gossamer thread—the trim, white sail was dragged down—rose up once, broken and torn, like a butterfly caught in a mill-stream—then disappeared.

"So it's all over with her, poor thing!"

"Who cares? We might have lost our lives," sharply said the other, an older and sickly-looking gentleman, dressed in mourning, to whom life did not seem a particularly pleasant thing, though he appeared to value it so highly.

They both scrambled up the Mythe without noticing John Halifax. Then the elder turned.

"But who pulled us ashore? Was it you, my young friend?"

John Halifax, emptying his soaked boots, answered, "I suppose so."

"Indeed, we owe you much."

"Not more than a crown will pay," said young Brithwood gruffly. "I know him, Cousin March. He works in Fletcher the Quaker's tanyard."

"Nonsense!" cried Mr. March, who had stood looking at the boy with a kindly, even half-sad air. "Impossible! Young man, will you tell me to whom I am so much obliged?"

"My name is John Halifax."

"Yes; but *what* are you?"

"What he said. Mr. Brithwood knows me well enough. I work in the tanyard."

"Oh!" Mr. March turned away with a resumption of dignity, though evidently both surprised and disappointed. Young Brithwood laughed.

"I told you so, cousin. Hey, lad!" eyeing John over, "you've been out at grass, and changed your coat for the better, but you're certainly the same lad that my curricle nearly ran over one day; you were driving a cart of skins—pah! I remember."

"So do I," said John fiercely; but when the youth's insolent laughter broke out again he controlled himself. The laughter ceased.

"Well, you've done me a good turn for an ill one, young—what's-your-name, so here's a guinea for you." He threw it towards him; it fell on the ground, and lay there.

"Nay, nay, Richard," expostulated the sickly gentleman, who, after all, *was* a gentleman. He stood apparently struggling with conflicting intentions, and not very easy in his mind. "My good fellow," he said at last, in a constrained voice, "I won't forget your bravery. If I could do anything for you—and meanwhile if a trifle like this"—and he slipped something into John's hand.

John returned it with a bow, merely saying "that he would rather not take any money."

The gentleman looked very much astonished. There was a little more of persistence on one side and resistance on the other; and then Mr. March put the guineas irresolutely back into his pocket, looking the while lingeringly at the boy—at his tall figure, and flushed, proud face.

"How old are you?"

"Fifteen, nearly."

"Ah!" it was almost a sigh. He turned away, and turned back again. "My name is March—Henry March; if you should ever——"

"Thank you, sir. Good-day."

"Good-day." I fancied he was half inclined to shake hands—but John did not, or would not, see it. Mr. March walked on, following young Brithwood; but at the stile he turned round once more and glanced at John. Then they disappeared.

"I'm glad they're gone: now we can be comfortable." He flung himself down, wrung out his wet stockings, laughed at me for being so afraid he would take cold, and so angry at young Brithwood's insults. I sat wrapped in my cloak, and watched him making idle circles in the sandy path with the rose switch he had cut.

A thought struck me. "John, hand me the stick, and I'll give you your first writing lesson."

So there, on the smooth gravel, and with the rose stem for a pen, I taught him how to form the letters of the alphabet and join them together. He learned very quickly—so quickly, that in a little while the simple copy-book that Mother Earth obliged us with was covered in all directions with "J O H N—John."

"Bravo!" he cried, as we turned homeward, he flourishing his gigantic pen, which had done such good service; "bravo! I have gained something to-day!"

Crossing the bridge over the Avon, we stood once more to look at the waters that were "out." They had risen considerably, even in that short time, and were now pouring in several new channels, one of which was alongside of the highroad; we stopped a good while watching it. The current was harmless enough, merely flooding a part of the Ham; but it awed us to see the fierce power of waters let loose. An old willow tree, about whose roots I had often watched the king-cups growing, was now in the centre of a stream as broad as the Avon by our tanyard, and thrice as rapid. The torrent rushed round it—impatient of the divisions its great roots caused—eager to undermine and tear it up. Inevitably, if the flood did not abate, within a few hours more there would be nothing left of the fine old tree.

"I don't quite like this," said John meditatively, as his quick eye swept down the course of the river, with the houses and wharves that abutted on it all along one bank. "Did you ever see the waters thus high before?"

"Yes, I believe I have; nobody minds it at Norton Bury; it is only the sudden thaw, my father says, and he ought to know, for he has had plenty of experience, the tanyard being so close to the river."

"I was thinking of that; but come, it's getting cold."

He took me safe home, and we parted cordially—nay, affectionately—at my own door.

"When will you come again, David?"

"When your father sends me."

And I felt that *he* felt that our intercourse was always to be limited to this. Nothing clandestine, nothing obtrusive, was possible, even for friendship's sake, to John Halifax.

My father came in late that evening; he looked tired and uneasy, and instead of going to bed, though it was after nine o'clock, sat down to his pipe in the chimney-corner.

"Is the river rising still, father? Will it do any harm to the tanyard?"

"What dost thee know about the tanyard?"

"Only John Halifax was saying——"

"John Halifax had better hold his tongue."

I held mine.

My father puffed away in silence till I came to bid him good-night. I think the sound of my crutches on the floor stirred him out of a long meditation, in which his ill-humour had ebbed away.

"Where didst thee go out to-day, Phineas?—thee and the lad I sent."

"To the Mythe;" and I told him the incident that had happened there. He listened without reply.

"Wasn't it a brave thing to do, father?"

"Um!" and a few meditative puffs. "Phineas, the lad thee hast such a hankering after is a good lad—a very decent lad—if thee doesn't make too much of him. Remember, he is but my servant; thee'rt my son—my only son."

Alas! my poor father, it was hard enough for him to have such an "only son" as I.

In the middle of the night—or else to me, lying awake, it seemed so—there was a knocking at our hall door. I slept on the ground flat, in a little room opposite the parlour. Ere I could well collect my thoughts, I saw my father pass, fully dressed, with a light in his hand. And, man of peace though he was, I was very sure I saw in the other—something which always lay near his strong box, at his bed's-head at night, because ten years ago a large sum had been stolen from him, and the burglar had gone free of punishment. The law refused to receive Abel Fletcher's testimony—he was "only a Quaker."

The knocking grew louder, as if the person had no time to hesitate at making a noise.

"Who's there?" called out my father; and at the answer he opened the front door, first shutting mine.

A minute afterwards I heard some one in my room. "Phineas, are you here?—don't be frightened."

I was not—as soon as his voice reached me, John's own familiar voice. "It's something about the tan-yard?"

"Yes; the waters are rising, and I have come to fetch your father; he may save a good deal yet.—I am ready, sir," in answer to a loud call.—" Now, Phineas. lie you down again—the night's bitter cold. Don't stir —you'll promise ?—I'll see after your father."

They went out of the house together, and did not return the whole night.

That night, February 5, 1795, was one long remembered at Norton Bury. Bridges were destroyed—boats carried away—houses inundated, or sapped at their foundations. The loss of life was small, but that of property was very great. Six hours did the work of ruin, and then the flood began to turn.

It was a long waiting until they came home—my father and John. At daybreak I saw them standing on the doorstep. A blessed sight !

" O father ! my dear father ! " and I drew him in, holding fast his hands—faster and closer than I had done since I was a child. He did not repel me.

" Thee'rt up early, and it's a cold morning for thee, my son. Go back to the fire."

His voice was gentle ; his ruddy countenance pale—two strange things in Abel Fletcher.

" Father, tell me what has befallen thee ? "

" Nothing, my son, save that the Giver of all worldly goods has seen fit to take back a portion of mine. I, like many another in this town, am poorer by some thousands than I went to bed last night."

He sat down. I knew he loved his money, for it had been hardly earned. I had not thought he would have borne its loss so quietly.

" Father, never mind ; it might have been worse."

" Of a surety. I should have lost everything I had in the world—save for—— Where is the lad ? What art thee standing outside for ? Come in, John, and shut the door."

John obeyed, though without advancing. He was cold and wet. I wanted him to sit down by the fireside.

" Ay, do, lad," said my father kindly.

John came.

I stood between the two—afraid to ask what they had

undergone; but sure, from the old man's grave face, and the lad's bright one—flushed all over with that excitement of danger so delicious to the young—that the peril had not been small.

"Jael," cried my father, rousing himself, "give us some breakfast, the lad and me—we have had a hard night's work together."

Jael brought the mug of ale and the bread and cheese; but either did not or could not notice that the meal had been ordered for more than one.

"Another plate," said my father sharply.

"The lad can go into the kitchen, Abel Fletcher; his breakfast is waiting there."

My father winced—even her master was sometimes rather afraid of Jael. But conscience or his will conquered.

"Woman, do as I desired. Bring another plate, and another mug of ale."

And so, to Jael's great wrath, and to my great joy, John Halifax was bidden, and sat down to the same board as his master. The fact made an ineffaceable impression on our household.

After breakfast, as we sat by the fire, in the pale haze of that February morning, my father, contrary to his wont, explained to me all his losses; and how, but for the timely warning he had received, the flood might have nearly ruined him.

"So it was well John came," I said, half afraid to say more.

"Ay, and the lad has been useful too; it is an old head on young shoulders."

John looked very proud of this praise, though it was grimly given. But directly after it some ill or suspicious thought seemed to come into Abel Fletcher's mind.

"Lad," suddenly turning round on John Halifax, "thee told me thee saw the river rising by the light of the moon. What wast *thee* doing then, out o' thy honest bed and thy quiet sleep, at eleven o'clock at night?"

John coloured violently; the quick young blood was

always ready enough to rise in his face. It spoke ill for him with my father.

"Answer. I will not be hard upon thee—to-night, at least."

"As you like, Abel Fletcher," answered the boy sturdily. "I was doing no harm. I was in the tan-yard."

"Thy business there ?"

"None at all. I was with the men—they were watching, and had a candle ; and I wanted to sit up, and had no light."

"What didst thee want to sit up for ?" pursued my father, keen and sharp as a ferret at a field-rat's hole, or a barrister hunting a witness in those courts of law that were never used by, though often used against, us Quakers.

John hesitated, and again his painful, falsely-accusing blushes tried him sore. "Sir, I'll tell you ; it's no disgrace. Though I'm such a big fellow, I can't write ; and your son was good enough to try and teach me. I was afraid of forgetting the letters ; so I tried to make them all over again, with a bit of chalk, on the bark shed wall. It did nobody any harm that I know of."

The boy's tone, even though it was rather quick and angry, won no reproof. At last my father said gently enough,—

"Is that all, lad ?"

"Yes."

Again Abel Fletcher fell into a brown study. We two lads talked softly to each other—afraid to interrupt. He smoked through a whole pipe—his great and almost his only luxury, and then again called out,—

"John Halifax."

"I'm here."

"It's time thee went away to thy work."

"I'm going this minute. Good-bye, Phineas. Good-day, sir. Is there anything you want done ?"

He stood before his master, cap in hand, with an honest manliness pleasant to see. Any master might have been proud of such a servant—any father of such a son. My poor father—no, he did not once look from John Halifax to me. He would not have owned for the world that half-smothered sigh, or murmured because Heaven had kept back from him—as, Heaven knows why, it often does from us all!—the one desire of the heart.

"John Halifax, thee hast been of great service to me this night. What reward shall I give thee?"

And instinctively his hand dived down into his pocket. John turned away.

"Thank you—I'd rather not. It is quite enough reward that I have been useful to my master, and that he acknowledges it."

My father thought a minute, and then offered his hand. "Thee'rt in the right, lad. I am very much obliged to thee, and I will not forget it."

And John—blushing brightly once more—went away, looking as proud as an emperor, and as happy as a poor man with a bag of gold.

"Is there nothing thou canst think of, Phineas, that would pleasure the lad?" said my father, after we had been talking some time—though not about John.

I had thought of something—something I had long desired, but which seemed then all but an impossibility. Even now it was with some doubt and hesitation that I made the suggestion that he should spend every Sunday at our house.

"Nonsense!—thee know'st naught of Norton Bury lads. He would not care. He had rather lounge about all First-day at street corners with his acquaintance."

"John has none, father. He knows nobody—cares for nobody—but me. Do let him come."

"We'll see about it."

My father never broke or retracted his word. So after that John Halifax came to us every Sunday; and for one day of the week, at least, was received in his master's household as our equal and my friend.

CHAPTER V.

SUMMERS and winters slipped by lazily enough, as the years seemed always to crawl round at Norton Bury. How things went in the outside world I little knew or cared. My father lived his life, mechanical and steady as clockwork, and we two, John Halifax and Phineas Fletcher, lived our lives—the one so active and busy, the other so useless and dull. Neither of us counted the days, nor looked backwards or forwards.

One June morning I woke to the consciousness that I was twenty years old, and that John Halifax was—a man; the difference between us being precisely as I have expressed it.

Our birthdays fell within a week of each other, and it was in remembering his—the one which advanced him to the dignity of eighteen—that I called to mind my own. I say, "advanced him to the dignity"—but, in truth, that is an idle speech; for any dignity which the maturity of eighteen may be supposed to confer he had already in possession. Manhood had come to him, both in character and demeanour, not as it comes to most young lads, an eagerly-desired and presumptuously-asserted claim, but as a rightful inheritance, to be received humbly, and worn simply and naturally. So naturally, that I never seemed to think of him as anything but a boy, until this one June Sunday, when, as before stated, I myself became twenty years old.

I was talking over that last fact, in a rather dreamy mood, as he and I sat in our long-familiar summer seat, the clematis arbour by the garden wall.

"It seems very strange, John, but so it is—I am actually twenty."

"Well, and what of that?"

I sat looking down into the river, which flowed on, as my years were flowing, monotonous, dark, and slow—as they must flow on for ever. John asked me what I was thinking of.

"Of myself: what a fine specimen of the noble *genus homo* I am."

I spoke bitterly, but John knew how to meet that mood. Very patient he was with it and with every ill mood of mine. And I was grateful, with that deep gratitude we feel to those who bear with us, and forgive us, and laugh at us, and correct us—all alike for love.

"Self-investigation is good on birthdays. Phineas, here goes for a catalogue of your qualities, internal and external."

"John, don't be foolish."

"I will, if I like; though perhaps not quite so foolish as some other people; so listen:—'*Imprimis*,' as saith Shakespeare—*Imprimis*, height, full five feet four; a stature historically appertaining to great men, including Alexander of Macedon and the First Consul."

"Oh, oh!" said I reproachfully; for this was our chief bone of contention—I hating, he rather admiring, the great ogre of the day, Napoleon Bonaparte.

"*Imprimis*, of a slight, delicate person, but not lame as once was."

"No, thank God!"

"Thin, rather——"

"Very—a mere skeleton!"

"Face elongated and pale——"

"Sallow, John, decidedly sallow."

"Be it so, sallow. Big eyes, much given to observation, which means hard staring. Take them off me, Phineas, or I'll not lie on the grass a minute longer. Thank you. To return: *Imprimis* and *finis* (I'm grand at Latin now, you see), long hair, which, since the powder tax, has resumed its original blackness, and is—any young damsel would say, only we count not a single one among our acquaintance—exceedingly bewitching."

I smiled, feeling myself colour a little too, weak invalid as I was. I was, nevertheless, twenty years old; and although Jael and Sally were the only specimens of the other sex which had risen on my horizon, yet once or twice, since I had read Shakespeare, I had had a boy's lovely dreams of the divinity of womanhood. They began, and ended—mere dreams. Soon dawned the bare, hard truth, that my character was too feeble and womanish to be likely to win any woman's reverence or love. Or, even had this been possible, one sickly as I was, stricken with hereditary disease, ought never to seek to perpetuate it by marriage. I therefore put from me, at once and for ever, every feeling of that kind; and during my whole life—I thank God!—have never faltered in my resolution. Friendship was given me for love—duty for happiness. So best, and I was satisfied.

This conviction, and the struggle succeeding it—for, though brief, it was but natural that it should have been a hard struggle—was the only secret that I had kept from John. It had happened some months now, and was quite over and gone, so that I could smile at his fun, and shake at him my "bewitching" black locks, calling him a foolish boy. And while I said it, the notion slowly dawning during the long gaze he had complained of, forced itself upon me, clear as daylight, that he was not a "boy" any longer.

"Now let me turn the tables. How old are *you*, John?"

"You know. Eighteen next week."

"And how tall?"

"Five feet eleven inches and a half." And, rising, he exhibited to its full advantage that very creditable altitude, more tall perhaps than graceful, at present; since, like most youths, he did not as yet quite know what to do with his legs and arms. But he was——

I cannot describe what he was. I could not then. I only remember that when I looked at him, and began jocularly "*Imprimis*," my heart came up into my throat and choked me.

It was almost with sadness that I said, "Ah, David, you are quite a young man now."

He smiled, of course only with pleasure, looking forward to the new world into which he was going forth; the world into which, as I knew well, I could never follow him.

"I am glad I look rather old for my years," said he, when, after a pause, he had again flung himself down on the grass. "It tells well in the tanyard. People would be slow to trust a clerk who looked a mere boy. Still, your father trusts me."

"He does indeed. You need never have any doubt of that. It was only yesterday he said to me that now he was no longer dissatisfied with your working at all sorts of studies, in leisure hours, since it made you none the worse man of business."

"No, I hope not, or I should be much ashamed. It would not be doing my duty to myself any more than to my master if I shirked his work for my own. I am glad he does not complain now, Phineas."

"On the contrary, I think he intends to give you a rise this midsummer. But oh!" I cried, recurring to a thought which would often come when I looked at the lad, though he always combated it so strongly that I often owned my prejudices were unjust, "how I wish you were something better than a clerk in a tanyard. I have a plan, John."

But what that plan was was fated to remain unrevealed. Jael came to us in the garden, looking very serious. She had been summoned, I knew, to a long conference with her master the day before—the subject of which she would not tell me, though she acknowledged it concerned myself. Ever since she had followed me about very softly, for her, and called me more than once, as when I was a child, "my dear." She now came with half-dolorous, half-angry looks, to summon me to an interview with my father and Dr. Jessop.

I caught her parting mutterings as she marched behind me: "Kill or cure, indeed," "No more fit than a baby," "Abel Fletcher be clean mad," "Hope Thomas Jessop will speak out plain, and tell him so," and the like. From these, and from her strange fit of tenderness, I guessed what was looming in the distance—a future which my father constantly held *in terrorem* over me, though successive illnesses had kept it in abeyance.

Alas, I knew that my poor father's hopes and plans were vain! I went into his presence with a heavy heart.

There is no need to detail that interview. Enough, that after it he set aside for ever his last lingering hope of having a son able to assist, and finally succeed him in his business, and that I set aside every dream of growing up to be a help and comfort to my father. It cost something on both our parts; but after that day's discussion we tacitly covered over the pain, and referred to it no more.

I came back into the garden, and told John Halifax all. He listened with his hand on my shoulder, and his grave, sweet look—dearer sympathy than any words! Though he added thereto a few, in his own wise way; then he and I also drew the curtain over an inevitable grief, and laid it in the peaceful chamber of silence.

When my father, Dr. Jessop, John Halifax, and I met at dinner, the subject had passed into seeming oblivion, and was never afterwards revived.

But dinner being over, and the chatty little doctor gone, while Abel Fletcher sat mutely smoking his pipe, and we two at the window maintained that respectful and decorous silence which in my young days was rigidly exacted by elders and superiors, I noticed my father's eyes frequently resting, with keen observance, upon John Halifax. Could it be that there had recurred to him a hint of mine, given faintly that morning, as faintly as if it had only just entered my mind, instead of having for months continually dwelt there, until a fitting moment should arrive? Could it be that this hint, which he had indignantly scouted at the time, was germinating in his acute brain, and might bear fruit in future days? I hoped so—I earnestly prayed so. And to that end I took no notice, but let it silently grow.

The June evening came and went. The service-bell rang out and ceased. First, deep shadows, and then a bright star, appeared over the Abbey tower. We watched it from the garden, where, Sunday after Sunday, in fine weather, we used to lounge, and talk over all manner of things in heaven and in earth, chiefly ending with the former, as on Sunday nights, with stars over our head, was natural and fit we should do.

"Phineas," said John, sitting on the grass with his hands upon his knees, and the one star, I think it was Jupiter, shining down into his eyes, deepening them into that peculiar look, worth any so-called "handsome eyes"—"Phineas, I wonder how soon we shall have to rise up from this quiet, easy life, and fight our battles in the world? Also, I wonder if we are ready for it?"

"I think you are."

"I don't know. I'm not clear how far I could resist doing anything wrong, if it were pleasant. So many wrong things are pleasant—just now, instead of rising to-morrow, and going into the little dark counting-house, and scratching paper from eight till six, shouldn't I like to break away!—dash out into the world, take to all sorts of wild freaks, do all sorts of grand things, and perhaps never come back to the tanning any more."

"Never any more?"

"No, no; I spoke hastily. I did not mean I ever should do such a wrong thing; but merely that I sometimes feel the wish to do it. I can't help it; it's my Apollyon that I have to fight with—everybody keeps a private Apollyon, I fancy. Now, Phineas, be content; Apollyon is beaten down."

He rose up, but I thought that, in the red glow of the twilight, he looked rather pale. He stretched his hand to help me up from the grass. We went into the house together silently.

After supper, when the chimes struck half-past nine, John prepared to leave as usual. He went to bid good-night to my father, who was sitting meditatively over the fireless hearth-place, sometimes poking the great bow-pot of fennel and asparagus, as in winter he did the coals; an instance of obliviousness which, in my sensible and acute father, argued very deep cogitation on some subject or other.

"Good-night," said John twice over, before his master heard him.

"Eh? Oh, good-night, good-night, lad! Stay, Halifax, what hast thee got to do to-morrow?"

"Not much, unless the Russian hides should come in; I cleared off the week's accounts last night as usual."

"Ay, to-morrow I shall look over all thy books and see how thee stand'st, and what further work thou art fit for. Therefore take a day's holiday if thee likes."

We thanked him warmly. "There, John," whispered I, "you may have your wish, and run wild to-morrow."

He said "the wish had gone out of him." So we planned a sweet lazy day under the midsummer sky, in some fields about a mile off, called the Vineyards.

The morning came, and we took our way thither, under the Abbey walls, and along a lane, shaded on one side by the "willows in the watercourses." We came out in those quiet hayfields, which, tradition says, had once grown wine for the rosy monks close by, and history avers, were afterwards watered by a darker stream than the blood of grapes. The Vineyards had been a battle-field; and under the long wavy grass and the roots of the wild apple trees slept many a Yorkist and Lancastrian. Sometimes an unusually deep furrow turned out a white bone—but more often the relics were undisturbed, and the meadows used as pastures or hayfields.

John and I lay down on some wind-rows, and sunned ourselves in the warm and delicious air. How beautiful everything was! so very still! with the Abbey tower—always the most picturesque point in our Norton Bury views—showing so near, that it almost seemed to rise up out of the fields and hedgerows.

"Well, David," and I turned to the long, lazy figure beside me, which had considerably flattened the hay, "are you satisfied?"

"Ay."

Thus we lounged out all the summer morning, recurring to a few of the infinitude of subjects we used to compare notes upon; though we were neither of us given to wordiness, and never talked but when we had something to say. Often—as on this day—we sat for hours in a pleasant dreaminess, scarcely exchanging a word; nevertheless, I could generally track John's thoughts, as they went wandering on, ay, as clearly as one might track a stream through a wood; sometimes—like to-day—I failed.

In the afternoon, when we had finished our bread and cheese—eaten slowly and with graceful dignity, in order to make dinner a more important and lengthy affair—he said abruptly,—

"Phineas, don't you think this field is rather dull? Shall we go somewhere else? Not if it tires you, though."

I protested the contrary, my health being much above the average this summer. But just as we were quitting the field, we met two rather odd-looking persons entering it, young-old persons they seemed, who might own to any age or any occupation. Their dress, especially that of the younger, amused us by its queer mixture of fashionableness and homeliness, such as gray ribbed stockings and shining paste shoe-buckles, rusty velvet small-clothes, and a coatee of blue cloth. But the wearer carried off this anomalous costume with an easy, condescending air, full of pleasantness, humour, and grace.

"Sir," said he, approaching John Halifax with a bow that I feel sure the "first gentleman of his day," as loyal folk then entitled the Prince Regent, could not have surpassed—"Sir, will you favour me by informing us how far it is to Coltham?"

"Ten miles, and the stage will pass here in three hours."

"Thank you; at present I have little to do with the—at least with *that* stage. Young gentlemen, excuse our continuing our dessert, in fact, I may say our dinner. Are you connoisseurs in turnips?"

He offered us—with a polite gesture—one of the "swedes" he was munching. I declined; but John, out of a deeper delicacy than I could boast, accepted it.

"One might dine worse," he said; "I have done, sometimes."

"It was a whim of mine, sir. But I am not the first remarkable person who has eaten turnips in your Norton Bury fields—ay, and turned field-preacher afterwards—the celebrated John Philip——"

Here the elder and less agreeable of the two wayfarers interposed with a nudge, indicating silence.

"My companion is right, sir," he continued. "I will not betray our illustrious friend by mentioning his surname; he is a great man now, and might not wish it generally known that he had dined off turnips. May I give you instead my own humble name?"

He gave it me; but I, Phineas Fletcher, shall copy his reticence, and not indulge the world therewith. It was a name wholly out of my sphere, both then and now; but I know it has since risen into note among the people of the world. I believe, too, its owner has carried up to the topmost height of celebrity always the gay, gentlemanly spirit and kindly heart which he showed when sitting with us and eating swedes. Still, I will not mention his surname—I will only call him "Mr. Charles."

"Now, having satisfactorily 'munched, and munched, and munched,' like the sailor's wife who had chestnuts in her lap—are you acquainted with my friend, Mr. William Shakespeare, young gentlemen?—I must try to fulfil the other duties of existence. You said the Coltham mail passed here in three hours? Very well. I have the honour of wishing you a very good day, Mr. ——"

"Halifax."

"And yours?"

"Fletcher."

"Any connection with him who went partnership with the worthy Beaumont?"

"My father has no partner, sir," said I. But John, whose reading had lately surpassed mine, and whom nothing ever puzzled, explained that I came from the same old stock as the brothers Phineas and Giles Fletcher.

Upon which Mr. Charles, who till now had somewhat overlooked me, took off his hat, and congratulated me on my illustrious descent.

"That man has evidently seen a good deal of the world," said John, smiling; "I wonder what the world is like!"

"Did you not see something of it as a child?"

"Only the worst and lowest side; not the one I want to see now. What business do you think that Mr. Charles is? A clever man, anyhow; I should like to see him again."

"So should I."

Thus talking at intervals and speculating upon our new acquaintance, we strolled along till we came to a spot called by the country people "The Bloody Meadow," from being, like several other places in the neighbourhood, the scene of one of those terrible slaughters chronicled in the Wars of the Roses. It was a sloping field, through the middle of which ran a little stream down to the meadow's end, where, fringed and hidden by a plantation of trees, the Avon flowed. Here, too, in all directions, the hayfields lay, either in green swathes, or tedded, or in the luxuriously-scented quiles. The lane was quite populous with wagons and haymakers—the men in their corduroys and blue hose—the women in their trim jackets and bright calamanco petticoats. There were more women than men by far, for the flower of the peasant youth of England had been drafted off to fight against "Bonyparty." Still haytime was a glorious season, when half our little town turned out and made holiday in the sunshine.

"I think we will go to a quieter place, John. There seems a crowd down in the meadow; and who is that man standing on the hay-cart, on the other side the stream?"

"Don't you remember the bright blue coat? 'Tis Mr. Charles. How he's talking and gesticulating! What can he be at?"

Without more ado, John leaped the low hedge, and ran

down the slope of the Bloody Meadow. I followed less quickly.

There, of a surety, stood our new friend, on one of the simple-fashioned hay-carts that we used about Norton Bury, a low framework on wheels, with a pole stuck at either of the four corners. He was bareheaded and his hair hung in graceful curls, well powdered. I only hope he had honestly paid the tax, which we were all then exclaiming against—so fondly does custom cling to deformity. Despite the powder, the blue coat, and the shabby velvet breeches, Mr. Charles was a very handsome and striking-looking man. No wonder the poor haymakers had collected from all parts to hear him harangue.

What was he haranguing upon ? Could it be, that like his friend, " John Philip," whoever that personage might be, his vocation was that of a field preacher ? It seemed like it, especially judging from the sanctified demeanour of the elder and inferior person who accompanied him ; and who sat in front of the cart, and folded his hands and groaned, after the most approved fashion of a Methodistical " revival."

We listened, expecting every minute to be disgusted and shocked : but no ! I must say this for Mr. Charles, that in no way did he trespass the bounds of reverence and decorum. His harangue, though given as a sermon, was strictly and simply a moral essay, such as might have emanated from any professor's chair. In fact, as I afterwards learnt, he had given for his text one which the simple rustics received in all respect, as coming from a higher and holier volume than Shakespeare :—

> " Mercy is twice blessed :
> It blesseth him that gives and him that takes.
> 'Tis mightiest in the mightiest."

And on that text did he dilate ; gradually warming with his subject, till his gestures—which at first had seemed burthened with a queer constraint, that now and then resulted in an irrepressible twitch of the corners of his flexible mouth—became those of a man beguiled into real earnestness. We of Norton Bury had never heard such eloquence.

"Who *can* he be, John? Isn't it wonderful?"

But John never heard me. His whole attention was riveted on the speaker. Such oratory—a compound of graceful action, polished language, and brilliant imagination, came to him as a positive revelation, a revelation from the world of intellect, the world which he longed after with all the ardour of youth.

What that harangue would have seemed like, could we have heard it with maturer ears, I know not; but at eighteen and twenty it literally dazzled us. No wonder it affected the rest of the audience. Feeble men, leaning on forks and rakes, shook their old heads sagely, as if they understood it all. And when the speaker alluded to the horrors of war—a subject which then came so bitterly home to every heart in Britain—many women melted into sobs and tears. At last, when the orator himself, moved by the pictures he had conjured up, paused suddenly, quite exhausted, and asked for a slight contribution "to help a deed of charity," there was a general rush towards him.

"No—no, my good people," said Mr. Charles, recovering his natural manner, though a little clouded, I thought, by a faint shade of remorse; "no, I will not take from any one more than a penny; and then only if they are quite sure they can spare it. Thank you, my worthy man. Thanks, my bonnie young lass—I hope your sweetheart will soon be back from the wars. Thank you all, my 'very worthy and approved good masters,' and a fair harvest to you!"

He bowed them away, in a dignified and graceful manner, still standing on the hay-cart. The honest folk trooped off, having no more time to waste, and left the field in possession of Mr. Charles, his co-mate, and ourselves; whom I do not think he had as yet noticed.

He descended from the cart. His companion burst into roars of laughter; but Mr. Charles looked grave.

"Poor, honest souls!" said he, wiping his brows—I am not sure that it was only his brows—"Hang me if I'll be at this trick again, Yates."

"It was a trick, then, sir," said John, advancing. "I am sorry for it."

"So am I, young man," returned the other, no way disconcerted; indeed, he seemed a person whose frank temper nothing could disconcert. "But starvation is—excuse me—unpleasant; and necessity has no law. It is of vital consequence that I should reach Coltham to-night; and after walking twenty miles one cannot easily walk ten more, and afterwards appear as Macbeth to an admiring audience."

"You are an actor?"

"I am, please your worship—

> "'A poor player,
> That struts and frets his hour upon the stage,
> And then is seen no more.'"

There was inexpressible pathos in his tone, and his fine face looked thin and worn—it did not take much to soften both John's feelings and mine towards the "poor player." Besides, we had lately been studying Shakespeare, who for the first time of reading generally sends all young people tragedy mad.

"You acted well to-day," said John; "all the folk here took you for a Methodist preacher."

"Yet I never meddled with theology—only common morality. You cannot say I did."

John thought a moment, and then answered,—

"No. But what put the scheme into your head?"

"The fact that, under a like necessity, the same amusing play was played out here years ago, as I told you, by John Philip—no, I will not conceal his name, the greatest actor and the truest gentleman our English stage has ever seen—John Philip Kemble."

And he raised his hat with sincere reverence. We too had heard—at least John had—of this wonderful man.

I saw the fascination of Mr. Charles's society was

strongly upon him. It was no wonder. More brilliant, more versatile talent I never saw. He turned "from grave to gay, from lively to severe"—appearing in all phases like the gentleman, the scholar, and the man of the world. And neither John nor I had ever met any one of these characters, all so irresistibly alluring at our age.

I say *our*, because though I followed where he led, I always did it of my own will likewise.

The afternoon began to wane, while we, with our two companions, yet sat talking by the brookside. Mr. Charles had washed his face and his travel-sore, blistered feet, and we had induced him, and the man he called Yates, to share our remnants of bread and cheese.

"Now," he said, starting up, "I am ready to do battle again, even with the Thane of Fife—who, to-night, is one Johnson, a fellow of six feet and twelve stone. What is the hour, Mr. Halifax?"

"Mr. Halifax" (I felt pleased to hear him for the first time so entitled) had, unfortunately, no watch among his worldly possessions, and candidly owned the fact. But he made a near guess by calculating the position of his unfailing timepiece, the sun. It was four o'clock.

"Then I must go. Will you not retract, young gentlemen? Surely you would not lose such a rare treat as 'Macbeth,' with—I will not say my humble self—but with that divine Siddons. Such a woman! Shakespeare himself might lean out of Elysium to watch her. You will join us?"

John made a silent, dolorous negative; as he had done once or twice before, when the actor urged us to accompany him to Coltham for a few hours only—we might be back by midnight easily.

"What do you think, Phineas?" said John, when we stood in the highroad, waiting for the coach; "I have money—and—we have so little pleasure—we would send word to your father. Do you think it would be wrong?"

I could not say; and to this minute, viewing the question nakedly in a strict and moral sense, I cannot say either whether or no it was an absolute crime; therefore, being accustomed to read my wrong or right in "David's" eyes, I remained perfectly passive.

We waited by the hedge-side for several minutes—Mr. Charles ceased his urging, half in dudgeon, save that he was too pleasant a man really to take offence at anything. His conversation was chiefly directed to me. John took no part therein, but strolled about plucking at the hedge.

When the stage appeared down the winding of the road I was utterly ignorant of what he meant us to do, or if he had any definite purpose at all.

It came—the coachman was hailed. Mr. Charles shook hands with us and mounted—paying his own fare and that of Yates with their handful of charity-pennies, which caused a few minutes' delay in counting, and a great deal of good-humoured joking, as good-humouredly borne.

Meanwhile, John put his two hands on my shoulders and looked hard into my face—his was slightly flushed and excited, I thought.

"Phineas, are you tired?"

"Not at all."

"Do you feel strong enough to go to Coltham? Would it do you any harm? Would you *like* to go?"

To all these hurried questions I answered with as hurried an affirmative. It was sufficient to me that he evidently liked to go.

"It is only for once—your father would not grudge us the pleasure, and he is too busy to be out of the tanyard before midnight. We will be home soon after that, if I carry you on my back all the ten miles. Come, mount, we'll go."

"Bravo!" cried Mr. Charles, and leaned over to help me up the coach's side. John followed, and the crisis was past.

But I noticed that for several miles he hardly spoke one word.

CHAPTER VI.

NEAR as we lived to Coltham, I had only been there once in my life; but John Halifax knew the town pretty well, having latterly, in addition to his clerkship, been employed by my father in going about the neighbourhood buying bark. I was amused when the coach stopped at an inn, which bore the ominous sign of the "Fleece," to see how well accustomed he seemed to be to the ways of the place. He deported himself with perfect self-possession; the waiter served him respectfully. He had evidently taken his position in the world—at least, our little world—he was no longer a boy, but a man. I was glad to see it; leaving everything in his hands, I lay down where he placed me in the inn parlour, and watched him giving his orders and walking about. Sometimes I thought his eyes were restless and unquiet, but his manner was as composed as usual.

Mr. Charles had left us, appointing a meeting at Coffee-house Yard, where the theatre then was.

"A poor barnlike place, I believe," said John, stopping in his walk up and down the room to place my cushions more easy; "they should build a new one, now Coltham is growing up into such a fashionable town. I wish I could take you to see the 'Well Walk,' with all the fine people promenading. But you must rest, Phineas."

I consented, being indeed rather weary.

"You will like to see Mrs. Siddons, whom we have so often talked about? She is not young now, Mr. Charles says, but magnificent still. She first came out in this same theatre more than twenty years ago. Yates saw her. I wonder, Phineas, if your father ever did?"

"Oh no! my father would not enter a playhouse for the world."

"What!"

"Nay, John, you need not look so troubled. You know he did not bring me up in the Society, and its restrictions are not binding upon me."

"True, true." And he resumed his walk, but not his cheerfulness. "If it were myself alone now, of course what I myself hold to be a lawful pleasure I have a right to enjoy; or, if not, being yet a lad and under a master—well, I will bear the consequences," added he, rather proudly; "but to share them—Phineas," turning suddenly to me, "would you like to go home? I'll take you."

I protested earnestly against any such thing; told him I was sure we were doing nothing wrong—which was, indeed, my belief; entreated him to be merry and enjoy himself, and succeeded so well, that in a few minutes we had started in a flutter of gaiety and excitement for Coffee-house Yard.

It was a poor place—little better than a barn, as Mr. Charles had said—built in a lane leading out of the principal street. This lane was almost blocked up with playgoers of all ranks and in all sorts of equipages, from the coach-and-six to the sedan-chair, mingled with a motley crowd on foot, all jostling, fighting, and screaming, till the place became a complete bear-garden.

"O John! take care!" and I clung to his arm.

"Never mind! I'm big enough and strong enough for any crowd. Hold on, Phineas." If I had been a woman, and the woman that he loved, he could not have been more tender over my weakness. The physical weakness—which, however humiliating to myself, and doubtless contemptible in most men's eyes—was yet dealt by the hand of Heaven, and, as such, regarded by John only with compassion.

The crowd grew denser and more formidable. I looked beyond it, up towards the low hills that rose in various directions round the town; how green and quiet they were in the still June evening! I only wished we were safe back again at Norton Bury.

But now there came a slight swaying in the crowd, as a sedan-chair was borne through—or attempted to be—for the effort failed. There was a scuffle; one of the bearers was knocked down and hurt. Some cried "Shame!"

others seemed to think this incident only added to the frolic. At last, in the midst of the confusion, a lady put her head out of the sedan and gazed around her.

It was a remarkable countenance; once seen, you could never forget it. Pale, rather large and hard in outline, an aquiline nose—full, passionate, yet sensitive lips—and very dark eyes. She spoke, and the voice belonged naturally to such a face. "Good people, let me pass—I am Sarah Siddons."

The crowd divided instantaneously, and in moving set up a cheer that must have rang through all the town. There was a minute's pause, while she bowed and smiled—such a smile!—and then the sedan curtain closed.

"Now's the time—only hold fast to me!" whispered John, as he sprang forward, dragging me after him. In another second he had caught up the pole dropped by the man who was hurt; and before I well knew what we were about we both stood safe inside the entrance of the theatre.

Mrs. Siddons stepped out, and turned to pay her bearers—a most simple action—but so elevated in the doing that even it, I thought, could not bring her to the level of common humanity. The tall, cloaked, and hooded figure, and the tones that issued thence, made her, even in that narrow passage, under the one flaring tallow candle, a veritable queen of tragedy—at least so she seemed to us two.

The one man was paid—overpaid, apparently, from his thankfulness—and she turned to John Halifax.

"I regret, young man, that you should have had so much trouble. Here is some requital."

He took the money, selected from it one silver coin, and returned the rest.

"I will keep this, madam, if you please, as a memento that I once had the honour of being useful to Mrs. Siddons."

She looked at him keenly, out of her wonderful dark eyes, then curtsied with grave dignity. "I thank you, sir," she said, and passed on.

A few minutes after some underling of the theatre found us out and brought us, "by Mrs. Siddons's desire," to the best places the house could afford.

It was a glorious night. At this distance of time, when I look back upon it, my old blood leaps and burns. I repeat, it was a glorious night!

Before the curtain rose we had time to glance about us on that scene, to both entirely new—the inside of a theatre. Shabby and small as the place was, it was filled with all the *beau monde* of Coltham, which then, patronized by royalty, rivalled even Bath in its fashion and folly. Such a dazzle of diamonds and spangled turbans and Prince of Wales' plumes. Such an odd mingling of costume, which was then in a transition state, the old ladies clinging tenaciously to the stately silken petticoats and long bodices, surmounted by the prim and decent *bouffantes*, while the younger belles had begun to flaunt in the French fashions of flimsy muslins—short-waisted, narrow-skirted. These we had already heard Jael furiously inveighing against: for Jael, Quakeress as she was, could not quite smother her original propensity towards the decoration of "the flesh," and betrayed a suppressed but profound interest in the same.

John and I quite agreed with her, that it was painful to see gentle English girls clad, or rather un-clad, after the fashion of our enemies across the Channel; now, unhappy nation! sunk to zero in politics, religion, and morals—where high-bred ladies went about dressed as heathen goddesses, with bare arms and bare sandalled feet, gaining none of the pure simplicity of the ancient world, and losing all the decorous dignity of our modern times.

We two—who had all a boy's mysterious reverence for womanhood in its most ideal, most beautiful form, and who, I believe, were, in our ignorance, expecting to behold in every woman an Imogen, a Juliet, or a Desdemona—felt no particular attraction towards the ungracefully attired, flaunting, simpering belles of Coltham.

But—the play began.

I am not going to follow it: all the world has heard of the Lady Macbeth of Mrs. Siddons. This, the first and last play I ever witnessed, stands out to my memory, after more than half a century, as clear as on that night. Still I can see her in her first scene, "reading a letter"—that wondrous woman, who, in spite of her modern black velvet and point lace, did not act, but *was*, Lady Macbeth: still I hear the awestruck, questioning, weirdlike tone, that sent an involuntary shudder through the house, as if supernatural things were abroad—"*They made themselves—air!*" And still there quivers through the silence that piteous cry of a strong heart broken—"*All the perfumes of Arabia will never sweeten this little hand!*"

Well, she is gone, like the brief three hours when we hung on her every breath, as if it could stay even the wheels of time. But they have whirled on—whirled her away with them into the infinite, and into earthly oblivion. People tell me that a new generation only smiles at the traditional glory of Sarah Siddons. They never saw her. For me, I shall go down to the grave worshipping her still.

Of him whom I call Mr. Charles I have little to say. John and I both smiled when we saw his fine frank face and manly bearing subdued into that poor, whining, sentimental craven, the stage Macbeth. Yet I believe he acted it well. But we irresistibly associated his idea with that of turnip-munching and hay-cart oratory. And when, during the first colloquy of Banquo with the witches, Macbeth took the opportunity of winking privately at us over the footlights, all the paraphernalia of the stage failed to make the murderous Thane of Cawdor aught else than our humorous and good-natured Mr. Charles. I never saw him after that night. He is still living—may his old age have been as peaceful as his youth was kind and gay!

The play ended. There was some buffoonery still to come, but we would not stay for that. We staggered, half-blind and dazzled, both in eyes and brain, out into the dark streets, John almost carrying me. Then we paused, and leaning against a post which was surmounted by one of the half-dozen oil lamps which illumined the town, tried to regain our mental equilibrium.

John was the first to do it. Passing his hand over his brow, he bared it to the fresh night air, and drew a deep, hard breath. He was very pale, I saw.

"John?"

He turned, and laid a hand on my shoulder. "What did you say? Are you cold?"

"No." He put his arm so as to shield the wind from me, nevertheless.

"Well," said he, after a pause, "we have had our pleasure, and it is over. Now we must go back to the old ways again. I wonder what o'clock it is?"

He was answered by a church clock striking, heard clearly over the silent town. I counted the strokes—*eleven!*

Horrified, we looked at one another by the light of the lamp. Until this minute we had taken no note of time. Eleven o'clock! How should we get home to Norton Bury that night?

For, now the excitement was over, I turned sick and faint; my limbs almost sank under me.

"What must we do, John?"

"Do! Oh! 'tis quite easy. You cannot walk—you shall not walk—we must hire a gig and drive home. I have enough money—all my month's wages—see!" He felt in his pockets one after the other; his countenance grew blank. "Why? where is my money gone to?"

Where, indeed! But that it was gone, and irretrievably—most likely stolen when we were so wedged in the crowd—there could be no manner of doubt. And I had not a groat. I had little use for money, and rarely carried any.

"Would not somebody trust us?" suggested I.

"I never asked anybody for credit in my life—and for a horse and gig—they'd laugh at me. Still—yes—stay here a minute, and I'll try."

He came back, though not immediately, and took my arm with a reckless laugh.

"It's of no use, Phineas—I'm not so respectable as I thought. What's to be done?"

Ay! what indeed! Here we were, two friendless youths, with not a penny in our pockets, and ten miles away from home. How to get there, and at midnight too, was a very serious question. We consulted a minute, and then John said firmly,—

"We must make the best of it and start. Every instant is precious. Your father will think we have fallen into some harm. Come, Phineas, I'll help you on."

His strong, cheery voice, added to the necessity of the circumstances, braced up my nerves. I took hold of his arm, and we marched on bravely through the shut-up town, and for a mile or two along the highroad leading to Norton Bury. There was a cool fresh breeze: and I often think one can walk so much farther by night than by day. For some time, listening to John's talk about the stars—he had lately added astronomy to the many things he tried to learn—and recalling with him all that we had heard and seen this day, I hardly felt my weariness.

But gradually it grew upon me; my pace lagged slower and slower—even the scented air of the midsummer night imparted no freshness. John wound his young arm, strong and firm as iron, round my waist, and we got on a while in that way.

"Keep up, Phineas. There's a hayrick near. I'll wrap you in my coat, and you shall rest there: an hour or two will not matter now—we shall get home by daybreak."

I feebly assented; but it seemed to me that we never should get home—at least I never should. For a short way more, I dragged myself—or rather, was dragged—along; then the stars, the shadowy fields, and the winding, white highroad mingled and faded from me. I lost all consciousness.

When I came to myself I was lying by a tiny brook at the roadside, my head resting on John's knees. He was bathing my forehead: I could not see him, but I heard his smothered moan.

"David, don't mind. I shall be well directly."

"O Phineas—Phineas; I thought I had killed you."

He said no more; but I fancied that under cover of the night he yielded to what his manhood might have been ashamed of—yet need not—a few tears.

I tried to rise. There was a faint streak in the east. "Why, it is daybreak! How far are we from Norton Bury?"

"Not very far. Don't stir a step. I shall carry you."

"Impossible!"

"Nonsense; I have done it for half a mile already. Come, mount! I am not going to have Jonathan's death laid at David's door."

And so, masking command with a jest, he had his way. What strength supported him I cannot tell, but he certainly carried me—with many rests between, and pauses, during which I walked a quarter of a mile or so—the whole way to Norton Bury.

The light broadened and broadened. When we reached my father's door, haggard and miserable, it was in the pale sunshine of a summer morning.

"Thank God!" murmured John, as he set me down at the foot of the steps. "You are safe at home."

"And you. You will come in—you would not leave me now?"

He thought a moment—then said "No!"

We looked up doubtfully at the house; there were no watchers there. All the windows were closed, as if the whole peaceful establishment were taking its sleep, prior to the early stirring of Norton Bury households. Even John's loud knocking was some time before it was answered.

I was too exhausted to feel much; but I know those five awful minutes seemed interminable. I could not have borne them, save for John's voice in my ear.

"Courage! I'll bear all the blame. We have committed no absolute sin, and have paid dearly for any folly. Courage!"

At the five minutes' end my father opened the door.

He was dressed as usual, looked as usual. Whether he had sat up watching, or had suffered any anxiety, I never found out.

He said nothing; merely opened the door, admitted us, and closed it behind us. But we were certain, from his face, that he knew all. It was so; some neighbour driving home from Coltham had taken pains to tell Abel Fletcher where he had seen his son—at the very last place a Friend's son ought to be seen—the playhouse. We knew that it was by no means to learn the truth, but to confront us with it, that my father—reaching the parlour, and opening the shutters that the hard daylight should shame us more and more—asked the stern question,—

"Phineas, where hast thee been?"

John answered for me. "At the theatre at Coltham. It was my fault. He went because I wished to go."

"And wherefore didst thee wish to go?"

"Wherefore?" The answer seemed hard to find. "Oh! Mr. Fletcher, were you never young like me?"

My father made no reply; John gathered courage.

"It was, as I say, all my fault. It might have been wrong—I think now that it was—but the temptation was hard. My life here is dull; I long sometimes for a little amusement—a little change."

"Thee shall have it."

That voice, slow and quiet as it was, struck us both dumb.

"And how long hast thee planned this, John Halifax?"

"Not a day—not an hour! It was a sudden freak of mine." (My father shook his head with contemptuous incredulity.) "Sir!—Abel Fletcher—did I ever tell you a lie? If you will not believe me, believe your own son. Ask Phineas—No, no, ask him nothing!" And he came in great distress to the sofa where I had fallen. "O Phineas! how cruel I have been to you!"

I tried to smile at him, being past speaking—but my father put John aside.

"Young man, *I* can take care of my son. Thee shalt not lead him into harm's way any more. Go—I have been mistaken in thee!"

If my father had gone into a passion, had accused us, reproached us, and stormed at us with all the ill-language that men of the world use! but that quiet, cold, irrevocable, "I have been mistaken in thee!" was ten times worse.

John lifted to him a mute look, from which all pride had ebbed away.

"I repeat, I have been mistaken in thee! Thee seemed a lad to my mind; I trusted thee. This day, by my son's wish, I meant to have bound thee 'prentice to me, and in good time to have taken thee into the business. Now——"

There was silence. At last John muttered, in a low, broken-hearted voice, "I deserve it all. I can go away. I might perhaps earn my living elsewhere; shall I?"

Abel Fletcher hesitated, looked at the poor lad before him (O David! how unlike to thee), then said, "No—I do not wish that. At least, not at present."

I cried out in the joy and relief of my heart. John came over to me, and we clasped hands.

"John, you will not go?"

"No, I will stay to redeem my character with your father. Be content, Phineas—I won't part with you."

"Young man, thou must," said my father, turning round.

"But——"

"I have said it, Phineas. I accuse him of no dishonesty, no crime, but of weakly yielding, and selfishly causing another to yield, to the temptation of the world. Therefore, as my clerk I retain him; as my son's companion—never!"

We felt that "never" was irrevocable.

Yet I tried, blindly and despairingly, to wrestle with it; I might as well have flung myself against a stone wall.

John stood perfectly silent.

"Don't, Phineas," he whispered at last; "never mind me. Your father is right—at least so far as he sees. Let me go—perhaps I may come back to you some time. If not——"

I moaned out bitter words—I hardly knew what I was saying. My father took no notice of them, only went to the door and called Jael.

Then, before the woman came, I had strength enough to bid John go.

"Good-bye—don't forget me, don't!"

"I will not," he said; "and if I live we shall be friends again. Good-bye, Phineas." He was gone.

After that day, though he kept his word, and remained in the tanyard, and though from time to time I heard of him—always accidentally—after that day for two long years I never once saw the face of John Halifax.

CHAPTER VII.

It was the year 1800, long known in English households as "the dear year." The present generation can have no conception of what a terrible time that was—War, Famine, and Tumult stalking hand-in-hand, and no one to stay them. For between the upper and lower classes there was a great gulf fixed; the rich ground the faces of the poor, the poor hated, yet meanly succumbed to, the rich. Neither had Christianity enough boldly to cross the line of demarcation, and prove, the humbler, that they were men—the higher and wiser, that they were gentlemen.

These troubles, which were everywhere abroad, reached us even in our quiet town of Norton Bury. For myself, personally, they touched me not, or, at least, only kept fluttering like evil birds outside the dear home-tabernacle, where I and Patience sat, keeping our solemn counsel together—for these two years had with me been very hard.

Though I had to bear so much bodily suffering that I was seldom told of any worldly cares, still I often fancied things were going ill both within and without our doors. Jael complained in an under-key of stinted housekeeping, or boasted aloud of her own ingenuity in making ends meet: and my father's brow grew continually heavier, graver, sterner; sometimes so stern that I dared not wage, what was, openly or secretly, the quiet but incessant crusade of my existence—the bringing back of John Halifax.

He still remained my father's clerk—nay, I sometimes thought he was even advancing in duties and trusts, for I heard of his being sent long journeys up and down England to buy grain—Abel Fletcher having added to his tanning business the flour-mill hard by, whose lazy whir was so familiar to John and me in our boyhood. But of these journeys my father never spoke; indeed, he rarely mentioned John at all. However he might employ and even trust him in business relations, I knew that in every other way he was inexorable.

And John Halifax was as inexorable as he. No underhand or clandestine friendship would he admit—no, not even for my sake. I knew quite well, that until he could walk in openly, honourably, proudly, he never would reenter my father's doors. Twice only he had written to me—on my two birthdays—my father himself giving me in silence the unsealed letters. They told me what I already was sure of—that I held, and always should hold, my steadfast place in his friendship. Nothing more.

One other fact I noticed: that a little lad, afterward discovered to be Jem Watkins, to whom had fallen the hard-working lot of the lost Bill, had somehow crept into our household as errand boy, or gardener's boy; and being "cute," and a "scholard," was greatly patronized by Jael. I noticed, too, that the said Jem, whenever he came in my way, in house or garden, was the most capital "little foot-page" that ever invalid had; knowing intuitively all my needs, and serving me with an unfailing devotion which quite surprised and puzzled me at the time. It did not afterwards.

Summer was passing. People began to watch with

anxious looks the thin harvest fields—as Jael often told me, when she came home from her afternoon walks. "It was piteous to see them," she said; "only July, and the quartern loaf nearly three shillings, and meal four shillings a peck."

And then she would glance at our flour-mill, where for several days a week the water-wheel was as quiet as on Sundays; for my father kept his grain locked up, waiting for what, he wisely judged, might be a worse harvest than the last. But Jael, though she said nothing, often looked at the flour-mill and shook her head. And after one market day—when she came in rather "flustered," saying there had been a mob outside the mill, until "that young man Halifax" had gone out and spoken to them—she never once allowed me to take my rare walk under the trees in the Abbey yard; nor, if she could help it, would she even let me sit watching the lazy Avon from the garden wall.

One Sunday—it was the first of August, for my father had just come back from the meeting, very much later than usual, and Jael said he had gone, as was his annual custom on that his wedding-day, to the Friends' burial-ground in St. Mary's Lane, where, far away from her own kindred and people, my poor young mother had been laid—on this one Sunday I began to see that things were going wrong. Abel Fletcher sat at dinner wearing the heavy, hard look which had grown upon his face not unmingled with the wrinkles planted by physical pain. For, with all his temperance, he could not quite keep down his hereditary enemy, gout; and this week it had clutched him pretty hard.

Dr. Jessop came in, and I stole away gladly enough, and sat for an hour in my old place in the garden, idly watching the stretch of meadow, pasture, and harvest land. Noticing, too, more as a pretty bit in the landscape than as a fact of vital importance, in how many places the half-ripe corn was already cut, and piled in thinly-scattered sheaves over the fields.

After the doctor left, my father sent for me and all his

household: in the which, creeping humbly after the womankind, was now numbered the lad Jem. That Abel Fletcher was not quite himself was proved by the fact that his unlighted pipe lay on the table, and his afternoon tankard of ale sank from foam to flatness untouched.

He first addressed Jael. "Woman, was it thee who cooked the dinner to-day?"

She gave a dignified affirmative.

"Thee must give us no more such dinners. No cakes, no pastry kickshaws, and only wheaten bread enough for absolute necessity. Our neighbours shall not say that Abel Fletcher has flour in his mill, and plenty in his house, while there is famine abroad in the land. So take heed."

"I do take heed," answered Jael staunchly. "Thee canst not say I waste a penny of thine. And for myself, do I not pity the poor? On First-day a woman cried after me about wasting good flour in starch—to-day, behold."

And with a spasmodic bridling up, she pointed to the *bouffante* which used to stand up stiffly round her withered old throat, and stick out in front like a pouter pigeon. Alas! its glory and starch were alike departed; it now appeared nothing but a heap of crumpled and yellowish muslin. Poor Jael! I knew this was the most heroic personal sacrifice she could have made, yet I could not help smiling; even my father did the same.

"Dost thee mock me, Abel Fletcher?" cried she angrily. "Preach not to others while the sin lies on thy own head."

And I am sure poor Jael was innocent of any jocular intention, as advancing sternly she pointed to her master's pate, where his long-worn powder was scarcely distinguishable from the snows of age. He bore the assault gravely and unshrinkingly, merely saying, "Woman, peace!"

"Nor while," pursued Jael, driven apparently to the last and most poisoned arrow in her quiver of wrath

—"while the poor folk be starving in scores about Norton Bury, and the rich folk there will not sell their wheat under famine price. Take heed to thyself, Abel Fletcher."

My father winced, either from a twinge of gout or conscience; and then Jael suddenly ceased the attack, sent the other servants out of the room, and tended her master as carefully as if she had not insulted him. In his fits of gout my father, unlike most men, became the quieter and easier to manage the more he suffered. He had a long fit of pain, which left him considerably exhausted. When, being at last relieved, he and I were sitting in the room alone, he said to me,—

"Phineas, the tanyard has thriven ill of late, and I thought the mill would make up for it. But if it will not it will not. Wouldst thee mind, my son, being left a little poor when I am gone?"

"Father!"

"Well, then, in a few days I will begin selling my wheat, as that lad has advised and begged me to do these weeks past. He is a sharp lad, and I am getting old. Perhaps he is right."

"Who, father?" I asked, rather hypocritically.

"Thee knowest well enough—John Halifax."

I thought it best to say no more; but I never let go one thread of hope which could draw me nearer to my heart's desire.

On the Monday morning my father went to the tanyard as usual. I spent the day in my bedroom, which looked over the garden, where I saw nothing but the waving of the trees and the birds hopping over the smooth grass; heard nothing but the soft chime, hour after hour, of the Abbey bells. What was passing in the world, in the town, or even in the next street, was to me faint as dreams.

At dinner-time I rose, went downstairs, and waited for my father; waited one, two, three hours. It was very strange. He never by any chance overstayed his time without sending a message home. So after some consideration as to whether I dared encroach upon his formal habits so much, and after much advice from Jael, who betrayed more anxiety than was at all warranted by the cause she assigned—namely, the spoiled dinner—I dispatched Jem Watkins to the tanyard to see after his master.

He came back with ill news. The lane leading to the tanyard was blocked up with a wild mob. Even the stolid, starved patience of our Norton Bury poor had come to an end at last—they had followed the example of many others. There was a bread riot in the town.

God only knows how terrible those "riots" were; when the people rose in desperation, not from some delusion of crazy, bloodthirsty "patriotism," but to get food for themselves, their wives, and children. God only knows what madness was in each individual heart of that concourse of poor wretches, styled "the mob," when every man took up arms, certain that there were before him but two alternatives, starving or—hanging.

The riot here was scarcely universal. Norton Bury was not a large place, and had always abundance of small-pox and fevers to keep the poor down numerically. Jem said it was chiefly about our mill and our tanyard that the disturbance lay.

"And where is my father?"

Jem "didn't know," and looked very much as if he didn't care.

"Jael, somebody must go at once and find my father."

"I am going," said Jael, who had already put on her cloak and hood. Of course, despite all her opposition, I went too.

The tanyard was deserted; the mob had divided, and gone, one half to our mill, the rest to another that was lower down the river. I asked of a poor frightened bark-cutter if she knew where my father was. She thought he was gone for the "millingtary;" but Mr. Halifax was at the mill now—she hoped no harm would come to Mr. Halifax.

Even in that moment of alarm I felt a sense of pleasure.

I had not been in the tanyard for nearly three years. I did not know John had come already to be called "Mr. Halifax."

There was nothing for me but to wait here till my father returned. He could not surely be so insane as to go to the mill—and John was there. Terribly was my heart divided, but my duty lay with my father.

Jael sat down in the shed, or marched restlessly between the tan pits. I went to the end of the yard, and looked down towards the mill. What a half-hour it was!

At last, exhausted, I sat down on the bark heap where John and I once sat as lads. He must now be more than twenty; I wondered if he were altered.

"O David! David!" I thought, as I listened eagerly for any sounds abroad in the town; "what should I do if any harm came to thee?"

This minute I heard a footstep crossing the yard. No, it was not my father's—it was firmer, quicker, younger. I sprang from the bark heap.

"Phineas!"

"John!"

What a grasp that was—both hands! and how fondly and proudly I looked up in his face—the still boyish face. But the figure was quite that of a man now.

For a minute we forgot ourselves in our joy, and then he let go my hands, saying hurriedly,—

"Where is your father?"

"I wish I knew! Gone for the soldiers, they say."

"No, not that—he would never do that. I must go and look for him. Good-bye."

"Nay, dear John!"

"Can't—can't," said he firmly; "not while your father forbids. I must go." And he was gone.

Though my heart rebelled, my conscience defended him; marvelling how it was that he who had never known his father should uphold so sternly the duty of filial obedience. I think it ought to act as a solemn warning to those who exact so much from the mere fact and name of parenthood, without having in any way fulfilled its duties, that orphans from birth often revere the ideal of that bond far more than those who have known it in reality. Always excepting those children to whose blessed lot it has fallen to have the ideal realized.

In a few minutes I saw him and my father enter the tanyard together. He was talking earnestly, and my father was listening—ay, listening—and to John Halifax! But whatever the argument was, it failed to move him. Greatly troubled, but staunch as a rock, my old father stood, resting his lame foot on a heap of hides. I went to meet him.

"Phineas," said John anxiously, "come and help me.—No, Abel Fletcher," he added, rather proudly, in reply to a sharp, suspicious glance at us both; "your son and I only met ten minutes ago, and have scarcely exchanged a word. But we cannot waste time over that matter now.—Phineas, help me to persuade your father to save his property. He will not call for the aid of the law, because he is a Friend. Besides, for the same reason, it might be useless asking."

"Verily!" said my father, with a bitter and meaning smile.

"But he might get his own men to defend his property, and need not do what he is bent on doing—go to the mill himself."

"Surely," was all Abel Fletcher said, planting his oaken stick firmly, as firmly as his will, and taking his way to the riverside, in the direction of the mill.

I caught his arm. "Father, don't go."

"My son," said he, turning on me one of his "iron looks," as I used to call them—tokens of a nature that might have ran molten once, and had settled into a hard, moulded mass, of which nothing could afterwards alter one form, or erase one line—"My son, no opposition. Any who try that with me fail. If those fellows had waited two days more, I would have sold all my wheat at a hundred shillings the quarter; now they shall have nothing. It will teach them wisdom another time. Get thee safe home, Phineas, my son; Jael, go thou likewise."

But neither went. John held me back as I was following my father.

"He will do it, Phineas, and I suppose he must. Please God, I'll take care no harm touches him—but you go home."

That was not to be thought of. Fortunately, the time was too brief for argument, so the discussion soon ended. He followed my father, and I followed him. For Jael, she disappeared.

There was a private path from the tanyard to the mill, along the riverside; by this we went in silence. When we reached the spot it was deserted; but farther down the river we heard a scuffling, and saw a number of men breaking down our garden wall.

"They think he is gone home," whispered John; "we'll get in here the safer. Quick, Phineas."

We crossed the little bridge; John took a key out of his pocket, and let us into the mill by a small door—the only entrance, and that was barred and trebly barred within. It had good need to be in such times.

The mill was a queer, musty, silent place, especially the machinery room, the sole flooring of which was the dark, dangerous stream. We stood there a good while—it was the safest place, having no windows. Then we followed my father to the top story, where he kept his bags of grain. There were very many; enough, in these times, to make a large fortune by—a cursed fortune wrung out of human lives.

"Oh! how could my father——"

"Hush!" whispered John, "it was for his son's sake, you know."

But while we stood, and with a meaning but rather grim smile Abel Fletcher counted his bags, worth almost as much as bags of gold—we heard a hammering at the door below. The rioters were come.

Miserable "rioters"! A handful of weak, starved men—pelting us with stones and words. One pistol-shot might have routed them all—but my father's doctrine of non-resistance forbade. Small as their force seemed, there was something at once formidable and pitiful in the low howl that reached us at times.

"Bring out the bags! Us mun have bread!"

"Throw down thy corn, Abel Fletcher!"

"Abel Fletcher *will* throw it down to ye, ye knaves," said my father, leaning out of the upper window; while a sound, half curses, half cheers of triumph, answered him from below.

"That is well," exclaimed John eagerly. "Thank you —thank you, Mr. Fletcher—I knew you would yield at last."

"Didst thee, lad?" said my father, stopping short.

"Not because they forced you—not to save your life —but because it was right."

"Help me with this bag," was all the reply.

It was a great weight, but not too great for John's young arm, nervous and strong. He hauled it up.

"Now, open the window—dash the panes through— it matters not. On to the window, I tell thee."

"But if I do, the bag will fall into the river. You cannot—oh no!—you cannot mean that!"

"Haul it up to the window, John Halifax."

But John remained immovable.

"I must do it myself then;" and in the desperate effort he made, somehow the bag of grain fell, and fell on his lame foot. Tortured into frenzy with the pain—or else, I will still believe, my old father would not have done such a deed—his failing strength seemed doubled and trebled. In an instant more he had got the bag half through the window, and the next sound we heard was its heavy splash in the river below.

Flung into the river, the precious wheat, and in the very sight of the famished rioters! A howl of fury and despair arose. Some plunged into the water ere the eddies left by the falling mass had ceased—but it was too late. A sharp substance in the river's bed had cut the bag, and we saw thrown up to the surface, and whirled down the Avon, thousands of dancing grains. A few of the men swam, or waded after them, clutching a handful here or there—but by the mill-pool the river ran swift, and the wheat had all soon disappeared, except what remained in the bag when it was drawn on shore. Over even that they fought like demons.

We could not look at them—John and I. He put his hand over his eyes, muttering the Name that, young man as he was, I had never yet heard irreverently and thoughtlessly on his lips. It was a sight that would move any one to cry for pity unto the Great Father of the human family.

Abel Fletcher sat on his remaining bags, in an exhaustion that I think was not all physical pain. The paroxysm of anger past, he, ever a just man, could not fail to be struck with what he had done. He seemed subdued, even to something like remorse.

John looked at him, and looked away. For a minute he listened in silence to the shouting outside, and then turned to my father.

"Sir, you must come now. Not a second to lose—they will fire the mill next."

"Let them."

"Let them?—and Phineas is here!"

My poor father! He rose at once.

We got him downstairs—he was very lame—his ruddy face all drawn and white with pain; but he did not speak one word of opposition, or utter a groan of complaint.

The flour-mill was built on piles, in the centre of the narrow river. It was only a few steps of bridge-work to either bank. The little door was on the Norton Bury side, and was hid from the opposite shore, where the rioters had now collected. In a minute we had crept forth, and dashed out of sight, in the narrow path which had been made from the mill to the tanyard.

"Will you take my arm? we must get on fast."

"Home?" said my father, as John led him passively along.

"No, sir, not home: they are there before you. Your life's not safe an hour—unless, indeed, you get soldiers to guard it."

Abel Fletcher gave a decided negative. The stern old Quaker held to his principles still.

"Then you must hide for a time—both of you. Come to my room. You will be secure there. Urge him, Phineas—for your sake and his own."

But my poor broken-down father needed no urging. Grasping more tightly both John's arm and mine, which, for the first time in his life, he leaned upon, he submitted to be led whither we chose. So, after this long interval of time, I once more stood in Sally Watkins' small attic; where, ever since I first brought him there, John Halifax had lived.

Sally knew not of our entrance; she was out, watching the rioters. No one saw us but Jem, and Jem's honour was safe as a rock. I knew that in the smile with which he pulled off his cap to "Mr. Halifax."

"Now," said John, hastily smoothing his bed, so that my father might lie down, and wrapping his cloak round me—"you must both be very still. You will likely have to spend the night here. Jem shall bring you a light and supper. You will make yourself easy, Abel Fletcher?"

"Ay." It was strange to see how decidedly, yet respectfully, John spoke, and how quietly my father answered.

"And Phineas"—he put his arm round my shoulder in his old way—"you will take care of yourself. Are you any stronger than you used to be?"

I clasped his hand without reply. My heart melted to hear that tender accent, so familiar once. All was happening for the best, if it only gave me back David.

"Now good-bye—I must be off."

"Whither?" said my father, rousing himself.

"To try and save the house and the tanyard—I fear we must give up the mill. No, don't hold me, Phineas. I run no risk: everybody knows me. Besides, I am young. There! see after your father. I shall come back in good time."

He grasped my hands warmly—then unloosed them;

and I heard his step descending the staircase. The room seemed to darken when he went away.

The evening passed very slowly. My father, exhausted with pain, lay on the bed and dozed. I sat watching the sky over the housetops, which met in the old angles, with the same blue peeps between. I half forgot all the day's events—it seemed but two weeks, instead of two years ago, that John and I sat in this attic window, conning our Shakespeare for the first time.

Ere twilight I examined John's room. It was a good deal changed; the furniture was improved; a score of ingenious little contrivances made the tiny attic into a cosy bed-chamber. One corner was full of shelves, laden with books, chiefly of a scientific and practical nature. John's taste did not lead him into the current literature of the day: Cowper, Akenside, and Peter Pindar were alike indifferent to him. I found among his books no poet but Shakespeare.

He evidently still practised his old mechanical arts. There was lying in the window a telescope—the cylinder made of pasteboard—into which the lenses were ingeniously fitted. A rough telescope stand, of common deal, stood on the ledge of the roof, from which the field of view must have been satisfactory enough to the young astronomer. Other fragments of skilful handiwork, chiefly meant for machinery on a Lilliputian scale, were strewn about the floor; and on a chair, just as he had left it that morning, stood a loom, very small in size, but perfect in its neat workmanship, with a few threads already woven, making some fabric not so very unlike cloth.

I had gone over all these things without noticing that my father was awake, and that his sharp eye had observed them likewise.

"The lad works hard," said he, half to himself. "He has useful hands and a clear head." I smiled, but took no notice whatever.

Evening began to close in—less peacefully than usual—over Norton Bury; for, whenever I ventured to open the window, we heard unusual and ominous sounds abroad in the town. I trembled inwardly. But John was prudent as well as brave; besides, "everybody knew him." Surely he was safe.

Faithfully, at supper-time, Jem entered. But he could tell us no news; he had kept watch all the time on the staircase by desire of "Mr. Halifax"—so he informed me. My father asked no questions—not even about his mill. From his look, sometimes, I fancied he yet beheld in fancy these starving men fighting over the precious food, destroyed so wilfully—nay, wickedly. Heaven forgive me, his son, if I too harshly use the word; for I think, till the day of his death, that cruel sight never wholly vanished from the eyes of my poor father.

Jem seemed talkatively inclined. He observed that "master was looking sprack agin; and warn't this a tidy room, like?"

I praised it; and supposed his mother was better off now?

"Ay, she be. Mr. Halifax pays her a good rent; and she sees 'un made comfortable. Not that he wants much, being out pretty much all day."

"What is he busy about of nights?"

"Larning," said Jem, with an awed look. "He's terrible wise. But for all that, sometimes he'll teach Charley and me a bit o' the Readamadeasy." (Reading-made-easy, I suppose, John's hopeful pupil meant.) "He's very kind o we, and to mother too. Her says, that her do, Mr. Halifax——"

"Send the fellow away, Phineas," muttered my father, turning his face to the wall.

I obeyed. But first I asked, in a whisper, if Jem had any idea when "Mr. Halifax" would be back.

"He said, maybe not till morning. Them's bad folk about. He was going to stop all night, either at your house or at the tanyard, for fear of a *blaze*."

The word made my father start; for in these times well we knew what poor folk meant by "a blaze."

"My house—my tanyard—I must get up this instant

—help me. He ought to come back—that lad Halifax. There's a score of my men at hand—Wilkes, and Johnson, and Jacob Baines—I say, Phineas—but thee know'st nothing."

He tried to dress, and to drag on his heavy shoes; but fell back, sick with exhaustion and pain. I made him lie down again on the bed.

"Phineas, lad," said he brokenly, "thy old father is getting as helpless as thee."

So we kept watch together all the night through; sometimes dozing, sometimes waking up at some slight noise below, or at the flicker of the long-wicked candle, which fear converted into the glare of some incendiary fire—doubtless our own home. Now and then I heard my father mutter something about "the lad being safe." I said nothing. I only prayed.

Thus the night wore away.

CHAPTER VIII.

After midnight—I know not how long, for I lost count of the hours by the Abbey chimes, and our light had gone out—after midnight I heard by my father's breathing that he was asleep. I was thankful to see it for his sake, and also for another reason.

I could not sleep—all my faculties were preternaturally alive; my weak body and timid mind became strong and active, able to compass anything. For that one night, at least, I felt myself a man.

My father was a very sound sleeper. I knew nothing would disturb him till daylight; therefore my divided duty was at an end. I left him, and crept downstairs into Sally Watkins' kitchen. It was silent; only the faithful warder, Jem, dozed over the dull fire. I touched him on the shoulder—at which he collared me and nearly knocked me down.

"Beg pardon, Mr. Phineas—hope I didn't hurt 'ee, sir?" cried he, all but whimpering; for Jem, a big lad of fifteen, was the most tender-hearted fellow imaginable. "I thought it were some of them folk that Mr. Halifax ha' gone among."

"Where is Mr. Halifax?"

"Doan't know, sir—wish I did! wouldn't be long a-finding out, though—on'y he says: 'Jem, you stop 'ere wi' they'" (pointing his thumb up the staircase). "So, Master Phineas, I stop."

And Jem settled himself with a doggedly obedient, but most dissatisfied, air down by the fireplace. It was evident nothing would move him thence: so he was as safe a guard over my poor old father's slumber as the mastiff in the tanyard, who was as brave as a lion and as docile as a child. My last lingering hesitation ended.

"Jem, lend me your coat and hat—I'm going out into the town."

Jem was so astonished that he stood with open mouth while I took the said garments from him, and unbolted the door. At last it seemed to occur to him that he ought to intercept me.

"But, sir, Mr. Halifax said——"

"I am going to look for Mr. Halifax."

And I escaped outside. Anything beyond his literal duty did not strike the faithful Jem. He stood on the door-sill, and gazed after me with a hopeless expression.

"I 'spose you mun have your way, sir; but Mr. Halifax said, 'Jem, you stop y'ere,'—and y'ere I stop."

He went in, and I heard him bolting the door, with a sullen determination, as if he would have kept guard against it—waiting for John—until doomsday.

I stole along the dark alley into the street. It was very silent—I need not have borrowed Jem's exterior in order to creep through a throng of maddened rioters. There was no sign of any such, except that under one of the three oil lamps that lit the night-darkness at Norton Bury lay a few smouldering hanks of hemp, well resined. They, then, had thought of that dreadful engine of destruction—fire. Had my terrors been true? Our house—and perhaps John within it!

On I ran, speeded by a dull murmur, which I fancied I heard; but still there was no one in the street—no one except the Abbey watchman lounging in his box. I roused him, and asked if all was safe?—where were the rioters?

"What rioters?"

"At Abel Fletcher's mill; they may be at his house now——"

"Ay, I think they be."

"And will not one man in the town help him; no constables—no law?"

"Oh! he's a Quaker; the law don't help Quakers."

That was the truth—the hard, grinding truth—in those days. Liberty, justice, were idle names to Nonconformists of every kind; and all they knew of the glorious constitution of English law was when its iron hand was turned against them.

I had forgotten this; bitterly I remembered it now. So wasting no more words, I flew along the churchyard until I saw, shining against the boles of the chestnut trees, a red light. It was one of the hempen torches. Now, at last, I had got in the midst of that small body of men, "the rioters."

They were a mere handful—not above two score—apparently the relics of the band which had attacked the mill, joined with a few plough-lads from the country around. But they were desperate; they had come up the Coltham road so quietly, that, except this faint murmur, neither I nor any one in the town could have told they were near. Wherever they had been ransacking, as yet they had not attacked my father's house; it stood upon the other side of the road—barred, black, silent.

I heard a muttering—"Th' old man bean't there." "Nobody knows where he be." No, thank God!

"Be us all y'ere?" said the man with the torch, holding it up so as to see round him. It was well then that I appeared as Jem Watkins. But no one noticed me except one man, who skulked behind a tree, and of whom I was rather afraid, as he was apparently intent on watching.

"Ready, lads? Now for the rosin! Blaze 'un out."

But in the eager scuffle the torch, the only one alight, was knocked down and trodden out. A volley of oaths arose, though whose fault it was no one seemed to know; but I missed my man from behind the tree—nor found him till after the angry throng had rushed on to the nearest lamp. One of them was left behind, standing close to our own railings. He looked round to see if none were by, and then sprang over the gate. Dark as it was, I thought I recognized him.

"John?"

"Phineas?" He was beside me in a bound. "How could you do——"

"I could do anything to-night. But you are safe; no one has harmed you. Oh, thank God, you are not hurt!"

And I clung to his arm—my friend, whom I had missed so long, so sorely.

He held me tight—his heart felt as mine, only more silently.

"Now, Phineas, we have a minute's time. I must have you safe—we must get into the house."

"Who is there?"

"Jael; she is as good as a host of constables; she has braved the fellows once to-night, but they're back again, or will be directly."

"And the mill?"

"Safe, as yet; I have had three of the tanyard men there since yesterday morning, though your father did not know. I have been going to and fro all night, between there and here, waiting till the rioters should come back from the Severn mills. Hist! here they are.—I say, Jael?"

He tapped at the window. In a few seconds Jael had unbarred the door, let us in, and closed it again securely, mounting guard behind it with something that looked very like my father's pistols, though I would not discredit her among our peaceful society by positively stating the fact.

"Bravo!" said John, when we stood all together in the barricaded house, and heard the threatening murmur of voices and feet outside. "Bravo, Jael! The wife of Heber the Kenite was no braver woman than you!"

She looked gratified, and followed John obediently from room to room.

"I have done all as thee bade me—thee art a sensible lad, John Halifax. We are secure, I think."

Secure? bolts and bars secure against fire? For that was threatening us now.

"They can't mean it—surely they can't mean it," repeated John, as the cry of "Burn 'un out!" rose louder and louder.

But they did mean it. From the attic window we watched them light torch after torch, sometimes throwing one at the house—but it fell harmless against the staunch oaken door, and blazed itself out on our stone steps. All it did was to show more plainly than even daylight had shown, the gaunt, ragged forms and pinched faces, furious with famine.

John as well as I recoiled at that miserable sight.

"I'll speak to them," he said. "Unbar the window, Jael;" and before I could hinder, he was leaning right out.—"Halloa, there!"

At his loud and commanding voice a wave of upturned faces surged forward, expectant.

"My men, do you know what you are about? To burn down a gentleman's house is—hanging."

There was a hush, and then a shout of derision.

"Not a Quaker's! nobody'll get hanged for burning out a Quaker!"

"That be true enough," muttered Jael between her teeth. "We must e'en fight, as Mordecai's people fought, hand to hand, until they slew their enemies."

"Fight!" repeated John, half to himself, as he stood at the now-closed window, against which more than one blazing torch began to rattle. "Fight—with these? What are you doing, Jael?"

For she had taken down a large Book—the last Book

in the house she would have taken under less critical circumstances, and with it was trying to stop up a broken pane.

"No, my good Jael, not this;" and he carefully replaced the volume; that volume, in which he might have read, as day after day, and year after year, we Christians generally do read, such plain words as these—"*Love your enemies;*" "*Bless them that curse you;*" "*Pray for them that despitefully use you and persecute you.*"

A minute or two John stood with his hand on the Book, thinking. Then he touched me on the shoulder.

"Phineas, I'm going to try a new plan—at least, one so old that it's almost new. Whether it succeeds or no, you'll bear me witness to your father that I did it for the best, and did it because I thought it right. Now for it."

To my horror, he threw up the window wide, and leant out.

"My men, I want to speak to you."

He might as well have spoken to the roaring sea. The only answer was a shower of missiles, which missed their aim. The rioters were too far off—our spiked iron railings, eight feet high or more, being a barrier which none had yet ventured to climb. But at length one random stone hit John on the chest.

I pulled him in, but he declared he was not hurt. Terrified, I implored him not to risk his life.

"Life is not always the first thing to be thought of," said he gently. "Don't be afraid—I shall come to no harm. But I *must* do what I think right, if it is to be done."

While he spoke, I could hardly hear him for the bellowings outside. More savage still grew the cry,—

"Burn 'em out! burn 'em out! They be only Quakers!"

"There's not a minute to lose—stop—let me think—Jael, is that a pistol?"

"Loaded," she said, handing it over to him with a kind of stern delight. Certainly, Jael was not meant to be a Friend.

John ran downstairs, and before I guessed his purpose, had unbolted the hall door, and stood on the flight of steps, in full view of the mob.

There was no bringing him back, so of course I followed. A pillar sheltered me. I do not think he saw me, though I stood close behind him.

So sudden had been his act, that even the rioters did not seem to have noticed, or clearly understood it, till the next lighted torch showed them the young man standing there, with his back to the door—*outside* the door.

The sight fairly confounded them. Even I felt that for the moment he was safe. They were awed—nay, paralyzed, by his daring.

But the storm raged too fiercely to be lulled, except for one brief minute. A confusion of voices burst out afresh,—

"Who be thee?" "It's one o' the Quakers." "No, he bean't." "Burn 'un anyhow." "Touch 'un if ye dare."

There was evidently a division arising. One big man, who had made himself very prominent all along, seemed trying to calm the tumult.

John stood his ground. Once a torch was flung at him—he stooped and picked it up. I thought he was going to hurl it back again, but he did not; he only threw it down, and stamped it out safely with his foot. This simple action had a wonderful effect on the crowd.

The big fellow advanced to the gate and called John by his name.

"Is that you, Jacob Baines? I am sorry to see you here."

"Be ye, sir?"

"What do you want?"

"Naught wi' thee. We wants Abel Fletcher. Where is 'um?"

"I shall certainly not tell you."

As John said this again, the noise arose, and again Jacob Baines seemed to have power to quiet the rest.

John Halifax never stirred. Evidently he was pretty well known. I caught many a stray sentence, such as "Don't hurt the lad." "He were kind to my lad, he were." "No, he be a real gentleman." "No, he comed here as poor as us," and the like. At length one voice, sharp and shrill, was heard above the rest.

"I zay, young man, didst ever know what it was to be pretty nigh vamished?"

"Ay, many a time."

The answer, so brief, so unexpected, struck a great hush into the throng. Then the same voice cried,—

"Speak up, man! we won't hurt 'ee! You be one o' we!"

"No, I am not one of you. I'd be ashamed to come in the night and burn my master's house down."

I expected an outbreak, but none came. They listened, as it were by compulsion, to the clear, manly voice that had not in it one shade of fear.

"What do you do it for?" John continued. "All because he would not sell you, or give you, his wheat. Even so—it was *his* wheat, not yours. May not a man do what he likes with his own?"

The argument seemed to strike home. There is always a lurking sense of rude justice in a mob—at least a British mob.

"Don't you see how foolish you were? You tried threats, too. Now you all know Mr. Fletcher; you are his men—some of you. He is not a man to be threatened."

This seemed to be taken rather angrily; but John went on speaking, as if he did not observe the fact.

"Nor am I one to be threatened neither. Look here—the first one of you who attempted to break into Mr. Fletcher's house I should most certainly have shot. But I'd rather not shoot you, poor, starving fellows! I know what it is to be hungry. I'm sorry for you—sorry from the bottom of my heart."

There was no mistaking that compassionate accent, nor the murmur which followed it.

"But what must us do, Mr. Halifax?" cried Jacob

Baines: "us be starved a'most. What's the good o' talking to we?"

John's countenance relaxed. I saw him lift his head and shake his hair back, with that pleased gesture I remember so well of old. He went down to the locked gate.

"Suppose I gave you something to eat, would you listen to me afterwards?"

There arose up a frenzied shout of assent. Poor wretches! they were fighting for no principle, true or false, only for bare life. They would have bartered their very souls for a mouthful of bread.

"You must promise to be peaceable," said John again, very resolutely, as soon as he could obtain a hearing. "You are Norton Bury folk; I know you. I could get every one of you hanged, even though Abel Fletcher is a Quaker. Mind, you'll be peaceable?"

"Ay—ay! Some'at to eat; give us some'at to eat."

John Halifax called out to Jael; bade her bring all the food of every kind that there was in the house, and give it to him out of the parlour window. She obeyed—I marvel now to think of it—but she implicitly obeyed. Only I heard her fix the bar to the closed front door, and go back, with a strange, sharp sob, to her station at the hall window.

"Now, my lads, come in!" and he unlocked the gate.

They came thronging up the steps, not more than two score, I imagined, in spite of the noise they had made. But two score of such famished, desperate men, God grant I may never again see!

John divided the food as well as he could among them; they fell to it like wild beasts. Meat, cooked or raw, loaves, vegetables, meal; all came alike, and were clutched, gnawed, and scrambled for in the fierce selfishness of hunger. Afterwards there was a call for drink.

"Water, Jael; bring them water."

"Beer!" shouted some.

"Water," repeated John. "Nothing but water. I'll have no drunkards rioting at my master's door."

And, either by chance or design, he let them hear the click of his pistol. But it was hardly needed. They were all cowed by a mightier weapon still—the best weapon a man can use—his own firm, indomitable will.

At length all the food we had in the house was consumed. John told them so; and they believed him. Little enough, indeed, was sufficient for some of them; wasted with long famine, they turned sick and faint, and dropped down even with bread in their mouths, unable to swallow it. Others gorged themselves to the full, and then lay along the steps, supine as satisfied brutes. Only a few sat and ate like rational human beings; and there was but one, the little, shrill-voiced man, who asked me if he might "take a bit o' bread to the old wench at home."

John, hearing, turned, and for the first time noticed me.

"Phineas, it was very wrong of you; but there is no danger now."

No, there was none—not even for Abel Fletcher's son. I stood safe by John's side, very happy, very proud.

"Well, my men," he said, looking round with a smile, "have you had enough to eat?"

"Oh, ay!" they all cried.

And one man added, "Thank the Lord!"

"That's right, Jacob Baines; and, another time, *trust* the Lord. You wouldn't, then, have been abroad this summer morning"—and he pointed to the dawn just reddening in the sky—"this quiet, blessed summer morning, burning and rioting, bringing yourselves to the gallows, and your children to starvation."

"They be nigh that a'ready," said Jacob sullenly. "Us men ha' gotten a meal, thankee for it; but what'll become o' the little 'uns at home? I say, Mr. Halifax," and he seemed waxing desperate again, "we must get some food somehow."

John turned away, his countenance very sad. Another of the men plucked at him from behind.

"Sir, when thee was a poor lad I lent thee a rug to sleep on; I doan't grudge 'ee getting on; you was born for a gentleman, sure-ly. But Master Fletcher be a hard man."

"And a just one," persisted John. "You that work for him, did he ever stint you of a halfpenny? If you had come to him and said, 'Master, times are hard, we can't live upon our wages,' he might—I don't say that he would—but he *might* even have given you the food you tried to steal."

"D'ye think he'd give it us now?" And Jacob Baines, the big, gaunt, savage fellow who had been the ringleader—the same, too, who had spoken of his "little 'uns"—came and looked steadily in John's face.

"I knew thee as a lad; thee'rt a young man now, as will be a father some o' these days. Oh! Mr. Halifax, may 'ee ne'er want a meal o' good meat for the missus and the babbies at home, if ee'll get a bit o' bread for our'n this day."

"My man, I'll try."

He called me aside, explained to me, and asked my advice and consent, as Abel Fletcher's son, to a plan that had come into his mind. It was to write orders, which each man presenting at our mill should receive a certain amount of flour.

"Do you think your father would agree?"

"I think he would."

"Yes," John added, pondering—"I am sure he would. And besides, if he does not give some, he may lose all. But he would not do it for fear of that. No, he is a just man—I am not afraid. Give me some paper, Jael."

He sat down as composedly as if he had been alone in the counting-house, and wrote. I looked over his shoulder, admiring his clear, firm handwriting, the precision, concentrativeness, and quickness with which he first seemed to arrange and then execute his ideas. He possessed to the full that "business" faculty, so frequently despised, but which, out of very ordinary material, often makes a clever man; and without which the cleverest man alive can never be altogether a great man.

When about to sign the orders, John suddenly stopped. "No; I had better not."

"Why so?"

"I have no right; your father might think it presumption."

"Presumption? after to-night!"

"Oh, that's nothing! Take the pen. It is your part to sign them, Phineas."

I obeyed.

"Isn't this better than hanging?" said John to the men, when he had distributed the little bits of paper—precious as pound notes—and made them all fully understand the same. "Why, there isn't another gentleman in Norton Bury, who, if you had come to burn *his* house down, would not have had the constables or the soldiers, have shot down one-half of you like mad dogs, and sent the other half to the county jail. Now, for all your misdoings, we let you go quietly home, well fed, and with food for children too. *Why*, think you?"

"I don't know," said Jacob Baines humbly.

"I'll tell you. Because Abel Fletcher is a Quaker and a Christian."

"Hurrah for Abel Fletcher! hurrah for the Quakers!" shouted they, waking up the echoes down Norton Bury streets; which, of a surety, had never echoed to *that* shout before. And so the riot was over.

John Halifax closed the hall door and came in—unsteadily—staggering. Jael placed a chair for him—worthy soul! she was wiping her old eyes. He sat down, shivering, speechless. I put my hand on his shoulder; he took it and pressed it hard.

"O Phineas, lad, I'm glad; glad it's safe over!"

"Yes, thank God!"

"Ay, indeed; thank God!"

He covered his eyes for a minute or two, then rose up pale, but quite himself again.

"Now let us go and fetch your father home."

We found him on John's bed, still asleep. But as we entered he woke. The daylight shone on his face—it looked ten years older since yesterday—he stared, bewildered and angry, at John Halifax.

"Eh, young man—oh! I remember. Where is my son—where's my Phineas?"

I fell on his neck as if I had been a child. And almost as if it had been a child's feeble head, mechanically he smoothed and patted mine.

"Thee art not hurt? Nor any one?"

"No," John answered; "nor is either the house or the tanyard injured."

He looked amazed. "How has that been?"

"Phineas will tell you. Or, stay—better wait till you are at home."

But my father insisted on hearing. I told the whole, without any comments on John's behaviour; he would not have liked it; and, besides, the facts spoke for themselves. I told the simple, plain story—nothing more.

Abel Fletcher listened at first in silence. As I proceeded he felt about for his hat, put it on, and drew its broad brim close down over his eyes. Not even when I told him of the flour we had promised in his name, the giving of which would, as we had calculated, cost him considerable loss, did he utter a word or move a muscle.

John at length asked him if he were satisfied.

"Quite satisfied."

But, having said this, he sat so long, his hands locked together on his knees, and his hat drawn down, hiding all the face except the rigid mouth and chin—sat so long, so motionless, that we became uneasy.

John spoke to him gently, almost as a son would have spoken.

"Are you very lame still? Could I help you to walk home?"

My father looked up, and slowly held out his hand.

"Thee hast been a good lad, and a kind lad to us; I thank thee."

There was no answer, none. But all the words in the world could not match that happy silence.

By degrees we got my father home. It was just such

another summer morning as the one, two years back, when we two had stood, exhausted and trembling, before that sternly-bolted door. We both thought of that day: I knew not if my father did also.

He entered, leaning heavily on John. He sat down in the very seat, in the very room, where he had so harshly judged us—judged him.

Something, perhaps, of that bitterness rankled in the young man's spirit now, for he stopped on the threshold.

"Come in," said my father, looking up.

"If I am welcome; not otherwise."

"Thee art welcome."

He came in—I drew him in—and sat down with us. But his manner was irresolute, his fingers closed and unclosed nervously. My father, too, sat leaning his head on his two hands, not unmoved. I stole up to him, and thanked him softly for the welcome he had given.

"There is nothing to thank me for," said he, with something of his old hardness. "What I once did was only justice—or I then believed so. What I have done, and am about to do, is still mere justice. John, how old art thee now?"

"Twenty."

"Then for one year from this time I will take thee as my 'prentice, though thee knowest already nearly as much of the business as I do. At twenty-one thee wilt be able to set up for thyself, or I may take thee into partnership—we'll see. But"—and he looked at me, then sternly, nay, fiercely, into John's steadfast eyes—"remember, thee hast in some measure taken that lad's place. May God deal with thee as thou dealest with my son Phineas—my only son!"

"Amen!" was the solemn answer.

And God, who sees us both now—ay, *now!* and, perhaps, not so far apart as some may deem—He knows whether or no John Halifax kept that vow.

CHAPTER IX.

"WELL done, Phineas—to walk round the garden without once resting! Now I call that grand, after an individual has been ill a month. However, you must calm your superabundant energies, and be quiet."

I was not unwilling, for I still felt very weak. But sickness did not now take that heavy, overpowering grip of me, mind and body, that it once used to do. It never did when John was by. He gave me strength, mentally and physically. He was life and health to me, with his brave cheerfulness—his way of turning all minor troubles into pleasantries, till they seemed to break and vanish away, sparkling, like the foam on the top of the wave. Yet, all the while one knew well that he could meet any great evil as gallantly as a good ship meets a heavy sea—breasting it, plunging through it, or riding over it, as only a good ship can.

When I recovered—just a month after the bread riot, and that month was a great triumph to John's kind care—I felt that if I always had him beside me I should never be ill any more; I said as much in a laughing sort of way.

"Very well; I shall keep you to that bargain. Now, sit down; listen to the newspaper, and improve your mind as to what the world is doing. It ought to be doing something, with the new century it began this year. Did it not seem very odd at first to have to write '1800'?"

"John, what a capital hand you write now!"

"Do I? That's somebody's credit. Do you remember my first lesson on the top of the Mythe?"

"I wonder what has become of those two gentlemen?"

"Oh! did you never hear? Young Mr. Brithwood is the squire now. He married, last month, Lady Somebody Something, a fine lady from abroad."

"And Mr. March—what of him?"

"I haven't the least idea. Come now, shall I read the paper?"

He read well, and I liked to listen to him. It was, I

remember, something about "the spacious new quadrangles, to be called Russell and Tavistock Squares, with elegantly laid out nursery grounds adjoining."

"It must be a fine place London."

"Ay; I should like to see it. Your father says, perhaps he shall have to send me, this winter, on business—won't that be fine? If only you would go too."

I shook my head. I had the strongest disinclination to stir from my quiet home, which now held within it, or about it, all I wished for and all I loved. It seemed as if any change must be to something worse.

"Nevertheless, you must have a change. Dr. Jessop insists upon it. Here have I been beating up and down the country for a week past—'Adventures in Search of a Country Residence'—and, do you know, I think I've found one at last. Shouldn't you like to hear about it?"

I assented, to please him.

"Such a nice, nice place, on the slope of Enderley Hill. A cottage—Rose Cottage—for it's all in a bush of cluster roses, up to the very roof."

"Where is Enderley?"

"Did you never hear of Enderley Flat, the highest table-land in England? Such a fresh, free, breezy spot—how the wind sweeps over it! I can feel it in my face still."

And even the description was refreshing, this heavy, sultry day, with not a breath of air moving across the level valley.

"Shouldn't you like to live on a hillside, to be at the top of everything, overlooking everything. Well, that's Enderley: the village lies just under the brow of the Flat."

"Is there a village?"

"A dozen cottages or so, at each door of which half a dozen white little heads and a dozen round eyes appeared staring at me. But oh, the blessed quiet and solitude of the place! No fights in filthy alleys! no tanyards—I mean," he added, correcting himself, "it's a thorough country spot; and I like the country better than the town."

"Do you, still? Would you really like to take to the 'shepherd's life and state,' upon which my namesake here is so eloquent? Let us see what he says."

And from the handful of books that usually lay strewn about wherever we two sat, I took up one he had lately got, with no small pains I was sure, and had had bound in its own proper colour, and presented it to me—"The Purple Island," and "Sicelides," of Phineas Fletcher. People seldom read this wise, tender, and sweet-voiced old fellow now; so I will even copy the verses I found for John to read.

"Here is the place. Thyrsis is just ending his 'broken lay.'

> "'Lest that the stealing night his later song might stay——'"

"Stop a minute," interrupted John. "Apropos of 'stealing night,' the sun is already down below the yew hedge. Are you cold?"

"Not a bit of it."

"Then we'll begin:—

> "'Thrice, oh, thrice happy, shepherd's life and state:
> When courts are happiness, unhappy pawns!'

"That's not clear," said John, laying down the book. "Now I do like poetry to be intelligible. A poet ought to see things more widely, and express them more vividly, than ordinary folk."

"Don't you perceive—he means the pawns on the chess-board—the common people."

"Phineas, don't say the common people—I'm a common person myself. But to continue:—

> "'His cottage low, and safely humble gate,
> Shuts out proud Fortune, with her scorns and fawns:
> No feared treason breaks his quiet sleep.
> Singing all day, his flocks he learns to keep,
> Himself as innocent as are his quiet sheep.'

("Not many sheep at Enderley, I fancy; the Flat chiefly abounds in donkeys. Well—)

"'No Serian worms he knows, that with their thread,
Drew out their silken lives—nor silken pride——'

"Which reminds me that——"

"David, how can you make me laugh at our reverend ancestor in this way? I'm ashamed of you."

"Only let me tell you this one fact—very interesting, you'll allow—that I saw a silken gown hanging up in the kitchen at Rose Cottage. Now, though Mrs. Tod is a decent, comely woman, I don't think it belonged to her."

"She may have lodgers."

"I think she said she had—an old gentleman—but *he* wouldn't wear a silk gown."

"His wife might. Now, do go on reading."

"Certainly; I only wish to draw a parallel between Thyrsis and ourselves in our future summer life at Enderley. So the old gentleman's wife may appropriate the 'silken pride,' while we emulate the shepherd.

"'His lambs' warm fleece well fits his little need——'

"I wear a tolerably good coat now, don't I, Phineas?"

"You are incorrigible."

Yet, through all his fun, I detected a certain undertone of seriousness, observable in him ever since my father's declaration of his intentions concerning him, had, so to speak, settled John's future career. He seemed aware of some crisis in his life, arrived or impending, which disturbed the generally even balance of his temperament.

"Nay, I'll be serious;" and passing over the unfinished verse, with another or two following, he began afresh, in a new place, and in an altogether changed tone.

"'His certain life, that never can deceive him,
Is full of thousand sweets and rich content;
The smooth-leaved beeches in the field receive him
With coolest shades till noontide's rage is spent;
His life is neither tost on boisterous seas
Of troublous worlds, nor lost in slothful ease.
Pleased and full blest he lives, when he his God can please.

"'His bed of wool yields safe and quiet sleeps,
While by his side his faithful spouse hath place;
His little son into his bosom creeps,
The lively image of his father's face;
Never his humble house or state torment him,
Less he could like, if less his God had sent him;
And when he dies, green turfs with grassy tomb content him.'"

John ceased. He was a good reader—but I had never heard him read like this before. Ending, one missed it like the breaking of music, or like the inner voice of one's own heart talking when nobody is by.

"David," I said, after a pause, "what are you thinking about?"

He started, with his old quick blush. "Oh, nothing. No, that's not quite true. I was thinking that, so far as happiness goes, this 'shepherd's' is my ideal of a happy life—ay, down to the 'grassy tomb.'"

"Your fancy leaps at once to the grassy tomb; but the shepherd enjoyed a few intermediate stages of felicity before that."

"I was thinking of those likewise."

"Then you do intend some day to have a 'faithful spouse and a little son'?"

"I hope so—God willing."

It may seem strange, but this was the first time our conversation had ever wandered in a similar direction. Though he was twenty and I twenty-two—to us both—and I thank Heaven that we could both look up in the face of Heaven and say so!—to us both, the follies and wickednesses of youth were, if not equally unknown, equally and alike hateful. Many may doubt, or smile at the fact; but I state it now, in my old age, with honour and pride, that we two young men that day trembled on the subject of love as shyly, as reverently, as delicately, as any two young maidens of innocent sixteen.

After John's serious "God willing," there was a good long silence. Afterwards I said,—

"Then you propose to marry?"

"Certainly! as soon as I can."

"Have you ever"—and, while speaking, I watched him narrowly, for a sudden possibility flashed across my mind—"Have you ever seen any one whom you would like for your wife?"

"No."

I was satisfied. John's single "No" was as conclusive as a score of asseverations.

We said no more; but after one of those pauses of conversation which were habitual to us—John used to say that the true test of friendship was to be able to sit or walk together for a whole hour in perfect silence, without wearying of one another's company—we again began talking about Enderley.

I soon found that in this plan my part was simply acquiescence; my father and John had already arranged it all. I was to be in charge of the latter; nothing could induce Abel Fletcher to leave, even for a day, his house, his garden, and his tanyard. We two young men were to set up for a month or two our bachelor establishment at Mrs. Tod's: John riding thrice a week over to Norton Bury to bring news of me, and to fulfil his duties at the tanyard. One could see plain enough—and very grateful to me was the sight—that whether or no Abel Fletcher acknowledged it, his right hand in all his business affairs was the lad John Halifax.

On a lovely August day we started for Enderley. It was about eight miles off, on a hilly, cross-country road. We lumbered slowly along in our post-chaise; I leaning back, enjoying the fresh air, the changing views, and chiefly to see how intensely John enjoyed them too.

He looked extremely well to-day—handsome, I was about to write; but John was never, even in his youth, "handsome." Nay, I have heard people call him "plain;" but that was not true. His face had that charm, perhaps the greatest, certainly the most lasting, either in women or men—of infinite variety. You were always finding out something—an expression strange as tender, or the track of a swift, brilliant thought, or an indication of feeling different from, perhaps deeper than, anything which appeared before. When you believed you had learnt it line by line it would startle you by a phase quite new, and beautiful as new. For it was not one of your impassive faces, whose owners count it pride to harden into a mass of stone those lineaments which nature made as the flesh and blood representation of the man's soul. True, it had its reticences, its sacred disguises, its noble powers of silence and self-control. It was a fair-written, open book; only, to read it clearly, you must come from its own country, and understand the same language.

For the rest, John was decidedly like the "David" whose name I still gave him now and then—"a goodly person;" tall, well-built, and strong. "The glory of a young man is his strength;" and so I used often to think, when I looked at him. He always dressed with extreme simplicity; generally in gray—he was fond of gray—and in something of our Quaker fashion. On this day, I remember, I noticed an especial carefulness of attire, at his age neither unnatural nor unbecoming. His well-fitting coat and long-flapped vest, garnished with the snowiest of lawn frills and ruffles; his knee-breeches, black silk hose, and shoes adorned with the largest and brightest of steel buckles, made up a costume which, quaint as it would now appear, still is, to my mind, the most suitable and graceful that a young man can wear. I never see any young men now who come at all near the picture which still remains in my mind's eye of John Halifax as he looked that day.

Once, with the natural sensitiveness of youth, especially of youth that has struggled up through so many opposing circumstances as his had done, he noticed my glance.

"Anything amiss about me, Phineas? You see I am not much used to holidays and holiday clothes."

"I have nothing to say against either you or your clothes," replied I, smiling.

"That's all right; I beg to state, it is entirely in honour of you and of Enderley that I have slipped off my tanyard husk, and put on the gentleman."

"You couldn't do that, John. You couldn't put on what you were born with."

He laughed—but I think he was pleased.

We had now come into a hilly region. John leaped out and gained the top of the steep road long before the post-chaise did. I watched him standing, balancing in his hands the riding-whip which had replaced the ever-lasting rose switch, or willow wand, of his boyhood. His figure was outlined sharply against the sky, his head thrown backward a little, as he gazed, evidently with the keenest zest, on the breezy Flat before him. His hair—a little darker than it used to be, but of the true Saxon colour still, and curly as ever—was blown about by the wind, under his broad hat. His whole appearance was full of life, health, energy, and enjoyment.

I thought any father might have been proud of such a son, any sister of such a brother, any young girl of such a lover. Ay, that last tie, the only one of the three that was possible to him—I wondered how long it would be before times changed and I ceased to be the only one who was proud of him.

We drove on a little farther, and came to the chief landmark of the high moorland—a quaint hostelry, called the "Bear." Bruin swung aloft pole in hand, brown and fierce, on an old-fashioned sign, as he and his progenitors had probably swung for two centuries or more.

"Is this Enderley ?" I asked.

"Not quite, but near it. You never saw the sea ? Well, from this point I can show you something very like it. Do you see that gleaming bit in the landscape far away ? That's water—that's our very own Severn, swelled to an estuary. But you must imagine the estuary—you can only get that tiny peep of water, glittering like a great diamond that some young Titaness has flung out of her necklace down among the hills."

"David, you are actually growing poetical."

"Am I ? Well, I do feel rather strange to-day—crazy like ; a high wind always sends me half crazy with delight. Did you ever feel such a breeze ? And there's something so gloriously free in this high level common—as flat as if my Titaness had found a little Mont Blanc, and amused herself with patting it down like a dough-cake."

"A very culinary goddess."

"Yes! but a goddess after all. And her dough-cake, her mushroom, her flattened Mont Blanc, is very fine. What a broad green sweep—nothing but sky and common, common and sky. This is Enderley Flat. We shall come to its edge soon, where it drops abruptly into such a pretty valley. There, look down—that's the church. We are on a level with the top of its tower.—Take care, my lad"—to the post-boy, who was crossing with difficulty the literally "pathless waste"—"don't lurch us into the quarry pits, or topple us at once down the slope, where we shall roll over and over—*facilis descensus Averni*—and lodge in Mrs. Tod's garden hedge."

"Mrs. Tod would feel flattered if she knew Latin. You don't look upon our future habitation as a sort of Avernus?"

John laughed merrily. "No, as I told you before, I like Enderley Hill. I can't tell why, but I like it. It seems as if I had known the place before. I feel as if we were going to have great happiness here."

And as he spoke, his unwonted buoyancy softened into a quietness of manner more befitting that word "happiness." Strange word! hardly in my vocabulary. Yet, when he uttered it, I seemed to understand it and to be content.

We wound a little way down the slope, and came in front of Rose Cottage. It was well named. I never in my life had seen such a bush of bloom. They hung in clusters—those roses—a dozen in a group; pressing their pinky cheeks together in a mass of family fragrance, pushing in at the parlour window, climbing up even to the very attic. There was a yellow jasmine over the porch at one front door, and a woodbine at the other; the cottage had two entrances, each distinct. But the general impression it gave, both as to sight and scent, was of roses—nothing but roses.

"How are you, Mrs. Tod?" as a comely, middle-aged body appeared at the right-hand doorway, dressed sprucely in one of those things Jael called a "coat and jacket," likewise a red calamanco petticoat tucked up at the pocket-holes.

"I be pretty fair, sir—be you the same? The children ha' not forgotten you—you see, Mr. Halifax."

"So much the better!" and he patted two or three little white heads, and tossed the youngest high up in the air. It looked very strange to see John with a child in his arms.

"Don't 'ee make more noise than 'ee can help, my lad," the good woman said to our post-boy, "because, sir, the sick gentleman bean't so well again to-day."

"I am sorry for it. We would not have driven up to the door had we known. Which is his room?"

Mrs. Tod pointed to a window not on our side of the house, but on the other. A hand was just closing the casement and pulling down the blind—a hand which, in the momentary glimpse we had of it, seemed less like a man's than a woman's.

When we were settled in the parlour John noticed this fact.

"It was the wife, most likely. Poor thing! how hard to be shut up indoors on such a summer evening as this!"

It did seem a sad sight—that closed window, outside which was the fresh, balmy air, the sunset, and the roses.

"And how do you like Enderley?" asked John, when, tea being over, I lay and rested, while he sat leaning his elbow on the window-sill, and his cheek against a bunch of those ever-intruding, inquisitive roses.

"It is very, very pretty, and so comfortable—almost like home."

"I feel as if it were home," John said, half to himself. "Do you know, I can hardly believe that I have only seen this place once before; it is so familiar. I seem to know quite well that slope of common before the door, with its black dots of furze bushes. And that wood below; what a clear line its top makes against the yellow sky! There, that high ground to the right; it's all dusky now, but it is such a view by daylight. And between it and Enderley is the prettiest valley, where the road slopes down just under those chestnut trees."

"How well you seem to know the place already."

"As I tell you, I like it. I hardly ever felt so content before. We will have a happy time, Phineas."

"Oh yes!" How—even if I had felt differently—could I say anything but "yes" to him then?

I lay until it grew quite dark, and I could only see a dim shape sitting at the window, instead of John's known face; then I bade him good-night, and retired. Directly afterwards, I heard him, as I knew he would, dash out of the house, and away up the Flat. In the deep quiet of this lonely spot I could distinguish, for several minutes, the diminishing sound of his footsteps along the loose, stony road; and the notes, clear and shrill, of his whistling. I think it was "Sally in our Alley," or some such pleasant old tune. At last it faded far off, and I fell into sleep and dreams.

CHAPTER X.

"THAT Mrs. Tod is an extraordinary woman. I repeat it—a most extraordinary woman."

And leaning his elbows on the table, from which the said extraordinary woman had just removed breakfast, John looked over to me with his own merry brown eyes.

"Wherefore, David?"

"She has a house full of children, yet manages to keep it quiet—and her own temper likewise. Astonishing patience! However people attain it who have to do with brats, *I* can't imagine."

"John! that's mean hypocrisy. I saw you myself half an hour ago holding the eldest Tod boy on a refractory donkey, and laughing till you could hardly stand."

"Did I?" said he, half ashamed. "Well, it was only to keep the little scamp from making a noise under the windows. And that reminds me of another remarkable virtue in Mrs. Tod—she can hold her tongue."

"How so?"

"In two whole days she has not communicated to us a single fact concerning our neighbours in the other half of Rose Cottage."

"Did you want to know?"

John laughingly denied; then allowed that he always had a certain pleasure in eliciting information on men and things.

"The wife being indicated, I suppose, by that very complimentary word 'thing.' But what possible interest can you have in either the old gentleman or the old lady?"

"Stop, Phineas: you have a bad habit of jumping at conclusions. And in our great dearth of occupation here, I think it might be all the better for you to take a little interest in your neighbours. So I've a great mind to indulge you with an important idea, suggestion, discovery. Hark 'ee, friend!"—and he put on an air of sentimental mystery, not a bad copy of our old acquaintance, Mr. Charles—"What if the—the individual should not be an old lady at all?"

"What! The old gentleman's wife?"

"Wife?—ahem! more jumping at conclusions. No; let us keep on the safe side, and call her the—individual. In short, the owner of that gray silk gown I saw hanging up in the kitchen. I've seen it again."

"The gray gown! When and where?"

"This morning, early. I walked after it across the Flat, a good way behind though; for I thought that it—well, let me say *she*—might not like to be watched or followed. She was trotting along very fast, and she carried a little basket—I fancy a basket of eggs."

"Capital housekeeper! excellent wife!"

"Once more—I have my doubts on that latter fact. She walked a great deal quicker and merrier than any wife ought to walk when her husband is ill!"

I could not help laughing at John's original notions of conjugal duty.

"Besides, Mrs. Tod always calls her invalid 'the old gentleman,' and I don't believe this was an elderly lady."

"Nay, old men do sometimes marry young women."

"Yes, but it is always a pity; and sometimes not quite right. No"—and I was amused to see how gravely and doggedly John kept to his point—"though this lady did not look like a sylph or a wood-nymph—being neither very small nor very slight, and having a comfortable woollen cloak and hood over the gray silk gown—still, I don't believe she's an old woman, or married either."

"How can you possibly tell? Did you see her face?"

"Of course not," he answered, rather indignantly. "I should not think it manly to chase a lady as a schoolboy does a butterfly, for the mere gratification of staring at her. I stayed on the top of the Flat till she had gone indoors."

"Into Rose Cottage?"

"Why—yes."

"She had, doubtless, gone to fetch new-laid eggs for her—I mean for the sick gentleman's breakfast. Kind soul!"

"You may jest, Phineas, but I think she is a kind soul. On her way home I saw her stop twice; once to speak to an old woman who was gathering sticks; and again, to scold a lad for thrashing a donkey."

"Did you hear her?"

"No; but I judge from the lad's penitent face as I passed him. I am sure she had been scolding him."

"Then she's not young, depend upon it. Your beautiful young creatures never scold."

"I'm not so sure of that," said John meditatively. "For my part, I should rather not cheat myself or be cheated after that manner. Perfection is impossible. Better see the young woman as she really is, bad and good together."

"The young woman! The fair divinity, you mean!"

"No"—shutting his mouth over the negative in his firm way—"I strongly object to divinities. How unpleasant it would be to woo an angel of perfection, and find her out at last to be only—only Mrs.——"

"Halifax," suggested I; at which he laughed, slightly colouring.

"But how woeful must be our dearth of subjects, when we talk such nonsense as this! What suggested it?"

"Your friend in the gray gown, I suppose."

"*Requiescat in pace!* May she enjoy her eggs! And now I must go saddle the brown mare, and be off to Norton Bury. A lovely day for a ride. How I shall dash along!"

He rose up cheerily. It was like morning sunshine only to see his face. No morbid follies had ever tainted his healthy nature, whatsoever romance was there—and never was there a thoroughly noble nature without some romance in it. But it lay deep down, calm and unawakened. His heart was as light and free as air.

Stooping over my easy-chair, he wheeled it to the window, in sight of the pleasant view.

"Now, Phineas, what more books do you want? You'll take a walk before dinner? You'll not be moping?"

No; why should I, who knew I had always, whether absent or present, the blessing, the infinite blessing, of being first in his thoughts and cares? Who, whether he expressed it or not—the best things never are expressed or expressible—knew by a thousand little daily acts like these, the depths and tenderness of his friendship, his brotherly love for me. As yet, I had it all. And God, who knows how little else I had, will pardon, if in my unspeakable thankfulness lurked a taint of selfish joy in my sole possession of such a priceless boon.

He lingered about, making me "all right," as he called it, and planning out my solitary day. With much merriment, too, for we were the gayest couple of young bachelors, when, as John said, "the duties of our responsible position" would allow.

"Responsible position! It's our good landlady who ought to talk about that. With two sets of lodgers, a husband, and an indefinite number of children. There's one of them got into mischief at last. Hark!"

"It's Jack, my namesake. Bless my life! I knew he would come to grief with that donkey.—Hey, lad! never mind. Get up again."

But soon he perceived that the accident was more serious; and disappeared like a shot, leaping out through the open window. The next minute I saw him carrying in the unlucky Jack, who was bleeding from a cut in the forehead, and screaming vociferously.

"Don't be frightened, Mrs. Tod; it is very slight—I saw it done.—Jack, my lad! be a man, and never mind it. Don't scream so; you alarm your mother."

But as soon as the good woman was satisfied that there was no real cause for terror, hers changed into hearty wrath against Jack for his carelessness, and for giving so much trouble to the gentleman.

"But he be always getting into mischief, sir—that boy. Three months back, the very day Mr. March came, he got playing with the carriage horse, and it kicked him and broke his arm. A deal he cares: he be just as sprack as ever. As I say to Tod—it bean't no use fretting over that boy."

"Have patience," answered John, who had again carried the unfortunate young scapegrace from our parlour into Mrs. Tod's kitchen—the centre room of the cottage; and was trying to divert the torrent of maternal indignation, while he helped her to plaster up the still ugly-looking wound. "Come, forgive the lad. He will be more sorry afterwards than if you had punished him."

"Do 'ee think so?" said the woman, as, struck either by the words, the manner, or the tone, she looked up straight at him. "Do 'ee really think so, Mr. Halifax?"

"I am sure of it. Nothing makes one so good as being forgiven when one has been naughty. Isn't it so, Jack, my namesake?"

"Jack ought to be proud o' that, sir," said the mother respectfully; "and there's some sense in what you say, too. You talk like my man does, o' Sundays. Tod be a Scotchman, Mr. Halifax; and they're good folks, the Scotch, and read their Bibles hard. There's a deal about forgiving in the Bible; isn't there, sir?"

"Exactly," John answered, smiling. "And so, Jack, you're safe this time; only you must not disobey your mother again, for the sake of donkeys or anything else."

"No, sir—thank'ee, sir," sobbed Jack humbly. "You be a gentleman; Mr. March bean't—he said it served me right for getting under his horses."

"Hold thy tongue!" said Jack's mother sharply; for the latch of the opposite door was just then lifted, and a lady stood there.

"Mrs. Tod, my father says——"

Seeing strangers, the lady paused. At the sound of her voice—a pleasant voice, though somewhat quick and decided in tone—John and I both involuntarily turned. We felt awkward; doubtful whether to stay or retire abruptly. She saved us the choice.

"Mrs. Tod, my father will take his soup at eleven. You will remember?"

"Yes, Miss March."

Upon which, Miss March shut the door at once, and vanished.

She wore a gray silken gown. I glanced at John, but he did not see me; his eyes were fixed on the door, which had disclosed and concealed the momentary picture. Its momentariness impressed it the more vividly on my memory—I have it there still.

A girl, in early but not precocious maturity, rather tall, of a figure built more for activity and energy than the mere fragility of sylph-like grace: dark-complexioned, dark-eyed, dark-haired—the whole colouring being of that soft darkness of tone which gives a sense of something at once warm and tender, strong, and womanly. Thorough woman she seemed—not a bit of the angel about her. Scarcely beautiful; and "pretty" would have been the very last word to have applied to her; but there was around her an atmosphere of freshness, health, and youth, pleasant as a breeze in spring.

For her attire, it was that notable gray silk gown—very simply made, with no fripperies or fandangos of any sort—reaching up to her throat and down to her wrists, where it had some kind of trimming of white fur, which made the skin beneath show exquisitely delicate.

"That is Miss March," said our landlady, when she had disappeared.

"Is it?" said John, removing his eyes from the shut door.

"She be very sensible-like, for a young body of seventeen; more sensible and pleasanter than her father, who is always ailing, and always grumbling. Poor gentleman!—most like he can't help it. But it be terrible hard for the daughter—bean't it, sir?"

"Very," said John. His laconism was extraordinary.

Still he kept standing by the kitchen table, waiting till the last bandage had been sewn on Jack's cut forehead, and even some minutes after his *protégé* had begun playing about as usual. It was I who had to suggest that we should not intrude in Mrs. Tod's kitchen any longer.

"No—certainly not. Come, Phineas. Mrs. Tod, I hope our presence did not inconvenience—the young lady?"

"Bless your heart, sir! nothing ever inconveniences she. There bean't a pleasanter young body alive. She'll often come into this kitchen—just as you did, gentlemen, and very happy to see you always," added Mrs. Tod curtsying. "When Mr. March is asleep she'll come and sit for half an hour, talking to Tod and me, and playing with the baby——"

Here, probably at sound of its name, the individual alluded to set up, from its cradle in the corner, such a terrific squall that we young men beat a precipitate retreat.

"So, John, your gray gown is discovered at last. She's young, certainly—but not exactly a beauty."

"I never said she was."

"A pleasant person, though; hearty, cheerful-looking, and strong. I can easily imagine her trotting over the common with her basket of eggs—chatting to the old woman, and scolding the naughty boy."

"Don't make fun of her. She must have a hard life with her old father."

Of course, seeing him take it up so seriously, I jested no more.

"By-the-bye, did not the father's name strike you? *March*—suppose it should turn out to be the very Mr. March you pulled out of Severn five years ago. What a romantic conjuncture of circumstances!"

"Nonsense," said John quickly—more quickly than he usually spoke to me; then came back to wish me a kind good-bye. "Take care of yourself, old fellow. It will be nightfall before I am back from Norton Bury."

I watched him mount, and ride slowly down the bit of common—turning once to look back at Rose Cottage, ere he finally disappeared between the chestnut trees: a goodly sight—for he was an admirable horseman.

When he was gone, I, glancing lazily up at Mr. March's window, saw a hand, and I fancied a white-furred wrist, pulling down the blind. It amused me to think Miss March might possibly have been watching him likewise.

I spent the whole long day alone in the cottage parlour, chiefly meditating; though more than once friendly Mrs. Tod broke in upon my solitude. She treated me in a motherly, free-and-easy way: not half so deferentially as she treated John Halifax.

The sun had gone down over Nunnely Hill, behind the four tall Italian poplars, which stood on the border of our bit of wilderness—three together, and one apart. They were our landmarks—and skymarks too—for the first sunbeam coming across the common struck their tops of a morning, and the broad western glimmer showed their forms distinctly until far in the night. They were just near enough for me to hear their faint rustling in windy weather; on calm days they stood up straight against the sky, like memorial columns. They were friends of mine—those four poplars; sometimes they almost seemed alive. We made acquaintance on this first night, when I sat watching for John; and we kept up the friendship ever afterwards.

It was nine o'clock before I heard the old mare's hoofs clattering up the road: joyfully I ran out.

David was not quite his youthful gay self that night; not quite, as he expressed it, "the David of the sheepfolds." He was very tired, and had what he called "the tanyard feeling," the oppression of business cares.

"Times are hard," said he, when we had finally shut out the starlight, and Mrs. Tod had lit candles, bade us good-night in her free, independent way, and "hoped Mr. Halifax had everything he wanted." She always seemed to consider him the head of our little *ménage*.

"The times are very hard," repeated John thoughtfully. "I don't see how your father can rightly be left with so many anxieties on his shoulders. I must manage to get to Norton Bury at least five days a week. You will have enough of solitude, I fear."

"And you will have little enough of the pleasant country life you planned, and which you seem so to delight in."

"Never mind—perhaps it's good for me. I have a life of hard work before me, and can't afford to get used to too much pleasure. But we'll make the most of every bit of time we have. How have you felt to-day? Strong?"

"Very strong. Now, what would you like us to do to-morrow?"

"I want to show you the common in early morning—the view there is so lovely."

"Of nature, or human nature?"

He half smiled, though only at my mischievousness. I could see it did not affect him in the least. "Nay, I know what you mean; but I had forgotten her, or, if not absolutely forgotten, she was not in my mind just then. We will go another way, as indeed I had intended: it might annoy the young lady, our meeting her again."

His grave, easy manner of treating and dismissing the

subject was a tacit reproach to me. I let the matter drop; we had much more serious topics afloat than gossip about our neighbours.

At seven next morning we were out on the Flat.

"I'm not going to let you stand here in the dews, Phineas. Come a little farther on, to my terrace, as I call it. There's a panorama!"

It was indeed. All around the high Flat a valley lay, like a moat, or as if some broad river had been dried up in its course, and, century after century, gradually converted into meadow, woodland, and town. For a little white town sat demurely at the bottom of the hollow, and a score or two of white cottages scattered themselves from this small nucleus of civilization over the opposite bank of this imaginary river, which was now a lovely hillside. Gorges, purple with shadow, yellow cornfields, and dark clumps of woodland dressed this broad hillside in many colours; its highest point, Nunnely Hill, forming the horizon where last night I had seen the sun go down, and which now was tinted with the tenderest western morning gray.

"Do you like this, Phineas? I do very much. A dear, smiling English valley, holding many a little nest of an English home. Fancy being patriarch over such a region, having the whole valley in one's hand, to do good to, or ill. You can't think what primitive people they are hereabouts—descendants from an old colony of Flemish cloth-weavers: they keep to the trade. Down in the valley—if one could see through the beech wood—is the grand support of the neighbourhood, a large cloth-mill!"

"That's quite in your line, John;" and I saw his face brighten up as it had done when, as a boy, he had talked to me about his machinery. "What has become of that wonderful little loom you made?"

"Oh! I have it still. But this is such a fine cloth-mill! I have been all over it. If the owner would put aside his old Flemish stolidity! I do believe he and his ancestors have gone on in the same way, and with almost the same machinery, ever since Queen Elizabeth's time. Now, just one or two of our modern improvements, such as—but I forget, you never could understand mechanics."

"You can, though. Explain clearly, and I'll try my best."

He did so, and so did I. I think he even managed to knock something of the matter into my stupid head, where it remained—for ten minutes! Much longer remained the impression of his energetic talk—his clear-headed way of putting before another what he understood so well himself. I marvelled how he had gained all his information.

"Oh! it's easy enough, when one has a natural propensity for catching hold of facts; and then, you know, I always had a weakness for machinery; I could stand for an hour watching a mill at work, especially if it's worked by a great water-wheel."

"Would you like to be a millowner?"

"Shouldn't I!"—with a sunshiny flash, which soon clouded over. "However, 'tis idle talking; one cannot choose one's calling—at least, very few can. After all, it isn't the trade that signifies—it's the man. I'm a tanner, and a capital tanner I intend to be. By-the-bye, I wonder if Mrs. Tod, who talks so much about 'gentlefolk,' knows that latter fact about you and me?"

"I think no; I hope not. O David! this one month at least let us get rid of the tanyard."

For I hated it more than ever now, in our quiet, free, Arcadian life; the very thought of it was insupportable, not only for myself, but for John.

He gently blamed me, yet, I think, he involuntarily felt much as I did, if he would have allowed himself so to feel.

"Who would guess now that I who stand here, delighting myself in this fresh air and pleasant view, this dewy common, all thick with flowers—what a pretty blue cluster that is at your foot, Phineas!—who would guess that all yesterday I had been stirring up tan-pits, handling raw hides? Faugh! I wonder the little harebells don't sicken in these, my hands—such ugly hands, too!"

"Nonsense, John! they're not so bad, indeed; and if they were, what does it matter?"

"You are right, lad; it does not matter. They have done me good service, and will yet, though they were not made for carrying nosegays."

"There is somebody besides yourself plucking posies on the Flat. See, how large the figure looks against the sky. It might be your Titaness, John—

"'Like Proserpina gathering flowers,
Herself the fairest——'

—no, not fairest; for I declare she looks very like your friend Gray-gown—I beg her pardon—Miss March."

"It is she," said John, so indifferently that I suspect that fact had presented itself to him for at least two minutes before I found it out.

"There's certainly a fatality about your meeting her."

"Not the least. She has this morning taken her walk in a different direction, as I did; and we both chanced again to hit upon the same," answered John, gravely and explanatorily. "Come away down the slope. We must not intrude upon a lady's enjoyments."

He carried me off, much against my will, for I had a great wish to see again that fresh young face, so earnest, cheerful, and good. Also, as I laboured in vain to convince my companion, the said face indicated an independent dignity which would doubtless make its owner perfectly indifferent whether her solitary walk were crossed by two gentlemen or two hundred.

John agreed to this; nevertheless he was inexorable. And, since he was "a man of the world"—having, in his journeys up and down the country for my father, occasionally fallen into "polite" society—I yielded the point to him, and submitted to his larger experience of good-breeding.

However, Fate, kinder than he, took the knot of etiquette into her own hands, and broke it.

Close to the cottage door, our two paths converging, and probably our breakfast hours likewise, brought us suddenly face to face with Miss March.

She saw us, and we had a distinct sight of her.

I was right: we and our contiguity were not of the smallest importance to Miss March. Her fresh morning roses did not deepen, nor her eyes droop, as she looked for a moment at us both—a quiet, maidenly look of mere observation. Of course no recognition passed; but there was a merry dimple beside her mouth, as if she quite well knew who we were, and owned to a little harmless feminine curiosity in observing us.

She had to pass our door, where stood Mrs. Tod and the baby. It stretched out its little arms to come to her, with that pretty, babyish gesture which I suppose no woman can resist. Miss March could not. She stopped, and began tossing up the child.

Truly, they made a pleasant picture, the two—she with her hooded cloak dropping off, showing her graceful shape, and her dark-brown hair, all gathered up in a mass of curls at the top of her head, as the fashion then was. As she stood, with her eyes sparkling, and the young blood flushing through her clear, brunette cheeks, I was not sure whether I had not judged too hastily in calling her "no beauty."

Probably, by his look, John thought the same.

She stood right before our wicket-gate; but she had evidently quite forgotten us, so happy was she with Mrs. Tod's bonny boy, until the landlady made some remark about "letting the gentlemen by." Then, with a slight start, drawing her hood back over her head, the young lady stepped aside.

In passing her, John raised his eyes, as was natural enough. For me, I could hardly take mine from her, such a pleasant creature was she to behold. She half smiled—he bowed, which she returned, courteously, and we both went indoors. I told him this was a good beginning of acquaintance with our neighbour.

"Not at all, no acquaintance; a mere civility between

two people living under the same roof. It will never be more."

"Probably not."

I am afraid John was disappointed at my "probably." I am afraid that when he stood at our window, contemplating the little group which filled up our wicket-gate, he missed some one out of the three—which, I suspect, was neither Mrs. Tod nor yet the baby.

"I like her face very much better now, David. Do you?"

It was a very curious fact, which I never noticed till afterwards, that though there had been some lapse of time before I hazarded this remark, we both intuitively supplied the noun to that indefinite personal pronoun.

"A good—nay, a noble face; though still, with those irregular features, I can't—really I can't—call her beautiful."

"Nor I."

"She bowed with remarkable grace, too. I think, John, for the first time in our lives, we may say we have seen a *lady*."

"Most certainly a lady."

"Nay, I only meant that, girl as she is, she is evidently accustomed to what is called 'society.' Which makes it the more likely that her father is the Mr. March who was cousin to the Brithwoods. An odd coincidence."

"A very odd coincidence."

After which brief reply John relapsed into taciturnity. More than once that morning we recurred to the subject of our neighbours—that is, I did—but John was rather saturnine and uncommunicative. Nay, when, as Mrs. Tod was removing the breakfast, I ventured to ask her a harmless question or two—who Mr. March was, and where he came from?—I was abruptly reproved, the very minute our good landlady had shut the door, for my tendency to "gossip."

At which I only laughed, and reminded him that he had ingeniously scolded me after, not before, I had gained the desired information—namely, that Mr. March was a gentleman of independent property—that he had no friends hereabouts, and that he usually lived in Wales.

"He cannot be our Mr. March, then."

"No," said John, with an air of great relief.

I was amused to see how seriously he took such a trifle; ay, many a time that day I laughed at him for evincing such great sympathy over our neighbours, and especially—which was plain enough to see, though he doubtless believed he entirely disguised it—for that interest which a young man of twenty would naturally take in a very charming and personable young woman. Ay, naturally, as I said to myself, for I admired her too, extremely.

It seems strange now to call to mind that morning and our light-hearted jests about Miss March. Strange that Destiny should often come thus, creeping like a child to our very doors; we hardly notice it, or send it away with a laugh; it comes so naturally, so simply, so accidentally, as it were, that we recognize it not. We cannot believe that the baby intruder is in reality the king of our fortunes, the ruler of our lives. But so it is continually; and since *it is*, it must be right.

We finished the morning by reading Shakespeare—"Romeo and Juliet"—at which the old folio seemed naturally to open. There is a time—a sweet time, too, though it does not last—when to every young mind the play of plays, the poem of poems, is "Romeo and Juliet." We were at that phase now.

John read it all through to me—not for the first time either; and then, thinking I had fallen asleep, he sat with the book on his knee, gazing out of the open window.

It was a warm summer day—breathless, soundless—a day for quietness and dreams. Sometimes a bee came buzzing among the roses, in and away again, like a happy thought. Nothing else was stirring; not a single bird was to be seen or heard, except that now and then came a coo of the wood-pigeons among the beech trees—a low, tender voice—reminding one of a mother's crooning over a cradled child; or of two true lovers standing clasped heart to heart, in the first embrace, which finds not, and needs not, a single word.

John sat listening. What was he thinking about? Why that strange quiver about his mouth?—why that wonderful new glow, that infinite depth of softness in his eyes?

I closed mine. He never knew I saw him. He thought I slept placidly through that half-hour, which seemed to him as brief as a minute. To me it was long—ah, so long! as I lay pondering with an intensity that was actual pain, on what must come some time, and, for all I knew, might even now be coming.

CHAPTER XI.

A WEEK slipped by. We had grown familiar with Enderley Hill—at least I had. As for John, he had little enough enjoyment of the pretty spot he had taken such a fancy to, being absent five days out of the seven; riding away when the morning sun had slid down to the boles of my four poplars, and never coming home till Venus peeped out over their heads at night. It was hard for him; but he bore the disappointment well.

With me one day went by just like another. In the mornings I crept out, climbed the hill behind Rose Cottage garden, and there lay a little under the verge of the Flat, in a sunny shelter, watching the ants running in and out of the numerous ant-hills there; or else I turned my observation to the short velvet herbage that grew everywhere hereabouts; for the common, so far from being barren, was a perfect sheet of greenest, softest turf, sowed with minute and rare flowers. Often a square foot of ground presented me with enough of beauty and variety in colour and form to criticize and contemplate for a full hour.

My human interests were not extensive. Sometimes the Enderley villagers, or the Tod children, who were a grade above these, and decidedly "respectable," would appear and have a game of play at the foot of the slope, their laughter rising up to where I lay. Or some old woman would come with her pails to the spring below, a curious and very old stone well, to which the cattle from the common often rushed down past me in bevies, and stood knee-deep, their mouths making glancing circles in the water as they drank.

Being out of doors almost all day, I saw very little of the inhabitants of our cottage. Once or twice a lady and gentleman passed, creeping at the foot of the slope so slowly, that I felt sure it must be Mr. March and his daughter. He was tall, with gray hair; I was not near enough to distinguish his features. She walked on the further side, supporting him with her arm. Her comfortable morning hood was put off, and she had on her head that ugly, stiff thing which ladies had lately taken to wearing, and which, Jael said, was called a "bonnet."

Except on these two occasions, I had no opportunity of making any observations on the manners and customs of our neighbours. Occasionally Mrs. Tod mentioned them in her social chatter, while laying the cloth; but it was always in the most cursory and trivial way, such as "Miss March having begged that the children might be kept quiet—Mrs. Tod hoped their noise didn't disturb *me?* but Mr. March was such a very fidgety gentleman—so particular in his dress, too—Why, Miss March had to iron his cravats with her own hands. Besides, if there was a pin awry in her dress he did make such a fuss—and, really, such an active, busy young lady couldn't look always as if she came trim out of a band-box. Mr. March wanted so much waiting on, he seemed to fancy he still had his big house in Wales, and his seven servants."

Mrs. Tod conversed as if she took it for granted I was fully acquainted with all the prior history of her inmates, or any others that she mentioned—a habit peculiar to Enderley folk with strangers. It was generally rather convenient, and it saved much listening; but in this case, I would rather have had it broken through. Sometimes

I felt strongly inclined to question her; but on consulting John, he gave his veto so decidedly against seeking out people's private affairs in such an illicit manner that I felt quite guilty, and began to doubt whether my sickly, useless, dreaming life was not inclining me to curiosity, gossip, and other small vices which we are accustomed —I know not why—to insult the other sex by describing as "womanish."

As I have said, the two cottages were built distinct, so that we could have neither sound nor sight of our neighbours, save upon the neutral ground of Mrs. Tod's kitchen; where, however, I might have felt inclined to venture, John's prohibition stopped me entirely.

Thus—save the two days when he was at home, when he put me on his mare's back, and led me far away, over common, and valley, and hill, for miles, only coming back at twilight—save those two blithe days, I spent the week in dignified solitude, and was very thankful for Sunday.

We determined to make it a long, lovely country Sunday; so we began it at six a.m. John took me a new walk across the common, where—he said, in answer to my question—we were quite certain *not* to meet Miss March.

"Do you experimentalize on the subject, that you calculate her paths with such nicety? Pray, have you ever met her again, for I know you have been out most mornings?"

"Morning is the only time I have for walking, you know, Phineas."

"Ah, true! You have little pleasure at Enderley. I almost wish we could go home."

"Don't think of such a thing. It is doing you a world of good. Indeed, we must not, on any account, go home."

I know, and knew then, that his anxiety was in earnest; that whatever other thoughts might lie underneath, the sincere thought of me was the one uppermost in his mind.

"Well, we'll stay—that is, if you are happy, John."

"Thoroughly happy; I like the dashing rides to Norton Bury. Above all, I like coming back. The minute I begin to climb Enderley Hill, the tanyard, and all belonging to it, drops off like an incubus, and I wake into free, beautiful life. Now, Phineas, confess; is not this common a lovely place, especially of a morning?"

"Ay," said I, smiling at his energy. "But you did not tell me whether you had met Miss March again."

"She has never once seen me."

"But you have seen her? Answer honestly."

"Why should I not? Yes, I have seen her—once or twice or so—but never in any way that could annoy her."

"That explains why you have become so well acquainted with the direction of her walks?"

He coloured deeply. "I hope, Phineas, you do not think that—that in any way I should intrude on or offend a lady?"

"Nay, don't take it so seriously—indeed, I meant nothing of the kind. It would be quite natural if a young man like you did use some pains to look at such a 'cunning piece of Nature's handiwork' as that apple-cheeked girl of seventeen."

"Russet apple. She is brown, you know—a real 'nut-browne mayde,'" said John, recovering his gay humour. "Certainly, I like to look at her. I have seen many a face that was more good-looking—never one that looked half so good."

"Sententious that;" yet I could not smile—he spoke with such earnestness. Besides, it was the truth. I myself would have walked half-way across the common any day for a glance at Miss March. Why not he?

"But, John, you never told me that you had seen her again!"

"Because you never asked me."

We were silent. Silent until we had walked along the whole length of a Roman encampment, the most perfect of the various fosses that seamed the Flat—tokens of many a battle fought on such capital battleground, and which John had this morning especially brought me to look at.

"Yes," I said at last, putting the ending affirmative

to a long train of thought, which was certainly not about Roman encampments; "yes, it is quite natural that you should admire her. It would even be quite natural, and not unlikely either, if she——"

"Pshaw!" interrupted he. "What nonsense you are talking! Impossible!" and setting his foot sharply upon a loose stone, he kicked it down into the ditch, where probably many a dead Roman had fallen before it in ages gone by.

The impetuous gesture—the energetic "impossible," struck me less than the quickness with which his mind had worked out my unexpressed thought—carrying it to a greater length than I myself had ever contemplated.

"Truly, no possibilities or impossibilities of *that* sort ever entered my head. I only thought you might admire her, and be unsettled thereby, as young men are when they take fancies. That would grieve me very much, John."

"Don't let it, then. Why, I have only seen her five times; I never spoke to her in my life, and most probably never shall do. Could any one be in a safer position? Besides," and his tone changed to extreme gravity, "I have too many worldly cares to think of; I can't afford the harmless little amusement of falling in love—so be easy, Phineas."

I smiled; and we began a discussion on camps and fosses, vallum and prætorium, the Danes, Saxons, and Normans, which, doubtless, we carried on to a most learned length; but at this distance of time, and indeed the very day after, I plead guilty to having forgotten all about it.

That long, quiet Sunday, when, I remember, the sun never came out all day, but the whole earth and sky melted together in a soft, gray haze; when we lay on the common and heard church-bells ringing, some distant, some near; and, after all was quiet, talked our own old Sabbath talks, of this world and the world to come; when, towards twilight, we went down into the beech wood below the house, and sat idly there among the pleasant-smelling ferns; when, from the morning to the evening, he devoted himself altogether to my comfort and amusement—to perfect which required of him no harder duty than to be near me always;—that Sunday was the last I ever had David altogether for my own—my very own.

It was natural, it was just, it was right. God forbid that in any way I should have murmured.

About ten o'clock—just as he was luring me out to see how grand the common looked under the black night, and we were wondering whether or no the household were in bed—Mrs. Tod came mysteriously into the parlour and shut the door after her. Her round, fresh face looked somewhat troubled.

"Mr. Halifax, might I speak a word to 'ee, sir?"

"With pleasure. Sit down, Mrs. Tod. There's nothing wrong with your children?"

"No, I thank 'ee. You are very kind, sir. No, it be about that poor Miss March."

I could see John's fingers twitch over the chair he was leaning on. "I hope——" he began, and stopped.

"Her father is dreadful bad to-night, and it's a good seven-mile walk to the doctor's at S——; and Miss March says—that is, she don't, for I bean't going to tell her a word about it—but I think, Mr. Halifax, if I might make so bold, it would be a great kindness in a young gentleman like you to lend Tod your mare to ride over and fetch the doctor."

"I will, gladly. At once?"

"Tod bean't come in yet."

"He shall have the mare with pleasure. Tell Miss March so—I mean, do not tell her, of course. It was very right of you to come to us in this way, Mrs. Tod. Really, it would be almost a treat to be ill in your house—you are so kind."

"Thank'ee, Mr. Halifax," said the honest landlady, greatly delighted. "But a body couldn't help doing anything for Miss March. You would think so yourself, if you only knew her."

"No doubt," returned John, more politely than warmly, I fancied, as he closed the door after the retreating figure of Mrs. Tod. But when he came and sat down again I saw he was rather thoughtful. He turned the books restlessly, one after the other, and could not settle to anything. To all my speculations about our sick neighbour, and our pearl of kind-hearted landladies, he only replied in monosyllables; at last he started up and said,—

"Phineas, I think I'll go myself."

"Where?"

"To fetch Dr. Brown. If Tod is not come in it would be but a common charity. And I know the way."

"But the dark night?"

"Oh, no matter; the mare will be safer under me than a stranger. And though I have taken good care that the three horses in the tanyard shall have the journey, turn and turn about, still it's a good pull from here to Norton Bury, and the mare's my favourite. I would rather take her myself."

I smiled at his numerous good reasons for doing such a very simple thing; and agreed that it was right and best he should do it.

"Then shall I call Mrs. Tod and inquire? Or perhaps it might make less fuss just to go and speak to her in the kitchen. Will you, Phineas, or shall I?"

Scarcely waiting my answer, we walked from our parlour into what I called the Debateable Land.

No one was there. We remained several minutes all alone, listening to the groaning overhead.

"That must be Mr. March, John."

"I hear. Good heavens! how hard for her. And she such a young thing, and alone," muttered he, as he stood gazing into the dull wood embers of the kitchen fire. I saw he was moved; but the expression on his face was one of pure and holy compassion. That at this moment no less unselfish feeling mingled with it I am sure.

Mrs. Tod appeared at the door leading to the other half of the cottage; she was apparently speaking to Miss

March on the staircase. We heard again those clear, quick, decided tones, but subdued to a half whisper.

"No, Mrs. Tod, I am not sorry you did it—on my father's account, 'tis best. Tell Mr.—the young gentleman—I forget his name—that I am very much obliged to him."

"I will, Miss March;—stay, he is just here.—Bless us! she has shut the door already. Won't you take a seat, Mr. Halifax? I'll stir up the fire in a minute, Mr. Fletcher. You are always welcome in my kitchen, young gentlemen." And Mrs. Tod bustled about, well aware what a cosy and cheerful old-fashioned kitchen it was, especially of evenings.

But when John explained the reason of our intrusion there was no end to her pleasure and gratitude. He was the kindest young gentleman that ever lived. She would tell Miss March so; as, indeed, she had done many a time.

"'Miss,' said I to her the very first day I set eyes on you, when I told her how you came hunting for lodgings (she often has a chat with me quite freely, being so lonesome-like, and knowing I to be too proud myself to forget that she's a born lady)—'Miss,' said I, 'who Mr. Halifax may be I don't know, but depend upon it he's a real gentleman.'"

I was the sole amused auditor of this speech, for John had vanished. In a few minutes more he had brought the mare round, and after a word or two with me was clattering down the road.

I wondered whether this time any white-furred wrist stirred the blind to watch him.

John was away a wonderfully short time, and the doctor rode back with him. They parted at the gate, and he came into our parlour, his cheeks all glowing with the ride. He only remarked "that the autumn nights were getting chill," and sat down. The kitchen clock struck one.

"You ought to have been in bed hours ago, Phineas. Will you not go? I shall sit up just a little while, to hear how Mr. March is."

"I should like to hear too. It is curious the interest that one learns to take in people that are absolute strangers, when shut up together in a lonely place like this, especially when they are in trouble."

"Ay, that's it," said he quickly. "It's the solitude, and their being in trouble. Did you hear anything more while I was away?"

"Only that Mr. March was rather better, and everybody had gone to bed except his daughter and Mrs. Tod."

"Hark! I think that's the doctor going away. I wonder if one might ask—no! they would think it intrusive. He must be better. But Dr. Brown told me that in one of these paroxysms he might—— Oh, that poor young thing!"

"Has she no relatives—no brothers or sisters? Dr. Brown surely knows."

"I did not like to ask, but I fancy not. However, that's not my business: my business is to get you off to bed, Phineas Fletcher, as quickly as possible."

"Wait one minute, John. Let us go and see if we can do anything more."

"Ay—if we can do anything more," repeated he, as we again recrossed the boundary line, and entered the Tod country.

All was quiet there. The kitchen fire burnt brightly, and a cricket sang in merry solitude on the hearth; the groans overhead were stilled, but we heard low talking, and presently stealthy footsteps crept downstairs. It was Mrs. Tod and Miss March.

We ought to have left the kitchen: I think John muttered something to that effect, and even made a slight movement towards the door; but—I don't know how it was—we stayed.

She came and stood by the fire, scarcely noticing us. Her fresh cheeks were faded, and she had the weary look of one who has watched for many hours. Some sort of white dimity gown that she wore added to this paleness.

"I think he is better, Mrs. Tod—decidedly better,"

said she, speaking quickly. "You ought to go to bed now. Let all the house be quiet. I hope you told Mr. —oh——"

She saw us, stopped, and for the moment the faintest tinge of her roses returned. Presently she acknowledged us, with a slight bend.

John came forward. I had expected some awkwardness on his part; but no—he was thinking too little of himself for that. His demeanour—earnest, gentle, kind—was the sublimation of all manly courtesy.

"I hope, *madam*,"—young men used the deferential word in those days always—"I do hope that Mr. March is better. We were unwilling to retire until we had heard."

"Thank you! My father is much better. You are very kind," said Miss March, with a maidenly dropping of the eyes.

"Indeed he is kind," broke in the warm-hearted Mrs. Tod. "He rode all the way to S——, his own self, to fetch the doctor."

"Did you, sir? I thought you only lent your horse."

"Oh! I like a night-ride. And you are sure, madam, that your father is better? Is there nothing else I can do for you?"

His sweet, grave manner, so much graver and older than his years, softened too with that quiet deference which marked at once the man who reverenced all women, simply for their womanhood—seemed entirely to reassure the young lady. This, and her own frankness of character, made her forget, as she apparently did, the fact that she was a young lady and he a young gentleman, meeting on unacknowledged neutral ground, perfect strangers, or knowing no more of one another than the mere surname.

Nature, sincerity, and simplicity conquered all trammels of formal custom. She held out her hand to him.

"I thank you very much, Mr. Halifax. If I wanted help I would ask you; indeed I would."

"Thank *you*. Good-night."

He pressed the hand with reverence—and was gone. I saw Miss March look after him: then she turned to speak and smile with me. A light word, an easy smile, as to a poor invalid whom she had often pitied out of the fullness of her womanly heart.

Soon I followed John into the parlour. He asked me no questions, made no remarks, only took his candle and went upstairs.

But, years afterwards, he confessed to me that the touch of that hand—it was a rather peculiar hand in the "feel" of it, as the children say, with a very soft palm, and fingers that had a habit of perpetually fluttering, like a little bird's wing—the touch of that hand was to the young man like a revelation of a new world.

CHAPTER XII.

THE next day John rode away earlier even than was his wont, I thought. He stayed but a little while talking with me. While Mrs. Tod was bustling over our breakfast he asked her, in a grave and unconcerned manner, "How Mr. March was this morning?" which was the only allusion he made to the previous night's occurrences.

I had a long, quiet day alone in the beech wood, close below our cottage, sitting by the little runnel, now worn to a thread with the summer weather, but singing still. It talked to me like a living thing.

When I came home in the evening Miss March stood in front of the cottage, with—strange to say—her father. But I had heard that his paroxysms were often of brief continuance, and that, like most confirmed valetudinarians, when real danger stared him in the face he put it from him, and was glad to be well.

Seeing me coming, Miss March whispered to him; he turned upon me a listless gaze from over his fur collar, and bowed languidly, without rising from his easy-chair. Yes, it was Mr. March—the very Mr. March we had met!

I knew him, changed though he was; but he did not know me in the least, as, indeed, was not likely.

His daughter came a step or two to meet me. "You are better, I see, Mr. Fletcher. Enderley is a most healthy place, as I try to persuade my father. This is Mr. Fletcher, sir, the gentleman who——"

"Was so obliging as to ride to S—— last night for me? Allow me to thank him myself."

I began to disclaim, and Miss March to explain; but we must both have been slightly incoherent, for I think the poor gentleman was never quite clear as to who it was that went for Dr. Brown. However, that mattered little, as his acknowledgments were evidently dictated more by a natural habit of courtesy than by any strong sense of service rendered.

"I am a very great invalid, sir.—My dear, will you explain to the gentleman?" And he leaned his head back wearily.

"My father has never recovered his ten years' residence in the West Indies."

"'Residence?' Pardon me, my dear, you forget I was governor of——"

"Oh yes! The climate is very trying there, Mr. Fletcher. But since he has been in England—five years only—he has been very much better. I hope he will be quite well in time."

Mr. March shook his head drearily. Poor man! the world of existence to him seemed to have melted lazily down into a mere nebula, of which the forlorn nucleus was—himself. What a life for any young creature—even his own daughter, to be bound to continually!

I could not help remarking the strong contrast between them. He, with his sallow, delicately-shaped features—the thin mouth, and long, straight nose, of that form I have heard called the "melancholy nose," which usually indicates a feeble, pensive, and hypochondriac temperament; while his daughter—but I have described her already.

"Mr. Fletcher is an invalid too, father," she said; so

gently that I could feel no pain in her noticing my infirmity; and took gratefully a seat she gave me beside that of Mr. March. She seemed inclined to talk to me; and her manner was perfectly easy, friendly, and kind.

We spoke of commonplace subjects, near at hand, and of the West Indian island, which its late "governor" was apparently by no means inclined to forget. I asked Miss March whether she had liked it.

"I was never there. Papa was obliged to leave me behind in Wales—poor mamma's country. Were you ever in Wales? I like it so! Indeed, I feel as if I belonged altogether to the mountains."

And saying this, she looked the very incarnation of the free mountain spirit—a little rugged, perhaps, and sharply outlined; but that would soften with time, and was better and wholesomer than any tame green level of soft perfection. At least, one inclined to think so, looking at her.

I liked Miss March very much, and was glad of it.

In retiring, with her father leaning on her arm, to which he hung trustingly and feebly as a child, she turned abruptly, and asked if she could lend me any books to read. I must find the days long and dull without my friend.

I assented with thanks; and shortly afterwards she brought me an armful of literature—enough to have caused any young damsel to have been dubbed a "blue," in those matter-of-fact days.

"I have no time to study much myself," said she in answer to my questions; "but I like those who do. Now, good-evening, for I must run. You and your friend can have any books of ours. You must not think"—and she turned back to tell me this—"that because my father said little he and I are not deeply grateful for the kindness Mr. Halifax showed us last night."

"It was a pleasure to John—it always is—to do a kind office for any one."

"I well believe that, Mr. Fletcher." And she left me.

When John came home I informed him of what had

passed. He listened, though he made no comment whatever. But all the evening he sat turning over Miss March's books, and reading either aloud or to himself fragments out of one—which I had expected he would have scouted, inasmuch as it was modern, not classical poetry—in fact, a collection of Lyrical Ballads, brought out that year by a young man named Mr. William Wordsworth, and some anonymous friend, conjointly. I had opened it, and found therein great nonsense; but John had better luck—he hit upon a short poem called "Love," by the Anonymous Friend, which he read, and I listened to, almost as if it had been Shakespeare. It was about a girl named Genevieve—a little simple story—everybody knows it now; but it was like a strange, low, mystic music, luring the very heart out of one's bosom, to us young visionaries then.

I wonder if Miss March knew the harm she did, and the mischief that has been done among young people in all ages (since Caxton's days), by the lending books, especially books of poetry.

The next day John was in a curious mood. Dreamy, lazy, mild; he sat poring indoors, instead of roaming abroad—in truth, was a changed lad. I told him so, and laid it all to the blame of the Anonymous Friend: who held him in such fascinated thrall that he only looked up once all the morning—which was when Mr. and Miss March went by. In the afternoon he submitted, lamb-like, to be led down to the beech wood—that the wonderful talking stream might hold forth to him as it did to me. But it could not—ah, no! it could not. Our lives, though so close, were yet as distinct as the musical living water and the motionless gray rock beside which it ran. The one swept joyfully on to its appointed course: the other—was what Heaven made it, abode where Heaven placed it, and likewise fulfilled its end.

Coming back out of the little wood, I took John a new way I had discovered, through the prettiest undulating meadow, half field, half orchard, where trees loaded with ripening cider apples and green crabs made a variety among the natural foresters. Under one of these, as we climbed the slope—for field, beech wood, and common formed a gradual ascent—we saw a vacant table laid.

"A pretty piece of rusticity—domestic Arcadia on a small scale," said John; "I should like to invite myself to tea with them. Who can they be?"

"Probably visitors. Resident country folks like their meals best under a decent roof-tree. I should not wonder if this were not one of Mr. March's vagaries."

"Don't say vagaries—he is an old man."

"Don't be reproachful—I shall say naught against him. Indeed, I have no opportunity, for there they both are coming hither from the house."

Sure enough they were—Miss March helping her father across the uneven bit of common to the gate which led to the field. Precisely at that gate we all four met.

"'Tis useless to escape them," whispered I to John.

"I do not wish—why should I?" he answered, and held the gate open for the father and daughter to go through. She looked up and acknowledged him, smiling. I thought that smile and his courteous, but far less frank, response to it, would have been all the greeting; but no! Mr. March's dull perceptions had somehow been brightened up. He stopped.

"Mr. Halifax, I believe?"

John bowed.

They stood a moment looking at one another; the tall, stalwart young man, so graceful and free in bearing, and the old man, languid, sickly, prematurely broken down.

"Sir," said the elder, and in his fixed gaze I fancied I detected something more than curiosity—something of the lingering pensiveness with which, years ago, he had turned back to look at John—as if the lad reminded him of some one he knew—"Sir, I have to thank you——"

"Indeed, no thanks are needed. I sincerely hope you are better to-day?"

Mr. March assented: but John's countenance apparently interested him so much that he forgot his usual complainings. "My daughter tells me you are our neighbours—I am happy to have such friendly ones.—My dear," in a half audible, pensive whisper to her, "I think your poor brother Walter would have grown up extremely like Mr.—Mr.——"

"Mr. Halifax, papa."

"Mr. Halifax, we are going to take tea under the trees there—my daughter's suggestion—she is so fond of rurality. Will you give us the pleasure of your company? You and—" here, I must confess, the second invitation came in reply to a glance of Miss March's—"your friend."

Of course we assented: I considerably amused, and not ill-pleased, to see how naturally it fell out that when John appeared in the scene, I, Phineas, subsided into the secondary character of John's "friend."

Very soon—so soon that our novel position seemed like an adventure out of the "Arabian Nights"—we found ourselves established under the apple tree, between whose branches the low sun stole in, kissing into red chestnut colour the hair of the "nut-browne mayde," as she sat, bare-headed, pouring into small white china cups that dainty luxury, tea. She had on—not the gray gown, but a white one, worked in delicate muslin. A bunch of those small pinky-white roses that grew in such clusters about our parlour window nestled, almost as if they were still growing, in her fair maiden bosom.

She apologized for little Jack's having "stolen" them from our domains for her—lucky Jack! and received some brief and rather incoherent answer from John about being "quite welcome."

He sat opposite her—I by her side—she had placed me there. It struck me as strange, that though her manner to us both was thoroughly frank and kind, it was a shade more frank, more kind, to me than to him. Also, I noted, that while she chatted gaily with me, John almost entirely confined his talk to her father.

But the young lady listened—ay, undoubtedly she listened—to every word that was said. I did not wonder at it: when his tongue was once unloosed few people could talk better than John Halifax. Not that he was one of your showy conversationalists; language was with him neither a science, an art, nor an accomplishment, but a mere vehicle for thought; the garb, always chosen as simplest and fittest, in which his ideas were clothed. His conversation was never wearisome, since he only spoke when he had something to say; and having said it, in the most concise and appropriate manner that suggested itself at the time, he was silent; and silence is a great and rare virtue at twenty years of age.

We talked a good deal about Wales; John had been there more than once in his journeyings; and this fact seemed to warm Miss March's manner, rather shy and reserved though it was, at least to him. She told us many an innocent tale of her life there—of her childish days, and of her dear old governess, whose name, I remember, was Cardigan. She seemed to have grown up solely under that lady's charge. It was not difficult to guess—though I forget whether she distinctly told us so—that "poor mamma" had died so early as to become a mere name to her orphan daughter. She evidently owed everything she was to this good governess.

"My dear," at last said Mr. March, rather testily, "you make rather too much of our excellent Jane Cardigan. She is going to be married, and she will not care for you now."

"Hush, papa, that is a secret at present. Pray, Mr. Halifax, do you know Norton Bury?"

The abruptness of the question startled John, so that he only answered in a hurried affirmative. Indeed, Mr. March left him no time for further explanation.

"I hate the place. My late wife's cousins, the Brithwoods of the Mythe, with whom I have had—ahem!—strong political differences—live there. And I was once nearly drowned in the Severn close by."

"Papa, don't speak of that, please," said Miss March hurriedly; so hurriedly that I am sure she did not notice what would otherwise have been plain enough—John's sudden and violent colour. But the flush died down again—he never spoke a word. And, of course, acting on his evident desire, neither did I.

"For my part," continued the young lady, "I have no dislike to Norton Bury. Indeed, I rather admired the place, if I remember right."

"You have been there?" Though it was the simplest question, John's sudden look at her, and the soft inflection of his voice, struck me as peculiar.

"Once, when I was about twelve years old. But we will talk of something papa likes better. I am sure papa enjoys this lovely evening. Hark! how the doves are cooing in the beech wood."

I asked her if she had ever been in the beech wood.

No; she was quite unacquainted with its mysteries—the fern glades, the woodbine tangles, and the stream, that, if you listened attentively, you could hear faintly gurgling even where we sat.

"I did not know there was a stream so near. I have generally taken my walks across the Flat," said Miss March, smiling, and then blushing at having done so, though it was the faintest blush imaginable.

Neither of us made any reply.

Mr. March settled himself to laziness and his arm-chair; the conversation fell to the three younger persons—I may say the two—for I also seceded, and left John master of the field. It was enough for me to sit listening to him and Miss March, as they gradually became more friendly; a circumstance natural enough, under the influence of that simple, solitary place, where all the pretences of etiquette seemed naturally to drop away, leaving nothing but the forms dictated and preserved by true manliness and true womanliness.

How young both looked, how happy in their frank, free youth, with the sun-rays slanting down upon them, making a glory round either head, and—as glory often does—dazzling painfully!

"Will you change seats with me, Miss March? The sun will not reach your eyes here."

She declined, refusing to punish any one for her convenience.

"It would not be punishment," said John, so gravely that one did not recognize it for a "pretty speech" till it had passed—and went on with their conversation. In the course of it he managed so carefully, and at the same time so carelessly, to interpose his broad hat between the sun and her, that the fiery old king went down in splendour before she noticed that she had been thus guarded and sheltered. Though she did not speak —why should she? of such a little thing—yet it was one of those "little things" which often touch a woman more than any words.

Miss March rose. "I should greatly like to hear your stream and its wonderful singing." (John Halifax had been telling how it held forth to me during my long, lonely days. "I wonder what it would say to me? Can we hear it from the bottom of this field?"

"Not clearly; we had better go into the wood." For I knew John would like that, though he was too great a hypocrite to second my proposal by a single word.

Miss March was more single-minded, or else had no reason for being the contrary. She agreed to my plan with childish eagerness. "Papa, you wouldn't miss me —I shall not be away five minutes.—Then, Mr. Fletcher, will you go with me?"

"And I will stay beside Mr. March, so that he will not be left alone," said John, reseating himself.

What did the lad do that for? Why did he sit watching us so intently, as I led Miss March down the meadow, and into the wood? It passed my comprehension.

The young girl walked with me, as she talked with me, in perfect simplicity and frankness, free from the smallest hesitation. Even as the women I have known have treated me all my life—showing me that sisterly trust and sisterly kindness which have compensated in a measure for the solitary fate which it pleased Heaven to lay upon me; which, in any case, conscience would have forced me to lay upon myself—that no woman should ever be more to me than a sister.

Yet I watched her with pleasure—this young girl, as she tripped on before me, noticing everything, enjoying everything. She talked to me a good deal too about myself, in her kindly way, asking what I did all day—and if I were not rather dull sometimes in this solitary country lodging.

"I am dull occasionally myself, or should be, if I had time to think about it. It is hard to be an only child."

I told her I had never found it so.

"But then you have your friend. Has Mr. Halifax any brothers or sisters?"

"None. No relatives living."

"Ah!" a compassionate ejaculation, as she pulled a woodbine spray, and began twisting it with those never-quiet fingers of hers. "You and he seem to be great friends?"

"John is a brother, friend, everything in the world to me."

"Is he? He must be very good. Indeed, he looks so," observed Miss March thoughtfully. "And I believe—at least I have often heard—that good men are rare."

I had no time to enter into that momentous question, when the origin of it himself appeared, breaking through the bushes to join us.

He apologized for so doing, saying Mr. March had sent him.

"You surely do not mean that you come upon compulsion? What an ill compliment to this lovely wood."

And the eyes of the "nut-browne mayde" were a little mischievous. John looked preternaturally grave, as he said, "I trust you do not object to my coming?"

She smiled—so merrily, that his slight haughtiness evaporated like mist before the sunbeams.

"I was obliged to startle you by jumping through the bushes, for I heard my own name. What terrible revelations has this friend of mine been making to you, Miss March?"

He spoke gaily; but I fancied he looked uneasy. The young lady only laughed.

"I have a great mind not to tell you, Mr. Halifax."

"Not when I ask you?"

He spoke so seriously that she could not choose but reply.

"Mr. Fletcher was telling me three simple facts:—First, that you were an orphan, without relatives. Secondly, that you were his dearest friend. Thirdly—well, I never compromise truth—that you were good."

"And you?"

"The first I was ignorant of; the second I had already guessed; the third—" He gazed at her intently. "The third I had likewise—not doubted."

John made some hurried acknowledgment. He looked greatly pleased—nay, more than pleased—happy. He walked forward by Miss March's side, taking his natural place in the conversation, while I as naturally and willingly fell behind. But I heard all they said, and joined in it now and then.

Thus, sometimes spoken to, and sometimes left silent, watching their two figures, and idly noting their comparative heights—her head came just above John's shoulder—I followed these young people through the quiet wood.

Let me say a word about that wood—dear and familiar as it was. Its like I have never since seen. It was small—so small that in its darkest depths you might catch the sunshine lighting up the branches of its outside trees. A young wood, too—composed wholly of smooth-barked beeches and sturdy Scotch firs, growing up side by side—the Adam and Eve in this forest Eden. No old folk were there—no gnarled and withered foresters—every tree rose up, upright in its youth, and perfect after its kind. There was as yet no choking undergrowth of vegetation; nothing but mosses, woodbine, and ferns; and between the boles of the trees you could trace vista after vista, as between the slender pillars of a cathedral aisle.

John pointed out all this to Miss March, especially noticing the peculiar character of the two species of trees—the masculine and feminine—fir and beech. She smiled at the fancy; and much graceful badinage went on between them. I had never before seen John in the company of women, and I marvelled to perceive the refinement of his language, and the poetic ideas it clothed. I forgot the truth—of whose saying was it?—"that once in his life every man becomes a poet."

They stood by the little rivulet, and he showed her how the water came from the spring above; the old well-head where the cattle drank; how it took its course merrily through the woods, till at the bottom of the valley below it grew into a wide stream.

"Small beginnings make great endings," observed Miss March sententiously.

John answered her with the happiest smile! He dipped his hollowed palm into the water and drank; she did the same. Then, in her free-hearted girlish fun, she formed a cup out of a broad leaf, which, by the greatest ingenuity, she managed to make contain about two teaspoonfuls of water for the space of half a minute, and held it to my mouth.

"I am like Rebecca at the well. Drink, Eleazer," she cried gaily.

John looked on. "I am very thirsty too," said he in a low voice.

The young girl hesitated a moment; then filled and offered to him the Arcadian cup. I fear he drank out of it a deeper and more subtle draught than that innocent water.

Both became somewhat grave, and stood, one on either side the stream, looking down upon it, letting its bubbling murmur have all the talk. What it said I know not: I only know that it did not, could not, say to those two what it said to me.

When we took leave of our acquaintances, Mr. March was extremely courteous, and declared our society would always be a pleasure to himself and his daughter.

"He always says so formally, 'my daughter,'" I observed, breaking the silence in which they had left us. "I wonder what her Christian name is?"

"I believe it is Ursula."

"How did you find that out?"

"It is written in one of her books."

"Ursula!" I repeated, wondering where I had heard it before. "A pretty name."

"A very pretty name."

When John fell into this echo mood I always found it best to fall into taciturnity.

CHAPTER XIII.

NEXT day the rain poured down incessantly, sweeping blindingly across the hills as I have rarely seen it sweep except at Enderley. The weather had apparently broken up, even thus early in the autumn; and for that day, and several days following, we had nothing but wind, rain, and storm. The sky was as dusky as Miss March's gray gown; broken sometimes in the evening by a rift of misty gold, gleaming over Nunnely Hill, as if to show us what September sunsets might have been.

John went every day to Norton Bury that week. His mind seemed restless—he was doubly kind and attentive to me; but every night I heard him go out in all the storm to walk upon the common. I longed to follow him, but it was best not.

On the Saturday morning, coming to breakfast, I heard him ask Mrs. Tod how Mr. March was. We knew the invalid had been ailing all the week, nor had we seen him or his daughter once.

Mrs. Tod shook her head ominously. "He is very bad, sir; badder than ever, I do think. She sits up wi' him best part of every night."

"I imagined so. I have seen her light burning."

"Law, Mr. Halifax! you don't be walking abroad of nights on the Flat? It's terrible bad for your health," cried the honest soul, who never disguised the fact that Mr. Halifax was her favourite of all her lodgers, save and except Miss March.

"Thank you for considering my health," he replied, smiling. "Only tell me, Mrs. Tod, can anything be done—can we do anything for that poor gentleman?"

"Nothing, sir—thank'ee all the same."

"If he should grow worse, let me go for Dr. Brown. I shall be at home all day."

"I'll tell Miss March of your kindness, sir," said Mrs. Tod, as with a troubled countenance she disappeared.

"Were you not going to Norton Bury to-day, John?"

"I was—but—as it is a matter of no moment, I have changed my mind. You have been left so much alone lately. Nay—I'll not disguise the truth; I had another reason."

"May I know it?"

"Of course you may. It is about our fellow-lodgers. Dr. Brown—I met him on the road this morning—told me that her father cannot live more than a few days—perhaps a few hours. And she does not know it."

He leaned on the mantelpiece. I could see he was very much affected.

So was I.

"Her relatives—surely they ought to be sent for?"

"She has none. Dr. Brown said she once told him so; none nearer than the Brithwoods of the Mythe—and we know what the Brithwoods are."

A young gentleman and his young wife—proverbially the gayest, proudest, most light-hearted of all our county families.

"Nay, Phineas, I will not have you trouble yourself. And, after all, they are mere strangers—mere strangers. Come, sit down to breakfast."

But he could not eat. He could not talk of ordinary things. Every minute he fell into abstractions. At length he said suddenly,—

"Phineas, I do think it is wicked, downright wicked, for a doctor to be afraid of telling a patient he is going to die—more wicked, perhaps, to keep the friends in ignorance until the last stunning blow falls. She ought to be told; she must be told; she may have many things to say to her poor father. And God help her! for such a stroke she ought to be a little prepared. It might kill her else!"

He rose up and walked about the room. The seal once taken from his reserve, he expressed himself to me freely, as he had used to do—perhaps because at this time his feelings required no disguise. The dreams which might have peopled that beautiful sunset wood necessarily faded in an atmosphere like this—filled with the solemn gloom of impending death.

At last he paused in his hurried walk, quieted, perhaps, by what he might have read in my ever-following eyes.

"I know you are as grieved as I am, Phineas. What can we do? Let us forget that they are strangers, and act as one Christian ought to another. Do *you* not think she ought to be told?"

"Most decidedly. They might get further advice."

"That would be vain. Dr. Brown says it is a hopeless case, has been so for long; but he would not believe it, nor have his daughter told. He clings to life desperately. How horrible for her!"

"You think most of her."

"I do," said he firmly. "He is reaping what he sowed, poor man! God knows, I pity him. But she is as good as an angel of heaven."

It was evident that, somehow or other, John had learnt a great deal about the father and daughter. However, now was not the time to question him. For at this moment, through the opened doors, we heard faint moans that pierced the whole house, and too surely came from the sick—possibly, the dying—man. Mrs. Tod, who had been seeing Dr. Brown to his horse, now entered our parlour, pale, with swollen eyes.

"Oh, Mr. Halifax!" and the kind soul burst out into crying afresh. John made her sit down, and gave her a glass of wine.

"I've been with them since four this morning, and it makes me weakly like," said she. "That poor Mr. March!—I didn't like him very much alive, but I do feel so sorry now he's a-dying."

Then he *was* dying.

"Does his daughter know?" I asked.

"No—no—I dare not tell her. Nobody dare."

"Does she not guess it?"

"Not a bit. Poor young body! she's never seen anybody so. She fancies him no worse than he has been, and has got over it. She *wouldn't* think else. She be a good daughter to him—that she be!"

We all sat silent; and then John said, in a low voice, "Mrs. Tod, she ought to be told—and you would be the best person to tell her."

But the soft-hearted landlady recoiled from the task. "If Tod were at home now—he that is so full o' wisdom learnt in 'the kirk'——"

"I think," said John, hastily interrupting, "that a woman would be the best. But if you object, and as Dr. Brown will not be here till to-morrow—and as there is no one else to perform such a trying duty—it seems —that is, I believe——" here his rather formal speech failed. He ended it abruptly—"If you like, I will tell her myself."

Mrs. Tod overwhelmed him with thankfulness.

"How shall I meet her, then? If it were done by chance it would be best."

"I'll manage it somehow. The house is very quiet; I've sent all the children away, except the baby. The baby 'll comfort her, poor dear, afterwards." And, again drying her honest eyes, Mrs. Tod ran out of the room.

We could do nothing at all that morning. The impending sorrow might have been our own, instead of that of people who three weeks ago were perfect strangers. We sat and talked—less, perhaps, of them individually, than of the dark Angel, whom face to face I at least had never yet known—who even now stood at the door of our little habitation, making its various inmates feel as one family, in the presence of the great leveller of all things—Death.

Hour by hour of that long day the rain fell down—pouring, pouring—shutting us up, as it were, from the world without, and obliterating every thought, save of what was happening under our one roof—that awful change which was taking place in the upper room, in the other half of the house, whence the moans descended, and whence Mrs. Tod came out from time to time, hurrying mournfully to inform "Mr. Halifax" how things went on.

It was nearly dusk before she told us Mr. March was asleep, that his daughter had at last been persuaded to come downstairs, and was standing drinking "a cup o' tea" by the kitchen fire.

"You must go now, sir; she'll not stop five minutes. Please go."

"I will," he answered; but he turned frightfully pale. "Phineas, don't let her see us both. Stay without the door If there were anybody to tell her this but me!"

"Do you hesitate?"

"No—no."

And he went out. I did not follow him; but I heard afterwards, both from himself and Mrs. Tod, what transpired.

She was standing so absorbed that she did not notice his entrance. She looked years older and sadder than the young girl who had stood by the stream-side less than a week ago. When she turned and spoke to John, it was with a manner also changed. No hesitation, no shyness; trouble had put aside both.

"Thank you, my father is indeed seriously ill. I am in great trouble, you see, though Mrs. Tod is very, very kind. Don't cry so, good Mrs. Tod; I can't cry, I dare not. If I once began I should never stop, and then how could I help my poor father? There now, there!"

She laid her hand, with its soft, fluttering motions, on the good woman's shoulder, and looked up at John. He said afterwards that those dry, tearless eyes smote him to the heart.

"Why does she sob so, Mr. Halifax? Papa will be better to-morrow, I am sure."

"I *hope* so," he answered, dwelling on the word; "we should always hope to the very last."

"The last?" with a quick, startled glance.

"And then we can only trust."

Something more than the *mere* words struck her. She examined him closely for a minute.

"You mean—yes—I understand what you mean. But you are mistaken. The doctor would have told me—if—if——" she shivered, and left the sentence unfinished.

"Dr. Brown was afraid—we were all afraid," broke in Mrs. Tod, sobbing. "Only Mr. Halifax, he said——"

Miss March turned abruptly to John. That woeful gaze of hers could be answered by no words. I believe he took her hand, but I cannot tell. One thing I can tell, for she said it to me herself afterwards, that he seemed to look down upon her like a strong, pitiful, comforting angel; a messenger sent by God.

Then she broke away, and flew upstairs. John came in again to me, and sat down. He did not speak for many minutes.

After an interval—I know not how long—we heard Mrs. Tod calling loudly for "Mr. Halifax." We both ran through the empty kitchen to the foot of the stairs that led to Mr. March's room.

Mr. March's room! Alas, he owned nothing now on this fleeting, perishable earth of ours. He had gone from it; the spirit stealing quietly away in sleep. He belonged now to the world everlasting.

Peace be to him! Whatever his life had been, he was *her* father.

Mrs. Tod sat half-way down the staircase, holding Ursula March across her knees. The poor creature was insensible, or nearly so. She—we learnt—had been composed under the terrible discovery made when she returned to his room; and when all restorative means failed, and the fact of death became certain, she had herself closed her father's eyes, and kissed him, then tried to walk from the room—but at the third step she dropped quietly down.

There she lay; physical weakness conquering the strong heart; she lay, overcome at last. There was no more to bear. Had there been, I think she would have been able to have borne it still.

John took her in his arms; I know not if he took her, or Mrs. Tod gave her to him—but there she was. He carried her across the kitchen into our own little parlour, and laid her down on my sofa.

"Shut the door, Phineas. Mrs. Tod, keep everybody out. She is waking now."

She did indeed open her eyes, with a long sigh, but closed them again. Then with an effort she sat upright, and looked at us all around.

"Oh, my dear, my dear!" moaned Mrs. Tod, clasping her, and sobbing over her like a child. "Cry, do cry!"

"I *can't*," she said, and lay down again.

We stood awed, watching that poor, pale face, on every line of which was written stunned, motionless, impassive grief. For John—two minutes of such a gaze as his might in a man's heart do the work of years.

"She must be roused," he said at last. "She *must* cry. Mrs. Tod, take her upstairs. Let her look at her father."

The word effected what he desired; what almost her life demanded. She clung round Mrs. Tod's neck in torrents of weeping.

"Now, Phineas, let us go away."

And he went, walking almost like one blindfold, straight out of the house, I following him.

CHAPTER XIV.

"I AM quite certain, Mrs. Tod, that it would be much better for her; and, if she consents, it shall be so," said John decisively.

We three were consulting, the morning after the death, on a plan which he and I had already settled between ourselves—namely, that we should leave our portion of the cottage entirely at Miss March's disposal, while we inhabited hers—save that locked and silent chamber wherein there was no complaining, no suffering now.

Either John's decision, or Mrs. Tod's reasoning, was successful; we received a message to the effect that Miss March would not refuse our "kindness." So we vacated; and all that long Sunday we sat in the parlour lately our neighbour's, heard the rain come down, and the church bells ring; the wind blowing autumn gales, and shaking all the windows, even that of the room overhead. It sounded awful *there*. We were very glad the poor young orphan was away.

On the Monday morning we heard going upstairs the heavy footsteps that every one at some time or other has shuddered at; then the hammering. Mrs. Tod came in, and told us that no one—not even his daughter—could be allowed to look at what had been "poor Mr. March" any more. All with him was ended.

"The funeral is to be soon. I wonder what she will do then, poor thing!"

John made me no answer.

"Is she left well provided for, do you think?"

"It is impossible to say."

His answers were terse and brief enough, but I could not help talking about the poor young creature, and wondering if she had any relative or friend to come to her in this sad time.

"She said—do you remember, when she was crying—that she had not a friend in the wide world?"

And this fact, which he expressed with a sort of

triumph, seemed to afford the greatest possible comfort to John.

But all our speculations were set at rest by a request brought this moment by Mrs. Tod—that Mr. Halifax would go with her to speak to Miss March.

"I! only I?" said John, starting.

"Only you, sir. She wants somebody to speak to about the funeral—and I said, 'There be Mr. Halifax, Miss March, the kindest gentleman;' and she said, 'If it wouldn't trouble him to come——'"

"Tell her I am coming."

When, after some time, he returned, he was very serious.

"Wait a minute, Phineas, and you shall hear; I feel confused, rather. It is so strange, her trusting me thus. I wish I could help her more."

Then he told me all that had passed—how he and Mrs. Tod had conjointly arranged the hasty funeral—how brave and composed she had been—that poor child, all alone!

"Has she indeed no one to help her?"

"No one. She might send for Mr. Brithwood, but he was not friendly with her father; she said she had rather ask this 'kindness' of me, because her father had liked me, and thought I resembled their Walter, who died."

"Poor Mr. March!—perhaps he is with Walter now. But, John, can you do all that is necessary for her? You are very young."

"She does not seem to feel that. She treats me as if I were a man of forty. Do I look so old and grave, Phineas?"

"Sometimes. And about the funeral?"

"It will be very simple. She is determined to go herself. She wishes to have no one besides Mrs. Tod, you, and me."

"Where is he to be buried?"

"In the little churchyard close by, which you and I have looked at many a time. Ah, Phineas, we did not think how soon we should be laying our dead there."

"Not *our* dead, thank God!"

But the next minute I understood. "*Our* dead"—the involuntary admission of that sole feeling, which makes one, erewhile a stranger, say to, or think of another, "All thine are mine, and mine are thine, henceforward and for ever."

I watched John as he stood by the fire; his thoughtful brow and firm-set lips contradicting the youthfulness of his looks. Few as were his years, he had learnt much in them. He was at heart a man, ready and able to design and carry out a man's work in the world. And in his whole aspect was such grave purity, such honest truth, that no wonder, young as they both were, and little as she knew of him, this poor orphan should not have feared to trust him entirely. And there is nothing that binds heart to heart, of lovers or friends, so quickly and so safely, as to trust and be trusted in time of trouble.

"Did she tell you any more, John? Anything of her circumstances?"

"No. But from something Mrs. Tod let fall, I fear"—and he vainly tried to disguise his extreme satisfaction—"that she will be left with little or nothing."

"Poor Miss March!"

"Why call her poor? She is not a woman to be pitied, but to be honoured. You would have thought so, had you seen her this morning. So gentle—so wise—so brave. Phineas,"—and I could see his lips tremble—"that was the kind of woman Solomon meant when he said, 'Her price was above rubies.'"

"I think so too. I doubt not that when she marries, Ursula March will be 'a crown to her husband.'"

My words, or the half sigh that accompanied them—I could not help it—seemed to startle John, but he made no remark. Nor did we recur to the subject again that day.

Two days after, our little company followed the coffin out of the woodbine porch—where we had last said good-bye to poor Mr. March—across the few yards of common, to the churchyard, scarcely larger than a cottage garden, where, at long intervals, the few Enderley dead were laid.

A small procession—the daughter first, supported by good Mrs. Tod; then John Halifax and I. So we buried him—the stranger who, at this time, and henceforth, seemed even, as John had expressed it, "our dead," our own.

We followed the orphan home. She had walked firmly, and stood by the graveside motionless, her hood drawn over her face. But when we came back to Rose Cottage door, and she gave a quick, startled glance up at the familiar window, we saw Mrs. Tod take her, unresisting, into her motherly arms—then we knew how it would be.

"Come away," said John, in a smothered voice—and we came away.

All that day we sat in our parlour—Mr. March's parlour that had been—where, through the no longer darkened casement, the unwonted sun poured in. We tried to settle to our ordinary ways, and feel as if this were like all other days—our old sunshiny days at Enderley. But it would not do. Some imperceptible but great change had taken place. It seemed a year since that Saturday afternoon, when we were drinking tea so merrily under the apple tree in the field.

We heard no more from Miss March that day. The next, we received a message of thanks for our "kindness." She had given way at last, Mrs. Tod said, and kept her chamber, not seriously ill, but in spirit thoroughly broken down. For three days more, when I went to meet John returning from Norton Bury, I could see that his first glance, as he rode up between the chestnut trees, was to the window of the room that had been mine. I always told him, without his asking, whatever Mrs. Tod had told me about her state; he used to listen, generally in silence, and then speak of something else. He hardly ever mentioned Miss March's name.

On the fourth morning I happened to ask him if he had told my father what had occurred here.

"No."

I looked surprised.

"Did you wish me to tell him? I will, if you like, Phineas."

"Oh no. He takes little interest in strangers."

Soon after, as he lingered about the parlour, John said,—

"Probably I may be late to-night. After business hours I want to have a little talk with your father."

He stood irresolutely by the fire. I knew by his countenance that there was something on his mind.

"David."

"Ay, lad."

"Will you not tell me first what you want to say to my father?"

"I can't stay now. To-night, perhaps. But, pshaw! what is there to be told? Nothing."

"Anything that concerns you can never be to me quite 'nothing.'"

"I know that," he said affectionately, and went out of the room.

When he came in he looked much more cheerful—stood switching his riding-whip after the old habit, and called upon me to admire his favourite brown mare.

"I do; and her master likewise. John, when you're on horseback you look like a young knight of the Middle Ages. Maybe some of the old Norman blood was in 'Guy Halifax, gentleman.'"

It was a dangerous allusion. He changed colour so rapidly and violently that I thought I had angered him.

"No—that would not matter—cannot—cannot—never shall. I am what God made me, and what, with His blessing, I will make myself."

He said no more, and very soon afterwards he rode away. But not before, as every day, I had noticed that wistful wandering glance up at the darkened window of the room, where, sad and alone, save for kindly Mrs. Tod, the young orphan lay.

In the evening, just before bedtime, he said to me,

with a rather sad smile, "Phineas, you wanted to know what it was that I wished to speak about to your father?"

"Ay, do tell me."

"It is hardly worth telling. Only to ask him how he set up in business for himself. He was, I believe, little older than I am now."

"Just twenty-one."

"And I shall be twenty-one next June."

"Are you thinking of setting up for yourself?"

"A likely matter!" and he laughed, rather bitterly, I thought, "when every trade requires capital, and the only trade I thoroughly understand, a very large one. No, no, Phineas; you'll not see me setting up a rival tanyard next year. My capital is *nil*."

"Except youth, health, courage, honour, honesty, and a few other such trifles."

"None of which I can coin into money, however. And your father has expressly told me that without money a tanner can do nothing."

"Unless, as was his own case, he was taken into some partnership where his services were so valuable as to be received instead of capital. True, my father earned little at first, scarcely more than you earn now; but he managed to live respectably, and, in course of time, to marry."

I avoided looking at John as I said the last word. He made no answer, but in a little time he came and leaned over my chair.

"Phineas, you are a wise counsellor—'a brother born for adversity.' I have been vexing myself a good deal about my future, but now I will take heart. Perhaps, some day, neither you nor any one else will be ashamed of me."

"No one could, even now, seeing you as you really are."

"As John Halifax, not as the tanner's 'prentice boy? Oh, lad—there the goad sticks. Here I forget everything unpleasant; I am my own free natural self; but the minute I get back to Norton Bury—however, it is a wrong, a wicked feeling, and must be kept down. Let us talk of something else."

"Of Miss March? She has been greatly better all day."

"She? No, not her to-night!" he said hurriedly. "Pah! I could almost fancy the odour of these hides on my hands still. Give me a candle."

He went upstairs, and only came down a few minutes before bedtime.

Next morning was Sunday. After the bells had done ringing, we saw a black-veiled figure pass our window. Poor girl!—going to church alone. We followed, taking care that she should not see us, either during service or afterwards. We did not see anything more of her that day.

On Monday a message came, saying that Miss March would be glad to speak with us both. Of course we went.

She was sitting quite alone, in our old parlour, very grave and pale, but perfectly composed. A little more womanly-looking in the dignity of her great grief, which, girl as she was, and young men as we were, seemed to be to her a shield transcending all worldly "proprieties."

As she rose, and we shook hands, in a silence only broken by the rustle of her black dress, not one of us thought—surely the most evil-minded gossip could not have dared to think—that there was anything strange in her receiving us here. We began to talk of common things—not *the* thing. She seemed to have fought through the worst of her trouble, and to have put it back into those deep, quiet chambers where all griefs go; never forgotten, never removed, but sealed up in silence, as it should be. Perhaps, too—for let us not exact more from nature than nature grants—the wide, wide difference in character, temperament, and sympathies between Miss March and her father unconsciously made his loss less a heart-loss, total and irremediable, than one of mere habit and instinctive feeling, which, the first shock over, would insensibly heal. Besides, she was young—young in life, in hope, in body, and soul; and youth, though it grieves passionately, cannot for ever grieve.

I saw, and rejoiced to see, that Miss March was in some degree herself again; at least, so much of her old self as was right, natural, and good for her to be.

She and John conversed a good deal. Her manner to him was easy and natural, as to a friend who deserved and possessed her warm gratitude; his was more constrained. Gradually, however, this wore away; there was something in her which, piercing all disguises, went at once to the heart of things. She seemed to hold in her hand the touchstone of truth.

He asked—no, I believe *I* asked her, how long she intended staying at Enderley.

"I can hardly tell. Once I understood that my cousin Richard Brithwood was left my guardian. This my fa—this was to have been altered, I believe. I wish it had been. You know Norton Bury, Mr. Halifax?"

"I live there."

"Indeed!" with some surprise. "Then you are probably acquainted with my cousin and his wife?"

"No; but I have seen them."

John gave these answers without lifting his eyes.

"Will you tell me candidly—for I know nothing of her, and it is rather important that I should learn—what sort of person is Lady Caroline?"

This frank question, put directly, and guarded by the battery of those innocent, girlish eyes, was a very hard question to be answered; for Norton Bury had said many ill-natured things of our young squire's wife, whom he married at Naples, from the house of the well-known Lady Hamilton.

"She was, you are aware, Lady Caroline Ravenel, the Earl of Luxmore's daughter."

"Yes, yes; but that does not signify. I know nothing of Lord Luxmore—I want to know what she is herself."

John hesitated, then answered, as he could with truth, "She is said to be very charitable to the poor, pleasant, and kind-hearted. But, if I may venture to hint as much, not exactly the friend whom I think Miss March would choose, or to whom she would like to be indebted for anything but courtesy."

"That was not my meaning. I need not be indebted to any one. Only, if she were a good woman, Lady Caroline would have been a great comfort and a useful adviser to one who is scarcely eighteen, and, I believe, an heiress."

"An heiress!" The colour flashed in a torrent over John's whole face, then left him pale. "I—pardon me—I thought it was otherwise. Allow me to—to express my pleasure——"

"It does not add to mine," said she, half sighing. "Jane Cardigan always told me riches brought many cares. Poor Jane! I wish I could go back to her—but that is impossible!"

A silence here intervened, which it was necessary some one should break.

"So much good can be done with a large fortune," I said.

"Yes. I know not if mine is very large; indeed, I never understood money matters, but have merely believed what—what I was told. However, be my fortune much or little, I will try to use it well."

"I am sure you will."

John said nothing; but his eyes, sad indeed, yet lit with a proud tenderness, rested upon her as she spoke. Soon after, he rose up to take leave.

"Do not go yet; I want to ask about Norton Bury. I had no idea you lived there. And Mr. Fletcher too?"

I replied in the affirmative.

"In what part of the town?"

"On the Coltham Road, near the Abbey."

"Ah, those Abbey chimes!—how I used to listen to them, night after night, when the pain kept me awake!"

"What pain?" asked John suddenly, alive to any suffering of hers.

Miss March smiled almost like her old smile. "Oh, I had nearly forgotten it, though it was very bad at the time; only that I cut my wrist rather dangerously with a bread-knife, in a struggle with my nurse."

"When was that?" eagerly inquired John.

For me, I said nothing. Already I guessed all. Alas! the tide of fate was running strong against my poor David. What could I do but stand aside and watch?

"When was it? Let me see—five, six years ago. But, indeed, 'tis nothing."

"Not exactly 'nothing.' Do tell me!"

And John stood, listening for her words, counting them even, as one would count, drop by drop, a vial of joy which is nearly empty, yet Time's remorseless hand still keeps on, pouring, pouring.

"Well, if you must know it, it was one of my naughtinesses—I was very naughty as a child. They would not let me have a piece of bread that I wanted to give away to a poor lad."

"Who stood opposite—under an alley—in the rain? Was it not so?"

"How could you know? But he looked so hungry; I was so sorry for him."

"Were you?" in a tone almost inaudible.

"I have often thought of him since, when I chanced to look at this mark."

"Let me look at it. May I?"

Taking her hand, he softly put back the sleeve, discovering, just above the wrist, a deep, discoloured seam. He gazed at it, his features all quivering, then, without a word either of adieu or apology, he quitted the room.

CHAPTER XV.

I WAS left with Miss March alone. She sat looking at the door where John had disappeared, in extreme surprise, not unmingled with a certain embarrassment.

"What does he mean, Mr. Fletcher? Can I have offended him in any way?"

"Indeed, no."

"Why did he go away?"

But that question, simple as it was in itself, and most simply put, involved so much, that I felt I had no right to answer it; while, at the same time, I had no possible right to use any of those disguises or prevarications which are always foolish and perilous, and very frequently wrong. Nor, even had I desired, was Miss March the woman to whom one dared offer the like; therefore I said to her plainly,—

"I know the reason. I would tell you, but I think John would prefer telling you himself."

"As he pleases," returned Miss March, a slight reserve tempering her frank manner; but it soon vanished, and she began talking to me in her usual friendly way, asking me many questions about the Brithwoods and about Norton Bury. I answered them freely—my only reservation being, that I took care not to give any information concerning ourselves.

Soon afterwards, as John did not return, I took leave of her, and went to our own parlour.

He was not there. He had left word with little Jack, who met him on the common, that he was gone a long walk, and should not return till dinner-time. Dinner-time came, but I had to dine alone. It was the first time I ever knew him break even such a trivial promise. My heart misgave me—I spent a miserable day. I was afraid to go in search of him, lest he should return to a dreary, empty parlour. Better, when he did come in, that he should find a cheerful hearth and—me.

Me, his friend and brother, who had loved him these six years better than anything else in the whole world. Yet what could I do now? Fate had taken the sceptre out of my hands—I was utterly powerless; I could neither give him comfort nor save him pain any more.

What I felt then, in those long, still hours, many a one has felt likewise; many a parent over a child, many a sister over a brother, many a friend over a friend. A feeling natural and universal. Let those who suffer take it patiently, as the common lot; let those who win hold the former ties in tenderest reverence, nor dare to flaunt the new bond cruelly in the face of the old.

Having said this, which, being the truth, it struck me as right to say, I will no more allude to the subject.

In the afternoon there occurred an incident. A coach-and-four, resplendent in liveries, stopped at the door; I knew it well, and so did all Norton Bury. It was empty; but Lady Caroline's own maid—so I heard afterwards—sat in the rumble, and Lady Caroline's own black-eyed Neapolitan page leaped down, bearing a large letter, which I concluded was for Miss March.

I was glad that John was not at home; glad that the coach, with all its fine paraphernalia, was away, empty as it had arrived, before John came in.

He did not come till it was nearly dusk. I was at the window, looking at my four poplar trees, as they pointed skywards like long fingers stretching up out of the gloom, when I saw him crossing the common. At first I was going to meet him at the gate, but on second thoughts I remained within, and only stirred up the fire, which could be seen shining ever so far.

"What a bright blaze! Nay, you have not waited dinner, I hope? Tea—yes, that's far better; I have had such a long walk, and am so tired."

The words were cheerful, so was the tone. *Too* cheerful—oh, by far! The sort of cheerfulness that strikes to a friend's heart, like the piping of soldiers as they go away back from a newly-filled grave.

"Where have you been, John?"

"All over Nunnely Hill. I must take you there—such expansive views. As Mrs. Tod informed me, quoting some local ballad, which she said was written by an uncle of hers,—

"'There you may spy
Twenty-three churches with the glass and the eye.'

Remarkable fact, isn't it?"

Thus he kept on talking all tea-time, incessantly, rapidly talking. It was enough to make one weep.

After tea I insisted on his taking my arm-chair; saying that after such a walk, in that raw day, he must be very cold.

"Not the least—quite the contrary—feel my hand." It was burning. "But I am tired—thoroughly tired."

He leaned back and shut his eyes. Oh, the utter weariness of body and soul that was written on his face!

"Why did you go out alone? John, you know that you have always me."

He looked up, smiling. But the momentary brightness passed. Alas! I was not enough to make him happy now.

We sat silent. I knew he would speak to me in time; but the gates of his heart were close locked. It seemed as if he dared not open them, lest the flood should burst forth and overwhelm us.

At nine o'clock Mrs. Tod came in with supper. She had always something or other to say, especially since the late events had drawn the whole household of Rose Cottage so closely together; now she was brimful of news.

She had been all that evening packing up for poor dear Miss March; though why she should call her "poor," truly, she didn't know. Who would have thought Mr. March had such grand relations? Had we seen Lady Caroline Brithwood's coach that came that day? Such a beautiful coach it was!—sent on purpose for Miss March—only she wouldn't go. "But now she has made up her mind, poor dear. She is leaving to-morrow."

When John heard this, he was helping Mrs. Tod, as usual, to fasten the heavy shutters. He stood, with his hand on the bolt, motionless, till the good woman was gone. Then he staggered to the mantelpiece, and leaned on it with both his elbows, his hands covering his face.

But there was no disguise now—no attempt to make it. A young man's first love—not first fancy, but first love—in all its passion, desperation, and pain—had come to him, as it comes to all. I saw him writhing under it

—saw, and could not help him. The next few silent minutes were very bitter to us both.

Then I said gently, " David ! "

" Well ? "

" I thought things were so."

" Yes."

" Suppose you were to talk to me a little—it might do you good."

" Another time. Let me go out—out into the air; I'm choking."

Snatching up his hat, he rushed from me. I did not dare to follow.

After waiting some time, and listening till all was quiet in the house, I could bear the suspense no longer, and went out.

I thought I should find him on the Flat—probably in his favourite walk, his " terrace," as he called it, where he had first seen, and must have seen many a day after, that girlish figure tripping lightly along through the morning sunshine and morning dew. I had a sort of instinct that he would be there now; so I climbed up the shortest way, often losing my footing; for it was a pitch-dark night, and the common looked as wide, and black, and still as a midnight sea.

John was not there; indeed, if he had been I could scarcely have seen him; I could see nothing but the void expanse of the Flat, or, looking down, the broad river of mist that rolled through the valley, on the other side of which twinkled a few cottage lights, like unearthly beacons from the farthest shore of an impassable flood.

Suddenly I remembered hearing Mrs. Tod say that, on account of its pits and quarries, the common was extremely dangerous after dark, except to those who knew it well. In a horrible dread I called out John's name—but nothing answered. I went on blindly, desperately, shouting as I went. At length, in one of the Roman fosses, I stumbled and fell. Some one came, darting with great leaps through the mist, and lifted me up.

"O David—David!"

"Phineas, is that you? You have come out this bitter night—why did you?"

His tenderness over me, even then, made me break down. I forgot my manhood, or else it slipped from me unawares. In the old Bible language, "I fell on his neck and wept."

Afterwards I was not sorry for this, because I think my weakness gave him strength. I think, amidst the whirl of passion that racked him, it was good for him to feel that the one crowning cup of life is not inevitably life's sole sustenance; that it was something to have a friend and brother who loved him with a love—like Jonathan's—"passing the love of women."

"I have been very wrong," he kept repeating, in a broken voice; "but I was not myself. I am better now. Come—let us go home."

He put his arm round me to keep me warm, and brought me safely into the house. He even sat down by the fire to talk with me. Whatever struggle there had been, I saw it was over, he looked his own self—only so very, very pale—and spoke in his natural voice; ay, even when mentioning *her*, which he was the first to do.

"She goes to-morrow, you are sure, Phineas?"

"I believe so. Shall you see her again?"

"If she desires it."

"Shall you say anything to her?"

"Nothing. If for a little while—not knowing or not thinking of all the truth—I felt I had strength to remove all impediments, I now see that even to dream of such things makes me a fool, or possibly worse—a knave. I will be neither—I will be a man."

I replied not; how could one answer such words?—calmly uttered, though each syllable must have been torn out like a piece of his heart.

"Did she say anything to you? Did she ask why I left her so abruptly this morning?"

"She did; I said you would probably tell her the reason yourself."

"I will. She must no longer be kept in ignorance about me or my position. I shall tell her the whole truth—save one thing. She need never know that."

I guessed by his broken voice what the "one thing" was which he counted as nothing; but which, I think, any true woman would have counted worth everything—the priceless gift of a good man's love. Love, that in such a nature as his, if once conceived, would last a lifetime. And she was not to know it! I felt sorry—ay, even sorry, for Ursula March.

"Do you not think I am right, Phineas?"

"Perhaps. I cannot say. You are the best judge."

"It is right," said he firmly. "There can be no possible hope for me; nothing remains but silence."

I did not quite agree with him. I could not see that to any young man, only twenty years old, with the world all before him, any love could be absolutely hopeless; especially to a young man like John Halifax. But as things now stood I deemed it best to leave him altogether to himself, offering neither advice nor opinion. What Providence willed, through *his* will, would happen: for me to interfere either way would be at once idle and perilous—nay, in some sense, exceedingly wrong.

So I kept my thoughts to myself, and preserved a total silence.

John broke it—talking to himself as if he had forgotten I was by.

"To think it was she who did it—that first kindness to a poor friendless boy. I never forgot it—never. It did me more good than I can tell. And that scar on her poor arm—her dear little tender arm; how this morning I would have given all the world to——"

He broke off—instinctively, as it were—with the sort of feeling every good man has, that the sacred passion, the inmost tenderness of his love, should be kept wholly between himself and the woman he has chosen.

I knew that too; knew that in his heart had grown up a secret, a necessity, a desire, stronger than any friendship—closer than the closest bond of brotherly love. Perhaps—I hardly know why—I sighed.

John turned round. "Phineas, you must not think—because of this—which you will understand for yourself, I hope, one day; you must not think I could ever think less, or feel less, about my brother."

He spoke earnestly, with a full heart. We clasped hands warmly and silently. Thus was healed my last lingering pain—I was thenceforward entirely satisfied.

I think we parted that night as we had never parted before; feeling that the trial of our friendship—the great trial, perhaps, of any friendship—had come and passed safely; that whatever new ties might gather round each, our two hearts would cleave together until death.

The next morning rose, as I have seen many a morning rise at Enderley—misty and gray; but oh, so heavenly fair! with a pearly network of dewy gossamer under foot, and overhead countless thistle-downs flying about, like fairy chariots hurrying out of sight of the sun, which had only mounted high enough above the Flat to touch the horizon of hills opposite, and the tops of my four poplars, leaving Rose Cottage and the valley below it all in morning shadow. John called me to go with him on the common; his voice sounded so cheerful outside my door that it was with a glad heart I rose and went.

He chose his old walk—his "terrace." No chance now of meeting the light figure coming tripping along the level hill. All that dream was now over. He did not speak of it—nor I. He seemed contented—or, at least, thoroughly calmed down; except that the sweet composure of his mien had settled into the harder gravity of manhood. The crisis and climax of youth had been gone through—he never could be a boy again.

We came to that part of John's terrace which overhung the churchyard. Both of us glanced instinctively down to the heap of loose red earth—the as yet nameless grave. Some one stood beside it—the only one who was likely to be there.

Even had I not recognized her, John's manner would

have told me who it was. A deadly paleness overspread his face—its quietness was gone—every feature trembled. It almost broke my heart to see how deeply this love had struck its roots down to the very core of his; twisting them with every fibre of his being. A love which, though it had sprung up so early, and come to maturity so fast, might yet be the curse of his whole existence. Save that no love conceived virtuously, for a good woman, be it ever so hopeless, can be rightly considered as a curse.

"Shall we go away?" I whispered—"a long walk—to the other side of the Flat? She will have left Rose Cottage soon."

"When?"

"Before noon, I heard. Come, David."

He suffered me to put my arm in his, and draw him away for a step or two, then turned.

"I can't, Phineas, I can't! I *must* look at her again—only for one minute—one little minute."

But he stayed—we were standing where she could not see us—till she had slowly left the grave. We heard the click of the churchyard gate; where she went afterward we could not discern.

John moved away. I asked him if we should take our walk now? But he did not seem to hear me; so I let him follow his own way—perhaps it might be for good—who could tell?

He descended from the Flat, and came quickly round the corner of the cottage. Miss March stood there, trying to find one fresh rose among the fast-withering clusters about what had been our parlour window and now was hers.

She saw us, acknowledged us, but hurriedly, and not without some momentary signs of agitation.

"The roses are all gone," she said rather sadly.

"Perhaps, higher up, I can reach one—shall I try?"

I marvelled to see that John's manner as he addressed her was just like his manner always with her.

"Thank you—that will do. I wanted to take some

away with me—I am leaving Rose Cottage to-day, Mr. Halifax."

"So I have heard."

He did not say "sorry to hear." I wondered did the omission strike her? But no—she evidently regarded us both as mere acquaintances, inevitably, perhaps even tenderly, bound up with this time; and as such, claiming a more than ordinary place in her regard and remembrance. No man with common sense or common feeling could for a moment dare to misinterpret the emotion she showed.

Re-entering the house, she asked us if we would come in with her; she had a few things to say to us. And then she again referred gratefully to our "kindness."

We all went once more—for the last time—into the little parlour.

"Yes—I am going away," said she mournfully.

"We hope all good will go with you—always and everywhere."

"Thank you, Mr. Fletcher."

It was strange, the grave tone our intercourse now invariably assumed. We might have been three old people, who had long fought with and endured the crosses of the world, instead of two young men and a young woman in the very dawn of life.

"Circumstances have fixed my plans since I saw you yesterday. I am going to reside for a time with my cousins, the Brithwoods. It seems best for me. Lady Caroline is very kind, and I am so lonely."

She said this not in any complaint, but as if accepting the fact, and making up her mind to endure it. A little more fragmentary conversation passed, chiefly between herself and me—John uttered scarcely a word. He sat by the window, half shading his face with his hand. Under that covert, the gaze which incessantly followed and dwelt on her face—oh, had she seen it!

The moments narrowed. Would he say what he had intended concerning his position in the world? Had she guessed or learned anything, or were we to her simply

Mr. Halifax and Mr. Fletcher—two "gentlemen" of Norton Bury? It appeared so.

"This is not a very long good-bye, I trust?" said she to me, with something more than courtesy. "I shall remain at the Mythe House some weeks, I believe. How long do you purpose staying at Enderley?"

I was uncertain.

"But your home is in Norton Bury? I hope—I trust, you will allow my cousin to express in his own house his thanks and mine for your great kindness during my trouble?"

Neither of us answered. Miss March looked surprised—hurt—nay, displeased; then her eye, resting on John, lost its haughtiness, and became humble and sweet.

"Mr. Halifax, I know nothing of my cousin, and I do know you. Will you tell me—candidly, as I know you will—whether there is anything in Mr. Brithwood which you think unworthy of your acquaintance?"

"He would think me unworthy of his," was the low, firm answer.

Miss March smiled incredulously. "Because you are not very rich? What can that signify? It is enough for me that my friends are gentlemen."

"Mr. Brithwood, and many others, would not allow my claim to that title."

Astonished—nay, somewhat more than astonished—the young gentlewoman drew back a little. "I do not quite understand you."

"Let me explain, then," and her involuntary gesture seeming to have brought back all honest dignity and manly pride, he faced her, once more himself. "It is right, Miss March, that you should know who and what I am, to whom you are giving the honour of your kindness. Perhaps you ought to have known before; but here at Enderley we seemed to be equals—friends."

"I have indeed felt it so."

"Then you will the sooner pardon my not telling you—what you never asked, and I was only too ready to forget—that we are *not* equals—that is, society would not regard us as such—and I doubt if even you yourself would wish us to be friends."

"Why not?"

"Because you are a gentlewoman and I am a tradesman."

The news was evidently a shock to her—it could not but be, reared as she had been. She sat—the eyelashes dropping over her flushed cheeks—perfectly silent.

John's voice grew firmer—prouder—no hesitation now.

"My calling is, as you will soon hear at Norton Bury, that of a tanner. I am apprentice to Abel Fletcher—Phineas's father."

"Mr. Fletcher!" She looked up at me—a mingled look of kindliness and pain.

"Ay, Phineas is a little less beneath your notice than I am. He is rich—he has been well educated; I have had to educate myself. I came to Norton Bury six years ago—a beggar boy. No, not quite that—for I never begged! I either worked or starved."

The earnestness, the passion of his tone, made Miss March lift her eyes, but they fell again.

"Yes, Phineas found me in an alley—starving. We stood in the rain, opposite the mayor's house. A little girl—you know her, Miss March—came to the door, and threw out to me a bit of bread."

Now indeed she started. "You—was that you?"

"It was I."

John paused, and his whole manner changed into softness as he resumed. "I never forgot that little girl. Many a time, when I was inclined to do wrong, she kept me right—the remembrance of her sweet face and her kindness."

That face was pressed down against the sofa where she sat. I think Miss March was all but weeping.

John continued.

"I am glad to have met her again—glad to have been able to do her some small good in return for the infinite good she once did me. I shall bid her farewell now—at once and altogether."

A quick, involuntary turn of the hidden face asked him "Why?"

"Because," John answered, "the world says we are not equals, and it would neither be for Miss March's honour nor mine did I try to force upon it the truth—which I may prove openly one day—that we *are* equals."

Miss March looked up at him—it were hard to say with what expression, of pleasure, or pride, or simple astonishment; perhaps a mingling of all—then her eyelids fell. She silently offered her hand, first to me and then to John. Whether she meant it as friendliness, or as a mere ceremony of adieu, I cannot tell. John took it as the latter, and rose.

His hand was on the door—but he could not go.

"Miss March," he said, "perhaps I may never see you again—at least, never as now. Let me look once more at that wrist which was hurt."

Her left arm was hanging over the sofa—the scar being visible enough. John took the hand, and held it firmly.

"Poor little hand—blessed little hand! May God bless it evermore."

Suddenly he pressed his lips to the place where the wound had been—a kiss long and close, such as only a lover's kiss could be. Surely she must have felt it—known it.

A moment afterward he was gone.

That day Miss March departed, and we remained at Enderley alone.

CHAPTER XVI.

It was winter-time. All the summer days at Enderley were gone, "like a dream when one awaketh." Of her who had been the beautiful centre of the dream we had never heard nor spoken since.

John and I were walking together along the road towards the Mythe; we could just see the frosty sunset reflected on the windows of the Mythe House, now closed for months, the family being away. The meadows alongside, where the Avon had overflowed and frozen, were a popular skating-ground; and the road was alive with lookers-on of every class. All Norton Bury seemed abroad; and half Norton Bury exchanged salutations with my companion, till I was amused to notice how large John's acquaintance had grown.

Among the rest there overtook us a little elderly lady, as prim and neat as an old maid, and as bright-looking as a happy matron. I saw at once who it was—Mrs. Jessop, our good doctor's new wife, and old love; whom he had lately brought home, to the great amazement and curiosity of Norton Bury.

"She seems to like you very much," I said; as, after a cordial greeting, which John returned rather formally, she trotted on.

"They were both very kind to me in London last month, as I think I told you."

"Ay!" It was one of the few things he had mentioned about that same London journey, for he had grown into a painful habit of silence now. Yet I dreaded to break it, lest any wounds rankling beneath might thereby be caused to smart once more. And our love to one another was too faithful for a little reserve to have power to influence it in any way.

We came once more upon the old lady, watching the skaters. She again spoke to John, and looked at me with her keen, kind, blue eyes.

"I think I know who your friend is, though you do not introduce him." (John hastily performed that ceremony). "Tom and I" (how funny to hear her call our old bachelor doctor "Tom"!) "were wondering what had become of you, Mr. Halifax. Are you stronger than you were in London?"

"Was he ill in London, madam?"

"No, indeed, Phineas! Or only enough to win for me Dr. and Mrs. Jessop's great kindness."

"Which you have never come to thank us for. Never crossed our door-sill since we returned home! Does not your conscience sting you for your ingratitude?"

He coloured deeply.

"Indeed, Mrs. Jessop, it was not ingratitude."

"I know it; I believe it," she answered, with much kindness. "Tell me what it was."

He hesitated.

"You ought to believe the warm interest we both take in you. Tell me the plain truth."

"I will. It is that your kindness to me in London was no reason for my intruding on you at Norton Bury. It might not be agreeable for you and Dr. Jessop to have my acquaintance here. I am a tradesman."

The little old lady's eyes brightened into something beyond mere kindness as she looked at him.

"Mr. Halifax, I thank you for that 'plain truth.' Truth is always best. Now for mine. I had heard you were a tradesman; I found out for myself that you were a gentleman. I do not think the two facts incompatible, nor does my husband. We shall be happy to see you at our house at all times and under all circumstances."

She offered him her hand. John bowed over it in silence, but it was long since I had seen him look more pleased.

"Well, then, suppose you come this evening, both of you?"

We assented; and on her further invitation John and I and the little old lady walked on together.

I could not help watching Mrs. Jessop with some amusement. Norton Bury said she had been a poor governess all her days; but that hard life had left no shadow on the cheerful sunset of her existence now. It was a frank, bright, happy face, in spite of its wrinkles and its somewhat hard Welsh features. And it was pleasant to hear her talk, even though she talked a good deal, and in a decidedly Welsh accent. Sometimes a tone or two reminded me slightly of—— Ay, it was easy to guess why John evidently liked the old lady.

"I know this road well, Mr. Halifax. Once I spent a summer here, with an old pupil, now grown up. I am going to-day to inquire about her at the Mythe House. The Brithwoods came home yesterday."

I was afraid to look at John. Even to me the news was startling. How I blessed Mrs. Jessop's innocent garrulousness.

"I hope they will remain here some time. I have a special interest in their stay. Not on Lady Caroline's account, though. She patronizes me very kindly; but I doubt if she ever forgets—what Tom says I am rather too proud of remembering—that I was the poor governess, Jane Cardigan."

"Jane Cardigan!" I exclaimed.

"What, Mr. Fletcher, you know my name! And really, now I think of it, I believe I have heard yours. Not from Tom, either. It couldn't possibly be—yes! it certainly was—how strange! Did you ever hear tell of a Miss Ursula March?"

The live crimson rushed madly over John's face. Mrs. Jessop saw it; she could not but see. At first she looked astounded, then exceedingly grave.

I replied "that we had had the honour of meeting Miss March last summer at Enderley."

"Yes," the old lady continued, somewhat formally. "Now I recollect, Miss March told me of the circumstance; of two gentlemen there, who were very kind to her when her father died; a Mr. Fletcher and his friend—was that Mr. Halifax?"

"It was," I answered: for John was speechless. Alas! I saw at once that all my hopes for him, all the design of my long silence on this subject, had been in vain. No, he had not forgotten her. It was not in his nature to forget.

Mrs. Jessop went on, still addressing herself to me.

"I am sure I ought, on behalf of my dear pupil, to offer you both my warmest thanks. Hers was a most trying position. She never told me of it till afterwards, poor child! I am thankful her trouble was softened to her by finding that *strangers*" (was it only my fancy that detected a slight stress on the word?)—"mere strangers could be at once so thoughtful and so kind."

"No one could be otherwise to Miss March. Is she well? Has she recovered from her trial?"

"I hope so. Happily, few sorrows, few feelings of any kind, take lasting hold at eighteen. She is a noble girl. She did her duty, and it was no light one, to him who is gone; now her life begins anew. It is sure to be prosperous—I trust it may be very happy. Now I must bid you both good-bye."

She stopped at the gates of the Mythe House; great iron gates, a barrier as proud and impassable as that which in these times the rich shut against the poor, the aristocrat against the plebeian. John, glancing once up at them, hurriedly moved on.

"Stay; you will come and see us, Mr. Halifax? Promise!"

"If you wish it."

"And promise, too, that under all circumstances you will tell me, as you did this morning, the 'plain truth'? Yes, I see you will. Good-bye."

The iron gates closed upon her, and against us. We took our silent way up to the Mythe to our favourite stile. There we leaned—still in silence, for many minutes.

"The wind is keen, Phineas; you must be cold."

Now I could speak to him—could ask him to tell me of his pain.

"It is so long since you have told me anything. It might do you good."

"Nothing can do me good. Nothing but bearing it. My God! what have I not borne! Five whole months to be dying of thirst, and not a drop of water to cool my tongue."

He bared his head and throat to the cutting wind—his chest heaved, his eyes seemed in a flame.

"God forgive me!—but I sometimes think I would give myself body and soul to the devil for one glimpse of her face, one touch of her little hand."

I made no answer. What answer could be made to such words as these? I waited—all I could do—till the paroxysm had gone by. Then I hinted—as indeed seemed not unlikely—that he might see her soon.

"Yes, a great way off, like that cloud up here. But

I want her near—close—in my home—at my heart. Phineas," he gasped, "talk to me—about something else—anything. Don't let me think, or I shall go clean mad."

And indeed he looked so. I was terrified. So quiet as I had always seen him when we met, so steadily as he had pursued his daily duties; and with all this underneath—this torment, conflict, despair, of a young man's love. It must come out—better it should.

"And you have gone on working all this while?"

"I was obliged. Nothing but work kept me in my senses. Besides"—and he laughed hoarsely—"I was safest in the tanyard. The thought of her could not come there. I was glad of it. I tried to be solely and altogether what I am—a 'prentice lad—a mere clown."

"Nay, that was wrong."

"Was it? Well, at last it struck me so. I thought I would be a gentleman again—just for a pretence, you know—a dream—a bit of the old dream back again. So I went to London."

"And met the Jessops there?"

"Yes; though I did not know she was Jane Cardigan. But I liked her—I liked my life with them. It was like breathing a higher air, the same air that—— Oh, Phineas, it was horrible to come back to my life here—to that accursed tanyard!"

I said nothing.

"You see, now"—and that hard laugh smote me to the heart again—"you see, Phineas, how wicked I am growing. You will have to cut my acquaintance presently."

"Tell me the rest—I mean, the rest of your life in London," I said, after a pause. "Did you ever hear of her?"

"Of course not; though I knew she was there. I saw it in the *Court Circular*. Fancy a lady whose name was in the *Court Circular* being inquired after by a tanner's lad! But I wanted to look at her—any beggar might do that, you know—so I watched in streets and parks, by theatre doors at nights, and by church doors on Sunday mornings; yet I never saw her once. Only think, not once for five whole months."

"John, how could you tell me you were happy?"

"I don't know. Perhaps because of my pride; perhaps because—— Ah, don't look so wretched! Why did you let me say all this? You are too good for such as I."

Of course I took no heed of idle words like these. I let him stand there, leaning against the stile, now and then grasping it with his nervous, muscular hands, as if he would tear it down; then I said quietly,—

"What do you intend to do?"

"Do? Nothing! What can I do? Though sometimes a score of wild plans rush into my mind, such as to run away to the Indies, like that young Warren Hastings we were talking of, come back twenty years hence a nabob, and—marry her."

"Marry her," I repeated mournfully.

"Ay, I could. That is what maddens me. If now she and I were to meet and stand together, equal man and woman, I could make her love me; I feel I could. Instead of crawling after her thus I would go boldly in at those very gates—do you think she is there?"

He trembled, actually trembled, at the mere thought of her being so near.

"Oh, it's hard, hard! I could despise myself. Why cannot I trust my manhood, my honest manhood that I was born with, go straight to her and tell her that I love her; that God meant her for me and me for her—true husband and true wife? Phineas, mark my words"—and, wild as his manner was, it had a certain force which sounded almost like prophecy—"if ever Ursula March marries she will be my wife—*my* wife!"

I could only murmur, "Heaven grant it!"

"But we shall never marry, neither one nor the other of us; we shall go on apart and alone till the next world. Perhaps she will come to me then: I may have her in my heart there."

John looked upward: there was in the west a broad,

red frosty cloud, and just beyond it, nay, all but resting on it, the new moon—a little, wintry, soft new moon. A sight that might well have hushed the maddest storm of passion: it hushed his. He stood, still looking up, for many minutes, then his eyes closed, the lashes all wet.

"We'll never speak of this again, Phineas; I'll not grieve thee any more; I'll try and be a better brother to thee for the future. Come along."

He drew my arm in his, and we went home.

Passing the tanyard, John proposed that we should call for my father. My poor father; now daily growing more sour and old, and daily leaning more and more upon John, who never ceased to respect, and make every one else respect, his master. Though still ostensibly a 'prentice, he had now the business almost entirely in his hands. It was pleasant to see how my father brightened up at his coming—how readily, when he turned homeward, he leaned upon John's strong arm, now the support of both him and me. Thus we walked through Norton Bury streets, where everybody knew us, and indeed, as it seemed to me this morning, nearly everybody greeted us—at least one of us; but my father walked along soberly and sternly, frowning at almost every salutation John Halifax received.

"Thee art making far too many friends, John. I warn thee!"

"Not *friends*—only friendly acquaintance," was the gentle answer: he was well used to turn away, daily and hourly, Abel Fletcher's wrath. But it was roused beyond control when Dr. Jessop's neat little carriage, and neatest of little wives, stopped at the curbstone and summoned John.

"I want you and Mr. Fletcher to come to us to-morrow instead of this evening. Lady Caroline Brithwood wishes to see you."

"Me?"

"Yes, you," smiled the old lady; "you, John Halifax, the hero of the people, who quelled the bread riots, and gave evidence thereupon to Mr. Pitt in London. Nay!

why didn't you tell me the wonderful story? Her ladyship is full of it. She will torment me till she sees you—I know her ways. For my sake, you *must* come."

Waiting no refusal, Mrs. Jessop drove on.

"What's that?" said my father sharply. "John, where art thee going?"

I knew this was the first warning-gun of a battle which broke out afresh every time John appeared in any livelier garb than his favourite gray, or was suspected of any more worldly associates than our quiet selves. He always took my father's attacks patiently—this time peculiarly so. He made no answer, but passed his hand once or twice over his brow, as if he could not see clearly.

Abel Fletcher repeated the question.

"Yes; that was Mrs. Jessop, sir."

"I know," grumbled my father. "The doctor is a fool in his old age. Who did she want thee to meet?"

"She!—Oh, Lady Caroline, you mean?"

"Lady Caroline wishes particularly to see John."

Abel Fletcher stopped, planted his stick in the ground, released his arm from John's, and eyed him from top to toe.

"Thee?—a woman of quality wanting to see *thee?* Young man, thee art a hypocrite."

"Sir!"

"I knew it! I foresaw how thy fine ways would end! Going to London—crawling at the heels of grand folk—despising thy honest trade—trying to make thyself appear a gentleman!"

"I hope I am a gentleman."

Words could not describe my father's horrified astonishment. "Oh, lad!" he cried; "poor, misguided lad!—the Lord have mercy upon thee!"

John smiled—his mind evidently full of other things. Abel Fletcher's anger grew.

"And thee wants to hang on to the tail of other 'gentlemen,' such as Richard Brithwood, forsooth!—a fox-hunting, drinking, dicing fool!"

I was shocked; I had not believed him so bad as that—the young squire—Miss March's cousin.

"Or," pursued my father, waxing hotter and hotter, "or a 'lady' such as his wife is, the Jezebel daughter of an Ahab father!—brought up in the impious atrocities of France, and the debaucheries of Naples, where, though she keeps it close here, she abode with that vile woman whom they call Lady Hamilton."

John started. Well he might, for even to our quiet town had come, all this winter, foul newspaper tales about Nelson and Lady Hamilton.

"Take care," he said, in much agitation. "Any taint upon a woman's fame harms not her alone but all connected with her. For God's sake, sir, whether it be true or not, do not whisper in Norton Bury that Lady Caroline Brithwood is a friend of Lady Hamilton."

"Pshaw! What is either woman to us?"

And my father climbed the steps to his own door, John following.

"Nay, young gentleman, my poor house is hardly good enough for such as thee."

John turned, cruelly galled, but recovered himself.

"You are unjust to me, Abel Fletcher; and you yourself will think so soon. May I come in?"

My father made no answer, and I brought John in as usual. In truth, we had both more to think of than Abel Fletcher's temporary displeasure. This strange chance—what might it imply?—to what might it not lead? But no: if I judged Mrs. Jessop aright, it neither implied, nor would lead to, what I saw John's fancy had at once sprang toward, and revelled in, madly. A lover's fancy—a lover's hope. Even I could see what will-o'-the-wisps they were.

But the doctor's good wife, Ursula's March's wise governess, would never lure a young man with such phantoms as these. I felt sure—certain—that if we met the Brithwoods we should meet no one else. Certain, even when, as we sat at our dish of tea, there came in two little dainty notes—the first invitations to worldly festivity that had ever tempted our Quaker household, and which Jael flung out of her fingers as if they had been coals from Gehenna. Notes, bidding us to a "little supper" at Dr. Jessop's, with Mr. and Lady Caroline Brithwood, of the Mythe House.

"Give them to your father, Phineas." And John vainly tried to hide the flash of his eye—the smiles that came and went like summer lightning. "To-morrow—you see, it is to-morrow."

Poor lad! he had forgotten every worldly thing in the hope of that to-morrow.

My father's sharp voice roused him. "Phineas, thee'lt stay at home. Tell the woman I say so."

"And John, father?"

"John may go to ruin if he chooses. He is his own master."

"I have been always." And the answer came less in pride than sadness. "I might have gone to ruin years ago, but for the mercy of Heaven and your kindness. Do not let us be at warfare now."

"All thy own fault, lad! Why cannot thee keep in thy own rank? Respect thyself. Be an honest tradesman, as I have been."

"And as I trust always to be. But that is only my calling, not me. I—John Halifax—am just the same, whether in the tanyard or Dr. Jessop's drawing-room. The one position cannot degrade, nor the other elevate me. I should not 'respect myself' if I believed otherwise."

"Eh?"—my father absolutely dropped his pipe in amazement. "Then thee thinkest thyself already quite a gentleman?"

"As I told you before, sir—I hope I am."

"Fit to associate with the finest folk in the land?"

"If they desire it, and I choose it, certainly."

Now, Abel Fletcher, like all honest men, liked honesty; and something in John's bold spirit, and free bright eye, seemed to-day to strike him more than ordinarily.

"Lad, lad, thee art young. But it won't last—no, it won't last."

He knocked the white ashes out of his pipe—it had been curling in brave wreaths to the very ceiling two minutes before—and sat musing.

"But about to-morrow?" persisted John, after watching him some little time. "I could go—I could have gone, without either your knowledge or permission; but I had rather deal openly with you. You know I always do. You have been the kindest master—the truest friend to me; I hope, as long as I live, rarely to oppose, and never to deceive you."

His manner—earnest, yet most respectful—his candid looks, under which lurked an evident anxiety and pain, might have mollified a harder man than Abel Fletcher.

"John, why dost thee want to go among those grand folk?"

"Not because they are grand folk. I have other reasons—strong reasons."

"Be honest. Tell me thy strong reasons."

Here was a strait.

"Why dost thee blush, young man? Is it aught thee art ashamed of?"

"Ashamed! No!"

"Is it a secret, then, the telling of which would be to thee, or to any else, dishonour?"

"Dishonour!" And the bright eye shot an indignant gleam.

"Then tell the truth."

"I will. I wish first to find out, for myself, whether Lady Caroline Brithwood is fitted to have under her charge one who is young—innocent—good."

"Has she such an one? One thee knows?"

"Yes."

"Man or woman?"

"Woman."

My father turned, and looked John full in the eyes. Stern as that look was, I traced in it a strange compassion.

"Lad, I thought so. Thee hast found the curse of man's life—woman."

To my amazement, John replied not a syllable. He seemed even as if he had forgotten himself and his own secret—thus, for what end I knew not, voluntarily betrayed—so absorbed was he in contemplating the old man. And truly, in all my life I had never seen such a convulsion pass over my father's face. It was like as if some one had touched and revived the torment of a long-hidden but never-to-be-healed wound. Not till years after did I understand the full meaning of John's gaze, or why he was so patient with my father.

The torment passed—ended in violent anger.

"Out with it. Who is deluding thee? Is it a matter of wedlock, or only——"

"Stop!" John cried, his face all on fire. "The lady——"

"It is a 'lady'! Now I see why thee would fain be a gentleman."

"O father—how can you?"

"So thee knowest it too—I see it in thy face. Wouldst thee be led away by him a second time? But thee shall not. I'll put thee under lock and key before thee shalt ruin thyself and disgrace thy father."

This was hard to bear; but I believe—it was John's teaching—that one ought to bear anything, however hard, from a just and worthy parent. And it was John himself who now grasped my hand, and whispered patience. John—who knew, what I myself, as I have said, did not learn for years, concerning my father's former history.

"Sir, you mistake; Phineas has nothing whatever to do with this matter. He is altogether blameless. So am I too, if you heard all."

"Tell me all; honour is bold—shame only is silent."

"I feel no shame—an honest love is no disgrace to any man. And my confessing it harms no one. She neither knows of it nor returns it."

As he said this, slowly, gravely, John moved a step back and sat down. His face was in shadow; but the fire shone on his hands, tightly locked together, motionless as stone.

My father was deeply moved. Heaven knows what ghosts of former days came and knocked at the old man's heart. We all three sat silent for a long time, then my father said,—

"Who is she?"

"I had rather not tell you. She is above me in worldly station."

"Ah!" a fierce exclamation. "But thee wouldst not humble thyself—ruin thy peace for life? Thee wouldst not marry her?"

"I would—if she had loved me. Even yet, if by any honourable means I can rise to her level, so as to be able to win her love, marry her I will."

That brave 'I will'—it seemed to carry its own fulfilment. Its indomitable resolution struck my father with wonder—nay, with a sort of awe.

"Do as thee thinks best, and God help thee," he said kindly. "Mayst thee never find thy desire a curse. Fear not, lad—I will keep thy counsel."

"I knew you would."

The subject ceased: my father's manner indicated that he wished it to cease. He re-lit his pipe, and puffed away, silently and sadly.

Years afterwards, when all that remained of Abel Fletcher was a green mound beside that other mound in the Friends' burying-ground in St. Mary's Lane, I learnt—what all Norton Bury, except myself, had long known—that my poor mother, the young, thoughtless creature whose married life had been so unhappy and so brief was by birth a "gentlewoman."

CHAPTER XVII.

Mrs. Jessop's drawing-room, ruddy with firelight, glittering with delicate wax candlelight; a few women in pale-coloured gauzy dresses, a few men, sublime in blue coats, gold buttons, yellow waistcoats, and smiles—this was all I noticed of the scene, which was quite a novel scene to me.

The doctor's wife had introduced us formally to all her guests, as the custom then was, especially in these small cosy supper-parties. How they greeted us I do not now remember; no doubt, with a kind of well-bred formal surprise; but society was generally formal then. My chief recollection is of Mrs. Jessop's saying pointedly and aloud, though with a smile playing under the corners of her good little mouth,—

"Mr. Halifax, it is kind of you to come; Lady Caroline Brithwood will be delighted. She longs to make your acquaintance."

After that everybody began to talk with extraordinary civility to Mr. Halifax.

For John, he soon took his place among them, with that modest self-possession which best becomes youth. Society's dangerous waters accordingly became smooth to him, as to a good swimmer who knows his own strength, trusts it, and struggles not.

"Mr. Brithwood and Lady Caroline will be late," I overheard the hostess say. "I think I told you that Miss March——"

But here the door was flung open, and the missing guests announced. John and I were in the alcove of the window; I heard his breathing behind me, but I dared not look at or speak to him. In truth, I was scarcely calmer than he. For though it must be clearly understood I never was "in love" with any woman, still the reflected glamour of those Enderley days had fallen on me. It often seems now as if I too had passed the golden gate, and looked far enough into youth's Eden to be able ever after to weep with those that wept without the doors.

No—she was not there.

We both sat down. I know not if I was thankful or sorry.

I had seldom seen the squire or Lady Caroline. He was a portly young man, pinched in by tight light-coloured garments. She was a lady rather past her first youth, but very handsome still, who floated about, leaving a general impression of pseudo-Greek draperies, gleaming arms and shoulders, sparkling jewellery, and equally sparkling smiles. These smiles seemed to fall just as redundantly upon the family physician, whom by a rare favour—for so, I suppose, it must have been—she was honouring with a visit, as if worthy Dr. Jessop were the noblest in the land. He, poor man, was all bows and scrapes and pretty speeches, in the which came more than the usual amount of references to the time which had made his fortune, the day when her Majesty Queen Charlotte had done him the honour to be graciously taken ill in passing through Norton Bury. Mrs. Jessop seemed to wear her honours as hostess to an earl's daughter very calmly indeed. She performed the ordinary courtesies, and then went over to talk with Mr. Brithwood. In their conversation I sought in vain the name of Ursula.

So it ended—the sickening expectation which I had read in the lad's face all day. He would not see her—perhaps it was best. Yet my heart bled when I looked at him. But such thoughts could not be indulged in now, especially as Mrs. Jessop's quick eyes seemed often upon him or me, with an expression that I could not make out at all, save that in such a good woman, whom Miss March so well loved, could lurk nothing evil or unkindly.

So I tried to turn my attention to the Brithwoods. One could not choose but look at her, this handsome Lady Caroline, whom half Norton Bury adored, the other half pursed up their lips at the mention of—but these were of the number she declined to "know." All that she did know—all that came within her influence, were irresistibly attracted, for to please seemed a part of her nature. To-night nearly every one present stole gradually into the circle round her; men and women alike charmed by the fascination of her ripe beauty, her lively manner, her exquisite smile and laugh.

I wondered what John thought of Lady Caroline Brithwood. She could not easily see him, even though her acute glance seemed to take in everything and everybody in the room. But on her entrance John had drawn back a little, and our half-dozen of fellow-guests, who had been conversing with him, crept shyly out of his way; as if, now the visible reality appeared, they were aghast at the great gulf that lay between John Halifax the tanner and the Brithwoods of the Mythe. A few even looked askance at our hostess, as though some terrible judgment must fall upon poor ignorant Mrs. Jessop, who had dared to amalgamate such opposite ranks.

So it came to pass, that while everybody gathered round the Brithwoods, John and I stood alone, and half concealed by the window.

Very soon I heard Lady Caroline's loud whisper,—

"Mrs. Jessop, my good friend, one moment. Where is your *jeune héros, l'homme du peuple?* I do not see him. Does he wear clouted shoes and woollen stockings? Has he a broad face and turned-up nose, like your *paysans anglais?*"

"Judge for yourself, my lady—he stands at your elbow.—Mr. Halifax, let me present you to Lady Caroline Brithwood."

If Lord Luxmore's fair daughter ever looked confounded in her life she certainly did at this minute.

"*Lui? Mon Dieu! Lui!*" And her shrug of amazement was stopped, her half-extended hand drawn back. No, it was quite impossible to patronize John Halifax.

He bowed gravely, she made a gracious curtsy; they met on equal terms, a lady and a gentleman.

Soon her lively manner returned. She buckled on her spurs for a new conquest, and left the already vanquished gentilities of Norton Bury to amuse themselves as they best might.

"I am enchanted to meet you, Mr. Halifax; I adore *le peuple.* Especially"—with a sly glance at her husband, who, with Tory Dr. Jessop, was vehemently exalting Mr. Pitt and abusing the First Consul, Bonaparte—"especially *le peuple français. Me comprenez vous?*"

"*Madame, je vous comprends.*"

Her ladyship looked surprised. French was not very common among the honest trading class, or indeed any but the higher classes in England.

"But," John continued, "I must dissent from Lady Caroline Brithwood, if she mingles the English people with *le peuple français*. They are a very different class of beings."

"Ah, *ça ira, ça ira*"—she laughed, humming beneath her breath a few notes out of that terrible song. "But you know French—let us talk in that language; we shall horrify no one then."

"I cannot speak it readily; I am chiefly self-taught."

"The best teaching. *Mon Dieu!* Truly you are made to be *un héros*—just the last touch of grace that a woman's hand gives—had you ever a woman for your friend?—and you would be complete. But I cannot flatter—plain, blunt honesty for me. You must—you shall be—*l'homme du peuple*. Were you born such? Who were your parents?"

I saw John hesitate; I knew how rarely he ever uttered those names written in the old Bible—how infinitely sacred they were to him. Could he blazon them out now, to gratify this woman's idle curiosity?

"Madam," he said gravely, "I was introduced to you simply as John Halifax. It seems to me that, so long as I do no discredit to it, the name suffices to the world."

"Ah—I see! I see!" But he, with his downcast eyes, did not detect the meaning smile that just flashed in hers, then was changed into a tone of soft sympathy. "You are right; rank is nothing—a cold, glittering marble, with no soul under. Give me the rich flesh-and-blood life of the people. *Liberté—fraternité—égalité*. I would rather be a *gamin* in Paris streets than my brother William at Luxmore Hall."

Thus talked she, sometimes in French, sometimes in English, the young man answering little. She only threw her shining arts abroad the more; she seemed determined to please. And Nature fitted her for it. Even if not born an earl's daughter, Lady Caroline would have been everywhere the magic centre of any society wherein she chose to move. Not that her conversation was brilliant or deep, but she said the most frivolous things in a way that made them appear witty; and the grand art, to charm by appearing charmed, was hers in perfection. She seemed to float altogether upon and among the pleasantnesses of life; pain, either endured or inflicted, was to her an impossibility.

Thus her character struck me on this first meeting, and thus, after many years, it strikes me still. I look back upon what she appeared that evening—lovely, gay, attractive—in the zenith of her rich maturity. What her old age was the world knows, or thinks it knows. But Heaven may be more merciful—I cannot tell. Whatever is now said of her, I can only say, "Poor Lady Caroline!"

It must have indicated a grain of pure gold at the bottom of the gold-seeming dross, that, from the first moment she saw him, she liked John Halifax.

They talked a long time. She drew him out, as a well-bred woman always can draw out a young man of sense. He looked pleased; he conversed well. Had he forgotten? No; the restless wandering of his eyes at the slightest sound in the room told how impossible it was he should forget. Yet he comported himself bravely, and I was proud that Ursula's kindred should see him as he was.

"Lady Caroline" (her ladyship turned, with a slightly bored expression, to her intrusive hostess), "I fear we must give up all expectation of our young friend to-night."

"I told you so. Post-travelling is very uncertain, and the Bath roads are not very good.—Have you ever visited Bath, Mr. Halifax?"

"But she is surely long on the road," pursued Mrs. Jessop, rather anxiously. "What attendants had she?"

"Her own maid, and our man Laplace. Nay, don't be alarmed, excellent and faithful *gouvernante!* I assure you your fair ex-pupil is quite safe. The *furore* about her has considerably abated since the heiress-hunters at Bath discovered the melancholy fact that Miss March——"

"Pardon me," interrupted the other; "we are among strangers. I assure you I am quite satisfied about my dear child."

"What a charming thing is affectionate fidelity," observed her ladyship, turning once more to John, with a sweet, lazy dropping of the eyelids.

The young man only bowed. They resumed their conversation—at least, she did, talking volubly; satisfied with monosyllabic answers.

It was now almost supper-time—held a glorious hour at Norton Bury parties. People began to look anxiously to the door.

"Before we adjourn," said Lady Caroline, "I must do what it will be difficult to accomplish after supper," and for the first time a sharp, sarcastic tone jarred in her smooth voice. "I must introduce you especially to my husband.—Mr. Brithwood?"

"Madam." He lounged up to her. They were a diverse pair. She, in her well-preserved beauty, and Gallic artificial grace—he, in his coarse, bloated youth, coarser and worse than the sensualism of middle age.

"Mr. Brithwood, let me introduce you to a new friend of mine."

The squire bowed rather awkwardly; proving the truth of what Norton Bury often whispered, that Richard Brithwood was more at home with grooms than gentlemen.

"He belongs to this your town—you must have heard of him, perhaps met him."

"I have more than once had the pleasure of meeting Mr. Brithwood, but he has doubtless forgotten it."

"By Jove! I have. What might your name be, sir?"

"John Halifax."

"What, Halifax the tanner?"

"The same."

"Phew!" He began a low whistle, and turned on his heel.

John changed colour a little. Lady Caroline laughed—a thoughtless, amused laugh, with a pleasant murmur of "*Bête!*"—"*Anglais!*"—Nevertheless, she whispered her husband,—

"*Mon ami*—you forget; I have introduced you to this gentleman."

"Gentleman indeed! Pooh! rubbish! Lady Caroline—I'm busy talking."

"And so are we, most pleasantly. I only called you as a matter of form, to ratify my invitation. Mr. Halifax will, I hope, dine with us next Sunday?"

"The devil he will!"

"Richard—you hurt me!"—with a little scream, as she pushed his rough fingers from her arm, so soft, and round, and fair.

"Madam, you must be crazy. The young man is a tradesman—a tanner. Not fit for *my* society."

"Precisely; I invite him for my own."

But the whispers and responses were alike unheeded by their object. For, at the doorway, entering with Mrs. Jessop, was a tall girl in deep mourning. We knew her—we both knew her—our dream at Enderley—our "nut-browne mayde."

John was near to the door—their eyes met. She bowed—he returned it. He was very pale. For Miss March, her face and neck were all in a glow. Neither spoke, nor offered more than this passing acknowledgment, and she moved on.

She came and sat down beside me, accidentally, I believe; but when she saw me she held out her hand. We exchanged a word or two—her manner was unaltered; but she spoke hurriedly, and her fingers had their old nervous twitch. She said this meeting was to her "unexpected," but "she was very glad to see me."

So she sat, and I looked sideways at her dropped eyes—her forehead with its coronet of chestnut curls. How would he bear the sight—he of whose heart mine was the mere faint echo? Yet truly an echo, repeating with cruel faithfulness every throb.

He kept his position, a little aloof from the Brithwoods, who were holding a slight altercation—though more of looks than words. John heeded them not. I was sure, though he had never looked directly towards us, that he had heard every syllable Miss March said to me.

The squire called across the room, in a patronizing tone: "My good fellow—that is, ahem! I say, young Halifax?"

"Were you addressing me, Mr. Brithwood?"

"I was. I want a quiet word or two—between ourselves."

"Certainly."

They stood face to face. The one seemed uncomfortable, the other was his natural self—a little graver, perhaps, as if he felt what was coming, and prepared to meet it, knowing in whose presence he had to prove himself—what Richard Brithwood, with all his broad acres, could never be—a gentleman.

Few could doubt that fact who looked at the two young men, as all were looking now.

"On my soul, it's awkward—I'll call at the tanyard and explain."

"I had rather you would explain here."

"Well, then, though it's a confounded unpleasant thing to say—and I really wish I had not been brought into such a position—you'll not heed my wife's nonsense?"

"I do not understand you."

"Come, it's no use running to cover in that way. Let's be open and plain. I mean no offence. You may be a very respectable young man for aught I know, still rank is rank. Of course Dr. Jessop asks whom he likes to his house—and, by George! I'm always civil to everybody—but really, in spite of my lady's likings, I can't well invite you to my table!"

"Nor could I humiliate myself by accepting any such invitation."

He said the words distinctly, so that the whole circle might have heard, and was turning away, when Mr.

Brithwood fired up—as an angry man does in a losing game.

"Humiliate yourself! What do you mean, sir? Wouldn't you be only too thankful to crawl into the houses of your betters, anyhow, by hook or by crook? Ha! ha! I know you would. It's always the way with you common folk, you rioters, you revolutionists. By the Lord! I wish you were all hanged."

The young blood rose fiercely in John's cheek, but he restrained himself. "Sir, I am neither a rioter nor a revolutionist."

"But you are a tradesman? You used to drive Fletcher's cart of skins."

"I did."

"And are you not—I remember you now—the very lad, the tanner's lad, that once pulled us ashore from the eger—Cousin March and me?"

I heard a quick exclamation beside me, and saw Ursula listening intently—I had not noticed how intently till now. Her eyes were fixed on John, waiting for his answer. It came.

"Your memory is correct; I was that lad."

"Thank'ee for it too. Lord! what a jolly life I should have missed! You got no reward, though. You threw away the guinea I offered you; come, I'll make it twenty guineas to-morrow."

The insult was too much. "Sir, you forget that whatever we may have been, to-night we meet as equals."

"Equals!"

"As guests in the same house—most certainly, for the time being, equals."

Richard Brithwood stared, literally dumb with fury. The standers-by were dumb too, though such *fracas* were then not uncommon even in drawing-rooms, and in women's presence, especially with men of Mr. Brithwood's stamp. His wife seemed quite used to it. She merely shrugged her shoulders and hummed a note or two of "*Ça ira*." It irritated the husband beyond all bounds.

"Hold your tongue, my lady. What, because a

'prentice lad once saved my life, and you choose to patronize him as you do many another vagabond, with your cursed liberty and equality, am I to have him at my table, and treat him as a gentleman? By ——, madam, never!"

He spoke savagely and loud. John was silent; he had locked his hands together convulsively; but it was easy to see that his blood was at boiling heat, and that, did he once slip the leash of his passions, it would go hard with Richard Brithwood.

The latter came up to him with clenched fist. "Now mark me, you—you vagabond!"

Ursula March crossed the room, and caught his arm, her eyes gleaming fire.

"Cousin, in my presence this gentleman shall be treated as a gentleman. He was kind to my father."

"Curse your father!"

John's right hand burst free; he clutched the savage by the shoulder.

"Be silent. You had better."

Brithwood shook off the grasp, turned and struck him; that last fatal insult, which offered from man to man, in those days, could only be wiped out with blood.

John staggered. For a moment he seemed as if he would have sprung on his adversary and felled him to the ground—but—he did not.

Some one whispered, "He won't fight. He is a Quaker."

"No!" he said, and stood erect; though he was ghastly pale, and his voice sounded hoarse and strange—"but I am a Christian. I shall not return blow for blow."

It was a new doctrine; foreign to the practice, if familiar to the ear, of Christian Norton Bury. No one answered him; all stared at him; one or two sheered off from him with contemptuous smiles. Then Ursula March stretched out her friendly hand. John took it, and grew calm in a moment.

There arose a murmur of "Mr. Brithwood is going."

"Let him go!" Miss March cried, anger still glowing in her eyes.

"Not so—it is not right. I will speak to him. May I?" John softly unclosed her detaining hand, and went up to Mr. Brithwood. "Sir, there is no need for you to leave this house—I am leaving it. You and I shall not meet again if I can help it."

His proud courtesy, his absolute dignity and calmness, completely overwhelmed his blustering adversary, who gazed open-mouthed, while John made his adieu to his host and to those he knew. The women gathered round him—woman's instinct is usually true. Even Lady Caroline, amid a flutter of regrets, declared she did not believe there was a man in the universe who would have borne so charmingly such a "degradation."

At the words Miss March fired up. "Madam," she said, in her impetuous young voice, "no insult offered to a man can ever degrade him; the only real degradation is when he degrades himself."

John, passing out at the doorway, caught her words. As he quitted the room, no crowned victor ever wore a look more joyful, more proud.

After a minute we followed him; the doctor's wife and I. But now the pride and joy had both faded.

"Mrs. Jessop, you see I am right," he murmured. "I ought not to have come here. It is a hard world for such as I. I shall never conquer it—never."

"Yes—you will." And Ursula stood by him, with crimsoned cheek, and eyes no longer flashing, but fearless still.

Mrs. Jessop put her arm round the young girl. "I also think you need not dread the world, Mr. Halifax, if you always act as you did to-night; though I grieve that things should have happened thus, if only for the sake of this my child."

"Have I done her any harm? oh!. tell me, have I done her any harm?"

"No!" cried Ursula, with the old impetuosity kindling anew in every feature of her noble face. "You have but showed me what I shall remember all my life—that a Christian only can be a true gentleman."

She understood him—he felt she did; understood him as, if a man be understood by one woman in the world, he—and she too—is strong, safe, and happy. They grasped hands once more, and gazed unhesitatingly into each other's eyes. All human passion for the time being set aside, these two recognized each in the other one aim, one purpose, one faith; something higher than love, something better than happiness. It must have been a blessed moment for both.

Mrs. Jessop did not interfere. She had herself known what true love was, if, as gossips said, she had kept constant to our worthy doctor for thirty years. But still she was a prudent woman, not unused to the world.

"You must go now," she said, laying her hand gently on John's arm.

"I am going. But she—what will she do?"

"Never mind me. Jane will take care of me," said Ursula, winding her arms round her old governess, and leaning her cheek down on Mrs. Jessop's shoulder.

We had never seen Miss March show fondness, that is, caressing fondness, to any one before. It revealed her in a new light; betraying the depths there were in her nature; infinite depths of softness and of love.

John watched her for a minute; a long, wild, greedy minute, then whispered hoarsely to me, "I must go."

We made a hasty adieu, and went out together into the night—the cold, bleak night, all blast and storm.

CHAPTER XVIII.

For weeks after then we went on in our usual way, Ursula March living within a stone's throw of us. She had left her cousin's, and come to reside with Dr. Jessop and his wife.

It was a very hard trial for John.

Neither of us again were invited by Mrs. Jessop. We

could not blame her; she held a precious charge, and Norton Bury was a horrible place for gossip. Already tale after tale had gone abroad about Miss March's "ingratitude" to her relations. Already tongue after tongue had repeated, in every possible form of lying, the anecdote of "young Halifax and the squire." Had it been "young Halifax and Miss March," I truly believe John could not have borne it.

As it was, though he saw her constantly, it was always by chance—a momentary glimpse at the window, or a passing acknowledgment in the street. I knew quite well when he had thus met her, whether he mentioned it or not—knew by the wild, troubled look, which did not wear off for hours.

I watched him closely, day by day, in an agony of doubt and pain.

For, though he said nothing, a great change was creeping over "the lad," as I still fondly called him. His strength, the glory of a young man, was going from him—he was becoming thin, weak, restless-eyed. That healthy energy and gentle composure, which had been so beautiful in him all his life through, were utterly lost.

"What am I to do with thee, David?" said I to him one evening, when he had come in, looking worse than usual—I knew why; for Ursula and her friend had just passed our house taking their pleasant walk in the spring twilight. "Thou art very ill, I fear?"

"Not at all. There is not the least thing the matter with me. Do let me alone."

Two minutes afterwards he begged my pardon for those sharp-spoken words.

"It was not *thee* that spoke, John," I said.

"No, you are right, it was not I. It was a sort of devil that lodges here:" he touched his breast. "The chamber he lives in is at times a burning hell."

He spoke in a low tone of great anguish. What could I answer? Nothing.

We stood at the window looking idly out. The chestnut trees in the Abbey yard were budding green; there came that faint, sweet sound of children at play, which one hears as the days begin to lengthen.

"It's a lovely evening," he said.

"John!" I looked him in the face. He could not palm off that kind deceit upon me. "You have heard something about her?"

"I have," he groaned. "She is leaving Norton Bury."

"Thank God!" I muttered.

John turned fiercely upon me—but only for a moment. "Perhaps I ought to say, 'Thank God.' This could not have lasted long, or it would have made me—what I pray His mercy to save me from, or to let me die. Oh, lad, if I could only die."

He bent down over the window-sill, crushing his forehead on his hands.

"John," I said, in this depth of despair snatching at an equally desperate hope, "what if, instead of keeping this silence, you were to go to her and tell her all?"

"I have thought of that: a noble thought, worthy of a poor 'prentice lad! Why, two several evenings I have been insane enough to walk to Dr. Jessop's door, which I have never entered, and—mark you well! they have never asked me to enter since that night. But each time ere I knocked my senses came back, and I went home—luckily having made myself neither a fool nor a knave."

There was no answer to this either. Alas! I knew as well as he did, that in the eye of the world's common sense, for a young man not twenty-one, a tradesman's apprentice, to ask the hand of a young gentlewoman, uncertain if she loved him, was most utter folly. Also, for a penniless youth to sue a lady with a fortune, even though it was (the Brithwoods took care to publish the fact) smaller than was at first supposed—would, in the eye of the world's honour, be not very much unlike knavery. There was no help—none!

"David," I groaned, "I would you had never seen her."

"Hush!—not a word like that. If you heard all I hear of her—daily—hourly—her unselfishness, her energy, her generous, warm heart! It is blessedness even to have known her. She is an angel—no, better than that, a woman! I did not want her for a saint in a shrine—I wanted her as a helpmeet, to walk with me in my daily life, to comfort me, strengthen me, make me pure and good. I could be a good man if I had her for my wife. Now——"

He rose and walked rapidly up and down. His looks were becoming altogether wild.

"Come, Phineas, suppose we go to meet her up the road—as I meet her almost every day. Sometimes she merely bends and smiles, sometimes she holds out her little hand, and 'hopes I am quite well!' And then they pass on, and I stand gaping and staring after them like an idiot. There—look—there they are now."

Ay! walking leisurely along the other side of the road—talking and smiling to one another, in their own merry, familiar way, were Mrs. Jessop and Miss March.

They were not thinking of us, not the least. Only just ere they passed our house Ursula turned slightly round and looked behind; a quiet, maidenly look, with the smile still lingering on her mouth. She saw nothing, and no one; for John had pulled me from the window, and placed himself out of sight. So, turning back again, she went on her way. They both disappeared.

"Now, Phineas, it is all ended."

"What do you mean?"

"I have looked on her for the last time."

"Nay—she is not going yet."

"But I am—fleeing from the devil and his angels. Hurrah, Phineas, lad! We'll have a merry night. To-morrow I am away to Bristol, to set sail for America."

He wrung my hands, with a long, loud, half-mad laugh, and then dropped heavily on a chair.

A few hours after he was lying on my bed, struck down by the first real sickness he had ever known. It was apparently a low aguish fever, which had been much about Norton Bury since the famine of last year. At least, so Jael said; and she was a wise doctoress, and had cured many. He would have no one else to attend him —seemed terrified at the mere mention of Dr. Jessop. I opposed him not at first, for well I knew, whatever the proximate cause of his sickness might be, its root was in that mental pang which no doctors could cure. So I trusted to the blessed quiet of a sickroom—often so healing to misery—to Jael's nursing, and his brother's love.

After a few days we called in a physician—a stranger from Coltham—who pronounced it to be this Norton Bury fever, caught through living, as he still persisted in doing, in his old attic, in that unhealthy alley where was Sally Watkins's house. It must have been coming on, the doctor said, for a long time; but it had no doubt now reached its crisis. He would be better soon.

But he did not get better. Days slid into weeks, and still he lay there, never complaining, scarcely appearing to suffer, except from the wasting of the fever; yet when I spoke of recovery he "turned his face unto the wall" —weary of living.

Once, when he had lain thus a whole morning, hardly speaking a word, I began to feel growing palpable the truth which day by day I had thrust behind me as some intangible, impossible dread—that ere now people had died of mere soul-sickness, without any bodily disease. I took up his poor hand that lay on the counterpane;— once, at Enderley, he had regretted its somewhat coarse strength: now Ursula's own was not thinner or whiter. He drew it back.

"O Phineas, lad, don't touch me—only let me rest."

The weak, querulous voice—that awful longing for rest! What if, despite all the physician's assurances, he might be sinking, sinking—my friend, my hope, my pride, all my comfort in this life—passing from it and from me into another, where, let me call never so wildly, he could not answer me any more, nor come back to me any more.

O God of mercy! if I were to be left in this world without my brother!

I had many a time thought over the leaving him, going

quietly away when it should please the Giver of all breath to recall mine, falling asleep, encompassed and sustained by his love until the last; then, a burden no longer, leaving him to work out a glorious life, whose rich web should include and bring to beautiful perfection all the poor broken threads in mine. But now, if this should be all vain, if he should go from me, not I from him—I slid down to the ground, to my knees, and the dumb cry of my agony went up on high.

How could I save him?

There seemed but one way; I sprang at it; stayed not to think if it were right or wrong, honourable or dishonourable. His life hung in the balance, and there was but one way; besides, had I not cried unto God for help?

I put aside the blind, and looked out of doors. For weeks I had not crossed the threshold; I almost started to find that it was spring. Everything looked lovely in the coloured twilight; a blackbird was singing loudly in the Abbey trees across the way; all things were fresh and glowing, laden with the hope of the advancing year. And there he lay on his sick-bed, dying!

All he said, as I drew the curtain back, was a faint moan—"No light! I can't bear the light! Do let me rest!"

In half an hour, without saying a word to human being, I was on my way to Ursula March.

She sat knitting in the summer-parlour alone. The doctor was out; Mrs. Jessop I saw down the long garden, bonneted and shawled, busy among her gooseberry bushes—so we were safe.

As I have said, Ursula sat knitting, but her eyes had a soft dreaminess. My entrance had evidently startled her, and driven some sweet, shy thought away.

But she met me cordially—said she was glad to see me—that she had not seen either of us lately; and the knitting-pins began to move quickly again.

Those dainty fingers—that soft, tremulous smile—I could have hated her!

"No wonder you did not see us, Miss March; John has been very ill, is ill now—almost dying."

I hurled the words at her, sharp as javelins, and watched to see them strike.

They struck—they wounded; I could see her shiver.

"Ill!—and no one ever told me!"

"You? How could it affect you? To me, now"—and my savage words, for they were savage, broke down in a burst of misery—"nothing in this world to me is worth a straw in comparison with John. If he dies——"

I let loose the flood of my misery. I dashed it over her, that she might see it—feel it; that it might enter all the fair and sightly chambers of her happy life, and make them desolate as mine. For was she not the cause?

Forgive me! I was cruel to thee, Ursula; and thou wert so good—so kind!

She rose, came to me, and took my hand. Hers was very cold, and her voice trembled much.

"Be comforted. He is young, and God is very merciful."

She could say no more, but sat down, nervously twisting and untwisting her fingers. There was in her looks a wild sorrow—a longing to escape from notice; but mine held her fast, mercilessly, as a snake holds a little bird. She sat cowering, almost like a bird, a poor, broken-winged, helpless little bird—whom the storm has overtaken.

Rising, she made an attempt to quit the room.

"I will call Mrs. Jessop: she may be of use——"

"She cannot. Stay!"

"Further advice, perhaps? Dr. Jessop—you must want help——"

"None save that which will never come. His bodily sickness is conquered—it is his mind. Oh, Miss March!"—and I looked up at her like a wretch begging for life—"do *you* not know of what my brother is dying?"

"Dying!" A long shudder passed over her, from head to foot—but I relented not.

"Think—a life like his, that might be made a blessing to all he loves—to all the world—is it to be sacrificed thus? It may be—I do not say it will—but it may be. While in health he could fight against this—this which I must not speak of; but now his health is gone. He cannot rally. Without some change, I see clearly even I, who love him better than any one can love him——"

She stirred a little here.

"Far better," I repeated; "for while John does *not* love me best, he to me is more than any one else in the world. Yet even I have given up hope, unless—— But I have no right to say more."

There was no need. She began to understand. A deep, soft red, sunrise colour, dawned all over her face and neck, nay, tinged her very arms—her delicate, bare arms. She looked at me once—just once—with a mute but keen inquiry.

"It is the truth, Miss March—ay, ever since last year. You will respect it? You will, you shall respect it?"

She bent her head in acquiescence—that was all. She had not uttered a single syllable. Her silence almost drove me wild.

"What! not one word? not one ordinary message from a friend to a friend?—one who is lying ill, too!"

Still silence.

"Better so!" I cried, made desperate at last. "Better, if it must be, that he should die and go to the God who made him—ay, made him, as you shall yet see, too noble a man to die for any woman's love."

I left her—left her where she sat, and went my way.

Of the hours that followed the less I say the better. My mind was in a tumult of pain, in which right and wrong were strangely confused. I could not decide—I can scarcely decide now—whether what I had done ought to have been done; I only know that I did it—did it under an impulse so sudden and impetuous that it seemed to me like the guidance of Providence. All I could do afterwards was to trust the result where we say we trust all things, and yet are for ever disquieting ourselves in vain—we of little faith!

I have said, and I say again, that I believe every true marriage—of which there is probably one in every five thousand of conjugal unions—is brought about by Heaven, and Heaven only; and that all human influence is powerless either to make or to mar that happy end. Therefore, to Heaven I left this marriage, if such it was destined to be. And so, after a season, I calmed myself enough to dare entering that quiet sick-chamber, where no one ever entered but Jael and me.

The old woman met me at the door.

"Come in gently, Phineas; I do think there is a change."

A change!—that awful word! I staggered rather than walked to John's bedside.

Ay, there was a change, but not *that* one—which made my blood run cold in my veins even to think of. Thank God for evermore for His great mercies—not *that* change!

John was sitting up in bed. New life shone in his eyes, in his whole aspect. Life and—no, not hope, but something far better, diviner.

"Phineas, how tired you look; it is time you were in bed."

The old way of speaking—the old, natural voice, as I had not heard it for weeks. I flung myself by the bedside—perhaps I wept outright—God knows! It is thought a shame for a man to weep; yet one Man wept, and that too was over His friend—His brother.

"You must not grieve over me any more, dear lad; to-morrow, please God! I mean to be quite well again."

Amidst all my joy I marvelled over what could be the cause of so miraculous a change.

"You would smile if I told you—only a dream."

No, I did not smile; for I believed in the Ruler of all our spirits, sleeping or waking.

"A dream so curious that I have scarcely lost the impression of it yet. Do you know, Phineas, she has been sitting by me, just where you sit now."

"She?"

"Ursula."

If I could express the tone in which he uttered the word, which had never fallen from his lips before—it was always either "Miss March," or the impersonal form used by all lovers to disguise the beloved name—"*Ursula*," spoken as no man speaks any woman's name save the one which is the music of his heart, which he foresees shall be the one fireside tune of his life, ever familiar, yet ever sweet.

"Yes, she sat there talking. She told me she knew I loved her—loved her so much that I was dying for her; that it was very wrong; that I must rise up and do my work in the world—do it for Heaven's sake, not for hers; that a true man should live, and live nobly, for the woman he loves—it is only a coward who dies for her."

I listened, wonderstruck—for these were the very words that Ursula March might have uttered; the very spirit that seemed to shine in her eyes that night—the last night she and John spoke to one another. I asked him if there was any more of the dream.

"Nothing clear. I thought we were on the Flat at Enderley, and I was following her; whether I reached her or not I cannot tell. And whether I ever shall reach her I cannot tell. But this I know, Phineas, I will do as she bade me; I will arise and walk."

And so he did. He slept quietly as an infant all that night. Next morning I found him up and dressed. Looking like a spectre, indeed, but with health, courage, and hope in his eyes. Even my father noticed it, when at dinner-time, with Jael's help—poor old Jael! how proud she was—John crawled downstairs.

"Why, thee art picking up, lad! Thee'lt be a man again in no time."

"I hope so. And a better man than ever I was before."

"Thee might be better, and thee might be worse. Anyhow, we couldn't do without thee, John.—Hey, Phineas! who's been meddling with my spectacles?"

The old man turned his back upon us, and busily read his newspaper upside down.

We never had a happier meal in our house than that dinner.

In the afternoon my father stayed at home—a rare thing for him to do; nay, more, he went and smoked his peaceful pipe in the garden. John lay on an extempore sofa, made of three of our high-backed chairs and the window-sill. I read to him—trying to keep his attention, and mine too, solely to the Great Plague of London and Daniel Defoe, when, just as I was stealthily glancing at his face, fancying it looked whiter and more sunken, that his smile was fading, and his thoughts were wandering, Jael burst in.

"John Halifax, there be a woman asking for thee."

No, John—no need for that start—that rush of impetuous blood to thy poor thin cheek, as if there were but one woman in all the world. No, it was only Mrs. Jessop.

At sight of him, standing up, tall and gaunt and pale, the good lady's eyes brimmed over.

"You have been very ill, my poor boy! Forgive me—but I am an old woman, you know. Lie down again."

With gentle force she compelled him, and sat down by his side.

"I had no idea—why did you not let us know—the doctor and me? How long have you been ill?"

"I am quite well now—I am indeed.—I shall be about again to-morrow, shall I not, Phineas?" and he looked eagerly to me for confirmation.

I gave it, firmly and proudly. I was glad she should know it—glad she should see that the priceless jewel of his heart would not lie tossing in the mire because a haughty girl scorned to wear it. Glad that she might one day find out there lived not the woman of whom John Halifax was not worthy.

"But you must be very careful—very careful of yourself indeed."

"He will, Mrs. Jessop. Or, if not, he has many to

take care of him. Many to whom his life is most precious and most dear."

I spoke perhaps more abruptly than I ought to have spoken to that good old lady, but her gentle answer seemed at once to understand and forgive me.

"I well believe that, Mr. Fletcher. And I think Mr. Halifax hardly knows how much we—we all—esteem him." And with a kind, motherly gesture she took John's hand. "You must make haste and get well now. My husband will come and see you to-morrow. For Ursula—" here she carefully busied herself in the depths of her pocket—"my dear child sends you this."

It was a little note—unsealed. The superscription was simply his name, in her clear, round, fair handwriting—"*John Halifax*."

His fingers closed over it convulsively. "I—she is—very kind." The words died away; the hand which grasped—ay, for more than a minute—the unopened letter, trembled like an aspen leaf.

"Yes, hers is a grateful nature," observed Mrs. Jessop, sedulously looking at and speaking to me. "I would not wish it otherwise—I would not wish her to forget those whose worth she proved in her season of trouble."

I was silent. The old lady's tongue likewise failed her. She took off her glove, wiped a finger across each eyelash, and sat still.

"Have you read your little note, Mr. Halifax?"

No answer.

"I will take your message back. She told me what she had said to you."

Ay, all the world might have read those simple lines :—

"MY DEAR FRIEND,—I did not know till yesterday that you had been ill. I have not forgotten how kind you were to my poor father. I should like to come and see you if you would allow me.—Yours sincerely,

"URSULA MARCH."

This was all the note. I saw it, more than thirty

years afterwards, yellow and faded, in the corner of his pocket-book.

"Well, what shall I say to my child?"

"Say"—he half rose, struggling to speak—"ask her to come."

He turned his head towards the window, and the sunshine glittered on two great drops, large as a child's tear.

Mrs. Jessop went away. And now for a long hour we waited, scarcely moving. John lay, his eyes sometimes closed, sometimes fixed dreamily on the bit of blue sky that shone out above the iron railings between the Abbey trees. More than once they wandered to the little letter, which lay buried in his hands. He felt it there—that was enough.

My father came in from the garden and settled to his afternoon doze; but I think John hardly noticed him—nor I. My poor old father! Yet we were all young once—let youth enjoy its day!

At length Ursula came. She stood at the parlour door, rosy with walking—a vision of youth and candid innocence, which blushed not, nor had need to blush, at any intent or act that was sanctified by the law of God, and by her own heart.

John rose to meet her. They did not speak, but only clasped hands.

He was not strong enough for disguises now—in his first look she might have seen, have felt, that I had told her the truth. For hers—but it dropped down, down, as Ursula March's clear glance had never dropped before. Then I knew how all would end.

Jael's voice broke in sharply. "Abel Fletcher, the doctor's wife is wanting thee down in the kitchen garden, and she says her green gooseberries bean't half as big as our'n."

My father awoke—rubbed his eyes—became aware of a lady's presence—rubbed them again, and sat staring.

John led Ursula to the old man's chair.

"Mr. Fletcher, this is Miss March, a friend of mine, who, hearing I was ill, out of her great kindness——"

His voice faltered. Miss March added, in a low tone, with downcast eyelids,—

"I am an orphan, and he was kind to my dear father."

Abel Fletcher nodded, adjusted his spectacles, eyed her all over, and nodded again—slowly, gravely, with a satisfied inspection. His hard gaze lingered, and softened while it lingered, on that young face, whereon was written simplicity, dignity, truth.

"If thee be a friend of John's, welcome to my house. Wilt thee sit down?"

Offering his hand, with a mixture of kindness and ceremonious grace that I had never before seen in my Quaker father, he placed her in his own arm-chair. How well I remember her sitting there, in her black silk pelisse, trimmed with the white fur she was so fond of wearing, and her riding-hat, the soft feathers of which drooped on her shoulder, trembling as she trembled! For she did tremble very much.

Gradually the old man's perception opened to the facts before him. He ceased his sharp scrutiny, and half smiled.

"Wilt thee stay and have a dish of tea with us?"

So it came to pass, I hardly remember how, that in an hour's space our parlour beheld the strangest sight it had beheld since—— Ah, no wonder that when she took her place at the table's foot, and gave him his dish of tea with her own hand—her pretty ringed lady's hand—my old father started, as if it had been another than Miss March who was sitting there. No wonder that, more than once, catching the sound of her low, quiet, gentlewomanlike speech, different from any female voices here, he turned round suddenly with a glance, half scared, half eager, as if she had been a ghost from the grave.

But Mrs. Jessop engaged him in talk, and, woman-hater as he was, he could not resist the pleasantness of the doctor's little wife. The doctor, too, came in after tea, and the old folk all settled themselves for a cosy chat, taking very little notice of us three.

Miss March sat at a little table near the window, admiring some hyacinths that Mrs. Jessop had brought us. A wise present; for all Norton Bury knew that if Abel Fletcher had a soft place in his heart it was for his garden and his flowers. These were very lovely; in colour and scent delicious to one who had been long ill. John lay looking at them and at her, as if, oblivious of past and future, his whole life were absorbed into that one exquisite hour.

For me—where I sat I do not clearly know, nor probably did any one else.

"There," said Miss March to herself, in a tone of almost childish satisfaction, as she arranged the last hyacinth to her liking.

"They are very beautiful," I heard John's voice answer, with a strange trembling in it. "It is growing too dark to judge of colours, but the scent is delicious, even here."

"I could move the table closer to you."

"Thank you—let me do it—will you sit down?"

She did so, after a very slight hesitation, by John's side. Neither spoke, but sat quietly there, with the sunset light on their two heads, softly touching them both, and then as softly melting away.

"There is a new moon to-night," Miss March remarked, appositely and gravely.

"Is there? Then I have been ill a whole month. For I remember noticing it through the trees the night when——"

He did not say what night, and she did not ask. To such a very unimportant conversation as they were apparently holding my involuntary listening could do no harm.

"You will be able to walk out soon, I hope," said Miss March again. "Norton Bury is a pretty town."

John asked suddenly, "Are you going to leave it?"

"Not yet—I do not know for certain—perhaps not at all. I mean," she added hurriedly, "that being independent, and having entirely separated from, and been given up by, my cousins, I prefer residing with Mrs. Jessop altogether."

"Of course—most natural." The words were formally spoken, and John did not speak again for some time.

"I hope——" said Ursula, breaking the pause, and then stopping, as if her own voice frightened her.

"What do you hope?"

"That long before this moon has grown old you will be quite strong again."

"Thank you. I hope so too. I have need for strength, God knows!" He sighed heavily.

"And you will have what you need, so as to do your work in the world. You must not be afraid."

"I am not afraid. I shall bear my burthen like other men. Every one has some inevitable burthen to bear."

"So I believe."

And now the room darkened so fast that I could not see them; but their voices seemed a great way off, as the children's voices playing at the old well-head used to sound to me when I lay under the brow of the Flat—in the dim twilights at Enderley.

"I intend," John said, "as soon as I am able, to leave Norton Bury, and go abroad for some time."

"Where?"

"To America. It is the best country for a young man who has neither money, nor kindred, nor position—nothing, in fact, but his own right hand with which to carve out his own fortunes—as I will, if I can."

She murmured something about this being "quite right."

"I am glad you think so." But his voice had resumed that formal tone which ever and anon mingled strangely with its low, deep tenderness. "In any case, I must quit England. I have reasons for so doing."

"What reasons?"

The question seemed to startle John—he did not reply at once.

"If you wish I will tell you; in order that, should I ever come back—or if I should not come back at all—you who were kind enough to be my friend will know I did not go away from mere youthful recklessness or love of change."

He waited, apparently for some answer—but it came not, and he continued,—

"I am going because there has befallen me a great trouble, which, while I stay here, I cannot get free from or overcome. I do not wish to sink under it—I had rather, as you said, 'Do my work in the world' as a man ought. No man has a right to say unto his Maker, 'My burthen is heavier than I can bear.' Do you not think so?"

"I do."

"Do you not think I am right in thus meeting, and trying to conquer, an inevitable ill?"

"*Is* it inevitable?"

"Hush!" John answered wildly. "Don't reason with me—you cannot judge—you do not know. It is enough that I must go. If I stay I shall become unworthy of myself, unworthy of—— Forgive me, I have no right to talk thus; but you called me 'friend,' and I would like you to think kindly of me always. Because—because——" And his voice shook—broke down utterly. "God love thee and take care of thee, wherever I may go!"

"John, stay!"

It was but a low, faint cry, like that of a little bird; but he heard it—felt it. In the silence of the dark she crept up to him, like a young bird to its mate, and he took her into the shelter of his love for evermore. At once all was made clear between them; for whatever the world might say, they were in the sight of Heaven equal, and she received as much as she gave.

* * * * * *

When Jael brought in lights the room seemed to me, at first, all in a wild dazzle. Then I saw John rise, and Miss March with him. Holding her hand, he led her across the room. His head was erect, his eyes shining—

his whole aspect that of a man who declares before all the world, " This is *my own*."

" Eh ? " said my father, gazing at them from over his spectacles.

John spoke brokenly, " We have no parents, neither she nor I. Bless her—for she has promised to be my wife."

And the old man blessed her with tears.

CHAPTER XIX.

" I HARDLY like taking thee out this wet day, Phineas—but it is a comfort to have thee."

Perhaps it was, for John was bent on a trying errand. He was going to communicate to Mr. Brithwood of the Mythe, Ursula's legal guardian and trustee, the fact that she had promised him her hand—him, John Halifax, the tanner. He did it—nay, insisted upon doing it—the day after he came of age, and just one week after they had been betrothed—this nineteenth of June, one thousand eight hundred and one.

We reached the iron gates of the Mythe House. John hesitated a minute, and then pulled the bell with a resolute hand.

" Do you remember the last time we stood here, John ? "

" I do, well ! "

But soon the happy smile faded from his lips, and left them pressed together in a firm, almost painful gravity. He was not only a lover but a man. And no man could go to meet what he knew he must meet in this house, and on this errand, altogether unmoved. One might foresee a good deal, even in the knowing side-glance of the servant, whom he startled with his name, " Mr. Halifax."

" Mr. Brithwood's busy, sir ; better come to-morrow," suggested the man, evidently knowing enough upon his master's affairs.

"I am sorry to trouble him—but I must see Mr. Brithwood to-day."

And John determinedly followed the man into the grand empty dining-room, where, on crimson velvet chairs, we sat and contemplated the great stag's head with its branching horns, the silver flagons and tankards, and the throstles hopping outside across the rainy lawn—at our full leisure, too, for the space of fifteen minutes.

"This will not do," said John, quietly enough, though this time it was with a less steady hand that he pulled the bell.

"Did you tell your master I was here?"

"Yes, sir." And the grin with which the footman came in somehow slid away from his mouth's corners.

"How soon may I have the honour of seeing him?"

"He says, sir, you must send up your business by me."

John paused, evidently subduing something within him, something unworthy of Ursula's lover, of Ursula's husband that was to be.

"Tell your master my business is solely with himself, and I must request to see him. It is important, say, or I would not thus intrude upon his time."

"Very well, sir."

Ere long the man brought word that Mr. Brithwood would be at liberty, for five minutes only, in the justice-room. We were led out, crossing the courtyard once more—where, just riding out, I saw two ladies, one of whom kissed her hand gaily to John Halifax—to the magistrate's office. There, safely separated from his own noble mansion, Mr. Brithwood administered justice. In the outer room a stout young fellow—a poacher, probably—sat heavily ironed, sullen and fierce; and by the door a girl with a child in her arms, and—God pity her!—no ring on her finger, stood crying; another ill-looking fellow, maudlin drunk, with a constable by him, called out to us as we passed for "a drop o' beer."

These were the people whom Richard Brithwood, Esquire, magistrate for the county of ——, had to judge and punish, according to his own sense of equity and his knowledge of his country's law.

He sat behind his office-table, thoroughly magisterial, dictating so energetically to his clerk behind him that we had both entered, and John had crossed the room, before he saw us, or seemed to see.

"Mr. Brithwood."

"Oh!—Mr. Halifax. Good-morning."

John returned the salutation, which was evidently meant to show that the giver bore no grudge; that, indeed, it was impossible so dignified a personage as Richard Brithwood, Esquire, in his public capacity, too, could bear a grudge against so inferior an individual as John Halifax.

"I should be glad, sir, of a few minutes' speech with you."

"Certainly—certainly; speak on;" and he lent a magisterial ear.

"Excuse me, my business is private," said John, looking at the clerk.

"No business is private here," returned the squire haughtily.

"Then shall I speak with you elsewhere? But I must have the honour of an interview with you, and immediately."

Whether Mr. Brithwood was seized with some indefinite alarm, he himself best knew why, or whether John's manner irresistibly compelled him to civility, as the stronger always compels the weaker, I cannot tell, but he signed to the clerk to leave the room.

"And, Jones, send back all the others to the lock-up house till to-morrow. Bless my life! it's near three o'clock. They can't expect to keep a gentleman's dinner waiting—these low fellows."

I suppose this referred only to the culprits outside. At all events, we chose to take it so.

"Now—you, sir—perhaps you'll dispatch your business; the sooner the better."

"It will not take long. It is a mere matter of form,

which nevertheless I felt it my duty to be the first to inform you. Mr. Brithwood, I have the honour of bearing a message to you from your cousin—Miss Ursula March."

"She's nothing to me—I never wish to see her face again, the—the vixen!"

"You will be kind enough, if you please, to avoid all such epithets—at least, in my hearing."

"Your hearing! And pray who are you, sir?"

"You know quite well who I am."

"Oh yes! And how goes the tanning? Any offers in the horse-flesh line? Always happy to meet you in the way of business. But what can you possibly have to do with me, or with any member of my family?"

John bit his lip; the squire's manner was extremely galling—more so, perhaps, in its outside civility than any gross rudeness.

"Mr. Brithwood, I was not speaking of myself, but of the lady whose message I have the honour to bring you."

"That lady, sir, has chosen to put herself away from her family, and her family can hold no further intercourse with her," said the squire loftily.

"I am aware of that," was the reply, with at least equal hauteur.

"Are you? And pray what right may *you* have to be acquainted with Miss March's private concerns?"

"The right—which, indeed, was the purport of her message to you—that in a few months I shall become her husband."

John said this very quietly—so quietly that, at first, the squire seemed hardly to credit his senses. At last he burst into a hoarse laugh.

"Well, that is the best joke I ever did hear."

"Pardon me; I am perfectly serious."

"Bah! how much money do you want, fellow? A pretty tale! You'll not get me to believe it—ha! ha! She wouldn't be so mad. To be sure, women have their fancies, as we know, and you're a likely young fellow enough; but to marry you——"

John sprang up, his whole frame quivering with fury. "Take care, sir; take care how you insult my *wife!*"

He stood over the wretch—the cowardly, shrinking wretch—he did not touch him, but he stood over him till, terrified out of his life, Richard Brithwood gasped out some apology.

"Sit down—pray sit down again. Let us proceed in our business.'

John Halifax sat down.

"So—my cousin is your wife, I think you were saying."

"She will be, some months hence. We were engaged a week ago, with the full knowledge and consent of Dr. and Mrs. Jessop, her nearest friends."

"And of yours?" asked Mr. Brithwood, with as much sarcasm as his blunt wits could furnish him.

"I have no relatives."

"So I always understood. And that being the case, may I ask the meaning of the visit? Where are your lawyers, your marriage settlements, hey? I say, young man—ha! ha! I should like to know what you can possibly want with me, Miss March's trustee?"

"Nothing whatever. Miss March, as you are aware, is by her father's will left perfectly free in her choice of marriage, and she has chosen. But since, under certain circumstances, I wish to act with perfect openness, I came to tell you, as her cousin and executor of this will, that she is about to become my wife."

And he lingered over that name, as if its very utterance strengthened and calmed him.

"May I inquire into those 'certain circumstances'?" asked the other, still derisively.

"You know them already. Miss March has a fortune and I have none; and though I wish that difference were on the other side—though it might and did hinder me from seeking her—yet now she is sought and won, it shall not hinder my marrying her."

"Likely not," sneered Mr. Brithwood.

John's passion was rising again.

"I repeat, it shall not hinder me. The world may say

what it chooses; we follow a higher law than the world —she and I. She knows me; she is not afraid to trust her whole life with me; am I to be afraid to trust her? Am I to be such a coward as not to dare to marry the woman I love, because the world might say I married her for her money?"

He stood, his clenched hand resting on the table, looking full into Richard Brithwood's face. The squire sat dumbfoundered at the young man's vehemence.

"Your pardon," John added, more calmly. "Perhaps I owe her some pardon too, for bringing her name thus into discussion; but I wished to have everything clear between myself and you, her nearest relative. You now know exactly how the matter stands. I will detain you no longer—I have nothing more to say."

"But I have," roared out the squire, at length recovering himself, seeing his opponent had quitted the field. "Stop a minute."

John paused at the door.

"Tell Ursula March she may marry you, or any other vagabond she pleases—it's no business of mine. But her fortune is my business, and it's in my hands too. Might's right, and possession's nine-tenths of the law. Not one penny shall she get out of my fingers as long as I can keep hold of it."

John bowed, his hand still on the door. "As you please, Mr. Brithwood. That was not the subject of our interview. Good-morning."

And we were away.

Re-crossing the iron gates, and out into the open road, John breathed freely.

"That's over—all is well."

"Do you think what he threatened is true? Can he do it?"

"Very likely; don't let us talk about that." And he walked on lightly, as if a load were taken off his mind, and body and soul leaped up to meet the glory of the summer sunshine, the freshness of the summer air.

"Oh! what a day is this!—after the rain, too! How she will enjoy it!"

And coming home through Norton Bury, we met her, walking with Mrs. Jessop. No need to dread that meeting now.

Yet she looked up, questioning, through her blushes. Of course he had told her where we were going to-day, her who had a right to know every one of his concerns now.

"Yes, dear, all is quite right. Do not be afraid."

Afraid, indeed! Not the least fear was in those clear eyes. Nothing but perfect content—perfect trust.

John drew her arm through his. "Come, we need not mind Norton Bury now," he said, smiling.

So they two walked forward, talking, as we could see, earnestly and rather seriously to one another, while Mrs. Jessop and I followed behind.

"Bless their dear hearts!" said the old lady, as she sat resting on the stile of a bean-field. "Well, we have all been young once."

Not all, good Mrs. Jessop, thought I; not all.

Yet surely it was most pleasant to see them, as it is to see all true lovers—young lovers, too, in the morning of their days. Pleasant to see written on every line of their happy faces the blessedness of Nature's law of love—love begun in youth-time, sincere and pure, free from all sentimental shams, or follies, or shames—love mutually plighted, the next strongest bond to that in which it will end, and is meant to end, God's holy ordinance of marriage.

We came back across the fields to tea at Mrs. Jessop's. It was John's custom to go there almost every evening, though certainly he could not be said to "go a-courting." Nothing could be more unlike it than his demeanour, or indeed the demeanour of both. They were very quiet lovers, never making much of one another "before folk." No whispering in corners, or stealing away down garden walks. No public show of caresses—caresses whose very sweetness must consist in their entire sacredness; at least, *I* should think so. No coquettish exactions, no testing of either's power over the other, in those perilous small quarrels which may be the renewal of passion, but are the death of true love.

No, our young people were well-behaved always. She sat at her work, and he made himself generally pleasant, falling in kindly to the Jessops' household ways. But whatever he was about, at Ursula's lightest movement, at the least sound of her voice, I could see him lift a quiet glance, as if always conscious of her presence; her who was the delight of his eyes.

To-night, more than ever before, this soft, invisible link seemed to be drawn closer between them, though they spoke little together, and even sat at opposite sides of the table; but whenever their looks met, one could trace a soft, smiling interchange, full of trust, and peace, and joy. He had evidently told her all that had happened to-day, and she was satisfied.

More, perhaps, than I was; for I knew how little John would have to live upon besides what means his wife brought him; but that was their own affair, and I had no business to make public my doubts or fears.

We all sat round the tea-table, talking gaily together, and then John left us, reluctantly enough; but he always made a point of going to the tanyard for an hour or two, in my father's stead, every evening. Ursula let him out at the front door; this was her right, silently claimed, which nobody either jested at or interfered with.

When she returned, and perhaps she had been away a minute or two longer than was absolutely necessary, there was a wonderful brightness on her young face; though she listened with a degree of attention, most creditable in its gravity, to a long dissertation of Mrs. Jessop's on the best and cheapest way of making jam and pickles.

"You know, my dear, you ought to begin and learn all about such things now."

"Yes," said Miss March, with a little droop of the head.

"I assure you"—turning to me—"she comes every day into the kitchen—never mind, my dear, one can say anything to Mr. Fletcher. And what lady need be ashamed of knowing how a dinner is cooked and a household kept in order?"

"Nay, she should rather be proud; I know John thinks so."

At this answer of mine Ursula half smiled; but there was a colour in her cheek, and a thoughtfulness in her eyes deeper than any that our conversation warranted or occasioned. I was planning how to divert Mrs. Jessop from the subject, when it was broken at once by a sudden entrance, which startled us all like a flash of lightning.

"Stole away! stole away! as my husband would say. Here have I come in the dusk, all through the streets, to Dr. Jessop's very door. How is she? Where is she, *ma petite?*"

"Caroline!"

"Ah! come forward. I haven't seen you for an age."

And Lady Caroline kissed her on both cheeks in her lively French fashion, which Ursula received patiently, and returned—no, I will not be certain whether she returned it or not.

"Pardon—how do you do, Mrs. Jessop, my dear woman? What trouble I have had in coming! Are you not glad to see me, Ursula?"

"Yes, very." In that sincere voice which never either falsified or exaggerated a syllable.

"Did you ever expect to see me again?"

"No, certainly I did not. And I would almost rather not see you now, if——"

"If Richard Brithwood did not approve of it? Bah! what notions you always had of marital supremacy! So, *ma chère*, you are going to be married yourself, I hear?"

"Yes."

"Why, how quietly you seem to take it! The news perfectly electrified me this morning. I always said that young man was *un héros de romans. Ma foi!* this is the prettiest little episode I ever heard of. Just King Cophetua and the beggar maid—only reversed. How do you feel, my Queen Cophetua?"

"I do not quite understand you, Caroline."

"Neither should I you, for the tale seems incredible. Only you gave me such an honest 'yes,' and I know you never tell even white lies. But it can't be true; at least, not certain. A little *affaire de cœur*, maybe—ah! I had several before I was twenty—very pleasant, chivalrous, romantic, and all that; and such a brave young fellow too! *Hélas!* love is sweet at your age!"—with a little sigh—"but marriage! My dear child, you are not surely promised to this youth?"

"I am."

"How sharply you say it! Nay, don't be angry. I liked him greatly. A very pretty fellow. But then he belongs to the people."

"So do I."

"Naughty child, you will not comprehend me. I mean the lower orders, the bourgeoisie. My husband says he is a tanner's 'prentice-boy."

"He was apprentice; he is now partner in Mr. Fletcher's tanyard."

"That is nearly as bad. And so you are actually going to marry a tanner?"

"I am going to marry Mr. Halifax. We will, if you please, cease to discuss him, Lady Caroline."

"*La belle sauvage!*" laughed the lady; and in the dusk I fancied I saw her reach over to pat Ursula's hand in her careless, pretty way. "Nay, I meant no harm."

"I am sure you did not; but we will change the subject."

"Not at all. I came to talk about it. I couldn't sleep till I had. *Je t'aime bien, tu le sais, ma petite Ursule.*"

"Thank you," said Ursula gently.

"And I would like well to see you married. Truly we women must marry, or be nothing at all. But as to marrying for love, as we used to think of, and as charming poets make believe — my dear, nowadays, *nous avons changé tout cela.*"

Ursula replied nothing.

"I suppose my friend the young bourgeois is very much in love with you? With *les beaux yeux de votre cassette*, Richard swears; but I know better. What of that? All men say they love one—but it will not last. It burns itself out. It will be over in a year, as we wives all know. Do we not, Mrs. Jessop? Ah! she is gone away."

Probably they thought I was away too—or else they took no notice of me—and went talking on.

"Jane would not have agreed with you, Cousin Caroline; she loved her husband very dearly when she was a girl. They were poor, and he was afraid to marry; so he let her go. That was wrong, I think."

"How wise we are growing in these things now!" laughed Lady Caroline. "But come, I am not interested in old turtle-doves. Say about yourself."

"I have nothing more to say."

"Nothing more? *Mon Dieu!* are you aware that Richard is furious; that he vows he will keep every sou he has of yours—law or no law—for as long as ever he can? He declared so this morning. Did young Halifax tell you?"

"Mr. Halifax has told me."

"'*Mr.* Halifax!' How proudly she says it. And are you still going to be married to him?"

"Yes."

"What! a bourgeois! a tradesman! with no more money than those sort of people usually have, I believe. You, who have had all sorts of comforts, have always lived as a gentlewoman. Truly, though I adore a love-marriage in theory, practically I think you are mad—quite mad, my dear."

"Do you?"

"And he too! Verily, what men are! Especially men in love. All selfish together."

"Caroline!"

"Isn't it selfish to drag a pretty creature down, and make her a drudge, a slave—a mere poor man's wife?"

"She is proud of being such!" burst in the indignant young voice. "Lady Caroline, you may say what you like to me—you were kind always, and I was fond of you—but you shall not say a word against Mr. Halifax. You do not know him—how could you?"

"And you do? Ah! *ma petite*, we all think that, till we find out to the contrary. And so he urges you to be married at once—rich or poor—at all risks, at all costs? How lover-like—how like a man! I guess it all. Half beseeches, half persuades——"

"He does not!" And the girl's voice was sharp with pain. "I would not have told you, but I must—for his sake. He asked me this afternoon if I was afraid of being poor; if I would like to wait, and let him work hard alone, till he could give me a home like that I was born to. He did, Caroline."

"And you answered?"

"No—a thousand times, no! He will have a hard battle to fight—would I let him fight it alone? when I can help him—when he says I can."

"Ah, child! you that know nothing of poverty, how can you bear it?"

"I will try."

"You that never ruled a house in your life——"

"I can learn."

"*Ciel!* 'tis wonderful! And this young man has no friends, no connections, no fortune! only himself?"

"Only himself," said Ursula, with a proud contempt.

"Will you tell me, my dear, why you marry him?"

"Because"—and Ursula spoke in low tones, that seemed wrung out of her almost against her will—"because I honour him, because I trust him; and, young as I am, I have seen enough of the world to be thankful that there is in it one man whom I can trust, can honour, entirely. Also—though I am often ashamed lest this be selfish—because when I was in trouble he helped me; when I was misjudged he believed in me; when I was sad and desolate he loved me. And I am proud of his love—I glory in it. No one shall take it from me—no one will—no one can, unless I cease to deserve it."

Lady Caroline was silent. Despite her will, you might hear a sigh breaking from some deep corner of that light, frivolous heart.

"*Bien! chacun à son goût!* But you have never stated one trifle—not unnecessary, perhaps, though most married folk get on quite well without it. 'Honour,' 'trust,'—pshaw! My child—do you *love* Mr. Halifax?"

No answer.

"Nay, why be shy? In England, they say, and among the people—no offence, *ma petite*—one does sometimes happen to care for the man one marries. Tell me, for I must be gone, do you love him? One word, whether or no?"

Just then the light coming in showed Ursula's face, beautiful with more than happiness, uplifted even with a religious thankfulness, as she said simply,—

"John knows."

CHAPTER XX.

In the late autumn John married Ursula March. He was twenty-one, and she eighteen. It was very young—too young, perhaps, prudent folk might say; and yet sometimes I think a double blessing falls on unions like this. A right and holy marriage, a true love-marriage, be it early or late, is—must be—sanctified and happy; yet those have the best chance of happiness who, meeting on the very threshold of life, enter upon its duties together; with free, fresh hearts, easily moulded the one to the other, rich in all the riches of youth, acute to enjoy, brave and hopeful to endure.

Such were these two—God bless them!

They were married quite privately, neither having any near kindred. Besides, John held strongly the opinion that so solemn a festival as marriage is only desecrated by outward show. And so, one golden autumn morning, Ursula walked quietly up the Abbey aisle in her plain white muslin gown; and John and she plighted their faithful vows, no one being present except the Jessops and I. They then went away for a brief holiday—went away without either pomp or tears, entirely happy—husband and wife together.

When I came home and said what had happened, my good father seemed little surprised. He had expressly desired not to be told anything of the wedding till all was over—he hated marriages.

"But since it is done, maybe 'tis as well," said he grimly. "She seems a kindly young thing; wise, even—for a woman."

"And pleasant too, father?"

"Ay, but favour is deceitful, and beauty vain. So the lad's gone;" and he looked round, as if missing John, who had lived in our house ever since his illness. "I thought as much, when he bade me good-night, and asked my leave to take a journey. So he's married and gone! Come, Phineas, sit thee down by thy old father; I am glad thee wilt always remain a bachelor."

We settled ourselves, my father and I; and while the old man smoked his meditative pipe, I sat thinking of the winter evenings when we two lads had read by the fireside; the summer days when we had lounged on the garden wall. He was a married man now, the head of a household; others had a right—the first, best, holiest right—to the love that used to be all mine; and though it was a marriage entirely happy and hopeful, though all that day and every day I rejoiced both with and for my brother, still it was rather sad to miss him from our house, to feel that his boyish days were quite over—that his boyish place would know him no more.

But of course I had fully overcome, or at least suppressed, this feeling when, John having brought his wife home, I went to see them in their own house.

I had seen it once before; it was an old dwelling-house, which my father bought with the flour-mill, situated in the middle of the town, the front windows looking on the street, the desolate garden behind shut in by four brick walls. A most unbridal-like abode. I feared they would find it so, even though John had been busy there the last two months, in early mornings and late evenings, keeping a comical secrecy over the matter as if he were jealous that any one but himself should lend an eye, or put a finger, to the dear task of making ready for his young wife.

They could not be great preparations, I knew, for the third of my father's business promised but a small income. Yet the gloomy outside being once passed, the house looked wonderfully bright and clean; the walls and doors newly painted and delicately stencilled—(" Master did all that himself," observed the proud little handmaid, Jenny—Jem Watkins's sweetheart. I had begged the place for her myself of Mrs. Ursula). Though only a few rooms were furnished, and that very simply, almost poorly, all was done with taste and care; the colours well mingled, the woodwork graceful and good.

They were out gardening, John Halifax and his wife——

Ay, his wife; he was a husband now. They looked so young, both of them, he kneeling, planting box-edging, she standing by him with her hand on his shoulder—the hand with the ring on it. He was laughing at something she had said, thy very laugh of old, David! Neither heard me come till I stood close by.

" Phineas, welcome, welcome! " He wrung my hand fervently, many times; so did Ursula, blushing rosy red. They both called me " brother," and both were as fond and warm as any brother and sister could be.

A few minutes after, Ursula—" Mrs. Halifax," as I said I ought to call her now—slipped away into the house, and John and I were left together. He glanced after his wife till she was out of sight, played with the spade, threw it down, placed his two hands on my shoulders, and looked hard in my face. He was trembling with deep emotion.

"Art thou happy, David?"

"Ay, lad, almost afraid of my happiness. God make me worthy of it, and of her!"

He lifted his eyes upwards; there was in them a new look, sweet and solemn, a look which expressed the satisfied content of a life now rounded and completed by that other dear life which it had received into and united with its own—making a full and perfect whole, which, however kindly and fondly it may look on friends and kindred outside, has no absolute need of any, but is complete in and sufficient to itself, as true marriage should be. A look unconsciously fulfilling the law—God's own law—that a man shall leave father and mother, brethren and companions, and shall cleave unto his wife, and "they two shall become one flesh."

And although I rejoiced in his joy, still I felt half sadly for a moment the vague, fine line of division which was thus for evermore drawn between him and me of no fault on either side, and of which he himself was unaware. It was but the right and natural law of things, the difference between the married and unmarried, which only the latter feel. Which, perhaps, the Divine One meant them to feel—that out of their great solitude of this world may grow a little inner Eden, where they may hear His voice, "walking in the garden in the cool of the day."

We went round John's garden; there was nothing Edenlike about it, being somewhat of a waste still, divided between ancient cabbage-beds, empty flower-beds, and great old orchard trees, very thinly laden with fruit.

"We'll make them bear better next year," said John hopefully. "We may have a very decent garden here in time." He looked round his little domain with the eye of a master, and put his arm, half proudly, half shyly, round his wife's shoulders—she had sidled up to him, ostensibly bringing him a letter, though possibly only for an excuse, because in those sweet early days they naturally liked to be in each other's sight continually.

It was very beautiful to see what a demure, soft, meek matronliness had come over the high spirit of the "nut-browne mayde."

"May I read?" she said, peeping over him.

"Of course you may, little one." A comical pet name for him to give her, who was anything but small. I could have smiled, remembering the time when John Halifax bowed to the stately and dignified young gentlewoman who stood at Mrs. Tod's door. To think he should ever have come to call Miss Ursula March "little one!"

But this was not exactly a time for jesting, since, on reading the letter, I saw the young wife flush an angry red, and then look grave. Until John, crumpling up the paper, and dropping it almost with a boyish frolic into the middle of a large rosemary bush, took his wife by both her hands, and gazed down into her troubled face, smiling.

"You surely don't mind this, love? We knew it all before. It can make no possible difference."

"No! But it is so wrong—so unjust. I never believed he dared do it—to you."

"Hear her, Phineas! She thinks nobody dare do anything ill to her husband—not even Richard Brithwood."

"He is a——"

"Hush, dear!—we will not talk about him; since, for all his threats, he can do us no harm, and, poor man! he never will be half as happy as we."

That was true. So Mr. Brithwood's insulting letter was left to moulder harmlessly away in the rosemary bush, and we all walked up and down the garden, talking over a thousand plans for making ends meet in that little household. To their young hopefulness even poverty itself became a jest; and was met cheerfully, like an honest, hard-featured, hard-handed friend, whose rough face was often kindly, and whose harsh grasp made one feel the strength of one's own.

"We mean," John said gaily, "to be two living Essays

on the Advantages of Poverty. We are not going to be afraid of it or ashamed of it. We don't care who knows it. We consider that our respectability lies solely in our two selves."

"But your neighbours?"

"Our neighbours may think of us exactly what they like. Half the sting of poverty is gone when one keeps house for one's own comfort, and not for the comments of one's neighbours."

"I should think not," Ursula cried, tossing back her head in merry defiance. "Besides, we are young, we have few wants, and we can easily reduce our wants to our havings."

"And no more gray silk gowns?" said her husband, half fondly, half sadly.

"You will not be so rude as to say I shall not look equally well in a cotton one? And as for being as happy in it—why, I know best."

He smiled at her once more—that tender, manly smile which made all soft and lustrous the inmost depths of his brown eyes; truly no woman need be afraid, with a smile like that to be the strength, the guidance, the sunshine of her home.

We went in, and the young mistress showed us her new house; we investigated and admired all, down to the very scullery; then we adjourned to the sitting-room—the only one—and, after tea, Ursula arranged her books, some on stained shelves, which she proudly informed me were of John's own making, and some on an old spinet, which he had picked up, and which, he said, was of no other use than to hold books, since she was not an accomplished young lady, and could neither sing nor play.

"But you don't dislike the spinet, Ursula? It caught my fancy. Do you know I have a faint remembrance that once, on such a thing as this, my mother used to play?"

He spoke in a low voice; Ursula stole up to him with a fond, awed look.

"You never told me anything about your mother?"

"Dear, I had little to tell. Long ago you knew whom you were going to marry—John Halifax, who had no friends, no kindred, whose parents left him nothing but his name,"

"And you cannot remember them?"

"My father not at all; my mother very little."

"And have you nothing belonging to them?"

"Only one thing. Should you like to see it?"

"Very much." She still spoke slowly, and with slight hesitation. "It was hard for him not to have known his parents," she added, when John had left the room. "I should like to have known them too. But still—when I know *him*——"

She smiled, tossed back the coronet of curls from her forehead—her proud, pure forehead, that would have worn a coronet of jewels more meekly than it now wore the unadorned honour of being John Halifax's wife. I wished he could have seen her.

That minute he reappeared.

"Here, Ursula, is all I have of my parents. No one has seen it, except Phineas there, until now."

He held in his hand the little Greek Testament which he had showed me years before. Carefully, and with the same fond, reverent look as when he was a boy, he undid the case, made of silk, with ribbon strings—doubtless a woman's work—it must have been his mother's. His wife touched it, softly and tenderly. He showed her the fly-leaf; she looked over the inscription, and then repeated it aloud.

"'*Guy Halifax, gentleman.*' I thought—I thought——"

Her manner betrayed a pleased surprise; she would not have been a woman, especially a woman reared in pride of birth, not to have felt and testified the like pleasure for a moment.

"You thought that I was only a labourer's son, or—nobody's. Well, does it signify?"

"No," she cried, as, clinging round his neck, and throwing her head back, she looked at him with all her heart in her eyes. "No, it does *not* signify. Were your father the king on his throne, or the beggar in the streets, it would be all the same to me; you would still be yourself—*my* husband—*my* John Halifax."

"God bless thee—my own wife that He has given me!" John murmured, through his close embrace.

They had altogether forgotten any one's presence, dear souls! so I kept them in that happy oblivion by slipping out to Jenny in the kitchen, and planning with her how we could at least spare Jem Watkins two days a week to help in the garden, under Mr. Halifax's orders.

"Only, Jenny," smiled I, with a warning finger, "no idling and chattering. Young folk must work hard if they want to come to the happy ending of your master and mistress."

The little maid grew the colour of her swain's pet peonies, and promised obedience. Conscientious Jem there was no fear of—all the rosy-cheeked damsels in Christendom would not have turned him aside from one iota of his duty to Mr. Halifax. Thus there was love in the parlour and love in the kitchen. But, I verily believe, the young married couple were served all the better for their kindness and sympathy to the humble pair of sweethearts in the rank below them.

John walked home with me—a pleasure I had hardly expected, but which was insisted upon both by him and Ursula. For from the very first of her betrothal there had been a thorough brother-and-sisterly bond established between her and me. Her womanly, generous nature would have scorned to do what, as I have heard, many young wives do—seek to make coldness between her husband and his old friends. No; secure in her riches, in her rightful possession of his whole heart, she took into hers everything that belonged to John, every one he cared for; to be for ever held sacred and beloved, being his, and therefore her own. Thus we were the very best of friends, my sister Ursula and me.

John and I talked a little about her—of her rosy looks, which he hoped would not fade in their town dwelling—and of good Mrs. Tod's wonderful delight at seeing her, when last week they had stayed two days in the dear old cottage at Enderley. But he seemed slow to speak about his wife, or to dilate on a joy so new that it was hardly to be breathed on, lest it might melt into air.

Only when, as we were crossing the street, a fine equipage passed, he looked after it with a smile.

"Gray ponies! she is so fond of long-tailed gray ponies. Poor child! when shall I be able to give her a carriage? Perhaps some day—who knows!"

He turned the conversation, and began telling me about the cloth-mill—his old place of resort—which he had been over once again when they were at Rose Cottage.

"And do you know, while I was looking at the machinery, a notion came into my head that, instead of that great water-wheel—you remember it?—it might be worked by steam."

"What sort of steam?"

"Phineas, your memory is no better, I see. Have you forgotten my telling you how, last year, some Scotch engineer tried to move boats by steam on the Forth and Clyde canal? Why should not the same power be turned to account in a cloth-mill? I know it could—I have got the plan of the machinery in my head already. I made a drawing of it last night, and showed it to Ursula; *she* understood it directly."

I smiled.

"And I do believe, by common patience and skill, a man might make his fortune with it at those Enderley cloth-mills."

"Suppose you try!" I said in half jest, and was surprised to see how seriously John took it.

"I wish I could try—if it were only practicable. Once or twice I have thought it might be. The mill belongs to Lord Luxmore. His steward works it. Now, if one could get to be a foreman or overseer——"

"Try—you can do anything you try."

"No, I must not think of it—she and I have agreed that I must not," said he steadily. "It's my weakness—my hobby, you know. But—no hobbies now. Above all, I must not, for a mere fancy, give up the work that lies under my hand. What of the tanyard, Phineas?"

"My father missed you, and grumbled after you a good deal. He looks anxious, I think. He vexes himself more than he needs about business."

"Don't let him. Keep him as much at home as you can. I'll manage the tanyard; you know—and he knows too—that everything which can be done for us all I shall do."

I looked up, surprised at the extreme earnestness of his manner.

"Surely, John——"

"Nay, there is nothing to be uneasy about—nothing more than there has been for this year past. All trade is bad just now. Never fear, we'll weather the storm—I'm not afraid."

Cheerfully as he spoke, I began to guess—what he already must have known—that our fortunes were as a slowly-leaking ship, of which the helm had slipped from my old father's feeble hand. But John had taken it—John stood firm at the wheel. Perhaps, with God's blessing, he might guide us safe to land.

I had not time to say more, when, with its pretty gray ponies, the curricle once more passed our way. Two ladies were in it: one leaned out and bowed. Presently a lackey came to beg Mr. Halifax would come and speak with Lady Caroline Brithwood.

"Shall you go, John?"

"Certainly—why not?" And he stepped forward to the carriage-side.

"Ah! delighted to see *mon beau cousin*.—This is he, Emma," turning to the lady who sat by her—oh, what a lovely face that lady had! no wonder it drove men mad; ay, even that brave man in whose honest life can be chronicled only this one sin, of being bewitched by her.

John caught the name—perhaps, too, he recognized the face—it was only too public, alas! His own took a sternness such as I had never before seen, and yet there was a trace of pity in it too.

"You are quite well. Indeed, he looks so—*n'est-ce pas, ma chère?*"

John bore gravely the eyes of the two ladies fixed on him, in rather too plain admiration—very gravely, too, he bowed.

"And what of our young bride, our treasure that we stole—nay, it was quite fair—quite fair. How is Ursula?"

"I thank you, Mrs. Halifax is well."

Lady Caroline smiled at the manner, courteous through all its coldness, which not ill became the young man. But she would not be repelled.

"I am delighted to have met you. Indeed, we must be friends. One's friends need not always be the same as one's husband's, eh, Emma? You will be enchanted with our fair bride. We must both seize the first opportunity, and come as disguised princesses to visit Mrs. Halifax."

"Again let me thank you, Lady Caroline. But——"

"No 'buts.' I am resolved. Mr. Brithwood will never find it out. And if he does—why, he may. I like you both; I intend us to be excellent friends, whenever I chance to be at Norton Bury. Don't be proud, and reject me, there's good people—the only good people I ever knew who were not disagreeable."

And leaning on her large ermine muff, she looked right into John's face, with the winning sweetness which Nature, not courts, lent to those fair features—already beginning to fade, already trying to hide by art their painful, premature decay.

John returned the look half sorrowfully; it was so hard to give back harshness to kindliness. But a light laugh from the other lady caught his ear, and his hesitation—if hesitation he had felt—was over.

"No, Lady Caroline, it cannot be. You will soon see yourself that it cannot. Living, as we do, in the same neighbourhood, we may meet occasionally by chance, and always, I hope, with kindly feeling; but under present circumstances—indeed, under any circumstances—intimacy between your house and ours would be impossible."

Lady Caroline shrugged her shoulders with a pretty air of pique. "As you will! I never trouble myself to court the friendship of any one. *Le jeu ne vaut pas la chandelle.*"

"Do not mistake me," John said earnestly. "Do not suppose I am ungrateful for your former kindness to my wife; but the difference between her and you—between your life and hers—is so extreme."

"*Vraiment!*" with another shrug and smile, rather a bitter one.

"Our two paths lie wide apart—wide as the poles; our house and our society would not suit you; and that my wife should ever enter yours"—glancing from one to the other of those two faces, painted with false roses, lit by false smiles—"No, Lady Caroline," he added firmly, "it is impossible."

She looked mortified for a moment, and then resumed her gaiety, which nothing could ever banish long.

"Hear him, Emma! So young and so unkindly! *Mais nous verrons.* You will change your mind. *Au revoir, mon beau cousin.*"

They drove off quickly, and were gone.

"John, what will Mrs. Halifax say?"

"My innocent girl! thank God she is safe away from them all—safe in a poor man's honest breast." He spoke with much emotion.

"Yet Lady Caroline——"

"Did you see who sat beside her?"

"That beautiful woman?"

"Poor soul! alas for her beauty! Phineas, that was Lady Hamilton."

He said no more, nor I. At my own door he left me, with his old merry laugh, his old familiar grasp of my shoulder.

"Lad, take care of thyself, though I'm not by to see. Remember, I am just as much thy tyrant as if I were living here still."

I smiled, and he went his way to his own quiet, blessed married home.

CHAPTER XXI.

THE winter and spring passed calmly by. I had much ill-health, and could go out very little; but they came constantly to me, John and Ursula, especially the latter. During this illness, when I learned to watch longingly for her kind face, and listen for her cheerful voice talking pleasantly and sisterly beside my chair, she taught me to give up "Mrs. Halifax," and call her Ursula. It was only by slow degrees I did so, truly; for she was not one of those gentle creatures whom, married or single, one calls instinctively by their Christian names. Her manner in girlhood was not exactly either "meek" or "gentle;" except towards him, the only one who ever ruled her, and to whom she was, through life, the meekest and tenderest of women. To every one else she comported herself, at least in youth, with a dignity and decision—a certain stand-offishness—so that, as I said, it was not quite easy to speak to or think of her as "Ursula." Afterwards, when seen in the light of a new character, for which Heaven destined and especially fitted her, and in which she appeared altogether beautiful—I began to give her another name—but it will come by-and-by.

In the long midsummer days, when our house was very quiet and rather dreary, I got into the habit of creeping over to John's home, and sitting for hours under the apple trees in his garden. It was now different from the wilderness he found it; the old trees were pruned and tended, and young ones planted. Mrs. Halifax called it proudly "our orchard," though the top of the tallest sapling could be reached with her hand. Then, in addition to the indigenous cabbages, came long rows of white-blossomed peas, big-headed cauliflowers, and all vegetables easy of cultivation. My father sent contributions from his celebrated gooseberry bushes, and his wall-fruit, the pride of Norton Bury; Mrs. Jessop stocked the borders from her great *parterres* of sweet-scented common flowers; so that, walled in as it was, and in the midst of a town likewise, it was growing into a very tolerable garden. Just the kind of garden that I love—half trim, half wild—fruits, flowers, and vegetables living in comfortable equality and fraternity, none being too choice to be harmed by their neighbours, none esteemed too mean to be restricted in their natural profusion. Oh, dear old-fashioned garden! full of sweet-williams and white-nancies, and larkspur and London-pride, and yard-wide beds of snowy saxifrage, and tall, pale evening primroses, and hollyhocks six or seven feet high, many-tinted, from yellow to darkest ruby colour; while for scents, large blushing cabbage-roses, pinks, gillyflowers, with here and there a great bush of southernwood or rosemary, or a border of thyme, or a sweet-brier hedge—a pleasant garden, where all colours and perfumes were blended together; ay, even a stray dandelion, that stood boldly up in his yellow waistcoat, like a young country bumpkin, who feels himself a decent lad in his way—or a plant of wild marjoram, that had somehow got in, and kept meekly in a corner of the bed, trying to turn into a respectable cultivated herb. Dear old garden!—such as one rarely sees nowadays!—I would give the finest modern pleasure-ground for the like of thee!

This was what John's garden became; its every inch and every flower still live in more memories than mine, and will for a generation yet; but I am speaking of it when it was young, like its gardeners. These were Mrs. Halifax and her husband, Jem and Jenny. The master could not do much; he had long, long hours in his business; but I used to watch Ursula, morning after morning, superintending her domain, with her faithful attendant Jem—Jem adored his "missis." Or else, when it was hot noon, I used to lie in their cool parlour, and listen to her voice and step about the house, teaching Jenny, or learning from her—for the young gentlewoman had much to learn, and was not ashamed of it either. She laughed at her own mistakes, and tried again; she never was idle or dull for a minute. She did a great deal in the house herself. Often she would sit chatting with me, having on her lap a coarse brown pan, shelling peas, slicing beans, picking gooseberries; her fingers—Miss March's fair fingers—looking fairer for the contrast with their unaccustomed work. Or else, in the summer evenings, she would be at the window sewing—always sewing—but so placed that with one glance she could see down the street where John was coming. Far, far off she always saw him; and at the sight her whole face would change and brighten, like a meadow when the sun comes out. Then she ran to open the door, and I could hear his low "my darling!" and a long, long pause in the hall.

They were very, very happy in those early days—those quiet days of poverty; when they visited nobody, and nobody visited them; when their whole world was bounded by the dark old house and the garden, with its four high walls.

One July night, I remember, John and I were walking up and down the paths by starlight. It was very hot weather, inclining one to stay without doors half the night. Ursula had been with us a good while, strolling about on her husband's arm; then he had sent her in to rest, and we two remained out together.

How soft they were, those faint, misty, summer stars! What a mysterious, perfumy haze they let fall over us! A haze through which all around seemed melting away in delicious intangible sweetness, in which the very sky above our heads—the shining, world-besprinkled sky—was a thing felt rather than seen.

"How strange all seems! how unreal!" said John in a low voice, when he had walked the length of the garden in silence. "Phineas, how very strange it seems!"

"What seems?"

"What ?—oh, everything." He hesitated a minute. "No, not everything—but something which to me seems now to fill and be mixed up with all I do, or think, or feel. Something you do not know—but to-night Ursula said I might tell you."

Nevertheless he was several minutes before he told me.

"This pear tree is full of fruit—is it not ? How thick they hang ; and yet it seems but yesterday that Ursula and I were standing here, trying to count the blossoms."

He stopped—touching a branch with his hand. His voice sank so I could hardly hear it.

"Do you know, Phineas, that when this tree is bare —we shall, if with God's blessing all goes well—we shall have—a little child."

I wrung his hand in silence.

"You cannot imagine how strange it feels. A child —hers and mine—little feet to go pattering about our house—a little voice to say—— Think, that by Christmas-time I shall be *a father*."

He sat down on the garden bench, and did not speak for a long time.

"I wonder," he said at last, "if, when I was born, *my* father was as young as I am ; whether he felt as I do now. You cannot think what an awful joy it is to be looking forward to a child ; a little soul of God's giving, to be made fit for His eternity. How shall we do it ! we that are both so ignorant, so young—she will be only just nineteen when, please God, her baby is born. Sometimes, of an evening, we sit for hours on this bench, she and I, talking of what we ought to do, and how we ought to rear the little thing, until we fall into silence, awed at the blessing that is coming to us."

"God will help you both, and make you wise."

"We trust He will ; and then we are not afraid."

A little while longer I sat by John's side, catching the dim outline of his face, half uplifted, looking towards those myriad worlds, which we are taught to believe, and do believe, are not more precious in the Almighty's sight than one living human soul.

But he said no more of the hope that was coming, or of the thoughts which, in the holy hush of that summer night, had risen out of the deep of his heart. And though after this time they never again formed themselves into words, yet he knew well that not a hope, or joy, or fear of his, whether understood or not, could be unshared by me.

In the winter, when the first snow lay on the ground, the little one came.

It was a girl—I think they had wished for a son; but they forgot all about it when the tiny maiden appeared. She was a pretty baby—at least, all the womenkind said so, from Mrs. Jessop down to Jael, who left our poor house to its own devices, and trod stately in Mrs. Halifax's, exhibiting to all beholders the mass of white draperies with the infinitesimal human morsel inside them, which she vehemently declared was the very image of its father.

For that young father——

But I—what can *I* say? How should *I* tell of the joy of a man over his first-born?

I did not see John till a day afterwards—when he came into our house, calm, happy, smiling. But Jael told me that when she first placed his baby in his arms he had wept like a child.

The little maiden grew with the snowdrops. Winter might have dropped her out of his very lap, so exceedingly fair, pale, and pure-looking was she. I had never seen, or at least never noticed, any young baby before; but she crept into my heart before I was aware. I seem to have a clear remembrance of all the data in her still and quiet infancy, from the time her week-old fingers, with their tiny pink nails—a ludicrous picture of her father's hand in little—made me smile as they closed over mine.

She was named Muriel—after the rather peculiar name of John's mother. Her own mother would have it so; only wishing out of her full heart, happy one! that there should be a slight alteration made in the second name. Therefore the baby was called Muriel Joy—Muriel Joy Halifax.

That name—beautiful, sacred, and never-to-be-forgotten among us—I write it now with tears.

* * * * * *

In December 1802 she was born—our Muriel. And on February 9th—alas! I have need to remember the date!—she formally received her name. We all dined at John's house—Dr. and Mrs. Jessop, my father and I.

It was the first time my father had taken a meal under any roof but his own for twenty years. We had not expected him, since, when asked and entreated, he only shook his head; but just when we were all sitting down to the table, Ursula at the foot, her cheeks flushed, and her lips dimpling with a housewifely delight that everything was so nice and neat, she startled us by a little cry of pleasure. And there, in the doorway, stood my father!

His broad figure, but slightly bent even now, his smooth-shaven face, withered, but of a pale brown still, with the hard lines softening down, and the keen eyes kinder than they used to be; dressed carefully in his First-day clothes, the stainless white kerchief supporting his large chin, his Quaker's hat in one hand, his stick in the other, looking in at us, a half-amused twitch mingling with the gravity of his mouth—thus he stood—thus I see thee, oh my dear old father!

The young couple seemed as if they never could welcome him enough. He only said, "I thank thee, John," "I thank thee, Ursula;" and took his place beside the latter, giving no reason why he had changed his mind and come. Simple as the dinner was—simple as befitted those who, their guests knew, could not honestly afford luxuries; though there were no ornaments, save the centre nosegay of laurustinus and white Christmas roses—I do not think King George himself ever sat down to a nobler feast.

Afterwards we drew merrily round the fire, or watched outside the window the thickly falling snow.

"It has not snowed these two months," said John—"never since the day our little girl was born."

And at that moment, as if she heard herself mentioned, and was indignant at our having forgotten her so long, the little maid upstairs set up a cry—that unmistakable child's cry which seems to change the whole atmosphere of a household.

My father gave a start—he had never seen or expressed a wish to see John's daughter. We knew he did not like babies. Again the little helpless wail; Ursula rose and stole away—Abel Fletcher looked after her with a curious expression, then began to say something about going back to the tanyard.

"Do not, pray do not leave us," John entreated; "Ursula wants to show you our little lady."

My father put out his hands in deprecation; or as if desiring to thrust from him a host of thronging, battling thoughts. Still came faintly down at intervals the tiny voice, dropping into a soft coo of pleasure, like a wood-dove in its nest—every mother knows the sound. And then Mrs. Halifax entered holding in her arms her little winter flower, her baby-daughter.

Abel Fletcher just looked at it and her—closed his eyes against both, and looked no more.

Ursula seemed pained a moment, but soon forgot it in the general admiration of her treasure.

"She might well come in a snowstorm," said Mrs. Jessop, taking the child. "She is just like snow, so soft and white."

"And as soundless—she hardly ever cries. She just lies in this way half the day over, cooing quietly, with her eyes shut. There, she has caught your dress fast. Now, was there ever a two months' old baby so quick at noticing things? And she does it all with her fingers—she touches everything—ah, take care, doctor," the mother added reproachfully, at a loud slam of the door, which made the baby tremble all over.

"I never knew a child so susceptible of sounds," said John, as he began talking to it and soothing it—how strange it was to see him! and yet it seemed quite natural already. "I think even now she knows the difference between her mother's voice and mine; and any sudden noise always startles her in this way."

"She must have astonishingly quick hearing," said the doctor, slightly annoyed. Ursula wisely began to talk of something else—showed Muriel's eyelashes, very long for such a baby—and descanted on the colour of her eyes, that fruitful and never-ending theme of mothers and friends.

"I think they are like her father's; yes, certainly like her father's. But we have not many opportunities of judging, for she is such a lazy young damsel, she hardly ever opens them—we should often fancy her asleep, but for that little soft coo; and then she will wake up all of a sudden. There now! do you see her? Come to the window, my beauty, and show Dr. Jessop your bonny brown eyes."

They were bonny eyes! lovely in shape and colour, delicately fringed; but there was something strange in their expression—or rather, in their want of it. Many babies have a round, vacant stare—but this was no stare, only a wide, full look—a look of quiet blankness—an *unseeing* look.

It caught Dr. Jessop's notice. I saw his air of vexed dignity change into a certain anxiety.

"Well, whose are they like—her father's or mine? His, I hope—it will be the better for her beauty. Nay, we'll excuse all compliments."

"I—I can't exactly tell. I could judge better by candlelight."

"We'll have candles."

"No—no! Had we not better put it off altogether till another day? I'll call in to-morrow and look at her eyes."

His manner was hesitating and troubled. John noticed it.

"Love, give her to me. Go and get us lights, will you?"

When she was gone, John took his baby to the window, gazed long and intently into her little face, then at Dr. Jessop. "Do you think—no—it's not possible—that there can be anything the matter with the child's eyes?"

Ursula, coming in, heard the last words.

"What was that you said about baby's eyes?"

No one answered her. All were gathered in a group at the window, the child being held on her father's lap, while Dr. Jessop was trying to open the small white lids, kept so continually closed. At last the baby uttered a little cry of pain—the mother darted forward, and clasped it almost savagely to her breast.

"I will not have my baby hurt! There is nothing wrong with her sweet eyes. Go away; you shall not touch her, John."

"Love!"

She melted at that low, fond word; leaning against his shoulder—trying to control her tears.

"It shocked me so—the bare thought of such a thing. Oh, husband, don't let her be looked at again."

"Only once again, my darling. It is best. Then we shall be quite satisfied. Phineas, give me the candle."

The words—caressing, and by strong constraint made calm and soothing—were yet firm. Ursula resisted no more, but let him take Muriel—little, unconscious, cooing dove! Lulled by her father's voice, she once more opened her eyes wide. Dr. Jessop passed the candle before them many times, once so close that it almost touched her face; but the full, quiet eyes never blenched nor closed. He set the light down.

"Doctor!" whispered the father, in a wild appeal against—ay, it was against certainty. He snatched the candle, and tried the experiment himself.

"She does not see at all. Can she be blind?"

"Born blind."

Yes, those pretty baby eyes were dark—quite dark. There was nothing painful nor unnatural in their look, save, perhaps, the blankness of gaze which I have before noticed. Outwardly, their organization was perfect; but in the fine inner mechanism was something wrong—something wanting. She never had seen—never would see—in this world.

"*Blind!*" The word was uttered softly, hardly above a breath, yet the mother heard it. She pushed every one aside, and took the child herself. Herself, with a desperate incredulity, she looked into those eyes, which never could look back either her agony or her love. Poor mother!

"John! John! O John!"—the name rising into a cry, as if he could surely help her. He came and took her in his arms—took both, wife and babe. She laid her head on his shoulder in bitter weeping. "O John! it is so hard. Our pretty one—our own little child!"

John did not speak, but only held her to him—close and fast. When she was a little calmer, he whispered to her the comfort—the sole comfort even her husband could give her—through whose will it was that this affliction came.

"And it is more an affliction to you than it will be to her, poor pet!" said Mrs. Jessop, as she wiped her friendly eyes. "She will not miss what she never knew. She may be a happy little child. Look how she lies and smiles."

But the mother could not take that consolation yet. She walked to and fro, and stood rocking her baby, mute indeed, but with tears falling in showers. Gradually her anguish wept itself away, or was smothered down, lest it should disturb the little creature asleep on her breast.

Some one came behind her, and placed her in the arm-chair gently. It was my father. He sat down by her, taking her hand.

"Grieve not, Ursula. I had a little brother who was blind. He was the happiest creature I ever knew."

My father sighed. We all marvelled to see the wonderful softness, even tenderness, which had come into him.

"Give me thy child for a minute." Ursula laid it across his knees; he put his hand solemnly on the baby breast. "God bless this little one! Ay, and she shall be blessed."

These words, spoken with as full assurance as the prophetic benediction of the departing patriarchs of old, struck us all. We looked at little Muriel, as if the blessing were already upon her; as if the mysterious touch which had sealed up her eyes for ever had left on her a sanctity like as of one who has been touched by the finger of God.

"Now, children, I must go home," said my father.

They did not detain us; it was indeed best that the poor young parents should be left alone.

"You will come again soon?" begged Ursula, tenderly clasping the hand which he had laid upon her curls as he rose with another murmured "God bless thee!"

"Perhaps. We never know. Be a good wife to thy husband, my girl. And, John, never be thou harsh to her, nor too hard upon her little failings. She is but young—but young."

He sighed again. It was plain to see he was thinking of another than Ursula.

As we walked down the street he spoke to me only once or twice, and then of things which startled me by their strangeness—things which had happened a long time ago; sayings and doings of mine in my childhood, which I had not the least idea he had either known of or remembered.

When we got indoors, I asked if I should come and sit with him till his bedtime.

"No—no; thee looks tired, and I have a business letter to write. Better go to thy bed as usual."

I bade him good-night, and was going, when he called me back.

"How old art thee, Phineas—twenty-four or five?"

"Twenty-five, father."

"Eh, so much?" He put his hand on my shoulder, and looked down on me kindly, even tenderly. "Thee art but weakly still, but thee must pick up, and live to be as old a man as thy father. Good-night. God be with thee, my son!"

I left him. I was happy. Once I had never expected my old father and I would have got on together so well, or loved one another so dearly.

In the middle of the night Jael came into my room, and sat down on my bed's foot, looking at me. I had been dreaming strangely about my own childish days and about my father and mother when we were young.

What Jael told me—by slow degrees, and as tenderly as when she was my nurse years ago—seemed at first so unreal as to be like a part of the dream.

At ten o'clock, when she had locked up the house, she had come as usual to the parlour door, to tell my father it was bedtime. He did not answer, being sitting with his back to the door, apparently busy writing. So she went away.

Half an hour afterwards she came again. He sat there still—he had not moved. One hand supported his head; the other, the fingers stiffly holding the pen, lay on the table. He seemed intently gazing on what he had written. It ran thus:—

"Good Friend,—To-morrow I shall be——"

But there the hand had stopped—for ever.

O dear father! on that to-morrow thou wert with God!

CHAPTER XXII.

It was the year 1812. I had lived for ten years as a brother in my adopted brother's house, whither he had brought me on the day of my father's funeral; entreating that I should never leave it again. For, as was shortly afterwards made clear, fate—say Providence—was now inevitably releasing him from a bond, from which, so long as my poor father lived, John would never have released himself. It was discovered that the profits of the tanning trade had long been merely nominal—that of necessity, for the support of our two families, the tanyard must be sold, and the business confined entirely to the flour-mill.

At this crisis, as if the change of all things broke her stout old heart, which never could bend to any new ways—Jael died. We laid her at my father's and mother's feet—poor old Jael! and that graveyard in St. Mary's Lane now covered over all who loved me, all who were of my youth day—my very own.

So thought I—or might have thought—but that John and Ursula then demanded with one voice, "Brother, come home."

I resisted long: for it is one of my decided opinions that married people ought to have no one, be the tie ever so close and dear, living permanently with them, to break the sacred duality—no, let me say the unity—of their home.

I wished to try and work for my living, if that were possible—if not, that out of the wreck of my father's trade might be found enough to keep me in some poor way. But John Halifax would not hear of that. And Ursula—she was sitting sewing, while the little one lay on her lap, cooing softly with shut eyes—Ursula took my hand to play with Muriel's. The baby fingers closed over mine. "See there, Phineas; *she* wants you too." So I stayed.

Perhaps it was on this account that better than all his other children, better than anything on earth except himself, I loved John's eldest daughter, little blind Muriel.

He had several children now. The dark old house and the square town garden were alive with their voices from morning till night. First, and loudest always, was Guy—born the year after Muriel. He was very like his mother, and her darling. After him came two more, Edwin and Walter. But Muriel still remained as "sister"—the only sister either given or desired.

If I could find a name to describe that child, it would

be not the one her happy mother gave her at her birth, but one more sacred, more tender. She was better than Joy—she was an embodied Peace.

Her motions were slow and tranquil—her voice soft—every expression of her little face extraordinarily serene. Whether creeping about the house, with a footfall silent as snow, or sitting among us, either knitting busily at her father's knee, or listening to his talk and the children's play, everywhere and always Muriel was the same. No one ever saw her angry, restless, or sad. The soft dark calm in which she lived seemed never broken by the troubles of this our troublous world.

She was, as I have said, from her very babyhood a living peace. And such she was to us all, during those ten struggling years, when our household had much to contend with, much to endure. If at night her father came home jaded and worn, sickened to the soul by the hard battle he had to fight daily, hourly, with the outside world, Muriel would come softly and creep into his bosom, and he was comforted. If, busying herself about, doing faithfully her portion too, that the husband when he came in of evenings might find all cheerful and never know how heavy had been the household cares during the day—if, at times, Ursula's voice took too sharp a tone, at sight of Muriel it softened at once. No one could speak any but soft and sweet words when the blind child was by.

Yet I think either parent would have looked amazed had any one pitied them for having a blind child. The loss—a loss only to them, and not to her, the darling!—became familiar, and ceased to wound; the blessedness was ever new. "*Ay, and she shall be blessed,*" had said my dear father. So she was. From her, or for her, her parents never had to endure a single pain. Even the sicknesses of infancy and childhood, of which the three others had their natural share, always passed her by, as if in pity. Nothing ever ailed Muriel.

The spring of 1812 was an era long remembered in our family. Scarlet fever went through the house—

safely, but leaving much care behind. When at last they all came round, and we were able to gather our pale little flock to a garden feast under the big old pear tree, it was with the trembling thankfulness of those who have gone through great perils, hardly dared to be recognized as such till they were over.

"Ay, thank God it is over!" said John, as he put his arm round his wife, and looked in her worn face, where still her own smile lingered—her bright, brave smile, that nothing could ever drive away. "And now we must try and make a little holiday for you."

"Nonsense! I am as well as possible. Did not Dr. Jessop tell me this morning I was looking younger than ever? I—a mother of a family, thirty years old?—Pray, Uncle Phineas, do I look my age?"

I could not say she did not—especially now. But she wore it so gracefully, so carelessly, that I saw—ay, and truly her husband saw—a sacred beauty about her jaded cheek, more lovely and lovable than all the bloom of her youth. Happy woman! who was not afraid of growing old.

"Love"—John usually called her "Love"—putting it at the beginning of a sentence, as if it had been her natural Christian name—which, as in all infant households, had been gradually dropped or merged into the universal title of "mother." My name for her was always emphatically "the mother"—the truest type of motherhood I ever knew.

"Love," her husband began again, after a long look in her face—ah, John, thine was altered too, but himself was the last thing *he* thought of—"say what you like —I know what we'll do, for the children's sake. Ah, that's her weak point—see, Phineas, she is yielding now. We'll go for three months to Longfield."

Now Longfield was the Utopia of our family, old and young. A very simple family we must have been—for this Longfield was only a small farmhouse, about six miles off, where once we had been to tea, and where ever since we had longed to live. For, pretty as our domain had grown, it was still in the middle of a town, and the children, like all naturally-reared children, craved after the freedom of the country—after cornfields, hayfields, nuttings, blackberryings—delights hitherto known only at rare intervals, when their father could spare a whole long day, and be at once the sun and the shield of the happy little band.

"Hearken, children! father says we shall go for three whole months to live at Longfield."

The three boys set up a shout of ecstasy.

"I'll swim boats down the stream, and catch and ride every one of the horses. Hurrah!" shouted Guy.

"And I'll see after the ducks and chickens, and watch all the threshing and winnowing," said Edwin, the practical and grave.

"And I'll get a 'ittle 'amb to p'ay wid me," lisped Walter—still the "baby"—or considered such, and petted accordingly.

"But what does my little daughter say?" said the father, turning—as he always turned, at the lightest touch of those soft, blind fingers, creeping along his coat sleeve. "What will Muriel do at Longfield?"

"Muriel will sit all day and hear the birds sing."

"So she shall, my blessing!" He often called her his "blessing," which in truth she was. To see her now leaning her cheek against his—the small soft face, almost a miniature of his own, the hair, a paler shade of the same bright colour, curling in the same elastic rings—they looked less like ordinary father and daughter than like a man and his good angel; the visible embodiment of the best half of his soul. So she was ever to him, this child of his youtn—his first-born and his dearest.

The Longfield plan being once started, father and mother and I began to consult together as to ways and means; what should be given up, and what increased, of our absolute luxuries, in order that the children might this summer—possibly every summer—have the glory of "living in the country." Of these domestic consultations there was never any dread, for they were always held in public. There were no secrets in our house. Father and mother, though sometimes holding different opinions, had but one thought, one aim—the family good. Thus, even in our lowest estate, there had been no bitterness in our poverty; we met it, looked it in the face, often even laughed at it. For it bound us all together, hand in hand; it taught us endurance, self-dependence, and, best of all lessons, self-renunciation. I think one's whole after-life is made easier and more blessed by having known what it was to be very poor when one was young.

Our fortunes were rising now, and any little pleasure did not take near so much contrivance. We found we could manage the Longfield visit—ay, and a horse for John to ride to and fro—without any worse sacrifice than that of leaving Jenny—now Mrs. Jem Watkins, but our cook still—in the house at Norton Bury, and doing with one servant instead of two. Also, though this was not publicly known till afterwards, by the mother's renouncing a long-promised silk dress—the only one since her marriage, in which she had determined to astonish John by choosing the same colour as that identical gray gown he had seen hanging up in the kitchen at Enderley.

"But one would give up anything," she said, "that the children might have such a treat, and that father might have rides backwards and forwards through green lanes all summer. Oh, how I wish we could always live in the country!"

"Do you?" And John looked—much as he had looked at long-tailed gray ponies in his bridegroom days—longing to give her everything she desired. "Well, perhaps we may manage it some time."

"When our ship comes in—namely, that money which Richard Brithwood will not pay, and John Halifax will not go to law to make him. Nay, father dear, I am not going to quarrel with any one of your crotchets." She spoke with a fond pride, as she did always, even when arguing against the too quixotic carrying out of the said crotchets. "Perhaps, as the reward of forbearance, the money will come some day when we least expect it; then John shall have his heart's desire, and start the cloth-mills at Enderley."

John smiled half sadly. Every man has a hobby—this was his, and had been for fifteen years. Not merely the making a fortune, as he still firmly believed it could be made, but the position of useful power, the wide range of influence, the infinite opportunities of doing good.

"No, love; I shall never be 'patriarch of the valley,' as Phineas used to call it. The yew hedge is too thick for me, eh, Phineas?"

"No!" cried Ursula—we had told her this little incident of our boyhood—"you have got half through it already. Everybody in Norton Bury knows and respects you. I am sure, Phineas, you might have heard a pin fall at the meeting last night when he spoke against hanging the Luddites. And such a shout as rose when he ended—oh, how proud I was!"

"Of the shout, love?"

"Nonsense!—but of the cause of it. Proud to see my husband defending the poor and the oppressed—proud to see him honoured and looked up to, more and more every year, till——"

"Till it may come at last to the prophecy in your birthday verse—'Her husband is known in the gates; he sitteth among the elders of the land.'"

Mrs. Halifax laughed at me for reminding her of this, but allowed that she would not dislike its being fulfilled.

"And it will be too. He is already 'known in the gates;' known far and near. Think how many of our neighbours come to John to settle their differences, instead of going to law! And how many poachers has he not persuaded out of their dishonest——"

"Illegal," corrected John.

"Well, their illegal ways, and made decent, respectable men of them! Then, see how he is consulted, and his opinion followed, by rich folk as well as poor folk, all about the neighbourhood. I am sure John is as popular, and has as much influence, as many a member of Parliament."

John smiled with an amused twitch about his mouth, but he said nothing. He rarely did say anything about himself—not even in his own household. The glory of his life was its unconsciousness—like our own silent Severn, however broad and grand its current might be, that course seemed the natural channel into which it flowed.

"There's Muriel," said the father, listening.

Often thus the child slipped away, and suddenly we heard all over the house the sweet sounds of "Muriel's voice," as some one had called the old harpsichord. When almost a baby she would feel her way to it, and find out first harmonies, then tunes, with that quickness and delicacy of ear peculiar to the blind.

"How well she plays! I wish I could buy her one of those new instruments they call 'pianofortes;' I was looking into the mechanism of one the other day."

"She would like an organ better. You should have seen her face in the Abbey church this morning."

"Hark! she has stopped playing. Guy, run and bring your sister here," said the father, ever yearning after his darling.

Guy came back with a wonderful story of two gentlemen in the parlour, one of whom had patted his head—"Such a grand gentleman, a great deal grander than father!"

That was true, as regarded the bright nankeens, the blue coat with gold buttons, and the showiest of cambric kerchiefs swathing him up to the very chin. To this "grand" personage John bowed formally, but his wife flushed up in surprised recognition.

"It is so long since I had the happiness of meeting Miss March, that I conclude Mrs. Halifax has forgotten me?"

"No, Lord Luxmore, allow me to introduce my husband."

And, I fancied, some of Miss March's old hauteur returned to the mother's softened and matronly mien—pride, but not for herself or in herself now. For, truly, as the two men stood together—though Lord Luxmore had been handsome in his youth, and was universally said to have as fine manners as the Prince Regent himself—any woman might well have held her head loftily, introducing John Halifax as "my husband."

Of the two, the nobleman was least at his ease, for the welcome of both Mr. and Mrs. Halifax, though courteous, was decidedly cold. They did not seem to feel—and, if rumour spoke true, I doubt if any honest, virtuous, middle-class fathers and mothers would have felt—that their house was greatly honoured or sanctified by the presence of the Earl of Luxmore.

But the nobleman was, as I have said, wonderfully fine-mannered. He broke the ice at once.

"Mr. Halifax, I have long wished to know you.—Mrs. Halifax, my daughter encouraged me to pay this impromptu visit."

Here ensued polite inquiries after Lady Caroline Brithwood; we learned that she was just returned from abroad, and was entertaining, at the Mythe House, her father and brother.

"Pardon—I was forgetting my son—Lord Ravenel."

The youth thus presented merely bowed. He was about eighteen or so, tall and spare, with thin features and large soft eyes. He soon retreated to the garden door, where he stood, watching the boys play, and shyly attempting to make friends with Muriel.

"I believe Ravenel has seen you years ago, Mrs. Halifax. His sister made a great pet of him as a child. He has just completed his education—at the College of St. Omer, was it not, William?"

"The Catholic college of St. Omer," repeated the boy.

"Tut—what matters!" said the father sharply. "Mr. Halifax, do not imagine we are a Catholic family still. I hope the next Earl of Luxmore will be able to take the oaths and his seat, whether or no we get Emancipation. By-the-bye, you uphold the Bill?"

John assented; expressing his conviction, then unhappily a rare one, that every one's conscience is free; and that all men of blameless life ought to be protected by, and allowed to serve the State, whatever be their religious opinions.

"Mr. Halifax, I entirely agree with you. A wise man esteems all faiths alike worthless."

"Excuse me, my lord, that was the very last thing I meant to say. I hold every man's faith so sacred, that no other man has a right to interfere with it, or to question it. The matter lies solely between himself and his Maker."

"Exactly! What facility of expression your husband has, Mrs. Halifax! He must be—indeed, I have heard he is—a first-rate public speaker."

The wife smiled, wifelike; but John said hurriedly,—

"I have no pretension or ambition of the kind. I merely now and then try to put plain truths, or what I believe to be such, before the people, in a form they are able to understand."

"Ay, that is it. My dear sir, the people have no more brains than the head of my cane (his Royal Highness's gift, Mrs. Halifax); they must be led or driven, like a flock of sheep. We"—a lordly "we!"—"are their proper shepherds. But, then, we want a middle class—at least, an occasional voice from it, a——"

"A shepherd's dog, to give tongue," said John dryly. "In short, a public orator. In the House, or out of it?"

"Both." And the earl tapped his boot with that royal cane, smiling. "Yes; I see you apprehend me. But, before we commence that somewhat delicate subject, there was another on which I desired my agent, Mr. Brown, to obtain your valuable opinion."

"You mean, when, yesterday, he offered me, by your lordship's express desire, the lease, lately fallen in, of your cloth-mills at Enderley?"

Now, John had not told us that!—why, his manner too plainly showed.

"And all will be arranged, I trust? Brown says you have long wished to take the mills; I shall be most happy to have you for a tenant."

"My lord, as I told your agent, it is impossible. We will say no more about it."

John crossed over to his wife with a cheerful air. She sat looking grave and sad.

Lord Luxmore had the reputation of being a keen-witted, diplomatic personage; undoubtedly he had, or could assume, that winning charm of manner which had descended in perfection to his daughter. Both qualities it pleased him to exercise now. He rose, addressing with kindly frankness the husband and wife.

"If I may ask—being a most sincere well-wisher of yours, and a sort of connection of Mrs. Halifax's, too—why is it impossible?"

"I have no wish to disguise the reason; it is because I have no capital."

Lord Luxmore looked surprised. "Surely—excuse me, but I had the honour of being well acquainted with the late Mr. March—surely, your wife's fortune——"

Ursula rose in her old impetuous way. "His wife's fortune!—(John, let me say it!—I will, I must!)—of his wife's fortune, Lord Luxmore, he has never received one farthing. Richard Brithwood keeps it back; and my husband would work day and night for me and our children rather than go to law."

"Oh, on principle, I suppose? I have heard of such opinions," said the earl, with the slightest perceptible sneer. "And you agree with him?"

"I do, heartily. I would rather we lived poor all our days than that he should wear his life out, trouble his spirit, perhaps even soil his conscience, by squabbling with a bad man over money matters."

It was good to see Ursula as she spoke; good to see the look that husband and his wife interchanged—husband and wife, different in many points, yet so blessedly, so safely *one!* Then John said in his quiet way,—

"Love, perhaps another subject than our own affairs would be more interesting to Lord Luxmore."

"Not at all—not at all!" And the earl was evidently puzzled and annoyed. "Such extraordinary conduct," he muttered: "so very—ahem!—unwise. If the matter were known—caught up by those newspapers—I must really have a little conversation with Brithwood."

The conversation paused, and John changed it entirely by making some remarks on the present minister, Mr Percival.

"I liked his last speech much. He seems a clear-headed, honest man, for all his dogged opposition to the Bill."

"He will never oppose it more."

"Nay, I think he will, my lord—to the death."

"That may be—and yet——" his lordship smiled. "Mr. Halifax, I have just had news by a carrier-pigeon—my birds fly well—most important news for us and our party. Yesterday, in the lobby of the House of Commons, Mr. Percival was shot."

We all started. An hour ago we had been reading his speech. Mr. Percival shot!

"O John," cried the mother, her eyes full of tears; "his poor wife—his fatherless children!"

And for many minutes they stood, hearing the lamentable history, and looking at their little ones at play in the garden; thinking, as many an English father and mother did that day, of the stately house in London, where the widow and orphans bewailed their dead. He might or might not be a great statesman, but he was undoubtedly a good man; many still remember the shock of his untimely death, and how, whether or not they liked him living, all the honest hearts of England mourned for Mr. Percival.

Possibly that number did not include the Earl of Luxmore.

"*Requiescat in pace!* I shall propose the canonization of poor Bellingham. For now Percival is dead, there will be an immediate election; and on that election depends Catholic Emancipation. Mr. Halifax," turning quickly round to him, "you would be of great use to us in Parliament."

"Should I?"

"Will you—I like plain speaking—will you enter it?"

Enter Parliament! John Halifax in Parliament! His wife and I were both astounded by the suddenness of the possibility, which, however, John himself seemed to receive as no novel idea.

Lord Luxmore continued, "I assure you nothing is more easy; I can bring you in at once, for a borough near here—my family borough."

"Which you wish to be held by some convenient person till Lord Ravenel comes of age? So Mr. Brown informed me yesterday."

Lord Luxmore slightly frowned. Such transactions, as common then in the service of the country as they still are in the service of the Church, were yet generally glossed over, as if a certain discredit attached to them. The young lord seemed to feel it; at sound of his name he turned round to listen, and turned back again, blushing scarlet. Not so the earl, his father.

"Brown is—(may I offer you a pinch, Mr. Halifax?—what, not the Prince Regent's own mixture?)—Brown is indeed a worthy fellow, but too hasty in his conclusions. As it happens, my son is yet undecided between the Church—that is, the priesthood, and politics. But to our conversation—Mrs. Halifax, may I not enlist you on my side? We could easily remove all difficulties, such as qualification, etc. Would you not like to see your husband member for the old and honourable borough of Kingswell?"

"Kingswell!" It was a tumble-down village, where John held and managed for me the sole remnant of landed property which my poor father had left me. "Kingswell! why, there are not a dozen houses in the place."

"The fewer the better, my dear madam. The election would cost me scarcely any—trouble; and the country be vastly the gainer by your husband's talents and probity. Of course, he will give up the—I forget what is his business now—and live independent. He is made to shine as a politician: it will be both happiness and honour to myself to have in some way contributed to that end.—Mr. Halifax, you will accept my borough?"

"Not on any consideration your lordship could offer me."

Lord Luxmore scarcely credited his ears. "My dear sir—you are the most extraordinary—may I again inquire your reasons?"

"I have several; one will suffice. Though I wish to gain influence—power perhaps; still the last thing I should desire would be political influence."

"You might possibly escape that unwelcome possession," returned the earl. "Half the House of Commons is made up of harmless dummies, who vote as we bid them."

"A character, my lord, for which I am decidedly unfitted. Until political conscience ceases to be a thing of traffic, until the people are allowed honestly to choose their own honest representatives, I must decline being of that number. Shall we dismiss the subject?"

"With pleasure, sir."

And courtesy being met by courtesy, the question so momentous was passed over, and merged into trivialities. Perhaps the earl, who, as his pleasures palled, was understood to be fixing his keen wits upon the pet profligacy of old age, politics—saw clearly enough that in these chaotic days of contending parties, when the maddened outcry of the "people" was just being heard and listened to, it might be as well not to make an enemy of this young man, who, with a few more, stood as it were midway in the gulf, now slowly beginning to narrow, between the commonalty and the aristocracy.

He stayed some time longer, and then bowed himself away with a gracious condescension worthy of the Prince of Wales himself, carrying with him the shy, gentle Lord Ravenel, who had spoken scarcely six words the whole time.

When he was gone, the father and mother seemed both relieved.

"Truly, John, he has gained little by his visit, and I hope it may be long before we see an earl in our quiet house again. Come in to dinner, my children."

But his lordship had left an uncomfortable impression behind him. It lasted even until that quiet hour—often the quietest and happiest of our day—when, the children being all in bed, we elders closed in round the fire.

Ursula and I sat there, longer alone than usual.

"John is late to-night," she said more than once; and I could see her start, listening to every foot under the window, every touch at the door-bell; not stirring, though: she knew his foot and his ring quite well always.

"There he is!" we both said at once—much relieved; and John came in.

Brightness always came in with him. Whatever cares he had without—and they were heavy enough, God knows—they always seemed to slip off the moment he entered his own door; and whatever slight cares we had at home, we put them aside; as they could not but be put aside—nay, forgotten—at the sight of him.

"Well, Uncle Phineas!—Children all right, my darling? A fire; I'm glad of it. Truly to-night is as cold as November."

"John, if you have a weakness, it is for fire. You're a regular salamander."

He laughed—warming his hands at the blaze. "Yes, I would rather be hungry than cold, any day. Love, our one extravagance is certainly coals. A grand fire this! I do like it so!"

She called him "foolish;" but smoothed down with a quiet kiss the forehead he lifted up to her as she stood beside him, looking as if she would any day have converted the whole house into fuel for his own private and particular benefit.

"Little ones all in bed, of course?"

"Indeed, they would have lain awake half the night—those naughty boys—talking of Longfield. You never saw children so delighted."

"Are they?" I thought the tone was rather sad, and that the father sat listening with less interest than usual to the pleasant little household chronicle, always wonderful and always new, which it was his custom to ask for and have, night after night, when he came home—saying it was to him, after his day's toil, like a "babbling o' green fields." Soon it stopped.

"John, dear, you are very tired?"

"Rather."

"Have you been very busy all day?"

"Very busy."

I understood, almost as well as his wife did, what those brief answers indicated; so, stealing away to the table where Guy's blurred copy-book and Edwin's astonishing addition sums were greatly in need of Uncle Phineas, I left the fireside corner to those two. Soon John settled himself in my easy-chair, and then one saw how very weary he was—weary in body and soul alike—weary as we seldom beheld him. It went to my heart to watch the listless stretch of his large, strong frame—the sharp lines about his mouth—lines which ought not to have come there in his two-and-thirty years. And his eyes—they hardly looked like John's eyes, as they gazed in a sort of dull quietude, too anxious to be dreamy, into the red coals—and nowhere else.

At last he roused himself, and took up his wife's work.

"More little coats! Love, you are always sewing."

"Mothers must, you know. And I think never did boys outgrow their things like our boys. It is pleasant, too. If only clothes did not wear out so fast."

"Ah!" A sigh—from the very depths of the father's heart.

"Not a bit too fast for my clever fingers, though," said Ursula quickly. "Look, John, at this lovely braiding. But I'm not going to do any more of it. I shall certainly have no time to waste over fineries at Longfield."

Her husband took up the fanciful work, admired it, and laid it down again. After a pause he said,—

"Should you be very much disappointed if—if we do not go to Longfield after all?"

"Not go to Longfield!" The involuntary exclamation showed how deep her longing had been.

"Because I am afraid—it is hard, I know—but I am afraid we cannot manage it. Are you very sorry?"

"Yes," she said, frankly and truthfully. "Not so much for myself, but—the children."

"Ay, the poor children."

Ursula stitched away rapidly for some moments, till the grieved look faded out of her face; then she turned it, all cheerful once more, to her husband. "Now, John, tell me. Never mind about the children. Tell me."

He told her, as was his habit at all times, of some losses which had to-day befallen him—bad debts in his business—which would make it, if not impracticable, at least imprudent, to enter on any new expenses that year. Nay, he must, if possible, retrench a little. Ursula listened, without question, comment, or complaint.

"Is that all?" she said at last, very gently.

"All."

"Then never mind. I do not. We will find some other pleasures for the children. We have so many pleasures, ay, all of us. Husband, it is not so hard to give up this one."

He said, in a whisper, low almost as a lover's, "I could give up anything in the world but them and thee."

So, with a brief information to me at supper-time—"Uncle Phineas, did you hear? we cannot go to Longfield"—the renunciation was made, and the subject ended. For this year, at least, our Arcadian dream was over.

But John's troubled looks did not pass away. It seemed as if this night his long toil had come to that crisis when the strongest man breaks down—or trembles within a hair's breadth of breaking down; conscious too, horribly conscious, that if so, himself will be the least part of the universal ruin. His face was haggard, his movements irritable and restless; he started nervously at every sound. Sometimes even a hasty word, an uneasiness about trifles, showed how strong was the effort he made at self-control. Ursula, usually by far the most quick-tempered of the two, became to-night mild and patient. She neither watched nor questioned him—wise woman as she was; she only sat still, busying herself over her work, speaking now and then of little things, lest he should notice her anxiety about him. He did at last.

"Nay, I am not ill; do not be afraid. Only my head aches so—let me lay it here as the children do."

His wife made a place for it on her shoulder; there it rested—the poor tired head, until gradually the hard and painful expression of the features relaxed, and it became John's own natural face—as quiet as any of the little faces on their pillows upstairs, whence, doubtless, slumber had long banished all anticipation of Longfield. At last he too fell asleep.

Ursula held up her finger, that I might not stir. The clock in the corner, and the soft sobbing of the flame on the hearth, were the only sounds in the parlour. She sewed on quietly to the end of her work; then let it drop on her lap, and sat still. Her cheek leaned itself softly against John's hair, and in her eyes, which seemed so intently contemplating the little frock, I saw large bright tears gather—fall. But her look was serene, nay, happy; as if she thought of these beloved ones, husband and children—her very own—preserved to her in health and peace—ay, and in that which is better than either, the unity of love. For that priceless blessing, for the comfort of being *his* comfort, for the sweetness of bringing up these his children in the fear of God and in the honour of their father—she, true wife and mother as she was, would not have exchanged the wealth of the whole world.

"What's that?" We all started, as a sudden ring at the bell pealed through the house, waking John, and frightening the very children in their beds. All for a mere letter too, brought by a lackey of Lord Luxmore's. Having—somewhat indignantly—ascertained this fact, the mother ran upstairs to quiet her little ones. When she came down, John still stood with the letter in his hand. He had not told me what it was; when I chanced to ask he answered in a low tone, "Presently!" On his wife's entrance, he gave her the letter without a word.

Well might it startle her into a cry of joy. Truly the dealings of Heaven to us were wonderful!

"Mr. John Halifax.

"SIR,—Your wife, Ursula Halifax, having some time since attained the age fixed by her late father as her majority, I will, within a month after date, pay over to your order all moneys, principal and interest, accruing to her, and hitherto left in my hands as trustee, according to the will of the late Henry March, Esquire.—I am, sir, yours, etc., RICHARD BRITHWOOD."

"Wonderful—wonderful!"

It was all I could say. That one bad man, for his own purposes, should influence another bad man to an act of justice—and that their double evil should be made to work out our good! Also, that this should come just in our time of need—when John's strength seemed ready to fail.

"O John—John! Now you need not work so hard!"

That was his wife's first cry, as she clung to him almost in tears.

He, too, was a good deal agitated. This sudden lifting of the burthen made him feel how heavy it had been—how terrible the responsibility—how sickening the fear.

"Thank God! In any case, you are quite safe now—you and the children!"

He sat down, very pale. His wife knelt beside him,

and put her arms around his neck—I quietly went out of the room.

When I came in again, they were standing by the fireside—both cheerful, as two people to whom had happened such unexpected good fortune might naturally be expected to appear. I offered my congratulations in rather a comical vein than otherwise; we all of us had caught John's habit of putting things in a comic light whenever he felt them keenly.

"Yes, he is a rich man now—mind you treat your brother with extra respect, Phineas."

"And your sister too.

"'For she sall walk in silk attire,
And siller hae to spare.'

She's quite young and handsome still, isn't she? How magnificent she'll look in that gray silk gown!"

"John, you ought to be ashamed of yourself! you—the father of a family! you—that are to be the largest millowner at Enderley——"

He looked at her fondly, half deprecatingly. "Not till I have made you and the children all safe—as I said."

"We are safe—quite safe—when we have you. O Phineas! make him see it as I do. Make him understand that it will be the happiest day in his wife's life when she knows him happy in his heart's desire."

We sat a little while longer, talking over the strange change in our fortunes—for they wished to make me feel that now, as ever, what was theirs was mine; then Ursula took her candle to depart.

"Love!" John cried, calling her back as she shut the door, and watching her stand there patient—watching with something of the old mischievous twinkle in his eyes. "Mrs. Halifax, when shall I have the honour of ordering your long-tailed gray ponies?"

CHAPTER XXIII.

Not many weeks afterwards we went to live at Longfield, which henceforth became the family home for many years.

Longfield! happy Longfield! little nest of love, and joy, and peace—where the children grew up, and we grew old—where season after season brought some new change ripening in us and around us—where summer and winter, day and night, the hand of God's providence was over our roof, blessing our goings out and our comings in, our basket and our store; crowning us with the richest blessing of all, that we were made a household where "brethren dwelt together in unity." Beloved Longfield! my heart, slow pulsing as befits one near the grave, thrills warm and young as I remember thee!

Yet how shall I describe it—the familiar spot—so familiar that it seems to need no description at all.

It was but a small place when we first came there. It led out of the high road by a field gate—the White Gate—from which a narrow path wound down to a stream, thence up a green slope to the house—a mere farmhouse, nothing more. It had one parlour, three decent bedrooms, kitchen, and outhouses. We built extempore chambers out of the barn and cheese-room. In one of these the boys, Guy and Edwin, slept, against the low roof of which the father generally knocked his head every morning when he came to call the lads. Its windows were open all summer round, and birds and bats used oftentimes to fly in, to the great delight of the youthful inmates.

Another infinite pleasure to the little folk was that for the first year the farmhouse kitchen was made our dining-room. There, through the open door, Edwin's pigeons, Muriel's two doves, and sometimes a stately hen, walked in and out at pleasure. Whether our live stock, brought up in the law of kindness, were as well-trained and well-behaved as our children, I cannot tell;

but certain it is that we never found any harm from this system, necessitated by our early straits at Longfield—this " liberty, fraternity, and equality."

Those words, in themselves true and lovely, but wrested to such false meaning, whose fatal sound was now dying out of Europe, merged in the equally false and fatal shout of " *Gloire ! gloire !* " remind me of an event which I believe was the first that broke the delicious monotony of our new life.

It was one September morning. Mrs. Halifax, the children, and I were down at the stream, planning a bridge across it, and a sort of stable, where John's horse might be put up—the mother had steadily resisted the long-tailed gray ponies. For with all the necessary improvements at Longfield, with the large settlement that John insisted upon making on his wife and children before he would use in his business any portion of her fortune, we found we were by no means so rich as to make any great change in our way of life advisable. And, after all, the mother's best luxuries were to see her children merry and strong, her husband's face lightened of its care, and to know he was now placed beyond doubt in the position he had always longed for ; for was he not this very day gone to sign the lease of Enderley Mills ?

Mrs. Halifax had just looked at her watch, and she and I were wondering, with quite a childish pleasure, whether he were not now signing the important deed, when Guy came running to say a coach-and-four was trying to enter the White Gate.

" Who can it be ? But they must be stopped, or they'll spoil John's new gravel road that he takes such pride in.—Uncle Phineas, would you mind going to see ? "

Who should I see but almost the last person I expected —who had not been beheld, hardly spoken of, in our household these ten years—Lady Caroline Brithwood, in her travelling habit of green cloth, her velvet riding-hat, with its Prince of Wales feathers, gayer than ever—though her pretty face was withering under the paint, and her lively manner growing coarse and bold.

"Is this Longfield? Does Mr. Halifax—— *Mon Dieu*, Mr. Fletcher, is that you?"

She held out her hand with the frankest condescension, and in the brightest humour in the world. She insisted on sending on the carriage, and accompanying me down to the stream, for a "surprise"—a "scene."

Mrs. Halifax, seeing the coach drive on, had evidently forgotten all about it. She stood in the little dell which the stream had made, Walter in her arms—her figure thrown back, so as to poise the child's weight. Her right hand kept firm hold of Guy, who was paddling barefoot in the stream. Edwin, the only one of the boys who never gave any trouble, was soberly digging away beside little Muriel.

The lady clapped her hands. "*Brava! bravissima!* a charming family picture, Mrs. Halifax."

"Lady Caroline!"

Ursula left her children, and came to greet her old acquaintance, whom she had never once seen since she was Ursula Halifax. Perhaps that fact touched her, and it was with a kind of involuntary tenderness that she looked into the sickly face, where all the smiles could not hide the wrinkles.

"It is many years since we met, and we are both somewhat altered, Cousin Caroline."

"You are, with those three great boys. The little girl yours also? Oh yes, I remember William told me—poor little thing!" And with uneasy awe she turned from our blind Muriel, our child of peace.

"Will you come up to the house? My husband has only ridden over to Enderley; he will be home soon."

"And glad to see me, I wonder? For I am rather afraid of that husband of yours—eh, Ursula? Yet I should greatly like to stay."

Ursula laughed, and repeated the welcome. She was so happy herself, she longed to distribute her happiness. They walked, the children following, towards the house.

Under the great walnut tree, by the sunk fence which guarded the flower garden from the sheep and cows, Mrs.

Halifax stopped and pointed down the green slope of the field, across the valley, to the wooded hills opposite.

"Isn't it a pretty view?" said Guy, creeping up and touching the stranger's gown. Our children had lived too much in an atmosphere of love to know either shyness or fear.

"Very pretty, my little friend."

"That's One-tree Hill. Father is going to take us all a walk there this afternoon."

"Do you like going walks with your father?"

"Oh, don't we!" An electric smile ran through the whole circle. It told enough of the blessed home-tale.

Lady Caroline laughed a sharp laugh. "Eh, my dear, I see how things are. You don't regret having married John Halifax the tanner?"

"Regret!"

"Nay, be not impetuous. I always said he was a noble fellow—so does the earl now. And William—you can't think what a hero your husband is to William."

"Lord Ravenel?"

"Ay, my little brother that was—growing a young man now—a frightful bigot, wanting to make our house as Catholic as when two or three of us lost our heads for King James. But he is a good boy—poor William! I had rather not talk about him."

Ursula inquired courteously if her Cousin Richard were well.

"Bah! I suppose he is; he is always well. His late astonishing honesty to Mr. Halifax cost him a fit of gout—*mais n'importe*. If they meet, I suppose all things will be smooth between them?"

"My husband never had any ill-feeling to Mr. Brithwood."

"I should not bear him an undying enmity if he had. But you see 'tis election time, and the earl wishes to put in a gentleman, a friend of ours, for Kingswell. Mr. Halifax owns some cottages there, eh?"

"Mr. Fletcher does. My husband transacts business——"

"Stop! stop!" cried Lady Caroline. "I don't understand business; I only know that they want your husband to be friendly with mine. Is this plain enough?"

"Certainly; be under no apprehension. Mr. Halifax never bears malice against any one. Was this the reason of your visit, Lady Caroline?"

"Eh—*mon Dieu!* what would become of us if we were all as straightforward as you, Mistress Ursula? But it sounds charming—in the country. No, my dear; I came—nay, I hardly know why. Probably because I liked to come—my usual reason for most actions. Is that your *salle à manger?* Won't you ask me to dinner, *ma cousine?*"

"Of course," the mother said, though I fancied, afterwards, the invitation rather weighed upon her mind, probably from the doubt whether or no John would like it. But in little things, as in great, she had always this safe trust in him—that conscientiously to do what she felt to be right was the surest way to be right in her husband's eyes.

So Lady Caroline was our guest for the day—a novel guest—but she made herself at once familiar and pleasant. Guy, a little gentleman from his cradle, installed himself her admiring knight attendant everywhere; Edwin brought her to see his pigeons; Walter, with sweet, shy blushes, offered her "a 'ittle f'ower!" and the three, as the greatest of all favours, insisted on escorting her to pay a visit to the beautiful calf not a week old.

Laughing, she followed the boys; telling them how lately in Sicily she had been presented to a week-old prince, son of Louis Philippe, the young Duke of Orleans, and the Princess Marie-Amelie. "And truly, children, he was not half so pretty as your little calf. Ursula, I am sick of courts sometimes. I would turn shepherdess myself, if we could find a tolerable Arcadia."

"Is there any Arcadia like home?"

"Home!" Her face expressed the utmost loathing, fear, and scorn. I remembered hearing that the squire since his return from abroad had grown just like his father—was drunk every day and all day long. "Is your husband altered, Ursula? He must be quite a young man still. Oh, what it is to be young!"

"John looks much older, people say; but I don't see it."

"Arcadia again! Can such things be? especially in England, that paradise of husbands, where the first husband in the realm sets such an illustrious example. How do you stay-at-home British matrons feel towards my friend the Princess of Wales?"

"God help her, and make her as good a woman as she is a wronged and miserable wife," said Ursula sadly.

"*Query*, Can a 'good woman' be made out of a 'wronged and miserable wife'? If so, Mrs. Halifax, you should certainly take out a patent for the manufacture."

The subject touched too near home. Ursula wisely avoided it by inquiring if Lady Caroline meant to remain in England.

"*Cela dépend.*" She turned suddenly grave. "Your fresh air makes me feel weary. Shall we go indoors?"

Dinner was ready laid out—a plain meal, since neither the father nor any of us cared for table dainties; but I think if we had lived in a hut, and fed off wooden platters on potatoes and salt, our repast would have been fair and orderly, and our hut the neatest that a hut could be. For the mother of the family had in perfection almost the best genius a woman can have—the genius of tidiness.

We were not in the least ashamed of our simple dinner-table, where no difference was ever made for anybody. We had little plate, but plenty of snow-white napery and pretty china; and what with the scents of the flower garden on one side, and the green waving of the elm tree on the other, it was as good as dining out of doors.

The boys were still gathered round Lady Caroline, in the little closet off the dining-room where lessons were learnt; Muriel sat as usual on the door-sill, petting one of her doves that used to come and perch on her head and her shoulder of their own accord, when I heard the child say to herself,—

"Father's coming."

"Where, darling?"

"Up the farmyard way. There—he is on the gravel walk. He has stopped, I dare say it is to pull some of the jessamine that grows over the well. Now, fly away, dove! Father's here."

And the next minute a general shout echoed, "Father's here!"

He stood in the doorway, lifting one after the other up in his arms, having a kiss and a merry word for all—this good father!

O solemn name, which Deity Himself claims and owns! Happy these children who, in its fullest sense, could understand the word "father!" to whom, from the dawn of their little lives, their father was what all fathers should be—the truest representative here on earth of that Father in heaven, who is at once justice, wisdom, and perfect love.

Happy, too—most blessed among women—the woman who gave her children such a father!

Ursula came—for his eye was wandering in search of her—and received the embrace without which he never left her or returned.

"All rightly settled, John?"

"Quite settled."

"I am so glad." With a second kiss, not often bestowed in public, as congratulation. He was going to tell more, when Ursula said, rather hesitatingly, "We have a visitor to-day."

Lady Caroline came out of her corner, laughing. "You did not expect me, I see. Am I welcome?"

"Any welcome that Mrs. Halifax has given is also mine."

But John's manner, though polite, was somewhat constrained; and he felt, as it seemed to my observant eye, more surprise than gratification in this incursion on his quiet home. Also I noticed that when Lady Caroline, in the height of her condescension, would have Muriel close to her at dinner, he involuntarily drew his little daughter to her accustomed place beside himself.

"She always sits here, thank you."

The table-talk was chiefly between the lady and her host; she rarely talked to women when a man was to be had. Conversation veered between the Emperor Napoleon and Lord Wellington, Lord William Bentinck, and Sardinian policy, the conjugal squabbles of Carlton House, and the one absorbing political question of this year—Catholic Emancipation.

"You are a stanch supporter of the Bill, my father says. Of course, you aid him in the Kingswell election to-morrow?"

"I can scarcely call it an election," returned John. He had been commenting on it to us that morning rather severely. An election! it was merely a talk in the King's Head parlour, a nomination, and show of hands by some dozen poor labourers, tenants of Mr. Brithwood and Lord Luxmore, who got a few pounds apiece for their services—and the thing was done.

"Who is the nominee, Lady Caroline?"

"A young gentleman of small fortune, but excellent parts, who returned with us from Naples."

The lady's manner being rather more formal than she generally used, John looked up quickly.

"The election being to-morrow, of course his name is no secret?"

"Oh no! Vermilye. Mr. Gerard Vermilye. Do you know him?"

"I have heard of him." As he spoke—either intentionally or no—John looked full at Lady Caroline. She dropped her eyes and began playing with her bracelets. Both immediately quitted the subject of Kingswell election.

Soon after we rose from table; and Guy, who had all dinner-time fixed his admiring gaze upon the "pretty lady," insisted on taking her down the garden and gathering for her a magnificent arum lily, the mother's favourite lily. I suggested gaining permission first, and was sent to ask the question.

I found John and his wife in serious, even painful conversation.

"Love," he was saying, "I have known it for very long; but if she had not come here, I would never have grieved you by telling it."

"Perhaps it is not true," cried Ursula warmly. "The world is ready enough to invent cruel falsehoods about us women."

"'Us women!' Don't say that, Ursula. I will not have my wife named in the same breath with *her*."

"John!"

"I will not, I say. You don't know what it costs me even to see her touch your hand."

"John!"

The soft tone recalled him to his better self.

"Forgive me! but I would not have the least taint come near this wife of mine. I could not bear to think of her holding intercourse with a light woman—a woman false to her husband."

"I do not believe it. Caroline was foolish, she was never wicked. Listen! If this were true, how could she be laughing with our children now? O John!—think—she has no children."

The deep pity passed from Ursula's heart to her husband's. John clasped fondly the two hands that were laid on his shoulders, as, looking up in his face, the happy wife pleaded silently for one whom all the world knew was so wronged and so unhappy.

"We will wait a little before we judge. Love, you are a better Christian than I."

All afternoon they both showed more than courtesy—kindness—to this woman, at whom, as any one out of our retired household would have known, and as John did know well, all the world was already pointing the finger, on account of Mr. Gerard Vermilye. She, on her part, with her chameleon power of seizing and sunning herself in the delight of the moment, was in a state of the highest enjoyment. She turned "shepherdess," fed the poultry with Edwin, pulled off her jewelled ornaments, and gave them to Walter for playthings—nay, she even washed off her rouge at the spring, and came in with faint natural roses upon her faded cheeks. So happy she seemed, so innocently, childishly happy, that more than once I saw John and Ursula exchange satisfied looks, rejoicing that they had followed after the divine charity which "thinketh no evil."

After tea we all turned out, as was our wont on summer evenings; the children playing about; while the father and mother strolled up and down the sloping field path, arm in arm like lovers, or sometimes he fondly leaning upon her. Thus they would walk and talk together in the twilight for hours.

Lady Caroline pointed to them. "Look! Adam and Eve modernized; Baucis and Philemon when they were young. *Bon Dieu!* what it is to be young!"

She said this in a gasp, as if wild with terror of the days that were coming upon her—the dark days.

"People are always young," I answered, "who love one another as these do."

"Love! What an old-fashioned word. I hate it! It is so—what would you say in English?—so *déchirant.* I would not cultivate *une grande passion* for the world."

I smiled at the idea of the bond between Mr. and Mrs. Halifax taking the Frenchified character of "*une grande passion.*"

"But home-love, married love, love among children and at the fireside—you believe in that?"

She turned upon me her beautiful eyes; they had a scared look, like a bird's driven right into the fowler's net.

"*C'est impossible—impossible!*"

The word hissed itself out between her shut teeth—"*impossible.*" Then she walked quickly on, and was her lively self once more.

When the evening closed, and the younger children were gone to bed, she became rather restless about the non-appearance of her coach. At last a lackey arrived on foot. She angrily inquired why a carriage had not been sent for her?

"Master didn't give orders, my lady," answered the man, somewhat rudely.

Lady Caroline turned pale—with anger or fear—perhaps both.

"You have not properly answered your mistress's question," said Mr. Halifax.

"Master says, sir—begging my lady's pardon for repeating it—but he says, 'My lady went out against his will, and she may come home when and how she likes.'"

"My lady" burst out laughing, and laughed violently and long.

"Tell him I will. Be sure you tell him I will. It is the last and the easiest obedience."

John sent the lackey out of the room, and Ursula said something about "not speaking thus before a servant."

"Before a servant! Why, my dear, we furnish entertainment for our whole establishment, my husband and I. We are at the Mythe what the Prince Regent and the Princess of Wales are to the country at large. We divide our people between us; I fascinate—he bribes. Ha! ha! Well done, Richard Brithwood! I may come home 'when and how I like'! Truly, I'll use that kind permission."

Her eyes glittered with an evil fire, her cheeks were hot and red.

"Mrs. Halifax, I shall be thrown on your hospitality for an hour or two longer. Could you send a letter for me?"

"To your husband? Certainly."

"My husband? Never! Yes, to *my husband*." The first part of the sentence was full of fierce contempt; the latter, smothered, and slowly desperate. "Tell me, Ursula, what constitutes a man one's husband? Brutality, tyranny—the tyranny which the law sanctions? Or kindness, sympathy, devotion, everything that makes life beautiful—everything that constitutes happiness and——"

"Sin."

The word in her ear was so low that she started as if conscience only had uttered it—conscience, to whom only her intents were known.

John came forward, speaking gravely, but not unkindly.

"Lady Caroline, I am deeply grieved that this should have happened in my house, and through your visiting us against your husband's will."

"His will!"

"Pardon me; but I think a wife is bound to the very last to obey in all things, not absolutely wrong, her husband's will. I am glad you thought of writing to Mr. Brithwood."

She shook her head in mocking denial.

"May I ask, then—since I am to have the honour of sending it—to whom is this letter?"

"To—" I think she would have told a falsehood, if John's eyes had not been so keenly fixed upon her—"to —a friend."

"Friends are at all times dangerous to a lady who——"

"Hates her husband—ha! ha! Especially male friends?"

"Especially male friends."

Here Guy, who had lingered out of his little bed most unlawfully—hovering about, ready to do any chivalrous duty to his idol of the day—came up to bid her goodnight, and held up his rosy mouth eagerly.

"I—kiss a little child! I!" And from her violent laughter she burst into a passion of tears.

The mother signed me to carry Guy away. She and John took Lady Caroline into the parlour and shut the door.

Of course I did not then learn what passed, but I did afterwards.

Lady Caroline's tears were evanescent, like all her emotions. Soon she became composed—asked again for writing materials—then countermanded the request.

"No, I will wait till to-morrow. Ursula, you will take me in for the night?"

Mrs. Halifax looked appealingly at her husband, but he gave no assent.

"Lady Caroline, you should willingly stay, were it not, as you must know, so fatal a step. In your position, you should be most careful to leave the world and your husband no single handle against you."

"Mr. Halifax, what right have you——"

"None, save that of an honest man, who sees a woman cruelly wronged, and desperate with her wrong, who would thankfully save her if he could."

"Save me? From what—or whom?"

"From Mr. Gerard Vermilye, who is now waiting down the road, and whom, if Lady Caroline Brithwood once flies to, or even sees, at this crisis, she loses her place among honourable English matrons for ever."

John said this with no air of virtuous anger or contempt, but as the simple statement of a fact. The convicted woman dropped her face between her hands.

Ursula, greatly shocked, was some time before she spoke.

"Is it true, Caroline?"

"What is true?"

"That which my husband has heard of you?"

"Yes," she cried, springing up, and dashing back her beautiful hair—beautiful still, though she must have been five or six and thirty at least—"yes, it is true—it shall be true. I will break my bonds and live the life I was made for. I would have done it long ago but for—no matter. Why, Ursula, he adores me; young and handsome as he is, he adores me. He will give me my youth back again—ay, he will."

And she sang out a French chanson, something about "*la liberté et ses plaisirs, la jeunesse, l'amour.*"

The mother grew sterner—any such wife and mother would. Then and there compassion might have died out of even her good heart had it not been for the sudden noise overhead of children's feet—children's chattering. Once more the pitiful thought came—"She has no children."

"Caroline," she said, catching her gown as she passed, "when I was with you, you had a child which only breathed and died. It died spotless. When you die, how dare you meet that little baby?"

The singing changed to sobbing. "I had forgotten. My little baby! Oh, *mon Dieu, mon Dieu!*"

Mrs. Halifax, taking in earnest those meaningless French ejaculations, whispered something about Him who alone can comfort and help us all.

"Him! I never knew Him, if indeed He be. No, no, there is no after-life."

Ursula turned away in horror. "John, what shall we do with her? No home!—no husband!—no God!"

"He never leaves Himself without a witness. Look, love."

The wretched woman sat rocking to and fro, weeping and wringing her hands. "It was cruel—cruel! You should not have spoken about my baby. Now——"

"Tell me—just one word—I will not believe anybody's word except your own. Caroline, are you—still innocent?"

Lady Caroline shrank from her touch. "Don't hold me so. You may have one standard of virtue, I another."

"Still, tell me."

"And if I did, you, an 'honourable English matron'—was not that your husband's word?—would turn from me most likely?"

"She will not," John said. "She has been happy, and you most miserable."

"Oh, most miserable."

That bitter groan went to both their hearts. Ursula leaned over her, herself almost in tears. "Cousin Caroline, John says true—I will not turn from you. I know you have been sinned against—cruelly—cruelly. Only tell me that you yourself have not sinned."

"I *have* 'sinned,' as you call it."

Ursula started—drew closer to her husband. Neither spoke.

"Mrs. Halifax, why don't you take away your hand?"

"I?—let me think. This is terrible. O John!"

Again Lady Caroline said, in her sharp, bold tone, "Take away your hand."

"Husband, shall I?"

"No."

For some minutes they stood together, both silent, with this poor woman. I call her "poor," as did they, knowing that if a sufferer needs pity, how tenfold more does a sinner!

John spoke first. "Cousin Caroline." She lifted up her head in amazement. "We are your cousins, and we wish to be your friends, my wife and I. Will you listen to us?"

She sobbed still, but less violently.

"Only, first—you must promise to renounce for ever guilt and disgrace."

"I feel it none. He is an honourable gentleman—he loves me, and I love him. That is the true marriage. No, I will make you no such promise. Let me go."

"Pardon me—not yet. I cannot suffer my wife's kinswoman to elope from my own house without trying to prevent it."

"Prevent!—sir!—Mr. Halifax! You forget who you are, and who I am—the daughter of the Earl of Luxmore."

"Were you the King's daughter it would make no difference. I will save you in spite of yourself, if I can. I have already spoken to Mr. Vermilye, and he has gone away."

"Gone away! the only living soul that loves me. Gone away! I must follow him—quick—quick."

"You cannot. He is miles distant by this time. He is afraid lest this story should come out to-morrow at Kingswell; and to be an M.P. and safe from arrest is better to Mr. Vermilye than even yourself, Lady Caroline."

John's wife, unaccustomed to hear him take that cool, worldly, half-sarcastic tone, turned to him somewhat reproachfully; but he judged best. For the moment this tone had more weight with the woman of the world than any homilies. She began to be afraid of Mr. Halifax. Impulse, rather than resolution, guided her, and even these impulses were feeble and easily governed. She sat down again, muttering,—

"My will is free. You cannot control me."

"Only so far as my conscience justifies me in preventing a crime."

"A crime?"

"It would be such. No sophistries of French philosophy on your part, no cruelty on your husband's, can abrogate the one law, which if you disown it as God's, is still man's—being necessary for the peace, honour, and safety of society."

"What law?"

"*Thou shalt not commit adultery.*"

People do not often utter this plain Bible word. It made Ursula start, even when spoken solemnly by her own husband. It tore from the self-convicted woman all the sentimental disguises with which the world then hid, and still hides, its corruptions. Her sin arose and stared her blackly in the face—*as sin.* She cowered before it.

"Am I—*that?* And William will know it. Poor William!" She looked up at Ursula—for the first time with the guilty look; hitherto it had been only one of pain or despair. "Nobody knows it, except you. Don't tell William. I would have gone long ago, but for him. He is a good boy. Don't let him guess his sister was——"

She left the word unspoken. Shame seemed to crush her down to the earth—shame, the precursor of saving penitence—at least, John thought so. He quitted the room, leaving her to the ministry of his other self, his wife. As he sat down with me, and told me in a few words what indeed I had already more than half guessed, I could not but notice the expression of his own face. And I recognized how a man can be at once righteous to judge, tender to pity, and strong to save—a man the principle of whose life is, as John's was, that it should be made " conformable to the image " of Him who was Himself on earth the image of God.

Ursula came out and called her husband. They talked some time together. I guessed, from what I heard, that she wished Lady Caroline to stay the night here, but that he with better judgment was urging the necessity of her returning to the protection of her husband's home without an hour's delay.

" It is her only chance of saving her reputation. She must do it. Tell her so, Ursula."

After a few minutes, Mrs. Halifax came out again.

" I have persuaded her at last. She says she will do whatever you think best. Only, before she goes, she wants to look at the children. May she ? "

" Poor soul !—yes," John murmured, turning away.

Stepping out of sight, we saw the poor lady pass through the quiet, empty house into the children's bedroom. We heard her smothered sob, at times, the whole way.

Then I went down to the stream, and helped John to saddle his horse with Mrs. Halifax's old saddle—in her girlish days Ursula used to be very fond of riding.

" She can ride back again from the Mythe," said John. " She wishes to go, and it is best she should ; so that nothing need be said, except that Lady Caroline spent a day at Longfield, and that my wife and I accompanied her safe home."

While he spoke, the two ladies came down the field path. I fancied I heard, even now, a faint echo of that peculiarly sweet and careless laugh, indicating how light were all impressions on a temperament so plastic and weak—so easily remoulded by the very next influence that fate might throw across her perilous way.

John Halifax assisted her on horseback, took the bridle under one arm, and gave the other to his wife. Thus they passed up the path, and out at the White Gate.

I delayed a little while, listening to the wind, and to

the prattle of the stream, that went singing along in daylight or in darkness by our happy home at Longfield. And I sighed to myself, "Poor Lady Caroline!"

CHAPTER XXIV.

MIDNIGHT though it was, I sat up until John and his wife came home. They said scarcely anything, but straightway retired. In the morning all went on in the house as usual, and no one ever knew of this night's episode except us three.

In the morning Guy looked wistfully around him, asking for the "pretty lady;" and being told that she was gone, and that he would not be likely to see her again, seemed disappointed for a minute; but soon he went down to play at the stream, and forgot all.

Once or twice I fancied the mother's clear voice about the house was rarer than its wont; that her quick, active, cheerful presence—penetrating every nook, and visiting every creature, as with the freshness of an April wind—was this day softer and sadder; but she did not say anything to me, nor I to her.

John had ridden off early—to the flour-mill, which he still kept on, together with the house at Norton Bury—he always disliked giving up any old associations. At dinner-time he came home, saying he was going out again immediately.

Ursula looked uneasy. A few minutes after she followed me under the walnut tree, where I was sitting with Muriel, and asked me if I would go with John to Kingswell.

"The election takes place to-day, and he thinks it right to be there. He will meet Mr. Brithwood and Lord Luxmore; and though there is not the slightest need—my husband can do all that he has to do alone—still, for my own satisfaction, I would like his brother to be near him."

They invariably called me their brother now, and it

seemed as if the name had been mine by right of blood always.

Of course, I went to Kingswell, riding John's brown mare, he himself walking by my side. It was not often that we were thus alone together, and I enjoyed it much. All the old days seemed to come back again as we passed along the quiet roads and green lanes, just as when we were boys together, when I had none I cared for but David, and David cared only for me. The natural growth of things had made a difference in this, but our affection had changed its outward form only, not its essence. I often think that all loves and friendships need a certain three days' burial before we can be quite sure of their truth and immortality. Mine—it happened just after John's marriage, and I may confess it now—had likewise its entombment, bitter as brief. Many cruel hours sat I in darkness, weeping at the door of its sepulchre, thinking that I should never see it again; but in the dawn of the morning it rose, and I met it in the desolate garden, different, yet the very same. And after that it walked with me continually, secure and imperishable evermore.

I rode, and John sauntered beside me along the foot-path, now and then plucking a leaf or branch off the hedge, and playing with it, as was his habit when a lad. Often I caught the old smile—not one of his three boys, not even handsome Guy, had their father's smile.

He was telling me about Enderley Mill, and all his plans there, in the which he seemed very happy. At last his long life of duty was merging into the life he loved. He looked as proud and pleased as a boy in talking of the new inventions he meant to apply in cloth-weaving; and how he and his wife had agreed together to live for some years to come at little Longfield, strictly within their settled income, that all the remainder of his capital might go to the improvement of Enderley Mills and mill people.

"I shall be master of nearly a hundred men and women. Think what good we may do! She has half a dozen plans on foot already—bless her dear heart!"

It was easy to guess whom he referred to—the one who went hand-in-hand with him in everything.

"Was the dinner in the barn next Monday her plan too?"

"Partly. I thought we would begin a sort of yearly festival for the old tanyard people, and those about the flour-mill, and the Kingswell tenants. Ah, Phineas, wasn't I right about those Kingswell folk?"

These were about a dozen poor families whom, when our mortgage fell in, he had lured out of Sally Watkins's miserable alley to these old houses, where they had at least fresh country air, and space enough to live wholesomely and decently, instead of herding together like pigs in a sty.

"You ought to be proud of your tenants, Phineas. I assure you, they form quite a contrast to their neighbours, who are Lord Luxmore's."

"And his voters likewise, I suppose?—the 'free and independent burgesses' who are to send Mr. Vermilye to Parliament?"

"If they can," said John, biting his lip with that resolute, half-combative air which I now saw in him at times, roused by things which continually met him in his dealings with the world—things repugnant alike to his feelings and his principles, but which he had still to endure, not having risen high enough to oppose, single-handed, the great mass of social corruption which at this crisis of English history kept gathering and gathering, until out of the very horror and loathsomeness of it an outcry for purification arose.

"Do you know, Phineas, I might last week have sold your houses for double price? They are valuable, this election year, since your five tenants are the only voters in Kingswell who are not likewise tenants of Lord Luxmore. Don't you see how the matter stands?"

It was not difficult, for that sort of game was played all over England, connived at, or at least winked at, by those who had political influence to sell or obtain, until the Reform Bill opened up the election system in all its rottenness and enormity.

"Of course I knew you would not sell your houses; and I shall use every possible influence I have to prevent your tenants selling their votes. Whatever may be the consequence, the sort of thing that this Kingswell election bids fair to be is what any honest Englishman ought to set his face against, and prevent if he can."

"Can you?"

"I do not feel sure, but I mean to try. First, for simple right and conscience; secondly, because if Mr. Vermilye is not saved from arrest by being placed in Parliament, he will be outlawed and driven safe out of the country. You see?"

Ay, I did, only too well. Though I foresaw that whatever John was about to do, it must necessarily be something that would run directly counter to Lord Luxmore—and he had only just signed the lease of Enderley Mills. Still, if right to be done, he ought to do it at all risks, at all costs; and I knew his wife would say so.

We came to the foot of Kingswell Hill, and saw the little hamlet, with its gray old houses, its small, ancient church, guarded by enormous yew trees, and clothed with ivy that indicated centuries of growth.

A carriage overtook us here; in it were two gentlemen, one of whom bowed in a friendly manner to John. He returned it.

"This is well; I shall have one honest gentleman to deal with to-day."

"Who is he?"

"Sir Ralph Oldtower, from whom I bought Longfield. An excellent man—I like him—even his fine old Norman face, like one of his knightly ancestors on the tomb in Kingswell Church. There's something pleasant about his stiff courtesy and his stanch Toryism; for he fully believes in it, and acts up to his belief. A true English gentleman, and I respect him."

"Yet, John, Norton Bury calls you a democrat."

"So I am, for I belong to the people. But I nevertheless uphold a true aristocracy—the *best men* of the country. Do you remember our Greeks of old? These ought to govern, and will govern one day, whether their patent of nobility be births and titles, or only honesty and brains."

Thus he talked on, and I liked to hear him, for talking was rare in his busy life of constant action. I liked to observe how during these ten years his mind had brooded over many things; how it had grown, strengthened, and settled itself, enlarging both its vision and its aspirations; as a man does who, his heart at rest in a happy home, has time and will to look out from thence into the troublous world outside, ready to do his work there likewise. That John was able to do it—ay, beyond most men—few would doubt who looked into his face, strong with the strength of an intellect which owed all its development to himself alone, calm with the wisdom which, if a man is ever to be wise, comes to him after he has crossed the line of thirty years. In that face, where day by day Time was writing its fit lessons—beautiful, because they were so fit—I ceased to miss the boyish grace, and rejoiced in the manhood present, in the old age that was to be.

It seemed almost too short a journey when, putting his hand on the mare's bridle—the creature loved him, and turned to lick his arm the minute he came near—John stopped me to see the view from across Kingswell churchyard.

"Look, what a broad valley, rich in woods, and meadow-land, and corn. How quiet and blue lie the Welsh hills far away! It does one good to look at them. Nay, it brings back a little bit of me which rarely comes uppermost now, as it used to come long ago, when we read your namesake, and Shakespeare, and that Anonymous Friend who has since made such a noise in the world. I delight in him still. Think of a man of business liking Coleridge."

"I don't see why he should not."

"Nor I. Well, my poetic tastes may come out more

at Enderley. Or perhaps when I am an old man, and have fought the good fight, and—— Holloa, there! Matthew Hales, have they made you drunk already?"

The man—he was an old workman of ours—touched his hat, and tried to walk steadily past "the master," who looked at once both stern and sad.

"I thought it would be so! I doubt if there is a voter in all Kingswell who has not got a bribe."

"It is the same everywhere," I said. "What can one man do against it single-handed?"

"Single-handed or not, every man ought to do what he can. And no man knows how much he can do till he tries."

So saying, he went into the large parlour of the Luxmore Arms, where the election was going on.

A very simple thing that election! Sir Ralph Oldtower, who was sheriff, sat at a table, with his son, the grave-looking young man who had been with him in the carriage; near them were Mr. Brithwood of the Mythe and the Earl of Luxmore.

The room was pretty well filled with farmers' labourers and the like. We entered, making little noise; but John's head was taller than most heads present; the sheriff saw him at once, and bowed courteously. So did young Mr. Herbert Oldtower, so did the Earl of Luxmore. Richard Brithwood alone took no notice, but turned his back and looked another way.

It was now many years since I had seen the squire, Lady Caroline's husband. He had fulfilled the promise of his youth, and grown into a bloated, coarse-featured, middle-aged man; such a man as one rarely meets with nowadays; for even I, Phineas Fletcher, have lived to see so great a change in manners and morals, that intemperance, instead of being the usual characteristic of "a gentleman," has become a rare failing, a universally-contemned disgrace.

"Less noise there!" growled Mr. Brithwood. "Silence, you fellows at the door! Now, Sir Ralph, let's get the business over, and be back for dinner."

Sir Ralph turned his stately gray head to the light, put on his gold spectacles, and began to read the writ of election. As he finished, the small audience set up a feeble cheer.

The sheriff acknowledged it, then leaned over the table talking with rather frosty civility to Lord Luxmore. Their acquaintance seemed solely that of business. People whispered that Sir Ralph never forgot that the Oldtowers were Crusaders when the Ravenels were—nobody. Also the baronet, whose ancestors were all honourable men and stainless women, found it hard to overlook a certain royal bar-sinister, which had originated the Luxmore earldom, together with a few other blots which had tarnished that scutcheon since. So folk said; but probably Sir Ralph's high principle was at least as strong as his pride, and that the real cause of his dislike was founded on the too well-known character of the Earl of Luxmore.

They ceased talking; the sheriff rose, and briefly stated that Richard Brithwood, Esquire, of the Mythe, would nominate a candidate.

The candidate was Gerard Vermilye, Esquire; at the mention of whose name one Norton Bury man broke into a hoarse laugh, which was quenched by his immediate ejection from the meeting.

Then Mr. Thomas Brown, steward of the Earl of Luxmore, seconded the nomination.

After a few words between the sheriff, his son, and Lord Luxmore, the result of which seemed rather unsatisfactory than otherwise, Sir Ralph Oldtower again rose.

"Gentlemen and electors, there being no other candidate proposed, nothing is left me but to declare Gerard Vermilye, Esquire——"

John Halifax made his way to the table. "Sir Ralph, pardon my interruption, but may I speak a few words?"

Mr. Brithwood started up with an angry oath.

"My good sir," said the baronet, with a look of reprehension which proved him of the minority who thought swearing ungentlemanly.

"By ——, Sir Ralph, you shall not hear that low fellow!"

"Excuse me, I must, if he has a right to be heard. Mr. Halifax, you are a freeman of Kingswell?"

"I am."

This fact surprised none more than myself.

Brithwood furiously exclaimed that it was a falsehood. "The fellow does not belong to this neighbourhood at all. He was picked up in Norton Bury streets—a beggar, a thief, for all I know."

"You do know very well, Mr. Brithwood.—Sir Ralph, I was never either a beggar or a thief. I began life as a working lad—a farm labourer—until Mr. Fletcher, the tanner, took me into his employ."

"So I have always understood," said Sir Ralph courteously. "And next to the man who is fortunate enough to boast a noble origin I respect the man who is not ashamed of an ignoble one."

"That is not exactly my position either," said John, with a half smile. "But we are passing from the question in hand, which is simply my claim to be a freeman of this borough."

"On what grounds?"

"You will find in the charter a clause, seldom put in force, that the daughter of a freeman can confer the freedom on her husband. My wife's late father, Mr. Henry March, was a burgess of Kingswell. I claimed my rights, and registered this year. Ask your clerk, Sir Ralph, if I have not spoken correctly."

The old white-headed clerk allowed the fact.

Lord Luxmore looked considerably surprised, and politely incredulous still. His son-in-law broke out into loud abuse of this "knavery."

"I will pass over this ugly word, Mr. Brithwood, merely stating that——"

"We are quite satisfied," interrupted Lord Luxmore blandly. "My dear sir, may I request so useful a vote and so powerful an interest as yours for our friend, Mr. Vermilye?"

"My lord, I should be very sorry for you to misapprehend me for a moment. It is not my intention, except at the last extremity, to vote at all. If I do, it will certainly not be for Mr. Brithwood's nominee. Sir Ralph, I doubt if, under some circumstances, which by your permission I am about to state, Mr. Gerard Vermilye can keep his seat, even if elected."

A murmur arose from the crowd of mechanics and labourers, who, awed by such propinquity to gentry and even nobility, had hitherto hung sheepishly back; but now, like all English crowds, were quite ready to "follow the leader," especially one they knew.

"Hear him! hear the master!" was distinguishable on all sides. Mr. Brithwood looked too enraged for words; but Lord Luxmore, taking snuff with a sarcastic smile, said,—

"*Honores mutant mores!* I thought, Mr. Halifax, you eschewed politics?"

"Mere politics I do, but not honesty, justice, morality; and a few facts have reached my knowledge, though possibly not Lord Luxmore's, which make me feel that Mr. Vermilye's election would be an insult to all three. Therefore I oppose it."

A louder murmur rose.

"Silence, you scoundrels!" shouted Mr. Brithwood, adding his usual formula of speech, which a second time extorted the old baronet's grave rebuke.

"It seems, Sir Ralph, that democracy is rife in your neighbourhood. True, my acquaintance has not lain much among the commonalty, but still I was not aware that the people choose the member of Parliament."

"They do not, Lord Luxmore," returned the sheriff, somewhat haughtily. "But we always hear the people. Mr. Halifax, be brief. What have you to allege against Mr. Brithwood's nominee?"

"First, his qualification. He has not three hundred, nor one hundred a year. He is deeply in debt, at Norton Bury and elsewhere. Warrants are out against him; and only as an M.P. can he be safe from outlawry. Add to this, an offence common as daylight, yet which the law dare not wink at when made patent—that he has bribed, with great or small sums, every one of the fifteen electors of Kingswell, and I think I have said enough to convince any honest Englishman that Mr. Gerard Vermilye is not fit to represent them in Parliament."

Here a loud cheer broke from the crowd at the door and under the open windows, where, thick as bees, the villagers had now collected. They, the unvoting, and consequently unbribable portion of the community, began to hiss indignantly at the fifteen unlucky voters. For though bribery was, as John had truly said, "as common as daylight," still, if brought openly before the public, the said virtuous public generally condemned it, if they themselves had not been concerned therein.

The sheriff listened uneasily to a sound, very uncommon at elections, of the populace expressing an opinion contrary to that of the lord of the soil.

"Really, Mr. Brithwood, you must have been as ignorant as I was of the character of your nominee, or you would have chosen some one else. Herbert"—he turned to his son, who, until the late dissolution, had sat for some years as member for Norton Bury—"Herbert, are you acquainted with any of these facts?"

Mr. Herbert Oldtower looked uncomfortable.

"Answer," said his father. "No hesitation in a matter of right and wrong. Gentlemen, and my worthy friends, will you hear Mr. Oldtower, whom you all know? Herbert, are these accusations true?"

"I am afraid so," said the grave young man, more gravely.

"Mr. Brithwood, I regret extremely that this discovery was not made before. What do you purpose doing?"

"By the Lord that made me, nothing! The borough is Lord Luxmore's; I could nominate Satan himself if I chose. My man shall stand."

"I think," Lord Luxmore said, with meaning, "it would be better for all parties that Mr. Vermilye should stand."

"My lord," said the baronet; and one could see that not only rigid justice, but a certain obstinacy, marked his character, especially when anything jarred against his personal dignity or prejudices; "you forget that, however desirous I am to satisfy the family to whom this borough belongs, it is impossible for me to see with satisfaction—even though I cannot prevent—the election of any person so unfit to serve his Majesty. If, indeed, there were another candidate, so that the popular feeling might decide this very difficult matter——"

"Sir Ralph," said John Halifax determinedly, "this brings me to the purpose for which I spoke. Being a landholder, and likewise a freeman of this borough, I claim the right of nominating a second candidate."

Intense, overwhelming astonishment struck all present. Such a right had been so long unclaimed that everybody had forgotten it was a right at all. Sir Ralph and his clerk laid their venerable heads together for some minutes before they could come to any conclusion on the subject. At last the sheriff rose.

"I am bound to say that, though very uncommon, this proceeding is not illegal."

"Not illegal?" almost screamed Richard Brithwood.

"Not illegal. I therefore wait to hear Mr. Halifax's nomination. Sir, your candidate is, I hope, no democrat?"

"His political opinions differ from mine, but he is the only gentleman whom I in this emergency can name; and is one whom myself, and I believe all my neighbours, will be heartily glad to see once more in Parliament. I beg to nominate Mr. Herbert Oldtower."

A decided sensation at the upper half of the room. At the lower half a unanimous, involuntary cheer; for among our county families there were few so warmly respected as the Oldtowers.

Sir Ralph rose, much perplexed. "I trust that no one present will suppose I was aware of Mr. Halifax's intention. Nor, I understand, was Mr. Oldtower. My son must speak for himself."

Mr. Oldtower, with his accustomed gravity, accompanied by a not unbecoming modesty, said, that in this conjuncture, and being personally unacquainted with both Mr. Brithwood and the Earl of Luxmore, he felt no hesitation in accepting the honour offered to him.

"That being the case," said his father, though evidently annoyed, "I have only to fulfil my duty as public officer to the Crown."

Amidst some confusion, a show of hands was called for; and then a cry arose of "Go to the poll!"

"Go to the poll!" shouted Mr. Brithwood. "This is a family borough. There has not been a poll here these fifty years. Sir Ralph, your son's mad."

"Sir, insanity is not in the family of the Oldtowers. My position here is simply as sheriff of the county. If a poll be called for——"

"Excuse me, Sir Ralph, it would be hardly worth while. May I offer you——"

It was—only his snuff-box. But the earl's polite and meaning smile filled up the remainder of the sentence.

Sir Ralph Oldtower drew himself up haughtily, and the fire of youth flashed indignantly from his grand old eyes.

"Lord Luxmore seems not to understand the duties and principles of us country gentlemen," he said coldly, and turned away, addressing the general meeting. "Gentlemen, the poll will be held this afternoon, according to the suggestion of my neighbour here."

"Sir Ralph Oldtower has convenient neighbours," remarked Lord Luxmore.

"Of my neighbour, Mr. Halifax," repeated the old baronet, louder and more emphatically. "A gentleman"—he paused, as if doubtful whether in that title he were awarding a right or bestowing a courtesy, looked at John, and decided—"a gentleman for whom, ever since I have known him, I have entertained the highest respect."

It was the first public recognition of the position which for some time had been tacitly given to John Halifax in his own neighbourhood. Coming thus, from this upright and honourable old man, whose least merit it was to hold, and worthily, a baronetage centuries old, it made John's cheek glow with an honest gratification and a pardonable pride.

"Tell her," he said to me, when, the meeting having dispersed, he asked me to ride home and explain the reason of his detention at Kingswell—"Tell my wife all. She will be pleased, you know."

Ay, she was. Her face glowed and brightened as only a wife's can—a wife whose dearest pride is in her husband's honour.

Nevertheless, she hurried me back again as quickly as I came.

As I once more rode up Kingswell Hill, it seemed as if the whole parish were agog to see the novel sight. A contested election! truly, such a thing had not been known within the memory of the oldest inhabitant. The fifteen voters—I believe that was the number—were altogether bewildered by a sense of their own importance. Also, by a new and startling fact—which I found Mr. Halifax trying to impress upon a few of them, gathered under the great yew tree in the churchyard—that a man's vote ought to be the expression of his own conscientious opinion; and that for him to sell it was scarcely less vile than to traffic in the liberty of his son or the honour of his daughter. Among those who listened most earnestly was a man whom I had seen before to-day—Jacob Baines, once the ringleader of the bread riots, who had long worked steadily in the tanyard, and then at the flour-mill. He was the honestest and faithfulest of all John's people—illustrating unconsciously that Divine doctrine, that often they love most to whom most has been forgiven.

The poll was to be held in the church—a not uncommon usage in country boroughs, but which from its rarity struck great awe into the Kingswell folk. The churchwarden was placed in the clerk's desk to receive votes. Not far off, the sheriff sat in his family pew, bareheaded; by his grave and reverent manner imposing due decorum, which was carefully observed by all except Lord Luxmore and Mr. Brithwood.

These two, apparently sure of their cause, had recovered their spirits, and talked and laughed loudly on the other side of the church. It was a very small building, narrow and cruciform; every word said in it was distinctly audible throughout.

"My lord, gentlemen, and my friends all," said Sir Ralph, rising gravely, "let me hope that every one will respect the sanctity of this place."

Lord Luxmore, who had been going about with his dazzling diamond snuff-box, and equally dazzling smile, stopped in the middle of the aisle, bowed, replied, "With pleasure—certainly!" and walked inside the communion rail, as if believing that his presence there conveyed the highest compliment he could pay the spot.

The poll began in perfect silence. One after the other, three farmers went up and voted for Mr. Vermilye. There was snuff under their noses—probably something heavier than snuff in their pockets.

Then came up the big, gray-headed fellow I have before mentioned—Jacob Baines. He pulled his forelock to Sir Ralph rather shyly; possibly in his youth he had made the sheriff's acquaintance under less favourable circumstances. But he plucked up courage.

"Your honour, might a man say a word to 'ee?"

"Certainly; but be quick, my good fellow," replied the baronet, who was noted for his kindly manner to humble folk.

"Sir, I be a poor man. I lives in one o' my lord's houses. I hanna paid no rent for a year. Mr. Brown zays to me, he zays, 'Jacob, vote for Vermilye, and I'll forgive 'ee the rent, and here be two pound ten to start again wi'.' So, as I zays to Matthew Hales (he be Mr. Halifax's tenant, your honour, and my lord's steward ha' paid 'un nigh four pound for his vote), I sure us be poor men, and his lordship a lord and all that—it's no harm, I reckon."

"Holloa, cut it short, you rascal; you're stopping the poll. Vote, I say."

"Ay, ay, squire;" and the old fellow, who had some humour in him, pulled his hair again civilly to Mr. Brithwood. "Wait till I ha' got shut o' these."

And he counted out of his ragged pockets a handful of guineas. Poor fellow! how bright they looked; those guineas, that were food, clothing, life.

"Three was paid to I, two to Will Horrocks, and the rest to Matthew Hales. But, sir, we has changed our minds; and please, would 'ee give back the money to them as owns it?"

"Still, my honest friend——"

"Thank'ee, Sir Ralph, that's it: we be honest; we couldn't look the master in the face else. Twelve year ago, come Michaelmas, he kept some on us from starving—maybe worse. We bean't going to turn rascals on's hands now. Now I'll vote, sir—and it won't be for Vermilye."

A smothered murmur of applause greeted old Jacob, as he marched back down the aisle, where on the stone benches of the porch was seated a rural jury, who discussed not over-favourably the merits of Lord Luxmore's candidate.

"He owes a power o' money in Norton Bury—he do."

"Why doesn't he show his face at the 'lection, like a decent gen'leman?"

"Fear'd o' bailiffs!" suggested the one constable, old and rheumatic, who guarded the peace of Kingswell. "He's the biggest swindler in all England."

"Curse him!" muttered an old woman. "She was a bonny lass—my Sally! Curse him!"

All this while, Lord Luxmore sat in lazy dignity in the communion chair, apparently satisfied that as things always had been so they would continue to be; that despite the unheard-of absurdity of a contested election, his pocket-burgh was quite secure. It must have been, to say the least, a great surprise to his lordship when, the poll being closed, its result was found thus: Out of the fifteen votes, six were for Mr. Vermilye, nine for his opponent. Mr. Herbert Oldtower was therefore duly elected as member for the borough of Kingswell.

The earl received the announcement with dignified, incredulous silence; but Mr. Brithwood never spared language.

"It's a cheat—an infamous conspiracy! I will unseat him—by my soul I will!"

"You may find it difficult," said John Halifax, counting out the guineas deposited by Jacob Baines, and laying them in a heap before Mr. Brown, the steward. "Small as the number is, I believe any Committee of the House of Commons will decide that nine honester votes were never polled. But I regret, my lord—I regret deeply, Mr. Brithwood"—and there was a kind of pity in his eye—"that in this matter I have been forced, as it were, to become your opponent. Some day, perhaps, you may both do me the justice that I now can only look for from my own conscience."

"Very possibly," replied the earl, with a satirical bow. "I believe, gentlemen, our business is ended for to-day, and it is a long drive to Norton Bury. Sir Ralph, might we hope for the honour of your company? No?—Good-day, my friends.—Mr. Halifax, your servant."

"One word, my lord. Those workmen of mine, who are your tenants—I am aware what usually results when tenants in arrear vote against their landlords—if, without taking any harsher measures, your agent will be so kind as to apply to me for the rent——"

"Sir, my agent will use his own discretion."

"Then I rely on your lordship's kindliness—your sense of honour."

"Honour is only spoken of between equals," said the earl haughtily. "But on one thing Mr. Halifax may always rely—my excellent memory."

With a smile and bow as perfect as if he were victoriously quitting the field, Lord Luxmore departed. Soon not one remained of all those who had filled the church and churchyard, making there a tumult that is chronicled to this very day by some ancient villagers, who still think themselves greatly ill-used because the Reform Act has blotted out of the list of English boroughs the "loyal and independent" borough of Kingswell.

Sir Ralph Oldtower stood a good while talking with John; and finally, having sent his carriage on, walked with him down Kingswell Hill towards the manor house. I, riding alongside, caught fragments of their conversation.

"What you say is all true, Mr. Halifax; and you say it well. But what can we do? Our English constitution is perfect—that is, as perfect as anything human can be. Yet corruptions will arise; we regret, we even blame—but we cannot remove them. It is impossible."

"Do you think, Sir Ralph, that the Maker of this world—which, so far as we can see, He means like all other of His creations gradually to advance toward perfection—do you think He would justify us in pronouncing any good work therein 'impossible'?"

"You talk like a young man," said the baronet, half sadly. "Coming years will show you the world and the ways of it in a clearer light."

"I earnestly hope so."

Sir Ralph glanced sideways at him—perhaps with a sort of envy of the very youth which he thus charitably excused as a thing to be allowed for till riper wisdom came. Something might have smote the old man with a conviction that in this youth was strength and life, the spirit of the new generation then arising, before which the old worn-out generation would crumble into its natural dust. Dust of the dead ages, honourable dust, to be reverently inurned, and never parricidally profaned by us the living age, who in our turn must follow the same downward path. Dust, venerable and beloved—but still only dust.

The conversation ending, we took our diverse ways; Sir Ralph giving Mr. Halifax a hearty invitation to the manor house, and seeing him hesitate, added, that "Lady Oldtower would shortly have the honour of calling upon Mrs. Halifax."

John bowed. "But I ought to tell you, Sir Ralph, that my wife and I are very simple people—that we make no mere acquaintances, and only desire friends."

"It is fortunate that Lady Oldtower and myself share the same peculiarity." And, shaking hands with a stately cordiality, the old man took his leave.

"John, you have made a step in the world to-day."

"Have I?" he said absently, walking in deep thought, and pulling the hedge leaves as he went along.

"What will your wife say?"

"My wife? bless her!" and he seemed to be only speaking the conclusion of his thinking. "It will make no difference to her—though it might to me. She married me in my low estate—but some day, God willing, no lady in the land shall be higher than my Ursula."

Thus, as in all things, each thought most of the other, and both of Him—whose will was to them beyond all human love, ay, even such love as theirs.

Slowly, slowly, I watched the gray turrets of the manor house fade away in the dusk; the hills grew indistinct, and suddenly we saw the little twinkling light that we knew was the lamp in Longfield parlour shine out like a glow-worm across the misty fields.

"I wonder if the children are gone to bed, Phineas?"

And the fatherly eyes turned fondly to that pretty winking light; the fatherly heart began to hover over the dear little nest of home.

"Surely there's some one at the White Gate. Ursula!"

"John! Ah—it is you."

The mother did not express her feelings after the fashion of most women; but I knew by her waiting there, and by the nervous tremble of her hand, how great her anxiety had been.

"Is all safe, husband?"

"I think so. Mr. Oldtower is elected—*he* must fly the country."

"Then she is saved."

"Let us hope she is. Come, my darling!" and he wrapped his arm round her, for she was shivering. "We have done all we could, and must wait the rest. Come home. Oh!" with a lifted look and a closer strain, "thank God for home!"

CHAPTER XXV.

We always rose early at Longfield. It was lovely to see the morning sun climbing over One-tree Hill, catching the larch wood, and creeping down the broad slope of our field; thence up toward Redwood and Leckington —until, while the dews yet lay thick on our shadowed valley, Leckington Hill was all in a glow of light. Delicious, too, to hear the little ones running in and out, bright and merry as children ought to be in the first wholesome hours of the day—to see them feeding their chickens and petting their doves—calling every minute on father or mother to investigate and enjoy some wonder in farmyard or garden. And either was ever ready to listen to the smallest of these little mysteries, knowing that nothing in childhood is too trivial for the notice, too foolish for the sympathy, of those on whom the Father of all men has bestowed the holy dignity of parenthood.

I could see them now, standing among the flower-beds, out in the sunny morning, the father's tall head in the centre of the group—for he was always the important person during the brief hour or two that he was able to be at home. The mother close beside him, and both knotted round with an interlaced mass of little arms and little eager faces, each wanting to hear everything and to look at everything—everybody to be first and nobody last. None rested quiet or mute for a second, except the one who kept close as his shadow to her father's side, and unwittingly was treated by him less like the other children than like some stray spirit of another world, caught and held jealously, but without much outward notice, lest haply it might take alarm, and vanish back again unawares. Whenever he came home and did not see her waiting at the door, his first question was always, "Where's Muriel?"

Muriel's still face looked very bright this morning—the Monday morning after the election—because her father was going to be at home the whole day. It was the annual holiday he had planned for his workpeople. This only "dinner-party" we had ever given was in its character not unlike that memorable feast, to which were gathered the poor, the lame, the halt, and the blind—all who needed, and all who could not return, the kindness. There were great cooking preparations—everything that could make merry the heart of man—tea, to comfort the heart of woman, hard-working woman—and lots of bright pennies and silver groats to rejoice the very souls of youth.

Mrs. Halifax, Jem Watkins, and his Jenny were as busy as bees all morning. John did his best to help, but finally the mother pleaded how hard it was that the children should miss their holiday walk with him, so we were all dismissed from the scene of action, to spend a long, quiet two hours, lying under the great oak on One-tree Hill. The little ones played about till they were tired; then John took out the newspaper, and read about Ciudad Rodrigo and Lord Wellington's entry into Madrid—the battered eagles and the torn and bloody flags of Badajoz, which were on their way home to the Prince Regent.

"I wish the fighting were over, and peace were come," said Muriel.

But the boys wished quite otherwise; they already gloried in the accounts of battles, played domestic games of French and English, acted garden sieges and blockades.

"How strange and awful it seems, to sit on this green grass, looking down on our quiet valley, and then think of the fighting far away in Spain—perhaps this very minute, under this very sky. Boys, I'll never let either of you be a soldier."

"Poor little fellows!" said I, "they can remember nothing but war time."

"What would peace be like?" asked Muriel.

"A glorious time, my child—rejoicings everywhere, fathers and brothers coming home, work thriving, poor men's food made cheap, and all things prospering."

"I should like to live to see it. Shall I be a woman then, father?"

He started. Somehow she seemed so unlike an ordinary child, that while all the boys' future was merrily planned out—the mother often said, laughing, she knew exactly what sort of a young man Guy would be—none of us ever seemed to think of Muriel as a woman.

"Is Muriel anxious to be grown up? Is she not satisfied with being my little daughter always?"

"Always."

Her father drew her to him, and kissed her soft, shut, blind eyes. Then, sighing, he rose, and proposed that we should all go home.

This first feast at Longfield was a most merry day. The men and their families came about noon. Soon after, they all sat down to dinner; Jem Watkins's plan of the barn being universally scouted in favour of an open-air feast, in the shelter of a hayrick, under the mild blue September sky. Jem presided with a ponderous dignity which throughout the day furnished great private amusement to Ursula, John, and me.

In the afternoon, all rambled about as they liked—many under the ciceroneship of Master Edwin and Master Guy, who were very popular and grand indeed. Then the mother, with Walter clinging shy-eyed to her gown, went among the other poorer mothers there; talked to one, comforted another, counselled a third, and invariably listened to all. There was little of patronizing benevolence about her; she spoke freely, sometimes even with some sharpness, when reproving comment was needed; but her earnest kindness, her active goodness, darting at once to the truth and right of things, touched the women's hearts. While a few were a little wholesomely afraid of her—all recognized the influence of "the mistress," penetrating deep and sure, extending far and wide.

She laughed at me when I told her so—said it was all nonsense—that she only followed John's simple recipe for making his workpeople feel that he was a friend as well as a master.

"What is that?"

"To pay attention and consideration to all they say; and always to take care and remember to call them by their right Christian names."

I could not help smiling—it was an answer so like Mrs. Halifax, who never indulged in any verbal sentimentalism. Her part in the world was deeds.

It was already evening, when, having each contributed our quota, great or small, to the entertainment, we all came and sat on the long bench under the walnut tree. The sun went down red behind us, throwing a last glint on the upland field, where, from top to bottom, the young men and women were running in a long "thread-the-needle." Their voices and laughter came fairly down to us.

"I think they have had a happy day, John. They will work all the better to-morrow."

"I am quite sure of it."

"So am I," said Guy, who had been acting the young master all day, condescendingly stating his will and giving his opinion on every subject, greatly petted and looked up to by all, to the no small amusement of us elders.

"Why, my son?" asked the father, smiling.

But here Master Guy was posed, and everybody laughed at him. He coloured up with childish anger, and crept nearer his mother. She made a place for him at her side, looking appealingly at John.

"Guy has got out of his depth—we must help him into safe waters again," said the father. "Look here, my son, this is the reason—and it is well not to be 'quite sure' of a thing unless one knows the reason. Our people will work the better, because they will work from love. Not merely doing their duty, and obeying their master in a blind way, but feeling an interest in him and all that belongs to him; knowing that he feels the same in them. Knowing, too, that although, being their superior in many things, he is their master and they his servants, he never forgets that saying, which I read out of the Bible, children, this morning: '*One is your Master—even Christ, and all ye are brethren.*' Do you understand?"

I think they did, for he was accustomed to talk with them thus—even beyond their years. Not in the way of preachifying—for these little ones had in their childish days scarcely any so-called "religious instruction," save the daily chapter out of the New Testament, and the father's and mother's daily life, which was a simple and literal carrying out of the same. To that one test was brought all that was thought, or said, or done, in our household, where it often seemed as if the Master were as visibly obeyed and followed as in the household which He loved at Bethany.

As to what doctrinal creed we held, or what sect we belonged to, I can give but the plain answer which John gave to all such inquiries—that we were *Christians.*

After these words from the Holy Book (which the children always listened to with great reverence, as to the Book which their parents most loved and honoured, the reading and learning of which was granted as a high reward and favour, and never carelessly allowed, or—horrible to think!—inflicted as a punishment), we ceased smiling at Guy, who in his turn ceased to frown. The little storm blew over, as our domestic storms usually did, leaving a clear, free heaven. Loving one another, of course we quarrelled sometimes; but we always made it up again, because we loved one another.

"Father, I hear the click of the gate. There's somebody coming," said Muriel.

The father paused in a great romp with his sons—paused, as he ever did when his little daughter's soft voice was heard. "'Tis only a poor boy—who can he be?"

"One of the folk that come for milk most likely—but we have none to give away to-day. What do you want, my lad?"

The lad, who looked miserable and scared, opened his mouth with a stupid "Eh?"

Ursula repeated the question.

"I wants Jacob Baines."

"You'll find him with the rest, in front of that hay-rick, over his pipe and ale."

The lad was off like a shot.

"He is from Kingswell, I think. Can anything be the matter, John?"

"I will go and see. No, boys, no more games—I will be back presently."

He went, apparently rather anxious—as was easy to find out by only a glance at the face of Ursula. Soon she rose and went after him. I followed her.

We saw, close by the hayrick, a group of men angrily talking. The gossiping mothers were just joining them. Far off, in the field, the younger folk were still dancing merrily down their long line of "Thread-the-needle."

As we approached, we heard sobbing from one or two women, and loud curses from the men.

"What's amiss?" said Mr. Halifax, as he came in the midst—and both curses and sobbings were silenced. All began a confused tale of wrongs. "Stop, Jacob—I can't make it out."

"This lad ha' seen it all. And he bean't a liar in big things—speak up, Billy."

Somehow or other we extracted the news brought by ragged Billy, who on this day had been left in charge of the five dwellings rented of Lord Luxmore. During the owners' absence there had been a distraint for rent; every bit of the furniture was carried off; two or three aged and sick folk were left lying on the bare floor—and the poor families here would have to go home to nothing but their four walls.

Again, at repetition of the story, the women wept and the men swore.

"Be quiet," said Mr. Halifax again. But I saw that his honest English blood was boiling within him. "Jem" —and Jem Watkins started, so unusually sharp and commanding was his master's tone—"saddle the mare—quick. I shall ride to Kingswell, and thence to the sheriff's."

"God bless 'ee, sir!" sobbed Jacob Baines's widowed daughter-in-law, who had left, as I overheard her telling Mrs. Halifax, a sick child to-day at home.

Jacob Baines took up a heavy knobbed stick which happened to be leaning against the hayrick, and eyed it with savage meaning.

"Who be they as has done this, master?"

"Put that bludgeon down, Jacob."

The man hesitated—met his master's determined eye —and obeyed him, meek as a lamb.

"But what is us to do, sir?"

"Nothing. Stay here till I return—you shall come to no harm. You will trust me, my men?"

They gathered round him—those big, fierce-looking fellows, in whom was brute force enough to attack or resist anything—yet he made them listen to reason. He explained as much as he could of the injustice which had apparently been done them—injustice which had overstepped the law, and could only be met by keeping absolutely within the law.

"It is partly my fault that I did not pay the rent to-day—I will do so at once. I will get your goods back to-night, if I can. If not, you hale fellows can rough it, and we'll take the women and children in till morning —can we not, love?"

"Oh, readily!" said the mother. "Don't cry, my good women. Mary Baines, give me your baby. Cheer up, the master will set all right!"

John smiled at her in fond thanks—the wife who hindered him by no selfishness or weakness, but was his right hand and support in everything. As he mounted, she gave him his whip, whispering,—

"Take care of yourself, mind. Come back as soon as you can."

And lingeringly she watched him gallop down the field.

It was a strange three hours we passed in his absence. The misty night came down, and round about the house crept wailing the loud September wind. We brought the women into the kitchen—the men lit a fire in the farmyard, and sat sullenly round it. It was as much as I could do to persuade Guy and Edwin to go to bed, instead of watching that "beautiful blaze." There, more than once, I saw the mother standing, with a shawl over her head, and her white gown blowing, trying to reason into patience those poor fellows, savage with their wrongs.

"How far have they been wronged, Phineas? What is the strict law of the case? Will any harm come to John for interfering?"

I told her, no, so far as I knew. That the cruelty and illegality lay in the haste of the distraint, and in the goods having been carried off at once, giving no opportunity of redeeming them. It was easy to grind the faces of the poor, who had no helper.

"Never mind; my husband will see them righted—at all risks."

"But Lord Luxmore is his landlord."

She looked troubled. "I see what you mean. It is easy to make an enemy. No matter—I fear not. I fear nothing while John does what he feels to be right—as I know he will; the issue is in higher hands than ours or Lord Luxmore's.—But where's Muriel?"

For as we sat talking, the little girl—whom nothing could persuade to go to bed till her father came home—had slipped from my hand, and gone out into the blustering night. We found her standing all by herself under the walnut tree.

"I wanted to listen for father. When will he come?"

"Soon, I hope," answered the mother, with a sigh. "You must not stay out in the cold and the dark, my child."

"I am not cold, and I know no dark," said Muriel softly.

And thus so it was with her always. In her spirit, as in her outward life, so innocent and harmless, she knew no dark. No cold looks—no sorrowful sights—no winter—no age. The hand laid upon her dear eyes pressed eternal peace down on her soul. I believe she was, if ever human being was, purely and entirely happy. It was always sweet for us to know this—it is very sweet still, Muriel, our beloved!

We brought her within the house, but she persisted in sitting in her usual place on the door-sill, "waiting" for her father. It was she who first heard the White Gate swing, and told us he was coming.

Ursula ran down to the stream to meet him.

When they came up the path, it was not alone—John was helping a lame old woman, and his wife carried in her arms a sick child, on whom, when they entered the kitchen, Mary Baines threw herself in a passion of crying.

"What have they been doing to 'ee, Tommy?—'ee warn't like this when I left 'ee. Oh, they've been killing my lad, they have!"

"Hush!" said Mrs. Halifax; "we'll get him well again, please God. Listen to what the master's saying."

He was telling to the men who gathered round the kitchen door the results of his journey.

It was—as I had expected from his countenance the first minute he appeared—fruitless. He had found all things at Kingswell as stated. Then he rode to the sheriff's; but Sir Ralph was absent, sent for to Luxmore Hall on very painful business.

"My friends," said the master, stopping abruptly in his narrative, "for a few hours you must make up your minds to sit still and bear it. Every man has to learn that lesson at times. Your landlord has—I would rather be the poorest among you than Lord Luxmore this night. Be patient; we'll lodge you all somehow. To-morrow I will pay your rent—get your goods back—and you shall begin the world again, as my tenants, not Lord Luxmore's."

"Hurrah!" shouted the men, easily satisfied; as working people are, who have been used all their days to live from hand to mouth, and to whom the present is all in all. They followed the master, who settled them in the barn; and then came back to consult with his wife as to where the women could be stowed away. So, in a short time, the five homeless families were cheerily disposed of—all but Mary Baines and her sick boy.

"What can we do with them?" said John questioningly to Ursula.

"I see but one course. We must take him in; his mother says hunger is the chief thing that ails the lad. She fancies that he has had the measles; but our children have had it too, so there's no fear. Come upstairs, Mary Baines."

Passing, with a thankful look, the room where her own boys slept, the good mother established this forlorn young mother and her two children in a little closet outside the nursery door; cheered her with comfortable words; helped her ignorance with wise counsels—for Ursula was the general doctress of all the poor folk round. It was almost midnight before she came down to the parlour where John and I sat, he with little Muriel asleep in his arms. The child would gladly have slumbered away all night there, with the delicate, pale profile pressed close into his breast.

"Is all right, love? How tired you must be!" John put his left arm round his wife as she came and knelt by him in front of the cheerful fire.

"Tired? Oh, of course; but you can't think how comfortable they are upstairs. Only poor Mary Baines does nothing but cry, and keep telling me that nothing ails her lad but hunger. Are they so very poor?"

John did not immediately answer; I fancied he looked suddenly uneasy, and imperceptibly pressed his little girl closer to him.

"The lad seems very ill. Much worse than our children were with measles."

"Yet how they suffered, poor pets! especially Walter.

It was the thought of them made me pity her so. Surely I have not done wrong?"

"No—love; quite right and kind. Acting so, I think one need not fear. See, mother, how soundly Muriel sleeps. It's almost a pity to waken her—but we must go to bed now."

"Stay one minute," I said. "Tell us, John—I quite forgot to ask till now—what is that 'painful business' you mentioned, which called the sheriff to Lord Luxmore's?"

John glanced at his wife, leaning fondly against him, her face full of sweet peace, then at his little daughter asleep, then round the cheerful fire-lit room, outside which the autumn night-wind went howling furiously.

"Love, we that are so happy, we must not, dare not condemn."

She looked at him with a shocked inquiry. "You don't mean—no; it is impossible!"

"It is true. She has gone away."

Ursula sank down, hiding her face. "Horrible! And only two days since she was here, kissing our children."

We all three kept a long silence; then I ventured to ask when she went away.

"This morning early. They took—at least, Mr. Vermilye did—all the property of Lord Luxmore's that he could lay his hands upon—family jewels and money to a considerable amount. The earl is pursuing him now, not only as his daughter's seducer, but as a swindler and a thief."

"And Richard Brithwood?"

"Drinks—and drinks—and drinks. That is the beginning and the end of all."

There was no more to be said. She had dropped for ever out of her old life, as completely as a star out of the sky. Henceforth, for years and years, neither in our home, nor, I believe, in any other, was there the slightest mention made of Lady Caroline Brithwood.

All the next day John was from home, settling the Kingswell affair. The ejected tenants—our tenants now

—left us at last, giving a parting cheer for Mr. Halifax, the best master in all England.

Sitting down to tea, with no small relief that all was over, John asked his wife after the sick lad.

"He is very ill still, I think."

"Are you sure it is measles?"

"I imagine so; and I have seen nearly all childish diseases, except—no, *that* is quite impossible!" added the mother hastily. She cast an anxious glance on her little ones; her hand slightly shook as she poured out their cups of milk. "Do you think, John—it was hard to do it when the child is so ill—I ought to have sent them away with the others?"

"Certainly not. If it were anything dangerous, of course Mary Baines would have told us. What are the lad's symptoms?"

As Ursula informed him, I thought he looked more and more serious; but he did not let her see.

"Make your mind easy, love; a word from Dr. Jessop will decide all. I will fetch him after tea. Cheer up! Please God, no harm will come to our little ones!"

The mother brightened again; with her all the rest; and the tea-table clatter went on merry as ever. Then, it being a wet night, Mrs. Halifax gathered her boys round her knee for an evening chat over the kitchen fire; while through the open door, out of the dim parlour, came "Muriel's voice," as we called the harpsichord. It seemed sweeter than ever this night, like—as her father once said, but checked himself, and never said it afterwards—like Muriel talking with angels.

He sat listening a while, then, without any remark, put on his coat and went out to fetch the good doctor. I followed him down to the stream.

"Phineas," he said, "will you mind—don't notice it to the mother—but mind and keep her and the children downstairs till I come back?"

I promised. "Are you uneasy about Mary Baines's lad?"

"No; I have full trust in human means, and above

all, in—what I need not speak of. Still, precautions are wise. Do you remember that day when, rather against Ursula's wish, I vaccinated the children ?"

I remembered. Also that the virus had taken effect with all but Muriel; and we had lately talked of repeating the much-blamed and miraculous experiment upon her. I hinted this.

"Phineas, you mistake," he answered rather sharply. "She is quite safe—as safe as the others. I wrote to Dr. Jenner himself. But don't mention that I spoke about this."

"Why not ?"

"Because to-day I heard that they have had the smallpox at Kingswell."

I felt a cold shudder. Though inoculation and vaccination had made it less fatal among the upper classes, this frightful scourge still decimated the poor, especially children. Great was the obstinacy in refusing relief; and loud the outcry in Norton Bury, when Mr. Halifax, who had met and known Dr. Jenner in London—finding no practitioner that would do it, persisted in administering the vaccine virus himself to his children. But still, with a natural fear, he had kept them out of all risk of taking the smallpox until now.

"John, do you think——"

"No; I will not allow myself to think. Not a word of this at home, mind. Good-bye!"

He walked away, and I returned up the path heavily, as if a cloud of terror and dole were visibly hanging over our happy Longfield.

The doctor appeared; he went up to the sick lad; then he and Mr. Halifax were closeted together for a long time. After he was gone, John came into the kitchen, where Ursula sat with Walter on her knee. The child was in his little white night-gown, playing with his elder brothers, and warming his rosy toes.

The mother had recovered herself entirely; was content and gay. I saw John's glance at her, and then—and then I feared.

"What does the doctor say? The child will soon be well?"

"We must hope so."

"John, what do you mean? I thought the little fellow looked better when I went up to see him last. And there—I hear the poor mother upstairs crying."

"She may cry; she has need," said John bitterly. "She knew it all the while. She never thought of *our* children; but they are safe. Be content, love—please God, they are quite safe. Very few take it after vaccination."

"It—do you mean the smallpox? Has the lad got smallpox? Oh, God help us! My children—my children!"

She grew white as death; long shivers came over her from head to foot. The little boys, frightened, crept up to her; she clasped them all together in her arms, turning her head with a wild savage look, as if some one were stealing behind to take them from her.

Muriel, perceiving the silence, felt her way across the room, and touching her mother's face, said anxiously, "Has anybody been naughty?"

"No, my darling; no!"

"Then never mind. Father says nothing will harm us, except being naughty. Did you not, father?"

John snatched his little daughter up to his bosom, and called her for the hundredth time the name my poor old father had named her—the "blessed" child.

We all grew calmer; the mother wept a little, and it did her good; we comforted the boys and Muriel, telling them that in truth nothing was the matter, only we were afraid of their catching the little lad's sickness, and they must not go near him.

"Yes; she shall quit the house this minute—this very minute," said the mother sternly, but with a sort of wildness too.

Her husband made no immediate answer; but as she rose to leave the room, he detained her. "Ursula, do you know the child is all but dying?"

"Let him die! The wicked woman! She knew it, and she let me bring him among my children—my own poor children!"

"I would she had never come. But what is done, is done. Love, think—if *you* were turned out of doors this bleak, rainy night—with a dying child."

"Hush, hush!" She sank down with a sob.

"My darling!" whispered John, as he made her lean against him—her support and comfort in all things; "do you think my heart is not ready to break, like yours? But I trust in God. This trouble came upon us while we were doing right; let us do right still, and we need not fear. Humanly speaking, our children are safe; it is only our own terror which exaggerates the danger. They may not take the disease at all. Then, how could we answer it to our conscience if we turned out this poor soul, and *her* child died?"

"No, no!"

"We will use all precautions. The boys shall be moved to the other end of the house."

I proposed that they should occupy my room, as I had had smallpox, and was safe.

"Thank you, Phineas; and even should they take it, Dr. Jenner has assured me that in every case after vaccination it has been the very slightest form of the complaint. Be patient, love; trust in God, and have no fear."

Her husband's voice gradually calmed her. At last, she turned and clung round his neck, silently and long. Then she rose up and went about her usual duties, just as if this horrible dread were not upon us.

Mary Baines and her children stayed in the house. Next day, about noon, the little lad died.

It was the first death that had ever happened under our roof. It shocked us all very much, especially the children. We kept them far away on the other side of the house—out of the house, when possible—but still they would be coming back and looking up at the window, at which, as Muriel declared, the little sick boy "had turned into an angel and flown away." The mother allowed the fancy to remain; she thought it wrong and horrible that a child's first idea of death should be "putting into the pit-hole." Truer and more beautiful was Muriel's instinctive notion of "turning into an angel and flying away." So we arranged that the poor little body should be coffined and removed before the children rose next morning.

It was a very quiet tea-time. A sense of awe was upon the little ones, they knew not why. Many questions they asked about poor Tommy Baines, and where he had gone to, which the mother only answered after the simple manner of Scripture—he "was not, for God took him." But when they saw Mary Baines go crying down the field path, Muriel asked "why she cried? how could she cry, when it was God who had taken little Tommy?"

Afterwards she tried to learn of me privately, what sort of place it was he had gone to, and how he went; whether he had carried with him all his clothes, and especially the great bunch of woodbine she sent to him yesterday; and, above all, whether he had gone by himself, or if some of the "angels," which held so large a place in Muriel's thoughts, and of which she was ever talking, had come to fetch him and take care of him. She hoped—indeed, she felt sure—they had. She wished she had met them, or heard them about in the house.

And seeing how the child's mind was running on the subject, I thought it best to explain to her as simply as I could, the solemn putting off of life and putting on of immortality. I wished that my darling, who could never visibly behold death, should understand it as no image of terror, but only as a calm sleep and a joyful waking in another country, the glories of which eye had not seen nor ear heard.

"Eye has not seen!" repeated Muriel thoughtfully; "can people *see* there, Uncle Phineas?"

"Yes, my child. There is no darkness at all."

She paused a minute, and said earnestly, "I want to

go—I very much want to go. How long do you think it will be before the angels come for me?"

"Many, many years, my precious one," said I, shuddering; for truly she looked so like them, that I began to fear they were close at hand.

But a few minutes afterwards she was playing with her brothers and talking to her pet doves so sweet and humanlike that the fear passed away.

We sent the children early to bed that night, and sat long by the fire, consulting how best to remove infection, and almost satisfied that in these two days it could not have taken any great hold on the house. John was firm in his belief in Dr. Jenner and vaccination. We went to bed greatly comforted, and the household sank into quiet slumbers, even though under its roof slept, in deeper sleep, the little dead child.

That small closet, which was next to the nursery I occupied, safely shut out by it from the rest of the house, seemed very still now. I went to sleep thinking of it, and dreamed of it afterwards.

In the middle of the night a slight noise woke me, and I almost fancied I was dreaming still; for there I saw a little white figure gliding past my bed's foot; so softly and soundlessly—it might have been the ghost of a child—and it went into the dead child's room.

For a moment that superstitious instinct which I believe we all have paralyzed me. Then I tried to listen. There was most certainly a sound in the next room—a faint cry, quickly smothered—a very human cry. All the stories I had ever heard of supposed death and premature burial rushed horribly into my mind. Conquering alike my superstitious dread or fear of entering the infected room, I leaped out of bed, threw on some clothes, got a light, and went in.

There lay the little corpse, all safe and still—for ever. And like its own spirit watching in the night at the head of the forsaken clay, sat Muriel.

I snatched her up and ran with her out of the room in an agony of fear.

She hid her face on my shoulder, trembling. "I have not done wrong, have I? I wanted to know what it was like—that which you said was left of little Tommy. I touched it—it was so cold. O Uncle Phineas! *that* isn't poor little Tommy?"

"No, my blessed one—no, my dearest child! Don't think of it any more."

And, hardly knowing what was best to be done, I called John, and told him where I had found his little daughter. He never spoke, but snatched her out of my arms into his own, took her in his room, and shut the door.

From that time our fears never slumbered. For one whole week we waited, watching the children hour by hour, noting each change in each little face; then Muriel sickened.

It was I who had to tell her father, when, as he came home in the evening, I met him by the stream. It seemed to him almost like the stroke of death.

"O my God, not her! Any but her!" And by that I knew, what I had long guessed, that she was the dearest of all his children.

Edwin and Walter took the disease likewise, though lightly. No one was in absolute danger except Muriel. But for weeks we had what people call "sickness in the house;" that terrible overhanging shadow which mothers and fathers well know; under which one must live and move, never resting night nor day. This mother and father bore their portion, and bore it well. When she broke down, which was not often, he sustained her. If I were to tell of all he did—how, after being out all day, night after night he would sit up watching by and nursing each little fretful sufferer, patient as a woman, and pleasant as a child playmate—perhaps those who talk loftily of "the dignity of man" would smile. I pardon them.

The hardest minute of the twenty-four hours was, I think, that when, coming home, he caught sight of me afar off, waiting for him, as I always did, at the White

Gate; and many a time, as we walked down to the stream, I saw—what no one else saw but God. After such times I used often to ponder over what great love His must be, who, as the clearest revelation of it, and of its nature, calls Himself "the Father."

And He brought us safe through our time of anguish; He left us every one of our little ones.

One November Sunday, when all the fields were in a mist, and the rain came pouring softly and incessantly upon the patient earth, which had been so torn and dried up by east winds that she seemed glad enough to put aside the mockery of sunshine and melt in quiet tears, we once more gathered our flock together in thankfulness and joy.

Muriel came downstairs triumphantly in her father's arms, and lay on the sofa smiling; the firelight dancing on her small white face—white and unscarred. The disease had been kind to the blind child; she was, I think, more sweet-looking than ever. Older, perhaps; the round prettiness of childhood gone—but her whole appearance wore that inexpressible expression, in which, for want of a suitable word, we all embody our vague notions of the unknown world, and call "angelic."

"Does Muriel feel quite well—quite strong and well?" the father and mother both kept saying every now and then, as they looked at her. She always answered, "Quite well."

In the afternoon, when the boys were playing in the kitchen, and John and I were standing at the open door, listening to the dropping of the rain in the garden, we heard, after its long silence, Muriel's "voice."

"Father, listen!" whispered the mother, linking her arm through his as he stood at the door. Soft and slow came the notes of the old harpsichord—she was playing one of the Abbey anthems. Then it melted away into melodies we knew not—sweet and strange. Her parents looked at one another—their hearts were full of thankfulness and joy.

"And Mary Baines's little lad is in the churchyard."

CHAPTER XXVI.

"WHAT a comfort! the daylight is lengthening. I think this has been the very dreariest winter I ever knew. Has it not, my little daughter? Who brought her these violets?"

And John placed himself on a corner of my own particular arm-chair, where, somehow or other, Muriel always lay curled up at tea-time now—(ay, and many hours in the daytime, though we hardly noticed it at first). Taking between his hands the little face, which broke into smiles at the merest touch of the father's fingers, he asked her "when she intended to go a walk with him?"

"To-morrow."

"So we have said for a great many to-morrows, but it is always put off. What do you think, mother—is the little maid strong enough?"

Mrs. Halifax hesitated; said something about "east winds."

"Yet I think it would do her good if she braved east winds, and played out of doors as the boys do. Would you not like it, Muriel?"

The child shrank back with an involuntary "Oh no."

"That is because she is a little girl, necessarily less strong than the lads are. Is it not so, Uncle Phineas?" continued her father hastily, for I was watching them.

"Muriel will be quite strong when the warm weather comes. We have had such a severe winter. Every one of the children has suffered," said the mother, in a cheerful tone, as she poured out a cup of cream for her daughter, to whom was now given, by common consent, all the richest and rarest of the house.

"I think every one has," said John, looking round on his apple-cheeked boys; it must have been a sharp eye that detected any decrease of health or increase of suffering there. "But my plan will set all to rights. I spoke to Mrs. Tod yesterday. She will be ready to take us all in. Boys, shall you like going to Enderley? You shall go as soon as ever the larch wood is green."

For, at Longfield, already we began to make a natural almanac and chronological table. "When the may was out"—"When Guy found the first robin's nest"—"When the field was all cowslips"—and so on.

"Is it absolutely necessary we should go?" said the mother, who had a strong home-clinging, and already began to hold tiny Longfield as the apple of her eye.

"I think so, unless you will consent to let me go alone to Enderley."

She shook her head.

"What, with those troubles at the mills? How can you speak so lightly?"

"Not lightly, love—only cheerfully. The troubles must be borne; why not bear them with as good heart as possible? They cannot last—let Lord Luxmore do what he will. If, as I told you, we re-let Longfield for this one summer to Sir Ralph, we shall save enough to put the mill in thorough repair. If my landlord will not do it, I will; and add a steam-engine too."

Now the last was a daring scheme, discussed many a winter night by us three in Longfield parlour. At first Mrs. Halifax had looked grave—most women would, especially wives and mothers, in those days when every innovation was regarded with horror, and improvement and ruin were held synonymous. She might have thought so too, had she not believed in her husband. But now, at mention of the steam-engine, she looked up and smiled.

"Lady Oldtower asked me about it to-day. She said 'she hoped you would not ruin yourself, like Mr. Miller of Glasgow!' I said I was not afraid."

Her husband returned a bright look. "It is easier to make the world trust one, when one is trusted by one's own household."

"Ah! never fear; you will make your fortune yet, in spite of Lord Luxmore."

For, all winter, John had found out how many cares

come with an attained wish. Chiefly because, as the earl had said, his lordship possessed an "excellent memory." The Kingswell election had worked its results in a hundred small ways, wherein the heavy hand of the landlord could be laid upon the tenant. He bore up bravely against it; but hard was the struggle between might and right, oppression and stanch resistance. It would have gone harder, but for one whom John now began to call his "friend;" at least, one who invariably called Mr. Halifax so—our neighbour, Sir Ralph Oldtower.

"How often has Lady Oldtower been here, Ursula?"

"She called first, you remember, after our trouble with the children; she has been twice since, I think. To-day she wanted me to bring Muriel and take luncheon at the manor house. I shall not go—I told her so."

"But gently, I hope?—you are so very outspoken, love. You made her clearly understand that it is not from incivility we decline her invitations? Well, never mind! Some day we will take our place, and so shall our children, with any gentry in the land."

I think—though John rarely betrayed it—he had strongly this presentiment of future power, which may often be noticed in men who have carved out their own fortunes. They have in them the instinct to rise; and as surely as water regains its own level, so do they, from however low a source, ascend to theirs.

Not many weeks after, we removed in a body to Enderley. Though the chief reason was that John might be constantly on the spot, superintending his mills, yet I fancied I could detect a secondary reason, which he would not own even to himself; but which peered out unconsciously in his anxious looks. I saw it when he tried to rouse Muriel into energy, by telling her how much she would enjoy Enderley Hill; how sweet the primroses grew in the beech wood, and how wild and fresh the wind swept over the common, morning and night. His daily longing seemed to be to make her love the world, and the things therein. He used to turn away, almost in pain, from her smile, as she would listen to all he said, then steal off to the harpsichord, and begin that soft, dreamy music, which the children called "talking to angels."

We came to Enderley through the valley, where was John's cloth-mill. Many a time in our walks he and I had passed it, and stopped to listen to the drowsy fall of the miniature Niagara, or watch the incessant turning, turning of the great water-wheel. Little we thought he should ever own it, or that John would be pointing it out to his own boys, lecturing them on "under-shot" and "over-shot," as he used to lecture me.

It was sweet, though half melancholy, to see Enderley again; to climb the steep meadows and narrow mule-paths, up which he used to help me so kindly. He could not now; he had his little daughter in his arms. It had come, alas! to be a regular thing that Muriel should be carried up every slight ascent, and along every hard road. We paused half-way up on a low wall, where I had many a time rested, watching the sunset over Nunneley Hill—watching for John to come home. Every night—at least after Miss March went away—he usually found me sitting there.

He turned to me and smiled. "Dost remember, lad?" at which appellation Guy widely stared. But, for a minute, how strangely it brought back old times, when there were neither wife nor children—only he and I! This seat on the wall, with its small twilight picture of the valley below the mill, and Nunneley heights, with that sentinel row of sunset trees—was all mine—mine solely—for evermore.

"Enderley is just the same, Phineas. Twelve years have made no change—except in us." And he looked fondly at his wife, who stood a little way off, holding firmly on the wall, in a hazardous group, her three boys. "I think the chorus and comment on all life might be included in two brief phrases given by our friend Shakespeare, one to Hamlet, the other to Othello: '*'Tis very strange*,' and '*'Tis better as it is*.'"

"Ay, ay," said I thoughtfully. Better as it was; better a thousand times.

I went to Mrs. Halifax, and helped her to describe the prospect to the inquisitive boys; finally coaxing the refractory Guy up the winding road, where, just as if it had been yesterday, stood my old friends, my four Lombardy poplars, three together and one apart.

Mrs. Tod descried us afar off, and was waiting at the gate; a little stouter, a little rosier—that was all. In her delight she so absolutely forgot herself as to address the mother as Miss March; at which long-unspoken name Ursula started, her colour went and came, and her eyes turned restlessly towards the church hard by.

"It is all right, miss—ma'am, I mean. Tod bears in mind Mr. Halifax's orders, and has planted lots o' flower roots and evergreens."

"Yes, I know."

And when she had put all her little ones to bed—we, wondering where the mother was, went out towards the little churchyard, and found her quietly sitting there.

We were very happy at Enderley. Muriel brightened up before she had been there many days. She began to throw off her listlessness, and go about with me everywhere. It was the season she enjoyed most—the time of the singing of birds, and the springing of delicate-scented flowers. I myself never loved the beech wood better than did our Muriel. She used continually to tell us this was the happiest spring she had ever had in her life.

John was much occupied now. He left his Norton Bury business under efficient care, and devoted himself almost wholly to the cloth-mill. Early and late he was there. Very often Muriel and I followed him, and spent whole mornings in the mill meadows. Through them the stream on which the machinery depended was led by various contrivances, checked or increased in its flow, making small ponds, or locks, or waterfalls. We used to stay for hours listening to its murmur, to the sharp, strange cry of the swans that were kept there, and the twitter of the water-hen to her young among the reeds. Then the father would come to us and remain a few minutes—fondling Muriel, and telling me how things went on at the mill.

One morning, as we three sat there, on the brickwork of a little bridge, underneath an elm tree, round the roots of which the water made a pool so clear, that we could see a large pike lying like a black shadow half-way down, John suddenly said,—

"What is the matter with the stream? Do you notice, Phineas?"

"I have seen it gradually lowering—these two hours. I thought you were drawing off the water."

"Nothing of the kind—I must look after it. Good-bye, my little daughter. Don't cling so fast; father will be back soon—and isn't this a sweet, sunny place for a little maid to be lazy in?"

His tone was gay, but he had an anxious look. He walked rapidly down the meadows, and went into his mill. Then I saw him retracing his steps, examining where the stream entered the bounds of his property. Finally, he walked off towards the little town at the head of the valley—beyond which, buried in woods, lay Luxmore Hall. It was two hours more before we saw him again.

Then he came towards us, narrowly watching the stream. It had sunk more and more—the muddy bottom was showing plainly.

"Yes—that's it—it can be nothing else! I did not think he would have dared to do it."

"Do what, John? Who?"

"Lord Luxmore." He spoke in the smothered tones of violent passion. "Lord Luxmore has turned out of its course the stream that works my mill."

I tried to urge that such an act was improbable; in fact, against the law.

"Not against the law of the great against the little! Besides, he gives a decent colouring—says he only wants the use of the stream three days a week, to make fountains at Luxmore Hall. But I see what it is—I have seen it coming a whole year. He is determined to ruin me!"

John said this in much excitement. He hardly felt Muriel's tiny creeping hands.

"What does 'ruin' mean? Is anybody making father angry?"

"No, my sweet—not angry—only very, very miserable!"

He snatched her up, and buried his head in her soft, childish bosom. She kissed him and patted his hair.

"Never mind, dear father. You say nothing signifies, if we are only good. And father is always good."

"I wish I were."

He sat down with her on his knee; the murmur of the elm leaves and the slow dropping of the stream soothed him. By-and-by his spirit rose, as it always did, the heavier it was pressed down.

"No, Lord Luxmore shall not ruin me! I have thought of a scheme. But first I must speak to my people—I shall have to shorten wages for a time."

"How soon?"

"To-night. If it must be done—better done at once, before winter sets in. Poor fellows, it will go hard with them—they'll be hard upon me. But it is only temporary; I must reason them into patience, if I can; God knows, it is not they alone who want it."

He almost ground his teeth as he saw the sun shining on the far white wing of Luxmore Hall.

"Have you no way of righting yourself? If it is an unlawful act, why not go to law?"

"Phineas, you forget my principle—only mine, however; I do not force it upon any one else—my firm principle, that I will never go to law. Never! I would not like to have it said, in contradistinction to the old saying, 'See how these Christians *fight!*'"

I urged no more; since, whether abstractedly the question be right or wrong, there can be no doubt that what a man believes to be evil, to him it is evil.

"Now, Uncle Phineas, go you home with Muriel. Tell my wife what has occurred—say I will come to tea as soon as I can. But I may have some little trouble with my people here. She must not alarm herself."

No, the mother never did. She wasted no time in puerile apprehensions—it was not her nature; she had the rare feminine virtue of never "fidgeting"—at least, externally. What was to be borne—she bore: what was to be done—she did; but she rarely made any "fuss" about either her doings or her sufferings.

To-night she heard all my explanation; understood it, I think, more clearly than I did—probably from being better acquainted with her husband's plans and fears. She saw at once the position in which he was placed; a grave one, to judge by her countenance.

"Then you think John is right?"

"Of course I do."

I had not meant it as a question, or even a doubt. But it was pleasant to hear her thus answer. For, as I have said, Ursula was not a woman to be led blindfold, even by her husband. Sometimes they differed on minor points, and talked their differences lovingly out; but on any great question she had always this safe trust in him—that if one were right and the other wrong, the erring one was much more likely to be herself than John.

She said no more, but put the children to bed; then came downstairs with her bonnet on.

"Will you come with me, Phineas? Or are you too tired? I am going down to the mill."

She started, walking quickly—yet not so quick but that on the slope of the common she stooped to pick up a crying child, and send it home to its mother in Enderley village.

It was almost dark, and we met no one else except a young man, whom I had occasionally seen about of evenings. He was rather odd-looking, being invariably muffled up in a large cloak and a foreign sort of hat.

"Who is that watching our mills?" said Mrs. Halifax hastily.

I told her all I had seen of the person.

"A Papist, most likely—I mean a Catholic." (John objected to the opprobrious word "Papist.") "Mrs. Tod says there are a good many hidden hereabouts. They used to find shelter at Luxmore."

And that name set both our thoughts anxiously wandering; so that not until we reached the foot of the hill did I notice that the person had followed us almost to the mill gates.

In his empty mill, standing beside one of its silenced looms, we found the master. He was very much dejected—Ursula touched his arm before he even saw her.

"Well, love—you know what has happened?"

"Yes, John. But never mind."

"I would not—except for my poor people."

"What do you intend doing? That which you have wished to do all the year?"

"Our wishes come as a cross to us sometimes," he said, rather bitterly. "It is the only thing I can do. The water-power being so greatly lessened, I must either stop the mills or work them by steam."

"Do that, then. Set up your steam-engine."

"And have all the country down upon me for destroying hand labour? Have a new set of Luddites coming to burn my mill, and break my machinery? That is what Lord Luxmore wants. Did he not say he would ruin me? Worse than this—he is ruining my good name. If you had heard those poor people whom I sent away to-night! What must they, who will have short work these two months, and after that machinery work, which they fancy is taking the very bread out of their mouths —what must they think of the master?"

He spoke—as we rarely heard John speak; as worldly cares and worldly injustice cause even the best of men to speak sometimes.

"Poor people!" he added, "how can I blame them? I was actually dumb before them to-night, when they said I must take the cost of what I do—they must have bread for their children. But so must I for mine. Lord Luxmore is the cause of all."

Here I heard—or fancied I heard—out of the black shadow behind the loom, a heavy sigh. John and Ursula were too anxious to notice it.

"Could anything be done?" she said. "Just to keep things going till your steam-engine is ready? Will it cost much?"

"More than I like to think of. But it must be; nothing venture, nothing have. You and the children are secure anyhow, that's one comfort. But oh, my poor people at Enderley!"

Again Ursula asked if nothing could be done.

"Yes—I did think of one plan, but——"

"John, I know what you thought of."

She laid her hand on his arm, and looked straight up at him—eye to eye. Often, it seemed that from long habit they could read one another's minds in this way, clearly as a book. At last John said,—

"Would it be too hard a sacrifice, love?"

"How can you talk so! We could do it easily, by living in a plainer way; by giving up one or two trifles. Only outside things, you know. Why need we care for outside things?"

"Why, indeed?" he said, in a low, fond tone.

So I easily found out how they meant to settle the difficulty—namely, by setting aside a portion of the annual income which John, in his almost morbid anxiety lest his family should take harm by any possible non-success in his business, had settled upon his wife. Three months of little renunciations—three months of the old narrow way of living, as at Norton Bury—and the poor people at Enderley might have full wages, whether or no there was full work. Then in our quiet valley there would be no want, no murmurings, and, above all, no blaming of the master.

They decided it all—in fewer words than I have taken to write it—it was so easy to decide when both were of one mind.

"Now," said John, rising, as if a load were taken off his breast—"now, do what he will, Lord Luxmore cannot do me any harm."

"Husband, don't let us speak of Lord Luxmore."

Again that sigh—quite ghostly in the darkness. They heard it likewise this time.

"Who's there?"

"Only I. Mr. Halifax—don't be angry with me."

It was the softest, mildest voice—the voice of one long used to oppression; and the young man whom Ursula had supposed to be a Catholic appeared from behind the loom.

"I do not know you, sir. How came you to enter my mill?"

"I followed Mrs. Halifax. I have often watched her and your children. But you don't remember me."

Yes; when he came underneath the light of the one tallow candle, we all recognized the face—more wan than ever—with a sadder and more hopeless look in the large gray eyes.

"I am surprised to see you here, Lord Ravenel."

"Hush; I hate the very sound of the name. I would have renounced it long ago. I would have hid myself away from him and from the world, if he would have let me."

"He—do you mean your father?"

The boy—no, he was a young man now, but scarcely looked more than a boy—assented silently, as if afraid to utter the name.

"Would not your coming here displease him?" said John, always tenacious of trenching a hairbreadth upon any lawful authority.

"It matters not—he is away. He has left me these six months alone at Luxmore."

"Have you offended him?" asked Ursula, who had cast kindly looks on the thin face, which perhaps reminded her of another—now for ever banished from our sight, and his also.

"He hates me because I am a Catholic, and wish to become a monk."

The youth crossed himself, then started and looked round, in terror of observers. "You will not betray me? You are a good man, Mr. Halifax, and you spoke warmly for us. Tell me—I will keep your secret—are you a Catholic too?"

"No, indeed."

"Ah! I hoped you were. But you are sure you will not betray me?"

Mr. Halifax smiled at such a possibility. Yet, in truth, there was some reason for the young man's fears; since, even in those days, Catholics were hunted down both by law and by public opinion, as virulently as Protestant nonconformists. All who kept out of the pale of the national church were denounced as schismatics, deists, atheists—it was all one.

"But why do you wish to leave the world?"

"I am sick of it. There never was but one in it I cared for, or who cared for me—and now—*Sancta Maria, ora pro nobis.*"

His lips moved in a paroxysm of prayer—helpless, parrot-learnt, Latin prayer; yet, being in earnest, it seemed to do him good. The mother, as if she heard in fancy that pitiful cry, which rose to my memory too —"Poor William!—don't tell William!"—turned and spoke to him kindly, asking him if he would go home with us.

He looked exceedingly surprised. "I—you cannot mean it? After Lord Luxmore has done you all this evil?"

"Is that any reason why I should not do good to his son—that is, if I could? Can I?"

The lad lifted up those soft gray eyes, and then I remembered what his sister had said of Lord Ravenel's enthusiastic admiration of Mr. Halifax. "Oh, you could —you could."

"But I and mine are heretics, you know!"

"I will pray for you. Only let me come and see you —you and your children."

"Come, and welcome."

"Heartily welcome, Lord——"

"No—not that name, Mrs. Halifax. Call me as they used to call me at St. Omer—Brother Anselmo."

The mother was half inclined to smile; but John never smiled at any one's religious beliefs, howsoever foolish. He held in universal sacredness that one rare thing—sincerity.

So henceforward "Brother Anselmo" was almost domesticated at Rose Cottage. What would the earl have said, had a little bird flown over to London and told him that his only son, the heir-apparent to his title and political opinions, was in constant and open association—for clandestine acquaintance was against all our laws and rules—with John Halifax the millowner, John Halifax the radical, as he was still called sometimes; imbibing principles, modes of life and of thought, which, to say the least, were decidedly different from those of the house of Luxmore!

Above all, what would that noble parent have said, had he been aware that this, his only son, for whom, report whispered, he was already planning a splendid marriage—as grand in a financial point of view as that he planned for his only daughter—that Lord Ravenel was spending all the love of his loving nature in the half-paternal, half-loverlike sentiment which a young man will sometimes lavish on a mere child—upon John Halifax's little blind daughter, Muriel!

He said, "She made him good"—our child of peace. He would sit gazing on her almost as if she were his guardian angel—his patron saint. And the little maid in her quiet way was very fond of him; delighting in his company when her father was not by. But no one ever was to her like her father.

The chief bond between her and Lord Ravenel—or "Anselmo," as he would have us call him—was music. He taught her to play on the organ, in the empty church close by. There, during the long midsummer evenings, they two would sit for hours in the organ gallery, while I listened down below; hardly believing that such heavenly sounds could come from those small child fingers; almost ready to fancy she had called down some celestial harmonist to aid her in playing. Since, as we used to say—but by some instinct never said now —Muriel was so fond of "talking with the angels."

Just at this time her father saw somewhat less of her than usual. He was oppressed with business cares; daily, hourly vexations. Only twice a week the great water-wheel, the delight of our little Edwin as it had once been of his father, might be seen slowly turning; and the watercourses along the meadows, with their mechanically-forced channels, and their pretty sham cataracts, were almost always low or dry. It ceased to be a pleasure to walk in the green hollow, between the two grassy hills, which heretofore Muriel and I had liked even better than the Flat. Now she missed the noise of the water—the cry of the water-hens—the stirring of the reeds. Above all, she missed her father, who was too busy to come out of his mill to us, and hardly ever had a spare minute, even for his little daughter.

He was setting up that wonderful novelty—a steam-engine. He had already been to Manchester and elsewhere, and seen how the new power was applied by Arkwright, Hargreaves, and others; his own ingenuity and mechanical knowledge furnished the rest. He worked early and late—often with his own hands—aided by the men he brought with him from Manchester. For it was necessary to keep the secret—especially in our primitive valley—until the thing was complete. So the ignorant, simple mill people, when they came for their easy Saturday's wages, only stood and gaped at the mass of iron and the curiously-shaped brickwork, and wondered what on earth "the master" was about. But he was so thoroughly "the master," with all his kindness, that no one ventured either to question or interfere.

CHAPTER XXVII.

SUMMER waned. Already the beech wood began to turn red, and the little yellow autumn flowers to show themselves all over the common, while in the midst of them looked up the large purple eye of the ground thistle. The mornings grew hazy and dewy. We ceased to take Muriel out with us in our slow walk along John's favourite "terrace" before any one else was stirring. Her father at first missed her sorely, but always kept repeating that "early walks were not good for children." At last he gave up the walk altogether, and used to sit with her on his knee in front of the cottage till breakfast-time.

After that, saying with a kind of jealousy "that every one of us had more of his little daughter than he," he got into a habit of fetching her down to the mill every day at noon, and carrying her about in his arms, wherever he went, during the rest of his work.

Many a time I have seen the rough, coarse, blue-handed, blue-pinafored women of the mill stop and look wistfully after "master and little blind miss." I often think that the quiet way in which the Enderley mill people took the introduction of machinery, and the peaceableness with which they watched for weeks the setting up of the steam-engine, was partly owing to their strong impression of Mr. Halifax's goodness as a father, and the vague, almost superstitious interest which attached to the pale, sweet face of Muriel.

Enderley was growing dreary, and we began to anticipate the cosy fireside of Longfield.

"The children will all go home looking better than they came; do you not think so, Uncle Phineas? Especially Muriel?"

To that sentence I had to answer with a vague assent; after which I was fain to rise and walk away, thinking how blind love was—all love save mine, which had a gift for seeing the saddest side of things.

When I came back, I found the mother and daughter

talking mysteriously apart. I guessed what it was about, for I had overheard Ursula saying they had better tell the child—it would be "something for her to look forward to—something to amuse her next winter."

"It is a great secret, mind," the mother whispered, after its communication.

"Oh yes!" The tiny face, smaller than ever, I thought, flushed brightly. "But I would much rather have a little sister, if you please. Only"—and the child suddenly grew earnest—"will she be like me?"

"Possibly; sisters often are alike."

"No, I don't mean that; but—you know?" And Muriel touched her own eyes.

"I cannot tell, my daughter. In all things else, pray God she may be like you, Muriel, my darling—my child of peace!" said Ursula, embracing her with tears.

After this confidence, of which Muriel was very proud, and only condescended, upon gaining express permission, to reconfide it to me, she talked incessantly of the sister that was coming, until "little Maud"—the name she chose for her—became an absolute entity in the household.

The dignity and glory of being sole depositary of this momentous fact seemed for a time to put new life—bright human life—into this little maid of eleven years old. She grew quite womanly, as it were; tried to help her mother in a thousand little ways, and especially by her own solitary branch of feminine industry—poor darling! She set on a pair of the daintiest elfin socks that ever were knitted. I found them, years after—one finished, one with the needles (all rusty) stuck through the fine worsted ball, just as the child had laid it out of her hand. Ah, Muriel, Muriel!

The father took great delight in this change, in her resuming her simple work, and going about constantly with her mother.

"What a comfort she will be to Ursula one day—an eldest daughter always is. So will she; will she not, Uncle Phineas?"

I smiled assentingly. Alas ! his burthens were heavy enough ! I think I did right to smile.

"We must take her down with us to see the steam-engine first worked. I wish Ursula would have gone home without waiting for to-morrow. But there is no fear—my men are so quiet and good-humoured. What in most mills has been a day of outrage and dread is with us quite a festival. Boys, shall you like to come ? Edwin, my practical lad, my lad that is to carry on the mills—will you promise to hold fast by Uncle Phineas, if I let you see the steam-engine work ?"

Edwin lifted up from his slate bright, penetrating eyes. He was quite an old man in his ways—wise even from his babyhood, and quiet even when Guy snubbed him ; but I noticed he did not come to "kiss and make friends" so soon as Guy. And though Guy was much the naughtiest, we all loved him best. Poor Guy ! he had the frankest, warmest, tenderest boy heart, always struggling to be good, and never able to accomplish it.

"Father," cried Guy, "I want to see the steam-engine move ; but I'll not be a baby like Edwin ; I'll not hold Uncle Phineas's hand."

Hereupon ensued one of those summer storms which sometimes swept across the family horizon, in the midst of which Muriel and I stole out into the empty church, where, almost in the dark—which was no dark to her—for a long hour she sat and played. By-and-by the moon looked in, showing the great gilt pipes of the organ, and the little fairy figure sitting below.

Once or twice she stooped from the organ loft to ask me where was Brother Anselmo, who usually met us in the church of evenings, and whom to-night—this last night before the general household moved back to Longfield—we had fully expected.

At last he came, sat down by me, and listened. She was playing a fragment of one of his Catholic masses. When it ended, he called, "Muriel !"

Her soft, glad answer came down from the gallery.

"Child, play the 'Miserere' I taught you."

She obeyed, making the organ wail like a tormented soul. Truly, no tales I ever heard of young Wesley and the infant Mozart ever surpassed the wonderful playing of our blind child.

"Now, the 'Dies Iræ.'—It will come," he muttered, "to us all."

The child struck a few notes, heavy and dolorous, filling the church like a thunder-cloud, then suddenly left off, and opening the flute stop, burst into altogether different music.

"That is Handel—'I know that my Redeemer liveth.'"

Exquisitely she played it, the clear treble notes seemed to utter like a human voice the very words,—

"*I know that my Redeemer liveth, and He shall stand at the latter day upon the earth.*

"*And though worms destroy this body, yet in my flesh shall I see God.*"

With that she ceased.

"More, more!" we both cried.

"Not now—no more now."

And we heard her shutting up the stops and closing the organ lid.

"But my little Muriel has not finished her tune!"

"She will, some day," said the child.

So she came down from the organ loft, feeling her way along the aisles; and we all went out together, locking the church door.

Lord Ravenel was rather sad that night; he was going away from Luxmore for some time. We guessed why—because the earl was coming. Bidding us good-bye, he said mournfully to his little pet, "I wish I were not leaving you. Will you remember me, Muriel?"

"Stoop down; I want to see you."

This was her phrase for a way she had of passing her extremely sensitive fingers over the faces of those she liked. After which she always said she "saw" them.

"Yes; I shall remember you."

"And love me?"

"And love you, Brother Anselmo."

He kissed, not her cheek or mouth, but her little child hands, reverently, as if she had been the saint he worshipped, or, perhaps, the woman whom afterwards he would learn to adore. Then he went away.

"Truly," said the mother, in an amused aside to me, as with a kind of motherly pride she watched him walk hastily down between those chestnut trees, known of old—"truly, time flies fast. Things begin to look serious—eh, father? Five years hence we shall have that young man falling in love with Muriel."

But John and I looked at the still, soft face, half a child's and half an angel's.

"Hush!" he said, as if Ursula's fancy were profanity; then eagerly snatched it up and laughed, confessing how angry he should be if anybody dared to "fall in love" with Muriel.

Next day was the one fixed for the trial of the new steam-engine; which trial being successful, we were to start at once in a post-chaise for Longfield; for the mother longed to be at home, and so did we all.

There was rather a dolorous good-bye, and much lamenting from good Mrs. Tod, who, her own bairns grown up, thought there were no children worthy to compare with our children. And truly, as the three boys scampered down the road—their few regrets soon over, eager for anything new—three finer lads could not be seen in the whole country.

Mrs. Halifax looked after them proudly—mother-like, she gloried in her sons; while John, walking slowly, and assuring Mrs. Tod over and over again that we should all come back next summer, went down the steep hill, carrying, hidden under many wraps and nestled close to his warm shoulder, his little frail winter rose—his only daughter.

In front of the mill we found a considerable crowd; for the time being ripe, Mr. Halifax had made public the fact that he meant to work his looms by steam, the only way in which he could carry on the mill at all. The announcement had been received with great surprise and remarkable quietness, both by his own workpeople and all along Enderley valley. Still there was the usual amount of contemptuous scepticism, incident on any new experiment. Men were peering about the locked door of the engine-room with a surly curiosity; and one village oracle, to prove how impossible it was that such a thing as steam could work anything, had taken the trouble to light a fire in the yard and set thereon his wife's best tea-kettle, which, as she snatched angrily away, scalded him slightly, and caused him to limp away swearing, a painful illustration of the adage that "a little knowledge is a dangerous thing."

"Make way, my good people," said Mr. Halifax; and he crossed the mill yard, his wife on his arm, followed by an involuntary murmur of respect.

"He be a fine fellow, the master; he sticks at nothing," was the comment heard made upon him by one of his people, and probably it expressed the feeling of the rest. There are few things which give a man more power over his fellows than the thoroughly English quality of daring.

Perhaps this was the secret why John had as yet passed safely through the crisis which had been the destruction of so many millowners—namely, the introduction of a power which the mill people were convinced would ruin hand labour. Or else the folk in our valley, out of their very primitiveness, had more faith in the master; for certainly, as John passed through the small crowd, there was only one present who raised the old fatal cry of "Down with machinery!"

"Who said that?"

At the master's voice—at the flash of the master's eye—the little knot of workpeople drew back, and the malcontent, whoever he was, shrunk into silence.

Mr. Halifax walked past them, entered his mill, and unlocked the door of the room which he had turned into an engine-room, and where, along with the two men he had brought from Manchester, he had been busy almost night and day for this week past in setting up his machinery. They worked—as the Manchester fellows said they had often been obliged to work—under lock and key.

"Your folk be queer 'uns, Mr. Halifax. They say there's six devils inside on her, theer."

And the man pointed to the great boiler which had been built up in an outhouse adjoining.

"Six devils, say they? Well, I'll be Maister Michael Scott—eh, Phineas?—and make my devils work hard."

He laughed, but he was much excited. He went over, piece by piece, the complicated but delicate machinery; rubbed here and there at the brass-work, which shone as bright as a mirror; then stepped back, and eyed it with pride, almost with affection.

"Isn't it a pretty thing? If only I have set it up right—if it will but work."

His hands shook—his cheeks were burning—little Edwin came peering about at his knee; but he pushed the child hastily away; then he found some slight fault with the machinery, and while the workmen rectified it, stood watching them, breathless with anxiety. His wife came to his side.

"Don't speak to me—don't, Ursula. If it fails I am ruined."

"John!" She just whispered his name, and the soft, firm fold of her fingers closed round his, strengthening, cheering. Her husband faintly smiled.

"Here!" He unlocked the door, and called to the people outside. "Come in, two of you fellows, and see how my devils work. Now then!—Boys, keep out of the way; my little girl"—his voice softened—"my pet will not be frightened?—Now, my men—ready?"

He opened the valve.

With a strange noise, that made the two Enderley men spring back as if the six devils were really let loose upon them, the steam came rushing into the cylinder. There was a slight motion of the piston rod.

"All's right! it will work?"

No, it stopped.

John drew a deep breath.

It went on again, beginning to move slowly up and down, like the strong right arm of some automaton giant. Greater and lesser cogwheels caught up the motive power, revolving slowly and majestically, and with steady, regular rotation, or whirling round so fast you could hardly see that they stirred at all. Of a sudden a soul had been put into that wonderful creature of man's making, that inert mass of wood and metal, mysteriously combined. The monster was alive!

Speechless, John stood watching it. Their trial over, his energies collapsed; he sat down by his wife's side, and taking Muriel on his knee, bent his head over hers.

"Is all right, father?" the child whispered.

"All quite right, my own."

"You said you could do it, and you have done it," cried his wife, her eyes glowing with triumph, her head erect and proud.

John dropped his lower, lower still. "Yes," he murmured; "yes, thank God."

Then he opened the door, and let all the people in to see the wondrous sight.

They crowded in by dozens, staring about in blank wonder, gaping curiosity, ill-disguised alarm. John took pains to explain the machinery stage by stage, till some of the more intelligent caught up the principle, and made merry at the notion of "devils." But they all looked with great awe at the master, as if he were something more than man. They listened open-mouthed to every word he uttered, cramming the small engine-room till it was scarcely possible to breathe, but keeping at a respectful distance from the iron-armed monster, that went working, working on, as if ready and able to work on to everlasting.

John took his wife and children out into the open air. Muriel, who had stood for the last few minutes by her father's side, listening with a pleased look to the monotonous regular sound, like the breathing of the demon, was unwilling to go.

"I am very glad I was with you to-day—very glad, father," she kept saying.

He said, as often—twice as often—that next summer, when he came back to Enderley, she should be with him at the mills every day, and all day over, if she liked.

There was now nothing to be done but to hasten as quickly and merrily as possible to our well-beloved Longfield.

Waiting for the post-chaise, Mrs. Halifax and the boys sat down on the bridge over the defunct and silenced waterfall, on the muddy steps of which, where the stream used to dash musically over, weeds and long grasses, mingled with the drooping water-fern, were already beginning to grow.

"It looks desolate, but we need not mind that now," said Mrs. Halifax.

"No," her husband answered. "Steam power once obtained, I can apply it in any way I choose. My people will not hinder; they trust me, they like me."

"And, perhaps, are just a little afraid of you. No matter, it is a wholesome fear. I should not like to have married a man whom nobody was afraid of."

John smiled; he was looking at the horseman riding towards us along the highroad. "I do believe that is Lord Luxmore. I wonder whether he has heard of my steam-engine. Love, will you go back into the mill or not?"

"Certainly not." The mother seated herself on the bridge, her boys around her; John avouched, with an air like the mother of the Gracchi, or like the Highland woman who trained one son after another to fight and slay their enemy—their father's murderer.

"Don't jest," said Ursula. She was much more excited than her husband. Two angry spots burnt on her cheeks when Lord Luxmore came up, and, in passing, bowed.

Mrs. Halifax returned it haughtily enough. But at the moment a loud cheer broke out from the mill hard by, and "Hurrah for the master!" "Hurrah for Mr.

Halifax!" was distinctly heard. The mother smiled right proudly.

Lord Luxmore turned to his tenant—they might have been on the best terms imaginable from his bland air.

"What is that rather harsh noise I hear, Mr. Halifax?"

"It is my men cheering me."

"Oh, how charming! so grateful to the feelings. And *why* do they cheer you, may I ask?"

John briefly told him, speaking with perfect courtesy as he was addressed.

"And this steam-engine—I have heard of it before—will greatly advantage your mills?"

"It will, my lord. It renders me quite independent of your stream, of which the fountains at Luxmore can now have the full monopoly."

It would not have been human nature if a spice of harmless malice—even triumph—had not sparkled in John's eye as he said this. He was walking by the horse's side, as Lord Luxmore had politely requested him.

They went a little way up the hill together, out of sight of Mrs. Halifax, who was busy putting the two younger boys into the chaise.

"I did not quite understand. Would you do me the favour to repeat your sentence?"

"Merely, my lord, that your cutting off of the water-course has been to me one of the greatest advantages I ever had in my life, for which, whether meant or not, allow me to thank you."

The earl looked full in John's face without answering, then spurred his horse violently. The animal started off full speed.

"The children. Good God—the children!"

Guy was in the ditch bank gathering flowers; but Muriel——— For the first time in our lives we had forgotten Muriel.

She stood in the horse's path—the helpless, blind child. The next instant she was knocked down.

I never heard a curse on John Halifax's lips but once—that once. Lord Luxmore heard it too. The image of the frantic father, snatching up his darling from under the horse's heels, must have haunted the earl's good memory for many a day.

He dismounted, saying anxiously, "I hope the little girl is not injured? It was accident—you see—pure accident."

But John did not hear; he would scarcely have heard heaven's thunder. He knelt with the child in his arms by a little runnel in the ditch bank. When the water touched her she opened her eyes with that wide, momentary stare so painful to behold.

"My little darling!"

Muriel smiled, and nestled to him. "Indeed, I am not hurt, dear father."

Lord Luxmore, standing by, seemed much relieved, and again pressed his apologies.

No answer.

"Go away," sobbed out Guy, shaking both his fists in the nobleman's face. "Go away—or I'll kill you—wicked man! I would have done it if you had killed my sister."

Lord Luxmore laughed at the boy's fury, threw him a guinea, which Guy threw back at him with all his might, and rode placidly away.

"Guy—Guy," called the faint, soft voice which had more power over him than any other, except his mother's—"Guy must not be angry. Father, don't let him be angry."

But the father was wholly occupied in Muriel—looking in her face, and feeling all her little fragile limbs, to make sure that in no way she was injured.

It appeared not, though the escape seemed almost miraculous. John recurred, with a kind of trembling tenacity, to the old saying in our house, that "nothing ever harmed Muriel."

"Since it is safe over, and she can walk—you are sure you can, my pet?—I think we will not say anything about this to the mother—at least, not till we reach Longfield."

But it was too late. There was no deceiving the mother. Every change in every face struck her instantaneously. The minute we rejoined her she said,—

"John, something has happened to Muriel."

Then he told her, making as light of the accident as he could—as, indeed, for the first ten minutes we all believed, until alarmed by the extreme pallor and silence of the child.

Mrs. Halifax sat down by the roadside, bathed Muriel's forehead and smoothed her hair; but still the little curls lay motionless against the mother's breast, and still to every question she only answered "that she was not hurt."

All this while the post-chaise was waiting.

"What must be done?" I inquired of Ursula; for it was no use asking John anything.

"We must go back again to Enderley," she said decidedly.

So, giving Muriel into her father's arms, she led the way, and, a melancholy procession, we again ascended the hill to Rose Cottage door.

CHAPTER XXVIII.

WITHOUT any discussion, our plans were tacitly changed; no more was said about going home to dear Longfield. Every one felt, though no one trusted it to words, that the journey was impossible. For Muriel lay, day after day, on her little bed in an upper chamber, or was carried softly down in the middle of the day by her father, never complaining, but never attempting to move or talk. When we asked her if she felt ill, she always answered, "Oh no! only so very tired." Nothing more.

"She is dull for want of the others to play with her. The boys should not run out and leave their sister alone," said John, almost sharply, when one bright morning the lads' merry voices came down from the Flat, while he and I were sitting by Muriel's sofa in the still parlour.

"Father, let the boys play without me, please. Indeed, I do not mind. I had rather lie quiet here."

"But it is not good for my little girl always to be quiet, and it grieves father."

"Does it?" She roused herself, sat upright, and began to move her limbs, but wearily.

"That is right, my darling. Now let me see how well you can walk."

Muriel slipped to her feet and tried to cross the room, catching at table and chairs—now, alas! not only for guidance but actual support. At last she began to stagger, and said, half crying,—

"I can't walk, I am so tired. Oh, do take me in your arms, dear father."

Her father took her, looked long in her sightless face, then buried his against her shoulder, saying nothing. But I think in that moment he too saw, glittering and bare, the long-veiled hand which, for this year past, *I* had seen stretched out of the immutable heavens, claiming that which was its own. Ever after there was discernible in John's countenance a something which all the cares of his anxious yet happy life had never written there—an ineffaceable record, burnt in with fire.

He held her in his arms all day. He invented all sorts of tales and little amusements for her; and when she was tired of these he let her lie in his bosom and sleep. After her bedtime he asked me to go out with him on the Flat.

It was a misty night. The very cows and asses stood up large and spectral as shadows. There was not a single star to be seen.

We took our walk along the terrace and came back again, without exchanging a single word. Then John said hastily,—

"I am glad her mother was so busy to-day—too busy to notice."

"Yes," I answered, unconnected as his words were.

"Do you understand me, Phineas? Her mother must not on any account be led to imagine, or to fear—anything. You must not look as you looked this morning. You must not, Phineas."

He spoke almost angrily. I answered in a few quieting words. We were silent, until over the common we caught sight of the light in Muriel's window. Then I felt rather than heard the father's groan.

"O God! my only daughter—my dearest child!"

Yes, she was the dearest. I knew it. Strange mystery, that He should so often take, by death or otherwise, the *dearest*—always the dearest. Strange that He should hear us cry—us writhing in the dust, "O Father, anything, anything but this!" But our Father answers not; and meanwhile the desire of our eyes—be it a life, a love, or a blessing—slowly, slowly goes—is gone. And yet we have to believe in our Father. Perhaps of all trials to human faith this is the sorest. Thanks be to God if He puts into our hearts such love towards Him that even while He slays us we can trust Him still.

This father—this broken-hearted earthly father—could.

When we sat at the supper-table—Ursula, John, and I, the children being all in bed—no one could have told that there was any shadow over us, more than the sadly-familiar pain of the darling of the house being "not so strong as she used to be."

"But I think she will be, John. We shall have her quite about again before——"

The mother stopped, slightly smiling. It was, indeed, an especial mercy of Heaven which put that unaccountable blindness before her eyes, and gave her other duties and other cares to intercept the thought of Muriel. While, from morning till night, it was the incessant secret care of her husband, myself, and good Mrs. Tod to keep her out of her little daughter's sight, and prevent her mind from catching the danger of one single fear.

Thus, within a week or two, the mother lay down cheerfully upon her couch of pain, and gave another child to the household—a little sister to Muriel.

Muriel was the first to whom the news was told. Her father told it. His natural joy and thankfulness seemed for the moment to efface every other thought.

"She is come, darling! little Maud is come. I am very rich—for I have two daughters now."

"Muriel is glad, father." But she showed her gladness in a strangely quiet, meditative way, unlike a child—unlike even her old self.

"What are you thinking of, my pet?"

"That—though father has another daughter, I hope he will remember the first one sometimes."

"She is jealous!" cried John, in the curious delight with which he always detected in her any weakness, any fault, which brought her down to the safe level of humanity. "See, Uncle Phineas, our Muriel is actually jealous."

But Muriel only smiled.

That smile—so serene—so apart from every feeling or passion appertaining to us who are "of the earth, earthy," smote the father to the heart's core.

He sat down by her, and she crept up into his arms.

"What day is it, father?"

"The first of December."

"I am glad. Little Maud's birthday will be in the same month as mine."

"But you came in the snow, Muriel, and now it is warm and mild."

"There will be snow on my birthday though. There always is. The snow is fond of me, father. It would like me to lie down and be all covered over, so that you could not find me anywhere."

I heard John try to echo her weak, soft laugh.

"This month it will be eleven years since I was born, will it not, father?"

"Yes, my darling."

"What a long time! Then, when my little sister is as old as I am, I shall be—that is, I should have been—a woman grown. Fancy me twenty years old, as tall as mother, wearing a gown like her, talking and ordering, and busy about the house. How funny!" And she laughed again. "Oh no, father, I couldn't do it. I had better remain always your little Muriel, weak and small, who liked to creep close to you, and go to sleep in this way."

She ceased talking; very soon she was sound asleep. But—the father!

Muriel faded, though slowly. Sometimes she was so well for an hour or two that the Hand seemed drawn back into the clouds, till of a sudden again we discerned it there.

One Sunday—it was ten days or so after Maud's birth, and the weather had been so bitterly cold that the mother had herself forbidden our bringing Muriel to the other side of the house where she and the baby lay—Mrs. Tod was laying the dinner, and John stood at the window playing with his three boys.

He turned abruptly, and saw all the chairs placed round the table—all save one.

"Where is Muriel's chair, Mrs. Tod?"

"Sir, she says she feels so tired like she'd rather not come down to-day," answered Mrs. Tod hesitatingly.

"Not come down?"

"Maybe better not, Mr. Halifax. Look out at the snow. It'll be warmer for the dear child to-morrow."

"You are right. Yes, I had forgotten the snow. She shall come down to-morrow."

I caught Mrs. Tod's eyes; they were running over. She was too wise to speak of it—but she knew the truth as well as we.

This Sunday—I remember it well—was the first day we sat down to dinner with the one place vacant.

For a few days longer her father, every evening when he came in from the mills, persisted in carrying her down, as he had said, holding her on his knee during tea, then amusing her and letting the boys amuse her for half an hour or so before bedtime. But at the week's end even this ceased.

When Mrs. Halifax, quite convalescent, was brought

triumphantly to her old place at our happy Sunday dinner-table, and all the boys came pressing about her, vying which should get most kisses from little sister Maud, she looked round, surprised amidst her smiling, and asked,—

"Where is Muriel?"

"She seems to feel this bitter weather a good deal," John said, "and I thought it better she should not come down to dinner."

"No," added Guy, wondering and dolefully, "sister has not been down to dinner with us for a great many days."

The mother started, looked first at her husband, and then at me.

"Why did nobody tell me this?"

"Love—there was nothing new to be told."

"Has the child had any illness that I do not know of?"

"No."

"Has Dr. Jessop seen her?"

"Several times."

"Mother," said Guy, eager to comfort, for naughty as he was sometimes, he was the most tender-hearted of all the boys, especially to Muriel and to his mother, "sister isn't ill a bit, I know. She was laughing and talking with me just now—saying she knows she could carry baby a great deal better than I could. She is as merry as ever she can be."

The mother kissed him in her quick, eager way—the sole indication of that maternal love which was in her almost a passion. She looked more satisfied.

Nevertheless, when Mrs. Tod came into the parlour, she rose and put little Maud into her arms.

"Take baby, please, while I go up to see Muriel."

"Don't—now don't, please, Mrs. Halifax," cried earnestly the good woman.

Ursula turned very pale. "They ought to have told me," she muttered. "John, *you must* let me go and see my child."

"Presently—presently. Guy, run up and play with

Muriel. Phineas, take the others with you. You shall go upstairs in one minute, my darling wife!"

He turned us all out of the room, and shut the door. How he told her that which was necessary she should know—that which Dr. Jessop himself had told us this very morning—how the father and mother had borne this first open revelation of their unutterable grief—for ever remained unknown.

I was sitting by Muriel's bed when they came upstairs. The darling lay listening to her brother, who was squatted on her pillow, making all sorts of funny talk. There was a smile on her face; she looked quite rosy: I hoped Ursula might not notice, just for the time being, the great change the last few weeks had made.

But she did—who could ever blindfold a mother? For a moment I saw her recoil, then turn to her husband with a dumb, piteous, desperate look, as though to say, "Help me—my sorrow is more than I can bear!"

But Muriel, hearing the step, cried with a joyful cry, "Mother! it's my mother!"

The mother folded her to her breast.

Muriel shed a tear or two there, in a satisfied, peaceful way; the mother did not weep at all. Her self-command, so far as speech went, was miraculous. For her look—but then she knew the child was blind.

"Now," she said, "my pet will be good and not cry? It would do her harm. We must be very happy to-day."

"Oh yes." Then, in a fond whisper, "Please, I do so want to see little Maud."

"Who?" with an absent gaze.

"My little sister Maud—Maud that is to take my place, and be everybody's darling now."

"Hush, Muriel," said the father hoarsely.

A strangely soft smile broke over her face—and she was silent.

The new baby was carried upstairs proudly by Mrs. Tod, all the boys following. Quite a levee was held round the bed, where, laid close beside her, her weak hands being guided over the tiny face and form, Muriel first "saw" her little sister. She was greatly pleased. With a grave elder-sisterly air she felt all over the baby limbs, and when Maud set up an indignant cry, began hushing her with so quaint an imitation of motherliness that we were all amused.

"You'll be a capital nurse in a month or two, my pretty!" said Mrs. Tod.

Muriel only smiled. "How fat she is!—and look how fast her fingers take hold! And her head is so round, and her hair feels so soft—as soft as my doves' necks at Longfield. What colour is it? Like mine?"

It was; nearly the same shade. Maud bore, the mother declared, the strongest likeness to Muriel.

"I am so glad. But these?" touching her eyes anxiously.

"No—my darling. Not like you there," was the low answer.

"I am *very* glad. Please, little Maud, don't cry; it's only sister touching you. How wide open your eyes feel! I wonder"—with a thoughtful pause—"I wonder if you can see me. Little Maud, I should like you to see sister."

"She does see, of course. How she stares!" cried Guy. And then Edwin began to argue to the contrary, protesting that as kittens and puppies could not see at first, he believed little babies did not: which produced a warm altercation among the children gathered round the bed, while Muriel lay back quietly on her pillow, with her little sister fondly hugged to her breast.

The father and mother looked on. It was such a picture—these five darlings, these children which God had given them—a group perfect and complete in itself, like a root of daisies, or a branch of ripening fruit, which not one could be added to, or taken from——

No. I was sure, from the parents' smile, that, this once, Mercy had blinded their eyes, so that they saw nothing beyond the present moment.

The children were wildly happy. All the afternoon they kept up their innocent little games by Muriel's bedside, she sometimes sharing, sometimes listening apart. Only once or twice came that wistful, absent look, as if she were listening partly to us and partly to those we heard not; as if through the wide-open orbs the soul were straining at sights wonderful and new—sights unto which *her* eyes were the clear-seeing, and ours the blank and blind.

It seems strange now to remember that Sunday afternoon, and how merry we all were; how we drank tea in the queer bedroom at the top of the house; and how afterwards Muriel went to sleep in the twilight, with baby Maud in her arms. Mrs. Halifax sat beside the little bed, a sudden blazing up of the fire showing the intentness of her watch over these two, her eldest and youngest, fast aleep; their breathing so soft, one hardly knew which was frailest, the life slowly fading or the life but just begun. Their breaths seemed to mix and mingle, and the two faces, lying close together, to grow into a strange likeness each to each. At least we all fancied so.

Meanwhile, John kept his boys as still as mice in the broad window-seat, looking across the white snowy sheet, with black bushes peering out here and there, to the feathery beech wood, over the tops of which the new moon was going down. Such a little young moon! and how peacefully—nay, smilingly—she set among the snows!

The children watched her till the very last minute, when Guy startled the deep quiet of the room by exclaiming, "There—she's gone."

"Hush!"

"No, mother, I am awake," said Muriel. "Who is gone, Guy?"

"The moon—such a pretty little moon."

"Ah, Maud will see the moon some day." She dropped her cheek down again beside the baby sister, and was silent once more.

This is the only incident I remember of that peaceful, heavenly hour.

Maud broke upon its quietude by her waking and

wailing, and Muriel very unwillingly let the little sister go.

"I wish she might stay with me—just this one night; and to-morrow is my birthday. Please, mother, may she stay?"

"We will both stay, my darling. I shall not leave you again."

"I am so glad;" and once more she turned round, as if to go to sleep.

"Are you tired, my pet?" said John, looking intently at her.

"No, father."

"Shall I take your brothers downstairs?"

"Not yet, dear father."

"What would you like, then?"

"Only to lie here, this Sunday evening, among you all."

He asked her if she would like him to read aloud, as he generally did on Sunday evenings.

"Yes, please; and Guy will come and sit quiet on the bed beside me and listen. That will be pleasant. Guy was always very good to his sister—always."

"I don't know that," said Guy, in a conscience-stricken tone. "But I mean to be when I grow a big man—that I do."

No one answered. John opened the large Book—the Book he had taught all his children to long for and to love—and read out of it their favourite history of Joseph and his brethren. The mother sat by him at the fire-side, rocking Maud softly on her knees. Edwin and Walter settled themselves on the hearthrug, with great eyes intently fixed on their father. From behind him the candlelight fell softly down on the motionless figure in the bed, whose hand he held, and whose face he every now and then turned to look at—then, satisfied, continued to read.

In the reading his voice had a fatherly, flowing calm—as Jacob's might have had, when "the children were tender," and he gathered them all round him under the palm trees of Succoth—years before he cried unto the

Lord that bitter cry (which John hurried over as he read), "*If I am bereaved of my children, I am bereaved.*"

For an hour nearly we all sat thus—with the wind coming up the valley, howling in the beech wood, and shaking the casement as it passed outside. Within, the only sound was the father's voice. This ceased at last; he shut the Bible, and put it aside. The group—that last perfect household picture—was broken up. It melted away into things of the past, and became only a picture for evermore.

"Now, boys, it is full time to say good-night. There, go and kiss your sister."

"Which?" said Edwin, in his funny way. "We've got two now, and I don't know which is the biggest baby."

"I'll thrash you if you say that again," cried Guy. "Which, indeed? Maud is but the baby. Muriel will be always 'sister.'"

"Sister" faintly laughed as she answered his fond kiss. Guy was often thought to be her favourite brother.

"Now, off with you, boys; and go downstairs quietly—mind, I say quietly."

They obeyed—that is, as literally as boy nature can obey such an admonition. But an hour after I heard Guy and Edwin arguing vociferously in the dark on the respective merits and future treatment of their two sisters, Muriel and Maud.

John and I sat up late together that night. He could not rest, even though he told me he had left the mother and her two daughters as cosy as a nest of wood-pigeons. We listened to the wild night, till it had almost howled itself away; then our fire went out, and we came and sat over the last faggot in Mrs. Tod's kitchen—the old Debateable Land. We began talking of the long-ago time, and not of this time at all. The vivid present—never out of either mind for an instant—we in our conversation did not touch upon by at least ten years. Nor did we give expression to a thought which strongly oppressed me, and which I once or twice fancied I could detect in John likewise—how very like this night seemed to the night when Mr. March died; the same silentness in the house—the same windy whirl without—the same blaze of the wood fire on the same kitchen ceiling.

More than once I could almost have deluded myself that I heard the faint moans and footsteps overhead—that the staircase door would open, and we should see there Miss March, in her white gown, and her pale, steadfast look.

"I think the mother seemed very well and calm to-night," I said hesitatingly, as we were retiring.

"She is. God help her—and us all!"

"He will."

This was all we said.

He went upstairs the last thing, and brought down word that mother and children were all sound asleep.

"I think I may leave them until daylight to-morrow. And now, Uncle Phineas, go you to bed, for you look as tired as tired can be."

I went to bed; but all night long I had disturbed dreams, in which I pictured over and over again, first the night when Mr. March died—then the night at Longfield, when the little white ghost had crossed by my bed's foot into the room where Mary Baines's dead boy lay. And continually, towards morning, I fancied I heard through my window, which faced the church, the faint, distant sound of the organ, as when Muriel used to play it.

Long before it was light I rose. As I passed the boy's room Guy called out to me,—

"Halloa! Uncle Phineas, is it a fine morning?—for I want to go down into the wood and get a lot of beech nuts and fir cones for sister. It's her birthday to-day, you know."

It *was*, for her. But for us—O Muriel, our darling, darling child!

Let me hasten over the story of that morning, for my old heart quails before it still.

John went early to the room upstairs. It was very still. Ursula lay calmly asleep, with baby Maud in her bosom. On her other side, with eyes wide open to the daylight, lay—that which for more than ten years we had been used to call "blind Muriel." She saw now.

* * * * * *

The same day at evening we three were sitting in the parlour—we elders only; it was past the children's bed-time. Grief had spent itself dry; we were all very quiet. Even Ursula, when she came in from fetching the boys' candle, as had always been her custom, and though afterwards I thought I had heard her going up-stairs, likewise from habit—where there was no need to bid any mother's good-night now—even Ursula sat in the rocking-chair, nursing Maud, and trying to still her crying with a little foolish baby tune that had descended as a family lullaby from one to the other of the whole five—how sad it sounded!

John—who sat at the table, shading the light from his eyes, an open book lying before him, of which he never turned one page—looked up at her.

"Love, you must not tire yourself. Give me the child."

"No, no! Let me keep my baby—she comforts me so." And the mother burst into uncontrollable weeping.

John shut his book and came to her. He supported her on his bosom, saying a soothing word or two at intervals, or, when the paroxysm of her anguish was beyond all bounds, supporting her silently till it had gone by, never once letting her feel that, bitter as her sorrow was, his was heavier than hers.

Thus, during the whole of the day, had he been the stay and consolation of the household. For himself—the father's grief was altogether dumb.

At last Mrs. Halifax became more composed. She sat beside her husband, her hand in his, neither speaking, but gazing, as it were, into the face of this their great sorrow, and from thence up to the face of God. They felt that He could help them to bear it—ay, or anything else that it was His will to send—if they might thus bear it together.

We all three sat thus, and there had not been a sound

in the parlour for ever so long, when Mrs. Tod opened the door and beckoned me.

"He will come in—he's crazy-like, poor fellow! He has only just heard——"

She broke off with a sob. Lord Ravenel pushed her aside and stood at the door. We had not seen him since the day of that innocent jest about his "falling in love" with Muriel. Seeing us all so quiet, and the parlour looking as it always did when he used to come of evenings, the young man drew back, amazed.

"It is not true! No, it could not be true!" he muttered.

"It is true," said the father. "Come in."

The mother held out her hand to him. "Yes, come in. You were very fond of——"

Ah! that name!—now nothing but a name! For a little while we all wept sore.

Then we told him—it was Ursula who did it chiefly—all particulars about our darling. She told him, but calmly, as became one on whom had fallen the utmost sorrow and crowning consecration of motherhood—that of yielding up her child, a portion of her own being, to the corruption of the grave—of resigning the life which out of her own life had been created, unto the Creator of all.

Surely, distinct and peculiar from every other grief, every other renunciation, must be that of a woman who is thus chosen to give her very flesh and blood, the fruit of her own womb, unto the Lord!

This dignity, this sanctity, seemed gradually to fall upon the mourning mother, as she talked about her lost one, repeating often, "I tell you this, because you were so fond of Muriel."

He listened silently. At length he said, "I want to see Muriel."

The mother lit a candle, and he followed her upstairs.

Just the same homely room—half bedchamber, half nursery—the same little curtainless bed where, for a week past, we had been accustomed to see the wasted figure and small pale face lying, in smiling quietude, all day long.

It lay there still. In it, and in the room, was hardly any change. One of Walter's playthings was in a corner of the window-sill, and on the chest of drawers stood the nosegay of Christmas roses which Guy had brought for his sister yesterday morning. Nay, her shawl—a white, soft, furry shawl, that she was fond of wearing—remained still hanging up behind the door. One could almost fancy the little maid had just been said "good-night" to, and left to dream the childish dreams on her nursery pillow, where the small head rested so peacefully, with that pretty babyish nightcap tied over the pretty curls.

There she was, the child who had gone out of the number of our children—our earthly children—for ever.

Her mother sat down at the side of the bed, her father at its foot, looking at her. Lord Ravenel stood by, motionless; then stooping down, he kissed the small marble hand.

"Good-bye, good-bye, my little Muriel!"

And he left the room abruptly, in such an anguish of grief that the mother rose and followed him.

John went to the door and locked it, almost with a sort of impatience, then came back and stood by his darling, alone. Me he never saw—no, nor anything in the world except that little face, even in death so strangely like his own, the face which had been for eleven years the joy of his heart, the very apple of his eye.

For a long time he remained gazing, in a stupor of silence; then, sinking on his knee, he stretched out his arms across the bed, with a bitter cry,—

"Come back to me, my darling, my first-born! Come back to me, Muriel, my little daughter—my own little daughter!"

But thou wert with the angels, Muriel—Muriel!

CHAPTER XXIX.

WE went home, leaving all that was mortal of our darling sleeping at Enderley underneath the snows.

For twelve years after then we lived at Longfield; in such unbroken, uneventful peace, that looking back seems like looking back over a level sea, whose leagues of tiny ripples make one smooth glassy plain.

Let me recall—as the first wave that rose, ominous of change—a certain spring evening, when Mrs. Halifax and I were sitting, as was our wont, under the walnut tree. The same old walnut tree, hardly a bough altered, though many of its neighbours and kindred had grown from saplings into trees—even as some of us had grown from children almost into young men.

"Edwin is late home from Norton Bury," said Ursula.

"So is his father."

"No—this is just John's time. Hark! there are the carriage wheels!"

For Mr. Halifax, a prosperous man now, drove daily to and from his mills in as tasteful an equipage as any of the country gentry between here and Enderley.

His wife went down to the stream to meet him as usual, and they came up the field path together.

Both were changed from the John and Ursula of whom I last wrote. She, active and fresh-looking still, but settling into that fair largeness which is not unbecoming a lady of middle age, he inclined to a slight stoop, with the lines of his face more sharply defined, and the hair wearing away off his forehead up to the crown. Though still not a gray thread was discernible in the crisp locks at the back, which successively five little ones had pulled, and played with, and nestled in; not a sign of age, as yet, in "father's curls."

As soon as he had spoken to me, he looked round as usual for his children, and asked if the boys and Maud would be home to tea.

"I think Guy and Walter never do come home in time when they go over to the manor house."

"They're young—let them enjoy themselves," said the father, smiling. "And you know, love, of all our 'fine' friends, there are none you so heartily approve of as the Oldtowers."

These were not of the former race. Good old Sir Ralph had gone to his rest, and Sir Herbert reigned in his stead—Sir Herbert who, in his dignified gratitude, never forgot a certain election day, when he first made the personal acquaintance of Mr. Halifax. The manor house family brought several other "county families" to our notice, or us to theirs. These, when John's fortunes grew rapidly—as many another fortune grew, in the beginning of the thirty years' peace, when unknown petty manufacturers first rose into merchant princes and cotton lords—these gentry made a perceptible distinction, often amusing enough to us, between John Halifax, the tanner of Norton Bury, and Mr. Halifax, the prosperous owner of Enderley Mills. Some of them, too, were clever enough to discover what a pleasant and altogether "visitable" lady was Mrs. Halifax, daughter of the late Mr. March, a governor in the West Indies, and cousin of Mr. Brithwood of the Mythe. But Mrs. Halifax, with quiet tenacity, altogether declined being visited as anything but Mrs. Halifax, wife of John Halifax, tanner, or mill-owner, or whatever he might be. All honours and all civilities that did not come through him, and with him, were utterly valueless to her.

To this her peculiarity was added another of John's own—namely, that all his life he had been averse to what is called "society;" had eschewed "acquaintances," and—but most men might easily count upon their fingers the number of those who, during a lifetime, are found worthy of the sacred name of "friend." Consequently our circle of associations was far more limited than that of many families holding an equal position with us—on which circumstance our neighbours commented a good deal. But little we cared, no more than we had cared for the chit-chat of Norton Bury. Our whole hearts were bound up within our own home—our happy Longfield.

"I do think this place is growing prettier than ever," said John, when, tea being over—a rather quiet meal without a single child—we elders went out again to the walnut-tree bench. "Certainly, prettier than ever;" and his eye wandered over the quaint, low house, all odds and ends—for nearly every year something had been built, or something pulled down; then crossing the smooth bit of lawn, Jem Watkins's special pride, it rested on the sloping field, yellow with tall buttercups, wavy with growing grass. "Let me see—how long have we lived here? Phineas, you are the one for remembering dates. What year was it we came to Longfield?"

"Eighteen hundred and twelve. Thirteen years ago."

"Ah, so long!"

"Not too long," said Mrs. Halifax earnestly. "I hope we may end our days here. Do not you, John?"

He paused a little before answering. "Yes, I wish it; but I am not sure how far it would be right to do it."

"We will not open that subject again," said the mother uneasily. "I thought we had all made up our minds that little Longfield was a thousand times pleasanter than Beechwood, grand as it is. But John thinks he never can do enough for his people at Enderley."

"Not that alone, love. Other reasons combined. Do you know, Phineas," he continued musingly, as he watched the sun set over Leckington Hill, "sometimes I fancy my life is too easy—that I am not a wise steward of the riches that have multiplied so fast. By fifty a man so blest as I have been ought to have done really something of use in the world—and I am forty-five. Once I hoped to have done wonderful things ere I was forty-five; but somehow the desire faded."

His wife and I were silent. We both knew the truth; that calm as had flowed his outer existence, in which was omitted not one actual duty, still, for these twelve years, all the high aims which make the glory and charm of life as duties make its strength, all the active energies and noble ambitions which especially belong to the prime of manhood, in him had been, not dead perhaps, but sleeping. Sleeping, beyond the power of any human voice to waken them, under the daisies of a child's grave at Enderley.

I know not if this was right—but it was scarcely unnatural. In that heart, which loved as few men love, and remembered as few men remember, so deep a wound could never be thoroughly healed. A certain something in him seemed different ever after, as if a portion of the father's own life had been taken away with Muriel, and lay buried in the little dead bosom of his first-born, his dearest child.

"You forget," said Mrs. Halifax tenderly—"you forget, John, how much you have been doing, and intend to do. What with your improvements at Enderley and your Catholic Emancipation—your Abolition of Slavery and your Parliamentary Reform—why, there is hardly any scheme for good, public or private, to which you do not lend a helping hand."

"A helping purse, perhaps, which is an easier thing, much."

"I will not have you blaming yourself. Ask Phineas there—our household Solomon."

"Thank you, Ursula," said I, submitting to the not rare fortune of being loved and laughed at.

"Uncle Phineas, what better could John have done in all these years than look after his mills and educate his three sons?"

"Have them educated rather," corrected he, sensitive over his own painfully-gained and limited acquirements. Yet this feeling had made him doubly careful to give his boys every possible advantage of study, short of sending them from home, to which he had an invincible objection. And three finer lads, or better educated, there could not be found in the whole country.

"I think, John, Guy has quite got over his fancy of going to Cambridge with Ralph Oldtower."

"Yes; college life would not have done for Guy," said the father thoughtfully.

"Hush! we must not talk about them, for here come the children."

It was now a mere figure of speech to call them so, though in their home-taught, loving simplicity they would neither have been ashamed nor annoyed at the epithet—these two tall lads, who in the dusk looked as manlike as their father.

"Where is your sister, boys?"

"Maud stopped at the stream with Edwin," answered Guy, rather carelessly. His heart had kept its childish faith; the youngest, pet as she was, was never anything to him but "little Maud." One—whom the boys still talked of, softly and tenderly, in fireside evening talks, when the winter winds came and the snow was falling—one only was ever spoken of by Guy as "sister."

Maud, or Miss Halifax, as from the first she was naturally called—as naturally as our lost darling was never called anything else than Muriel—came up, hanging on Edwin's arm, which she was fond of doing, both because it happened to be the only arm low enough to suit her childish stature, and because she was more especially "Edwin's girl," and had been so always. She had grown out of the likeness that we longed for in her cradle days, or else we had grown out of the perception of it; for though the external resemblance in hair and complexion still remained, nothing could be more unlike in spirit than this sprightly elf, at once the plague and pet of the family, to our Muriel.

"Edwin's girl" stole away with him, merrily chattering. Guy sat down beside his mother, and slipped his arm round her waist. They still fondled her with a childlike simplicity—these her almost grown-up sons, who had never been sent to school for a day, and had never learned from other sons of far different mothers that a young man's chief manliness ought to consist in despising the tender charities of home.

"Guy, you foolish boy!" as she took his cap off and

pushed back his hair, trying not to look proud of his handsome face, " what have you been doing all day ? "

" Making myself agreeable, of course, mother."

" That he has," corroborated Walter, whose great object of hero-worship was his eldest brother. " He talked with Lady Oldtower, and he sang with Miss Oldtower and Miss Grace. Never was there such a fellow as our Guy."

" Nonsense ! " said his mother ; while Guy only laughed, too accustomed to this family admiration to be much disconcerted or harmed thereby.

" When does Ralph return to Cambridge ? "

" Not at all. He is going to leave college, and be off to help the Greeks. Father, do you know everybody is joining the Greeks ? Even Lord Byron is off with the rest. I only wish I were."

" Heaven forbid ! " muttered the mother.

" Why not ? I should have made a capital soldier, and liked it too, better than anything."

" Better than being my right hand at the mills, and your mother's at home ? Better than growing up to be our eldest son, our comfort and our hope ? I think not, Guy."

" You are right, father," was the answer, with an uneasy look. For this description seemed less what Guy was than what we desired him to be. With his easy, happy temper, generous but uncertain, and his showy, brilliant parts, he was not nearly so much to be depended on as the grave Edwin, who was already a thorough man of business, and plodded between Enderley Mills and a smaller one which had taken the place of the flour-mill at Norton Bury, with indomitable perseverance.

Guy fell into a brown study, not unnoticed by those anxious eyes, which lingered oftener upon his face than on that of any of her sons. Mrs. Halifax said, in her quick, decisive way, that it was " time to go in."

So the sunset picture outside changed to the home group within—the mother sitting at her little table, where the tall silver candlestick shed a subdued light on her work-basket, that never was empty, and her busy fingers, that never were still. The father sat beside her; he kept his old habit of liking to have her close to him—ay, even though he was falling into the middle-aged comforts of an arm-chair and newspaper. There he sat, sometimes reading aloud, or talking; sometimes lazily watching her, with silent, loving eyes, that saw beauty in his old wife still.

The young folk scattered themselves about the room. Guy and Walter at the unshuttered window—we had a habit of never hiding our home-light—were looking at the moon, and laying bets, *sotto voce*, upon how many minutes she would be in climbing over the oak on the top of One-tree Hill. Edwin sat, reading hard, his shoulders up to his ears, and his fingers stuck through his hair, developing the whole of his broad, knobbed, knotted forehead, where, Maud declared, the wrinkles had already begun to show. For Mistress Maud herself, she flitted about in all directions, interrupting everything, and doing nothing.

"Maud," said her father at last, "I am afraid you give a great deal of trouble to Uncle Phineas."

Uncle Phineas tried to soften the fact, but the little lady was certainly the most trying of his pupils. Her mother she had long escaped from, for the advantage of both. For, to tell the truth, while in the invisible atmosphere of moral training the mother's influence was invaluable, in the minor branch of lesson-learning there might have been found many a better teacher than Ursula Halifax. So the children's education was chiefly left to me, other tutors succeeding as was necessary; and it had just begun to be considered whether a lady governess ought not to "finish" the education of Miss Halifax. But always at home. Not for all the knowledge and all the accomplishments in the world would these parents have suffered either son or daughter—living souls entrusted them by the Divine Father—to be brought up anywhere out of their own sight, out of the shelter and safeguard of their own natural home.

"Love, when I was waiting to-day in Jessop's bank——"

(Ah! that was another change, to which we were even yet not familiar, the passing away of our good doctor and his wife, and his brother and heir turning the old dining-room into a "County Bank—open from ten till four.")

"While waiting there I heard of a lady who struck me as likely to be an excellent governess for Maud."

"Indeed!" said Mrs. Halifax, not over-enthusiastically. Maud became eager to know "what the lady was like?" I at the same time inquiring "who was she?"

"Who? I really did not ask," John answered, smiling. "But of what she is, Jessop gave me first-rate evidence—a good daughter, who teaches in Norton Bury anybody's children for any sort of pay, in order to maintain an ailing mother. Ursula, you would let her teach our Maud, I know?"

"Is she an Englishwoman?" For Mrs. Halifax, prejudiced by a certain French lady who had for a few months completely upset the peace of the manor house, and even slightly tainted her own favourite, pretty Grace Oldtower, had received coldly this governess plan from the beginning. "Would she have to live with us?"

"I think so, decidedly."

"Then it can't be. The house will not accommodate her. It will hardly hold even ourselves. No, we cannot take in anybody else at Longfield."

"But—we may have to leave Longfield."

The boys here turned to listen; for this question had already been mooted, as all family questions were. In our house we had no secrets: the young folk, being trusted, were ever trustworthy; and the parents, clean-handed and pure-hearted, had nothing that they were afraid to tell their children.

"Leave Longfield!" repeated Mrs. Halifax. "Surely—surely——" But glancing at her husband, her tone of impatience ceased.

He sat gazing into the fire with an anxious air.

"Don't let us discuss that question—at least, not to-night. It troubles you, John. Put it off till to-morrow."

No, that was never his habit. He was one of the very few who, a thing being to be done, will not trust it to uncertain "to-morrows." His wife saw that he wanted to talk to her, and listened.

"Yes, the question does trouble me a good deal. Whether, now that our children are growing up, and our income is doubling and trebling year by year, we ought to widen our circle of usefulness, or close it up permanently within the quiet bound of little Longfield. Love, which say you?"

"The latter, the latter—because it is far the happiest."

"I am afraid *not* the latter, because it *is* the happiest."

He spoke gently, laying his hand on his wife's shoulder, and looking down on her with that peculiar look which he always had when telling her things that he knew were sore to hear. I never saw that look on any living face save John's; but I have seen it once in a picture—of two Huguenot lovers. The woman is trying to fasten round the man's neck the white badge that will save him from the massacre (of St. Bartholomew); he, clasping her the while, gently puts it aside—not stern, but smiling. That quiet, tender smile, firmer than any frown, will, you feel sure, soon control the woman's anguish, so that she will sob out—any faithful woman would—"Go, die! Dearer to me than even thyself are thy honour and thy duty!"

When I saw this noble picture, it touched to the core this old heart of mine—for the painter, in that rare expression, might have caught John's. Just as in a few crises of his life I have seen it, and especially in this one, when he first told to his wife that determination which he had slowly come to—that it was both right and expedient for us to quit Longfield, our happy home for so many years, of which the mother loved every flower in the garden, every nook and stone in the walls.

"Leave Longfield!" she repeated again, with a bitter sigh.

"Leave Longfield!" echoed the children, first the youngest, then the eldest, but rather in curiosity than regret. Edwin's keen, bright eyes were just lifted from his book, and fell again; he was not a lad of much speech, or much demonstration of any kind.

"Boys, come and let us talk over the matter."

They came at once and joined in the circle; respectfully, yet with entire freedom, they looked towards their father—these, the sons of his youth, to whom he had been from their birth not only parent and head, but companion, guide, and familiar friend. They honoured him, they trusted him, they loved him; not, perhaps, in the exact way that they loved their mother; for it often seems Nature's own ordinance that a mother's influence should be strongest over her sons, while a father's is greatest over his daughters. But even a stranger could not glance from each to each of those attentive faces, so different, yet with a curious "family look" running through them all, without seeing in what deep, reverent affection, such as naturally takes the place of childish fondness, these youths held their father.

"Yes, I am afraid, after much serious thought on the matter, and much consultation with your mother here, that we ought to leave Longfield."

"So I think," said Mistress Maud, from her footstool; which putting forward of her important opinion shook us all from gravity to merriment, that compelled even Mrs. Halifax to join. Then, laying aside her work, and with it the saddened air with which she had bent over it, she drew her chair closer to her husband, slipping her hand in his, and leaning against his shoulder. Upon which Guy, who had at first watched his mother anxiously, doubtful whether or no his father's plan had her approval, and therefore ought to be assented to, relapsed into satisfied, undivided attention.

"I have again been over Beechwood Hall. You all remember Beechwood?"

Yes. It was the "great house" at Enderley, just on the slope of the hill, below Rose Cottage. The beech wood itself was part of its pleasure ground, and from its gardens honest James Tod, who had them in keeping, had brought many a pocketful of pears for the boys, many a sweet-scented nosegay for Muriel.

"Beechwood has been empty a great many years, father. Would it be a safe investment to buy it?"

"I think so, Edwin, my practical lad," answered the father, smiling. "What say you, children? Would you like living there?"

Each one made his or her comment. Guy's countenance brightened at the notion of "lots of shooting and fishing" about Enderley, especially at Luxmore; and Maud counted on the numerous visitors that would come to John Halifax, Esquire, of Beechwood Hall.

"Neither of which excellent reasons happen to be your father's," said Mrs. Halifax shortly. But John, often tenderer over youthful frivolities than she, answered,—

"I will tell you, boys, what are my reasons. When I was a young man, before your mother and I were married, indeed before I had ever seen her, I had strongly impressed on my mind the wish to gain influence in the world—riches if I could—but at all events influence. I thought I could use it well, better than most men; those can best help the poor who understand the poor. And I can; since, you know, when Uncle Phineas found me, I was——"

"Father," said Guy, flushing scarlet, "we may as well pass over that fact. We are gentlefolks now."

"We always were, my son."

The rebuke, out of its very mildness, cut the youth to the heart. He dropped his eyes, colouring now with a different and a holier shame.

"I know that. Please will you go on, father."

"And now," the father continued, speaking as much out of his own thoughts as aloud to his children—"now, twenty-five years of labour have won for me the position I desired. That is, I might have it for the claiming. I might take my place among the men who have lately risen from the people, to guide and help the people—the Cannings, Huskissons, Peels."

"Would you enter Parliament? Sir Herbert asked me to-day if you ever intended it. He said there was nothing you might not attain to if you would give yourself up entirely to politics."

"No, Guy, no. Wisdom, like charity, begins at home. Let me learn to rule in my own valley, among my own people, before I attempt to guide the State. And that brings me back again to the pros and cons about Beechwood Hall."

"Tell them, John; tell all out plainly to the children."

The reasons were—first, the advantage of the boys themselves; for John Halifax was not one of those philanthropists who would benefit all the world except their own household and their own kin. He wished—since the higher a man rises, the wider and nobler grows his sphere of usefulness—not only to lift himself, but his sons after him—lift them high enough to help on the ever-advancing tide of human improvement, among their own people first, and thence extending outward in the world whithersoever their talents or circumstances might call them.

"I understand," cried the eldest son, his eyes sparkling; "you want to found a family. And so it shall be. We will settle at Beechwood Hall; all coming generations shall live to the honour and glory of your name—our name——"

"My boy, there is only one Name to whose honour we should all live. One Name 'in whom all the generations of the earth are blessed.' In thus far only do I wish to 'found a family,' as you call it, that our light may shine before men—that we may be a city set on a hill—that we may say plainly unto all that ask us, 'For me and my house, we will serve the Lord.'"

It was not often that John Halifax spoke thus, adopting solemnly the literal language of the Book—his and our life's guide, no word of which was ever used lightly in our family. We all listened, as in his earnestness he rose, and standing upright in the firelight, spoke on.

"I believe, with His blessing, that one may 'serve the Lord' as well in wealth as in poverty, in a great house as in a cottage like this. I am not doubtful, even though my possessions are increased. I am not afraid of being a rich man. Nor a great man neither, if I were called to such a destiny."

"It may be—who knows?" said Ursula softly.

John caught his wife's eyes, and smiled.

"Love, you were a true prophet once, with a certain 'Yes, you will,' but now—— Children, you know when I married your mother I had nothing, and she gave up everything for me. I said I would yet make her as high as any lady in the land—in fortune I then meant, thinking it would make her happier; but she and I are wiser now. We know that we never can be happier than we were in the old house at Norton Bury, or in this little Longfield. By making her lady of Beechwood I should double her responsibilities and treble her cares, give her an infinitude of new duties, and no pleasures half so sweet as those we leave behind. Still, of herself and for herself, my wife shall decide."

Ursula looked up at him; tears stood in her eyes, though through them shone all the steadfastness of faithful love. "Thank you, John. I have decided. If you wish it, if you think it right, we will leave Longfield and go to Beechwood."

He stooped and kissed her forehead, saying only, "We will go."

Guy looked up half reproachfully, as if the father were exacting a sacrifice; but I question whether the greater sacrifice were not his who took rather than hers who gave.

So all was settled; we were to leave beloved Longfield. It was to be let, not sold—let to a person we knew, who would take jealous care of all that was ours, and we might come back and see it continually; but it would be ours—our own home—no more.

Very sad—sadder even than I had thought—was the

leaving all the familiar things—the orchard and the flower garden, the meadow and the stream, the woody hills beyond, every line and wave of which was pleasant and dear almost as our children's faces. Ay, almost as that face which for a year—one little year—had lived in sight of, but never beheld, their beauty; the child who one spring day had gone away merrily out of the white gate with her three brothers, and never came back to Longfield any more.

Perhaps this circumstance, that her fading away and her departure happened away from home, was the cause why her memory—the memory of our living Muriel in her human childhood—afterwards clung more especially about the house at Longfield. The other children altered imperceptibly, yet so swiftly, that from year to year we half forgot their old likenesses. But Muriel's never changed. Her image, only a shade, yet often more real than any of these living children, seemed perpetually among us. It crept through the house at dusk; in winter firelight it sat smiling in dim corners; in spring mornings it moved about the garden borders, with tiny soft footsteps neither seen nor heard. The others grew up—would be men and women shortly—but the one child that "was not" remained to us always a child.

I thought, even the last evening—the very last evening that John returned from Enderley, and his wife went down to the stream to meet him, and they came up the field together, as they had done for so many, many years—ay, even then I thought I saw his eyes turn to the spot where a little pale figure used to sit on the door-sill, listening and waiting for him, with her dove in her bosom. We never kept doves now.

And the same night, when all the household was in bed—even the mother, who had gone about with a restless activity, trying to persuade herself that there would be at least no possibility of accomplishing the flitting to-morrow—the last night, when John went as usual to fasten the house door, he stood a long time outside, looking down the valley.

"How quiet everything is! You can almost hear the tinkle of the stream. Poor old Longfield!" And I sighed, thinking we should never again have such another home.

John did not answer. He had been mechanically bending aside and training into its place a long shoot of wild clematis—virgin's bower—which Guy and Muriel had brought in from the fields and planted, a tiny root; it covered the whole front of the house now. Then he came and leaned beside me over the wicket-gate, looking fixedly up into the moonlight blue.

"I wonder if she knows we are leaving Longfield?"

"Who?" said I, for a moment forgetting.

"The child."

CHAPTER XXX.

FATHER and son—a goodly sight, as they paced side by side up and down the gravel walk (alas! the pretty field path belonged to days that were!)—up and down the broad, sunshiny walk, in front of the breakfast-room windows of Beechwood Hall.

It was early—little past eight o'clock; but we kept Longfield hours and Longfield ways still. And, besides, this was a grand day—the day of Guy's coming of age. Curious it seemed to watch him, as he walked along by his father, looking every inch "the young heir," and perhaps not unconscious that he did so; curious enough, remembering how meekly the boy had come into the world, at a certain old house at Norton Bury, one rainy December morning, twenty-one years ago.

It was a bright day to-day—bright as all our faces were, I think, as we gathered round the cosy breakfast-table. There, as heretofore, it was the mother's pride and the father's pleasure that not one face should be missing—that, summer and winter, all should assemble for an hour of family fun and family chat before the busy cares of the day; and by general consent, which had grown into habit, every one tried to keep unclouded this little bit of early sunshine, before the father and brothers went away. No sour or dreary looks, no painful topics, were ever brought to the breakfast-table.

Thus it was against all custom when Mr. Halifax, laying down his paper with a grave countenance, said,—

"This is very ill news. Ten bank failures in the *Gazette* to-day."

"But it will not harm us, father."

"Edwin is always thinking of 'us' and 'our business,'" remarked Guy, rather sharply. It was one of the slight—the very slight—jars in our household, that these two lads, excellent lads both, as they grew into manhood, did not exactly "pull together."

"Edwin is scarcely wrong in thinking of 'us,' since upon us depend so many," observed the father, in that quiet tone with which, when he did happen to interfere between his sons, he generally smoothed matters down and kept the balance even. "Yet though we are ourselves secure, I trust the losses everywhere around us make it the more necessary that we should not parade our good fortune by launching out into any of Guy's magnificences—eh, my boy?"

The youth looked down. It was well known in the family that since we came to Beechwood his pleasure-loving temperament had wanted all sorts of improvements on our style of living—foxhounds, dinner-parties, balls; that the father's ways, which, though extended to liberal hospitalities, forbade outward show, and made our life a thorough family life still, were somewhat distasteful to that most fascinating young gentleman, Guy Halifax, Esquire, heir of Beechwood Hall.

"You may call it 'magnificence,' or what you choose, but I know I should like to live a little more as our neighbours do. And I think we ought too—we that are known to be the wealthiest family——"

He stopped abruptly, for the door opened; and Guy had too much good taste and good feeling to discuss our riches before Maud's poor governess—the tall, grave, sad-looking, sad-clothed Miss Silver, the same whom John had seen at Mr. Jessop's bank, and who had been with us four months—ever since we came to Beechwood.

One of the boys rose and offered her a chair; for the parents set the example of treating her with entire respect—nay, would gladly have made her altogether one of the family, had she not been so very reserved.

Miss Silver came forward with the daily nosegay which Mrs. Halifax had confided to her superintendence.

"They are the best I can find, madam. I believe Watkins keeps all his greenhouse flowers for to-night."

"Thank you, my dear. These will do very well.—Yes, Guy, persuade Miss Silver to take your place by the fire. She looks so cold."

But Miss Silver, declining the kindness, passed on to her own seat opposite.

Ursula busied herself over the breakfast equipage rather nervously. Though an admirable person, Miss Silver in her extreme and all but repellent quietness was one whom the mother found it difficult to get on with. She was scrupulously kind to her, and the governess was as scrupulously exact in all courtesy and attention; still that impassable, self-contained demeanour, that great reticence—it might be shyness, it might be pride—sometimes, Ursula privately admitted, "fidgeted" her.

To-day was to be a general holiday for both masters and servants; a dinner at the mills; and in the evening something which, though we call it a tea-drinking, began to look, I was amused to see, exceedingly like a "ball." But on this occasion both parents had yielded to their young people's wishes, and half the neighbourhood had been invited by the universally-popular Mr. Guy Halifax to celebrate his coming of age.

"Only once in a way," said the mother, half ashamed of herself for thus indulging the boy, as, giving his shoulder a fond shake, she called him "a foolish fellow."

Then we all dispersed, Guy and Walter to ride to the manor house, Edwin vanishing with his sister, to whom he was giving daily Latin lessons in the schoolroom.

John asked me to take a walk on the hill with him.

"Go, Phineas," whispered his wife ; "it will do him good. And don't let him talk too much of old times. This is a hard week for him."

The mother's eyes were mournful, for Guy and "the child" had been born within a year and three days of each other; but she never hinted—it never would have struck her to hint—"this is a hard week for *me*."

That grief—the one great grief of their life—had come to her more wholesomely than to her husband: either because men, the very best of men, can only suffer, while women can endure, or because in the mysterious ordinance of nature Maud's baby lips had sucked away the bitterness of the pang from the bereaved mother, while her loss was yet new. It had never been left to rankle in that warm heart, which had room for every living child, while it cherished, in tenderness above all sorrow, the child that was no more.

John and I, in our walk, stood a moment by the low churchyard wall, and looked over at that plain white stone, where was inscribed her name, "Muriel Joy Halifax," a line out of that New Testament miracle-story she delighted in, "*Whereas I was blind, now I see*," and the date when *she saw*. Nothing more : it was not needed.

"December 5, 1813," said the father, reading the date. "She would have been quite a woman now. How strange! My little Muriel!"

And he walked thoughtfully along, almost in the same footprints where he had been used to carry his darling up the hillside to the brow of Enderley Flat. He seemed in fancy to bear her in his arms still—this little one, whom, as I have before said, Heaven in its compensating mercy, year by year, through all changes, had made the one treasure that none could take away—the one child left to be a child for ever.

I think, as we rested in the selfsame place, the sunshiny nook where we used to sit with her for hours together, the father's heart took this consolation so closely and surely into itself that memory altogether ceased to be pain. He began talking about the other children, especially Maud, and then of Miss Silver, her governess.

"I wish she were more likeable, John. It vexes me sometimes to see how coldly she returns the mother's kindness."

"Poor thing!—she has evidently not been used to kindness. You should have seen how amazed she looked yesterday when we paid her a little more than her salary, and my wife gave her a pretty silk dress to wear to-night. I hardly knew whether she would refuse it, or burst out crying—in girlish fashion."

"Is she a girl? Why, the boys say she looks thirty at least. Guy and Walter laugh amazingly at her dowdy dress and her solemn, haughty ways."

"That will not do, Phineas. I must speak to them. They ought to make allowance for poor Miss Silver, of whom I think most highly."

"I know you do; but do you heartily like her?"

"For most things, yes. And I sincerely respect her, or, of course, she would not be here. I think people should be as particular over choosing their daughter's governess as their son's wife; and having chosen, should show her almost equal honour."

"You'll have your sons choosing themselves wives soon, John. I fancy Guy has a soft place in his heart for that pretty Grace Oldtower."

But the father made no answer. He was always tenacious over the slightest approach to such jests as these. And besides just at this moment Mr. Brown, Lord Luxmore's steward, passed—riding solemnly along. He barely touched his hat to Mr. Halifax.

"Poor Mr. Brown! He has a grudge against me for those Mexican speculations I refused to embark in; he did, and lost everything but what he gets from Lord Luxmore. I do think, Phineas, the country has been running mad this year after speculation. There is sure to come a panic afterwards, and indeed it seems already beginning."

"But you are secure? You have not joined in the

mania, and the crash cannot harm you? Did I not hear you say that you were not afraid of losing a single penny?"

"Yes—unfortunately," with a troubled smile.

"John, what do you mean?"

"I mean, that to stand upright while one's neighbours are falling on all sides is a most trying position. Misfortune makes people unjust. The other day at the sessions I got cold looks enough from my brother magistrates—looks that would have set my blood boiling twenty years ago. And—you saw in the *Norton Bury Mercury* that article about 'grasping plebeian millionaires'—'wool-spinners, spinning out of their country's vitals.' That's meant for me, Phineas. Don't look incredulous. Yes—for me."

"How disgraceful!"

"Perhaps so—but to them more than to me. I feel sorry, because of the harm it may do me—especially among working people, who know nothing but what they hear, and believe everything that is told them. They see I thrive and others fail—that my mills are the only cloth-mills in full work, and I have more hands than I can employ. Every week I am obliged to send new-comers away. Then they raise the old cry—that my machinery has ruined labour. So, you see, for all that Guy says about our prosperity, his father does not sleep exactly upon a bed of roses."

"It is wicked—atrocious!"

"Not at all. Only natural—the penalty one has to pay for success. It will die out most likely; meantime, we will mind it as little as we can."

"But are you safe?—your life——" For a sudden fear crossed me—a fear not unwarranted by more than one event of this year—this terrible 1825.

"Safe?—yes"—and his eyes were lifted—"I believe my life is safe—if I have work to do. Still, for others' sake, I have carried this month past whenever I go to and from the Coltham bank, besides my cash-box—this."

He showed me, peering out of his breast-pocket, a small pistol.

I was greatly startled.

"Does your wife know?"

"Of course. But she knows too that nothing but the last extremity would force me to use it; also that my carrying it, and its being noised about that I do so, may prevent my ever having occasion to use it. God grant I never may! Don't let us talk about this."

He stopped, gazing with a sad abstraction down the sunshiny valley—most part of which was already his own property. For whatever capital he could spare from his business he never sunk in speculation, but took a patriarchal pleasure in investing it in land, chiefly for the benefit of his mills and those concerned therein.

"My poor people—they might have known me better! But I suppose one never attains one's desire without its being leavened with some bitterness. If there was one point I was anxious over in my youth, it was to keep up through life a name like the Chevalier Bayard—how folk would smile to hear of a tradesman emulating Bayard—'*Sans peur et sans reproche*'! And so things might be—ought to be. So perhaps they shall be yet, in spite of this calumny."

"How shall you meet it? What shall you do?"

"Nothing. Live it down."

He stood still, looking across the valley to where the frosty line of the hilltops met the steel-blue, steadfast sky. Yes, I felt sure he *would* "live it down."

We dismissed the subject, and spent an hour more in pleasant chat about many things. Passing homeward through the beech wood, where through the bare treetops a light snow was beginning to fall, John said musingly,—

"It will be a hard winter—we shall have to help our poor people a great deal. Christmas dinners will be much in request."

"There's a saying that the way to an Englishman's heart is through his stomach. So perhaps you'll get justice by spring."

"Don't be angry, Phineas. As I tell my wife, it is not worth while. Half the wrongs people do to us are through sheer ignorance. We must be patient. '*In your patience possess ye your souls.*'"

He said this, more to himself than aloud, as if carrying out the thread of his own thought. Mine following it, and observing him, involuntarily turned to another passage in our Book of books, about the blessedness of some men, even when reviled and persecuted.

Ay, and for all his many cares, John Halifax looked like a man who was "blessed."

Blessed, and happy too, throughout that day, especially in the midst of the mill-yard dinner—which reminded me forcibly of that feast at which guests were gathered out of the highways and hedges—guests such as John Halifax liked to have—guests who could not, by any possibility, "recompense" him. Yet it did one's heart good to hear the cheer that greeted the master, ay, and the young master too, who was to-day for the first time presented as such; as the firm henceforward was to be "Halifax and Son."

And full of smiling satisfaction was the father's look, when in the evening he stood in the midst of his children waiting for "Guy's visitors," as he pertinaciously declared them to be—these fine people, for whose entertainment our house had been these three days turned upside down; the sober old dining-room converted into a glittering ballroom, and the entrance-hall a very "bower of bliss"—all green boughs and Chinese lanterns. John protested he should not have known his own study again; and that, if these festive transformations were to happen frequently, he should soon not even know himself!

Yet for all that, and in spite of the comical horror he testified at this first *bouleversement* of our quiet home ways, I think he had a real pleasure in his children's delight; in wandering with them through the decorated rooms, tapestried with ivy and laurel, and arbor vitæ; in making them all pass in review before him, and admiring their handiwork and themselves.

A goodly group they made—our young folk; there were no "children" now—for even Maud, who was tall and womanly for her age, had bloomed out in a ball dress, all white muslin and camellias, and appeared every inch "Miss Halifax." Walter, too, had lately eschewed jackets, and began to borrow razors; while Edwin, though still small, had a keen, old-man-like look, which made him seem—as he was, indeed, in character—the eldest of the three. Altogether, they were "a fine family," such as any man might rejoice to see growing, or grown up, around him.

But my eyes naturally sought the father as he stood among his boys, taller than any of them, and possessing far more than they that quality for which John Halifax had always been remarkable—dignity. True, Nature had favoured him beyond most men, giving him the stately, handsome presence befitting middle age, throwing a kind of apostolic grace over the high, half-bald crown, and touching with a softened gray the still curly locks behind. But these were mere accidents; the true dignity lay in himself and his own personal character, independent of any exterior.

It was pleasant to watch him, and note how advancing years had given rather than taken away from his outward mien. As ever, he was distinguishable from other men, even to his dress—which had something of the Quaker about it still, in its sober colour, its rarely-changed fashion, and its exceeding neatness. Mrs. Halifax used now and then to laugh at him for being so particular over his daintiest of cambric and finest of lawn—but secretly she took the greatest pride in his appearance.

"John looks well to-night," she said, coming in and sitting down by me, her eyes following mine. One would not have guessed from her quiet gaze that she knew—what John had told me she knew this morning. But these two in their perfect union had a wonderful strength—a wonderful fearlessness. And she had learned from him—what perhaps originally was foreign to her impressible and somewhat anxious mind—that steadfast faith, which, while ready to meet every ill when the time comes, until the time waits cheerfully, and will not disquiet itself in vain.

Thus, for all their cares, her face as well as his was calm and bright. Bright, even with the prettiest girlish blush, when John came up to his wife and admired her—as indeed was not surprising.

She laughed at him, and declared she always intended to grow lovely in her old age. "I thought I ought to dress myself grandly, too, on Guy's birthday. Do you like me, John?"

"Very much; I like that black velvet gown, substantial, soft, and rich, without any show. And that lace frill round your throat—what sort of lace is it?"

"Valenciennes. When I was a girl, if I had a weakness, it was for black velvet and Valenciennes."

John smiled, with visible pleasure that she had even a "weakness" gratified now. "And you have put on my brooch at last, I see."

"Yes; but"—and she shook her head—"remember your promise!"

"Phineas, this wife of mine is a vain woman. She knows her own price is 'far above rubies'—or diamonds either. No, Mrs. Halifax, be not afraid; I shall give you no more jewels."

She did not need them. She stood amidst her three sons with the smile of a Cornelia. She felt her husband's eyes rest on her, with that quiet perfectness of love—better than any lover's love—

> "The fullness of a stream that knew no fall"—

the love of a husband who has been married nearly twenty-five years.

Here a troop of company arrived, and John left me to assume his duty as host.

No easy duty, as I soon perceived; for times were hard, and men's minds troubled. Every one, except the light-heeled, light-hearted youngsters, looked grave.

Many yet alive remember this year—1825—the panic year. War having ceased, commerce, in its worst form, started into sudden and unhealthy overgrowth. Speculations of all kinds sprang up like fungi, out of dead wood, flourished a little, and dropped away. Then came ruin, not of hundreds, but thousands, of all ranks and classes. This year, and this month in this year, the breaking of many established firms, especially bankers, told that the universal crash had just begun.

It was felt even in our retired country neighbourhood, and among our friendly guests this night, both gentle and simple—and there was a mixture of both, as only a man in Mr. Halifax's position could mix such heterogeneous elements—townspeople and country people, dissenters and church folk, professional men and men of business. John dared to do it—and did it. But though through his own personal influence many of different ranks whom he liked and respected, meeting in his own house, learned to like and respect one another, still, even to-night, he could not remove the cloud which seemed to hang over all—a cloud so heavy that none present liked referring to it. They hit upon all sorts of extraneous subjects, keeping far aloof from the one which evidently pressed upon all minds—the universal distress abroad, the fear that was knocking at almost every man's door but ours.

Of course the talk fell on our neighbours—country talk always does. I sat still, listening to Sir Herbert Oldtower, who was wondering that Lord Luxmore suffered the Hall to drop into disgraceful decay, and had begun cutting down the pine woods round it.

"Woods older than his title by many a century—downright sacrilege! And the property being entailed, too—actual robbery of the heir. But, I understand, anybody may do anything with Lord Ravenel—a mere selfish, cynical, idle voluptuary!"

"Indeed you are mistaken, Sir Herbert!" cried Mr. Jessop of Norton Bury—a very honest fellow was Josiah Jessop. "He banks with me—that is, there are some poor Catholics in this neighbourhood whom I pay—but, bless me! he told me not to tell. No, indeed. Cynical he may be; idle, perhaps—most men of fashion are—but Lord Ravenel is not the least like his father—is he, Mr. Halifax?"

"I have not seen Lord Ravenel for many years."

And as if, even to this day, the mention of the young man's name brought back thoughts of the last day we had seen him—a day which, its sadness having gone by, still kept its unspoken sacredness, distinct from all other days—John moved away and went and talked to a girl whom both he and the mother liked above most young girls we knew—simple, sunny-faced Grace Oldtower.

Dancing began. Spite of my Quaker education, or perhaps for that very reason, I delighted to see dancing. Dancing, such as it was then, when young folk moved breezily and lightly, as if they loved it; skimming like swallows down the long lines of the Triumph—gracefully winding in and out through the graceful country dance—lively always, but always decorous. In those days people did not think it necessary to the pleasures of dancing that any stranger should have liberty to snatch a shy, innocent girl round the waist, and whirl her about in mad waltz or awkward polka, till she stops, giddy and breathless, with burning cheek and tossed hair, looking—as I would not have liked to see our pretty Maud look.

No; though while watching the little lady to-night, I was inclined to say to her,—

> "When you do dance, I wish you
> A wave o' the sea, that you might ever do
> Nothing but that."

And in her unwearied spirits she seemed as if she would readily have responded to the wish.

We did not see Guy among the dancers, who were now forming in a somewhat confused square, in order to execute a new dance called quadrilles, of which Miss Grace Oldtower was to be the instructress.

"Where is Guy?" said the mother, who would have missed him among a room full of people. "Have you seen Guy anywhere, Miss Silver?"

Miss Silver, who sat playing tunes—she had declined dancing—turned, colouring visibly.

"Yes, I have seen him; he is in the study."

"Would you be so kind as to fetch him?"

The governess rose and crossed the room, with a stately walk—statelier than usual. Her silk gown, of some rich soft colour, fashioned after Mrs. Halifax's taste, and the chaplet of bay leaves, which Maud had insisted upon putting in her dark hair, made an astonishing change in Miss Silver. I could not help noticing it to Mrs. Halifax.

"Yes, indeed, she looks well. John says her features are fine; but, for my part, I don't care for your statuesque faces; I like colour—expression. See that bright little Grace Oldtower!—a thoroughly English rose; I like *her*. Poor Miss Silver! I wish——"

What, out of compunction for a certain sharpness with which she had spoken, Mrs. Halifax was about to wish, remained undeclared. For, just this minute, Guy entered, and leaning his handsome head and his tender *petits soins* over the "English rose," as his mother called her, led her out to the dancing.

We sat down and looked on.

"Guy dances lazily; he is rather pale too, I fancy."

"Tired, probably. He was out far too long on the ice to-day with Maud and Miss Silver. What a pretty creature his partner is!" added Ursula thoughtfully.

"The children are growing up fast," I said.

"Ay, indeed. To think that Guy is actually twenty-one—the age when his father was married!"

"Guy will be reminding you of that fact some day soon."

Mrs. Halifax smiled. "The sooner the better, if only he makes a worthy choice—if only he brings me a daughter whom I can love."

And I fancied there was love—motherly love—in the

eyes that followed through the graceful mazes of her dancing the bonny English rose.

Guy and his partner sat down beside us. His mother noticed that he had turned very pale again, and the lad owned to be in some pain: he had twisted his foot that morning in helping Maud and Miss Silver across the ice; but it was a mere trifle—not worth mentioning.

It passed over, with one or two anxious inquiries on the mother's part, and a soft, dewy shadow over the down-dropped cheek of the little Rose, who evidently did not like to think of any harm coming to her old playfellow. Then Sir Herbert appeared to lead Mrs. Halifax in to supper, Guy limped along with pretty Grace on his arm, and all the guests, just enough to fill our longest table in John's study, came thronging round in a buzz of mirthfulness.

Either the warm, hospitable atmosphere, or the sight of the merry youngsters, or the general influence of social pleasantness, had for the time being dispelled the cloud. But certainly it was dispelled. The master of the feast looked down two long lines of happy faces—his own as bright as theirs—down to where, at the foot of the table, the mother and mistress sat. She had been slightly nervous at times during the evening, but now she appeared thoroughly at ease and glad—glad to see her husband take his place at the head of his own hospitable board, in the midst of his own friends and his own people, honoured and beloved. It seemed a good omen—an omen that the bitter things outside would pass away.

How bitter they had been, and how sore the wife's heart still felt, I could see from the jealous way in which, smiling and cheerful as her demeanour was, she caught every look, every word of those around her which might chance to bear reference to her husband; in her quick avoidance of every topic connected with these disastrous times, and, above all, in her hurried grasp of a newspaper that some careless servant brought in fresh from the night mail, wet with sleet and snow.

"Do you get your country paper regularly?" asked some one at table. And then some others appeared to recollect the *Norton Bury Mercury*, and its virulent attacks on their host—for there ensued an awkward pause, during which I saw Ursula's face beginning to burn. But she conquered her wrath.

"There is often much interest in our provincial papers, Sir Herbert. My husband makes a point of taking them all in—bad and good—of every shade of politics. He believes it is only by hearing all sides that you can truly judge of the state of the country."

"Just as a physician must hear all symptoms before he decides on the patient's case. At least, so our good old friend Dr. Jessop used to say."

"Eh?" said Mr. Jessop the banker, catching his own name, and waking up from a brown study, in which he had seemed to see nothing—except, perhaps, the newspaper, which, in its printed cover, lay between himself and Mrs. Halifax. "Eh? did any one—— Oh, I beg pardon—beg pardon—Sir Herbert," hastily added the old man, who was a very meek and worthy soul, and had been perhaps more subdued than usual this evening.

"I was referring," said Sir Herbert, with his usual ponderous civility, "to your excellent brother, who was so much respected among us—for which respect, allow me to say, he did not leave us without an inheritor."

The old banker answered the formal bow with a kind of nervous hurry; and then Sir Herbert, with a loud premise of his right as the oldest friend of our family, tried to obtain silence for the customary speech, prefatory to the customary toast of "Health and prosperity to the heir of Beechwood."

There was great applause and filling of glasses; great smiling and whispering; everybody glancing at poor Guy, who turned red and white, and evidently wished himself a hundred miles off. In the confusion, I felt my sleeve touched, and saw leaning towards me, hidden by Maud's laughing happy face, the old banker. He held in his hand the newspaper which seemed to have so fascinated him.

"It's the *London Gazette*. Mr. Halifax gets it three hours before any of us. I may open it? It is important to me. Mrs. Halifax would excuse, eh?"

Of course she would. Especially if she had seen the old man's look, as his trembling fingers vainly tried to unfold the sheet without a single rustle betraying his surreptitious curiosity.

Sir Herbert rose, cleared his throat, and began,—

"Ladies and gentlemen, I speak as a father myself, and as son of a father whom—whom I will not refer to here, except to say that his good heart would have rejoiced to see this day. The high esteem in which Sir Ralph always held Mr. Halifax has descended, and will descend——"

Here some one called out,—

"Mr. Jessop! Look at Mr. Jessop!"

The old man had suddenly sank back, with a sort of choking groan. His eyes were staring blankly, his cheek was the colour of ashes. But when he saw every one looking at him, he tried desperately to recover himself.

"'Tis nothing. Nothing of the slightest moment. Eh?" clutching tightly at the paper which Mrs. Halifax was kindly removing out of his hand. "There's no news in it—none, I assure you."

But from his agitation—from the pitiful effort he made to disguise it—it was plain enough that there was news. Plain also, as in these dangerous and critical times men were only too quick to divine, in what that news consisted. Tidings which now made every newspaper a sight of fear—especially this—the *London Gazette*.

Edwin caught and read the fatal page—the fatal column—known only too well.

"W——'s have stopped payment."

W——'s was a great London house, the favourite banking-house in our county, with which many provincial banks, and Jessop's especially, were widely connected, and would be no one knew how widely involved.

"W——'s stopped payment!"

A murmur—a hush of momentary suspense, as the *Gazette* was passed hurriedly from hand to hand; and then our guests, one and all, sat looking at one another in breathless fear, suspicion, or assured dismay. For, as every one was aware (we knew our neighbours' affairs so well about innocent Enderley), there was not a single household of that merry little company upon whom, near or remote, the blow would not fall—except ours.

No polite disguise could gloss over the general consternation. Few thought of Jessop—only of themselves. Many a father turned pale; many a mother melted into smothered tears. More than one honest countenance that five minutes before had beamed like the rising sun, all friendliness and jocularity, I saw shrink into a wizened, worldly face, with greedy selfishness peering out of the corners of its eyes, eager to conceal its own alarms and dive as far as possible into the terrors of its neighbours.

"There will be a run on Jessop's bank to-morrow," I heard one person saying; glancing to where the poor old banker still sat, with a vacant, stupefied smile, assuring all around him that "nothing had happened; really, nothing."

"A run? I suppose so. Then it will be '*Sauve qui peut,*' and the devil take the hindmost."

"What say you to all this, Mr. Halifax?"

John still kept his place. He sat perfectly quiet, and had never spoken a syllable.

When Sir Herbert, who was the first to recover from the shock of these ill-tidings, called him by his name, Mr. Halifax looked quickly up. It was to see, instead of those two lines of happy faces, faces already gathering in troubled groups, faces angry, sullen, or miserable, all of which, with a vague distrust, seemed instinctively turned upon him.

"Mr. Halifax," said the baronet, and one could see how, in spite of his steadfast politeness, he too was not without his anxieties, "this is an unpleasant breaking-in upon your kindly hospitalities. I suppose, through this unpropitious event, each of us must make up our minds to some loss. Let me hope yours will be trifling."

John made no answer.

"Or, perhaps—though I can hardly hope anything so fortunate—perhaps this failure will not affect you at all?"

He waited—as did many others, for Mr. Halifax's reply, which was long in coming. However, since all seemed to expect it, it did come at last; but grave and sad, as if it were the announcement of some great misfortune.

"No, Sir Herbert; it will not affect me at all."

Sir Herbert, and not he alone, looked surprised—uneasily surprised. Some mutters there were of "congratulation." Then arose a troubled murmur of talking, in which the master of the house was forgotten; until the baronet said, "My friends, I think we are forgetting our courtesy. Allow me to give you without more delay—the toast I was about to propose—'Health, long life, and happiness to Mr. Guy Halifax.'"

And so poor Guy's birthday toast was drunk; almost in silence; and the few words he said in acknowledgment were just listened to, scarcely heard. Every one rose from table, and the festivities were over.

One by one all our guests began to make excuse. One by one, involuntarily perhaps, yet not the less painfully and plainly, they all shrunk away from us, as if in the universal trouble we, who had nothing to fear, had no part nor lot. Formal congratulations, given with pale lips and wandering eyes; brusque adieux, as some of the more honest or less courteous showed but too obviously how cruelly, even resentfully, they felt the inequalities of fortune; hasty departures, full of a dismay that rejected angrily every shadow of consolation—all these things John had to meet and to bear.

He met them with composure, scarcely speaking a word, as indeed what was there to say? To all the friendly speeches, real or pretended, he listened with a kind of sad gravity: of all harsher words than these—

and there were not a few—he took not the least notice, but held his place as master of the house; generously deaf and blind to everything that it were as well the master of the house should neither hear nor see.

At last he was left, a very pariah of prosperity, by his own hearth, quite alone.

The last carriage had rolled away; the tired household had gone to bed; there was no one in the study but me. John came in and stood leaning with both his arms against the fireplace, motionless and silent. He leant there so long, that at last I touched him.

"Well, Phineas!"

I saw this night's events had wounded him to the core.

"Are you thinking of these honest, friendly, disinterested guests of ours? Don't! They are not worth a single thought."

"Not an angry thought, certainly." And he smiled at my wrath—a sad smile.

"Ah, Phineas! now I begin to understand what is meant by the curse of prosperity."

CHAPTER XXXI.

A GREAT, eager, but doggedly-quiet crowd, of which each had his or her—for it was half women—individual terror to hide, his or her individual interest to fight for, and cared not a straw for that of any one else.

It was market-day, and this crowd was collected and collecting every minute, before the bank at Norton Bury. It included all classes, from the stout farmer's wife or market-woman, to the pale, frightened lady of "limited income," who had never been in such a throng before; from the aproned mechanic to the gentleman who sat in his carriage at the street corner, confident that whatever poor chance there was, his would be the best.

Everybody was, as I have said, extremely quiet. You heard none of the jokes that always rise in and circulate through a crowd; none of the loud outcries of a mob.

All were intent on themselves and their own business; on that fast-bolted red-baize door, and on the green blind of the windows, which informed them that it was "open from ten till four."

The abbey clock struck three-quarters. Then there was a slight stirring, a rustling here and there of paper, as some one drew out and examined his bank notes; openly, with small fear of theft—they were not worth stealing.

John and I, a little way off, stood looking on, where we had once watched a far different crowd; for Mr. Jessop owned the doctor's former house, and in sight of the green bank blinds were my dear old father's known windows.

Guy's birthday had fallen on a Saturday. This was Monday morning. We had driven over to Norton Bury, John and I, at an unusually early hour. He did not exactly tell me why, but it was not difficult to guess. Not difficult to perceive how strongly he was interested, even affected—as any man, knowing all the circumstances, could not but be affected—by the sight of that crowd, all the sadder for its being such a patient, decent, respectable crowd, out of which so large a proportion was women.

I noticed this latter fact to John.

"Yes, I was sure it would be so. Jessop's bank has such a number of small depositors and issues so many small notes. He cannot cash above half of them without some notice. If there comes a run, he may have to stop payment this very day; and then, how wide the misery would spread among the poor, God knows."

His eye wandered pitifully over the heaving mass of anxious faces blue with cold, and growing more and more despondent as every minute they turned with a common impulse from the closed bank door to the Abbey clock, glittering far up in the sunshiny atmosphere of morning.

Its finger touched the one heel of the great striding X—glided on to the other—the ten strokes fell leisurely and regularly upon the clear frosty air; then the chimes —Norton Bury was proud of its Abbey chimes—burst out in the tune of "Life let us cherish."

The bells went through all the tune, to the very last note—then ensued silence. The crowd were silent too —almost breathless with intent listening—but, alas! not to the merry Abbey chimes.

The bank door remained closed—not a rattle at the bolts, not a clerk's face peering out above the blind. The house was as shut up and desolate as if it were entirely empty.

Five whole minutes—by the Abbey clock—did that poor, patient crowd wait on the pavement. Then a murmur arose. One or two men hammered at the door; some frightened women, jostled in the press, began to scream.

John could bear it no longer. "Come along with me," he said hurriedly. "I must see Jessop—we can get in at the garden door."

This was a little gate round the corner of the street, well known to us both in those brief "courting days," when we came to tea of evenings, and found Mrs. Jessop and Ursula March in the garden watering the plants and tying up the roses. Nay, we passed out of it into the same summer parlour, where—I cannot tell if John ever knew of the incident, at all events he never mentioned it to me—there had been transacted a certain momentous event in Ursula's life and mine. Entering by the French window, there rose up to my mental vision, in vivid contrast to all present scenes, the picture of a young girl I had once seen sitting there, with head drooped, knitting. Could that day be twenty-five years ago?

No summer parlour now—its atmosphere was totally changed. It was a dull, dusty room, of which the only lively object was a large fire, the under half of which had burnt itself away unstirred into black dingy caverns. Before it, with breakfast untasted, sat Josiah Jessop—his feet on the fender, his elbows on his knees, the picture of despair.

"Mr. Jessop, my good friend!"

"No, I haven't a friend in the world, or shall not have an hour hence. Oh! it's you, Mr. Halifax? You have not an account to close? You don't hold any notes of mine, do you?"

John put his hand on the old man's shoulder, and repeated that he only came as a friend.

"Not the first 'friend' I have received this morning. I knew I should be early honoured with visitors;" and the banker attempted a dreary smile. "Sir Herbert and half a dozen more are waiting for me upstairs. The biggest fish must have the first bite—eh, you know?"

"I know," said John gloomily.

"Hark! those people outside will hammer my door down! Speak to them, Mr. Halifax—tell them I'm an old man—that I was always an honest man—always. If only they would give me time—hark!—just hark! Heaven help me! do they want to tear me in pieces?"

John went out for a few moments, then came back and sat down beside Mr. Jessop.

"Compose yourself"—the old man was shaking like an aspen leaf. "Tell me, if you have no objection to give me this confidence, exactly how your affairs stand."

With a gasp of helpless thankfulness, looking up in John's face, while his own quivered like a frightened child's, the banker obeyed. It seemed that great as was his loss by W——'s failure, it was not absolute ruin to him. In effect, he was at this moment perfectly solvent, and by calling in mortgages, etc., could meet both the accounts of the gentry who banked with him, together with all his own notes now afloat in the county, principally among the humbler ranks, petty tradespeople, and such like—if only both classes of customers would give him time to pay them.

"But they will not. There will be a run upon the bank, and then all's over with me. It's a hard case—solvent as I am—ready and able to pay every farthing—if only I had a week's time. As it is, I must stop payment to-day. Hark! they are at the door again! Mr. Halifax, for God's sake quiet them!"

"I will; only tell me first what sum, added to the cash you have available, would keep the bank open—just for a day or two."

At once guided and calmed, the old man's business faculties seemed to return. He began to calculate, and soon stated the sum he needed; I think it was three or four thousand pounds.

"Very well; I have thought of a plan. But first—those poor fellows outside. Thank Heaven, I am a rich man, and everybody knows it. Phineas, that inkstand, please."

He sat down and wrote: curiously the attitude and manner reminded me of his sitting down and writing at my father's table, after the bread riot—years and years ago. Soon a notice, signed by Josiah Jessop, and afterwards by himself, to the effect that the bank would open, "without fail," at one o'clock this day, was given by John to the astonished clerk to be posted in the window.

A responsive cheer outside showed how readily those outside had caught at even this gleam of hope. Also—how implicitly they trusted in the mere name of a gentleman who all over the county was known for "his word being as good as his bond"—John Halifax.

The banker breathed freer; but his respite was short: an imperative message came from the gentlemen abovestairs, desiring his presence. With a kind of blind dependence he looked towards John.

"Let me go in your stead. You can trust me to manage matters to the best of my power?"

The banker overwhelmed him with gratitude.

"Nay, that ought to be my word, standing in this house and remembering." His eyes turned to the two portraits—grimly-coloured daubs, yet with a certain apology of likeness too, which broadly smiled at one another from opposite walls—the only memorials now remaining of the good doctor and his cheery little old wife. "Come, Mr. Jessop, leave the matter with me; believe me, it is not only a pleasure, but a duty."

The old man melted into senile tears.

I do not know how John managed the provincial magnates, who were sitting in council considering how best to save, first themselves, then the bank lastly.—If the poor public outside had been made acquainted with that ominous "lastly"! Or if to the respectable conclave above-stairs, who would have recoiled indignantly at the vulgar word "jobbing," had been hinted a phrase—which ran oddly in and out of the nooks of my brain, keeping time to the murmur in the street, "*Vox populi, vox Dei*"—truly, I should have got little credit for my Latinity.

John came out in about half an hour with a cheerful countenance; told me he was going over to Coltham for an hour or two—would I wait his return?

"And all is settled?" I asked.

"Will be soon, I trust. I can't stay to tell you more now. Good-bye."

I was no man of business, and could assist in nothing. So I thought the best I could do was to pass the time in wandering up and down the familiar garden, idly watching the hoar-frost on the arbutus leaves, and on the dry stems of what had been dear little Mrs. Jessop's favourite roses—the same roses I had seen her among on that momentous evening—the evening when Ursula's bent neck flushed more crimson than the sunset itself, as I told her John Halifax was "too noble to die for any woman's love."

No—he had lived for it—earned it—won it. And musing over these long-ago times, my heart melted—foolish old heart that it was! with a trembling joy, to think that Providence had, in some way, used my poor useless hand to give to him this blessing—a man's chiefest blessing—of a virtuous and loving wife, which had crowned his life for all these wonderful years.

As it neared one o'clock, I could see my ancient friend the Abbey clock with not a wrinkle in his old face, staring at me through the bare Abbey trees. I began to feel rather anxious. I went into the deserted office; and thence, none forbidding, ensconced myself behind the sheltering bank blinds.

The crowd had scarcely moved; a very honest, patient, weary crowd, dense in the centre, thinning towards the edges. On its extremest verge, waiting in a curricle, was a gentleman, who seemed observing it with a lazy curiosity. I, having like himself apparently nothing better to do, observed this gentleman.

He was dressed in the height of the mode, combined with a novel and eccentric fashion, which had been lately set by that extraordinary young nobleman whom everybody talked about—my Lord Byron. His neckcloth was loose, his throat bare, and his hair fell long and untidy. His face, that of a man about thirty—I fancied I had seen it before, but could not recall where—was delicate, thin, with an expression at once cynical and melancholy. He sat in his carriage, wrapped in furs, or looked carelessly out on the scene before him, as if he had no interest therein—as if there was nothing in life worth living for.

"Poor fellow!" said I to myself, recalling the bright, busy, laughing faces of our growing up lads, recalling especially their father's—full of all that active energy and wise cheerfulness which gives zest to existence; God forbid any man should die till he has lived to learn it!—"poor fellow! I wish his moodiness could take a lesson from us at home!"

But the gentleman soon retired from my observation under his furs; for the sky had gloomed over, and snow began to fall. Those on the pavement shook it drearily off, and kept turning every minute to the Abbey clock—I feared it would take the patience of Job to enable them to hold out another quarter of an hour.

At length some determined hand again battered at the door. I fancied I heard a clerk speaking out of the first-floor window.

"Gentlemen"—how tremblingly polite the voice was!

—"Gentlemen, in five minutes—positively five minutes —the bank will——"

The rest of the speech was drowned and lost. Dashing round the street corner, the horses all in a foam, came our Beechwood carriage. Mr. Halifax leaped out.

Well might the crowd divide for him—well might they cheer him. For he carried a canvas bag—a great, ugly, grimy-coloured bag—a precious, precious bag, with the consolation—perhaps the life—of hundreds in it!

I knew, almost by intuition, what he had done—what, in one or two instances, was afterwards done by other rich and generous Englishmen, during the crisis of this year.

The bank door flew open like magic. The crowd came pushing in; but when John called out to them, "Good people, pray let me pass!" they yielded and suffered him to go in first. He went right up to the desk, behind which, flanked by a tolerable array of similar canvas bags, full of gold—but nevertheless waiting in mortal fear, and as white as his own neckcloth—the old banker stood.

"Mr. Jessop," John said, in a loud, distinct voice, that all might hear him, "I have the pleasure to open an account with you. I feel satisfied that in these dangerous times no credit is more safe than yours. Allow me to pay in to-day the sum of five thousand pounds."

"Five thousand pounds!"

The rumour of it was repeated from mouth to mouth. In a small provincial bank such a sum seemed unlimited. It gave universal confidence. Many who had been scrambling, swearing, almost fighting, to reach the counter and receive gold for their notes, put them again into their pockets, uncashed. Others, chiefly women, got them cashed with a trembling hand—nay, with tears of joy. A few who had come to close accounts changed their minds, and even paid money in. All were satisfied—the run upon the bank ceased.

Mr. Halifax stood aside, looking on. After the first murmur of surprise and pleasure no one seemed to take any notice of him, or of what he had done. Only one old widow woman, as she slipped three bright guineas under the lid of her market-basket, dropped him a curtsy in passing by.

"It's your doing, Mr. Halifax. The Lord reward you, sir."

"Thank you," he said, and shook her by the hand.

I thought to myself, watching the many that came and went unmindful, "*only this Samaritan!*"

No—one person more, standing by, addressed him by name. "This is indeed your doing, and an act of benevolence which I believe no man alive would have done except Mr. Halifax."

And the gentleman who spoke—the same I had seen outside in his curricle—held out a friendly hand.

"I see you do not remember me. My name is Ravenel."

"Lord Ravenel!"

John uttered this exclamation—and no more. I saw that this sudden meeting had brought back, with a cruel tide of memory, the last time they met—by the small nursery bed, in that upper chamber at Enderley.

However, this feeling shortly passed away, as must needs be; and we all three began to converse together.

While he talked, something of the old "Anselmo" came back into Lord Ravenel's face, especially when John asked him if he would drive over with us to Enderley.

"Enderley—how strange the word sounds!—yet I should like to see the place again. Poor old Enderley!"

Irresolutely—all his gestures seemed dreamy and irresolute—he drew his hand across his eyes—the same white, long-fingered, womanish hand which had used to guide Muriel's over the organ keys.

"Yes—I think I will go back with you to Enderley. But first I must speak to Mr. Jessop here."

It was about some poor Catholic families, who, as we had before learnt, had long been his pensioners.

"You are a Catholic still, then?" I asked. "We heard the contrary."

"Did you? Oh, of course. One hears such wonderful facts about oneself. Probably you heard also that I have been to the Holy Land, and turned Jew—called at Constantinople, and come back a Mohammedan."

"But are you of your old faith?" John said. "Still a sincere Catholic?"

"If you take Catholic in its original sense, certainly. I am a Universalist. I believe everything—and nothing. Let us change the subject." The contemptuous scepticism of his manner altered as he inquired after Mrs. Halifax and the children. "No longer children now, I suppose?"

"Scarcely. Guy and Walter are as tall as yourself; and my daughter——"

"Your daughter?"—with a start—"oh yes, I recollect. Baby Maud. Is she at all like—like——"

"No."

Neither said more than this; but it seemed as if their hearts warmed to one another, knitted by the same tender remembrance.

We drove home. Lord Ravenel muffled himself up in his furs, complaining bitterly of the snow and sleet.

"Yes, the winter is setting in sharply," John replied, as he reined in his horses at the turnpike gate. "This will be a hard Christmas for many."

"Ay, indeed, sir," said the gatekeeper, touching his hat. "And if I might make so bold—it's a dark night, and the road's lonely," he added, in a mysterious whisper.

"Thank you, my friend. I am aware of all that." But as John drove on, he remained for some time very silent.

On, across the bleak country, with the snow pelting in our faces—along roads so deserted, that our carriage wheels made the only sound audible, and that might have been heard distinctly for miles.

All of a sudden the horses were pulled up. Three or four ill-looking figures had started out of a ditch bank, and caught hold of the reins.

"Holloa there! What do you want?"

"Money."

"Let go my horses! They're spirited beasts. You'll get trampled on."

"Who cares?"

This brief colloquy passed in less than a minute. It showed at once our position—miles away from any house—on this desolate moor; showed plainly our danger—John's danger.

He himself did not seem to recognize it. He stood upright on the box seat, the whip in his hand.

"Get away, you fellows, or I must drive over you!"

"Thee'd better!" With a yell, one of the men leaped up and clung to the neck of the plunging mare—then was dashed to the ground between her feet. The poor wretch uttered one groan and no more. John sprang out of his carriage, caught the mare's head, and backed her.

"Hold off!—the poor fellow is killed, or may be in a minute. Hold off, I say."

If ever these men, planning perhaps their first ill-deed, were struck dumb with astonishment, it was to see the gentleman they were intending to rob take up their comrade in his arms, drag him towards the carriage lamps, rub snow in his face, and chafe his heavy hands. But all in vain. The blood trickled down from a wound in the temples—the head, with its open mouth dropping, fell back upon John's knee.

"He is quite dead."

The others gathered round in silence, watching Mr. Halifax, as he still knelt, with the dead man's head leaning against him, mournfully regarding it.

"I think I know him. Where does his wife live?"

Some one pointed across the moor to a light, faint as a glow-worm. "Take that rug out of my carriage—wrap him in it." The order was at once obeyed. "Now carry him home. I will follow presently."

"Surely not," expostulated Lord Ravenel, who had got out of the carriage and stood, shivering and much shocked, beside Mr. Halifax. "You would not surely put yourself in the power of these scoundrels? What brutes they are—the lower orders!"

"Not altogether—when you know them. Phineas, will you drive Lord Ravenel on to Beechwood?"

"Excuse me—certainly not," said Lord Ravenel, with dignity. "We will stay to see the result of the affair. What a singular man Mr. Halifax is, and always was!" he added thoughtfully, as he muffled himself up again in his furs, and relapsed into silence.

Soon, following the track of those black figures across the snow, we came to a cluster of peat huts, alongside of the moorland road. John took one of the carriage lamps in his hand, and went in, without saying a word. To my surprise Lord Ravenel presently dismounted and followed him. I was left with the reins in my hand, and two or three of those ill-visaged men hovered about the carriage; but no one attempted to do me any harm. Nay, when John reappeared, after a lapse of some minutes, one of them civilly picked up the whip and put it into his hand.

"Thank you. Now, my men, tell me what did you want with me just now?"

"Money," cried one. "Work," shouted another.

"And a likely way you went about to get it! Stopping me in the dark, on a lonely road, just like common robbers. I did not think any Enderley men would have done a thing so cowardly."

"We bean't cowards," was the surly answer. "Thee carries pistols, Mr. Halifax."

"You forced me to do it. My life is as precious to my wife and children as—as that poor fellow's to his." John stopped. "God help us, my men! it's a hard world for us all sometimes. Why did you not know me better? Why not come to my house and ask honestly for a dinner and a half-crown?—you should have had both, any day."

"Thank'ee, sir," was the general cry. "And, sir," begged one old man, "you'll hush up the crowner's 'quest—you and this gentleman here. You won't put us in jail for taking to the road, Mr. Halifax?"

"No; unless you attack me again. But I am not afraid

—I'll trust you. Look here!" He took the pistol out of his breast-pocket, cocked it, and fired its two barrels harmlessly into the air. "Now, good-night; and if ever I carry firearms again, it will be your fault, not mine."

So saying, he held the carriage door open for Lord Ravenel, who took his place with a subdued and thoughtful air; then, mounting the box-seat, John drove, in somewhat melancholy silence, across the snowy, starlit moors to Beechwood.

CHAPTER XXXII.

In the home-light.

It was a scene—glowing almost as those evening pictures at Longfield. Those pictures, photographed on memory by the summer sun of our lives, and which no paler after-sun could have power to reproduce. Nothing earthly is ever reproduced in the same form. I suppose Heaven meant it to be so; that in the perpetual progression of our existence we should be reconciled to loss, and taught that change itself is but another form for aspiration. Aspiration which never can rest, or ought to rest, in anything short of the One absolute Perfection—the One all-satisfying Good "*in whom is no variableness, neither shadow of turning.*"

I say this to excuse myself for thoughts which at times made me grave—even in the happy home-light of John's study, where, for several weeks after the last incident I have recorded, the family were in the habit of gathering every evening. For poor Guy was a captive. The "mere trifle" had turned out to be a sprained foot, which, happening to a tall and strong young man, became serious. He bore his imprisonment restlessly enough at first, but afterwards grew more reconciled—took to reading, drawing, and society—and even began to interest himself in the pursuits of his sister Maud, who every morning had her lessons in the study.

Miss Silver first proposed this. She had evinced more feeling than was usual to her since Guy's accident;

showed him many little feminine kindnesses—out of compunction it seemed; and altogether was much improved. Of evenings, as now, she always made one of the "young people," who were generally grouped together round Guy's sofa—Edwin, Walter, and little Maud. The father and mother sat opposite—as usual, side by side, he with his newspaper, she with her work. Or sometimes, falling into pleasant idleness, they would slip hand in hand, and sit talking to one another in an undertone, or silently and smilingly watch the humours of their children.

For me, I generally took to my nook in the chimney-corner—it was a very ancient fireplace, with settles on each side, and dogs instead of a grate, upon which many a faggot hissed and crackled its merry brief life away. Nothing could be more cheery and comfortable than this old-fashioned, low-roofed room, three sides of which were peopled with books—all the books which John had gathered up during the course of his life. Perhaps it was their long-familiar, friendly faces which made this his favourite room, his own especial domain. But he did not keep it tabooed from his family; he liked to have them about him, even in his studious hours.

So, of evenings, we all sat together as now, each busy, and none interrupting the rest. At intervals, flashes of talk or laughter broke out, chiefly from Guy, Walter, or Maud, when Edwin would look up from his everlasting book, and even the grave governess relax into a smile. Since she had learnt to smile, it became more and more apparent how very handsome Miss Silver was. "Handsome" is, I think, the fittest word for her; that correctness of form and colour which attracts the eye chiefly, and perhaps the eye of men rather than of women—at least, Mrs. Halifax could never be brought to see it. But, then, her peculiar taste was for slender, small brunettes, like Grace Oldtower; whereas Miss Silver was large and fair.

Fair, in every sense, most decidedly. And now that she evidently began to pay a little more attention to her dress and her looks, we found out that she was also young.

"Only twenty-one to-day, Guy says," I remarked one day to Ursula.

"How did Guy know it?"

"I believe he discovered the wonderful secret from Maud."

"Maud and her brother Guy have grown wonderful friends since his illness. Do you not think so?"

"Yes, I found the two of them—and even Miss Silver—as merry as possible, when I came into the study this morning."

"Did you?" said the mother, with an involuntary glance at the group opposite.

There was nothing particular to observe. They all sat in most harmless quietude, Edwin reading, Maud at his feet, playing with the cat, Miss Silver busy at a piece of that delicate muslin-work with which young women then used to ornament their gowns. Guy had been drawing a pattern from it, and now leant back upon his sofa, shading off the fire with his hand, and from behind it gazing, as I had often seen him gaze lately, with a curious intentness, at the young governess.

"Guy," said his mother (and Guy started), "what were you thinking about?"

"Oh, nothing that is——" Here, by some accident, Miss Silver quitted the room. "Mother, come over here, I want your opinion. There, sit down—though it's nothing of the least importance."

Nevertheless it was with some hesitation that he brought out the mighty question—namely, that it was Miss Silver's birthday to-day; that he thought we ought to remember it, and give her some trifle as a present.

"And I was considering this large 'Flora' I ordered from London—she would like it extremely; she is so fond of botany."

"What do you know about botany?" said Edwin, sharply and rather irrelevantly as it seemed, till I remembered how he plumed himself upon his knowledge of this science, and how he had persisted in taking Maud, and her governess also, long wintry walks across the country, "in order to study the cryptogamia."

Guy vouchsafed no answer to his brother; he was too much absorbed in turning over the pages of the beautiful "Flora" on his knee.

"What do you say, all of you? Father, don't you think she would like it? Then, suppose you give it to her?"

At this inopportune moment Miss Silver returned.

She might have been aware that she was under discussion—at least so much of discussion as was implied by Guy's eager words and his mother's silence, for she looked around her uneasily, and was about to retire.

"Do not go," Guy exclaimed anxiously.

"Pray do not," his mother added; "we were just talking about you, Miss Silver. My son hopes you will accept this book from him, and from us all, with all kind birthday wishes."

And rising, with a little more gravity than was her wont, Mrs. Halifax touched the girl's forehead with her lips, and gave her the present.

Miss Silver coloured and drew back. "You are very good, but indeed I would much rather not have it."

"Why so? Do you dislike gifts, or this gift in particular?"

"Oh no; certainly not."

"Then," said John, as he too came forward and shook hands with her with an air of hearty kindness, "pray take the book. Do let us show how much we respect you; how entirely we regard you as one of the family."

Guy turned a look of grateful pleasure to his father; but Miss Silver, colouring more than ever, still held back.

"No, I cannot; indeed, I cannot."

"Why can you not?"

"For several reasons."

"Give me only one of them—as much as can be expected from a young lady," said Mr. Halifax good-humouredly.

"Mr. Guy ordered the 'Flora' for himself. I must not allow him to renounce his pleasure for me."

"It would not be renouncing it if *you* had it," returned the lad, in a low tone, at which once more his younger brother looked up angrily.

"What folly about nothing! How can one read with such a clatter going on?"

"You old bookworm. You care for nothing and nobody but yourself," Guy answered, laughing. But Edwin, really incensed, rose and settled himself in the far corner of the room.

"Edwin is right," said the father, in a tone which indicated his determination to end the discussion, a tone which even Miss Silver obeyed. "My dear young lady, I hope you will like your book; Guy, write her name in it at once."

Guy willingly obeyed, but was a good while over the task; his mother came and looked over his shoulder.

"Louisa Eugénie—how did you know that, Guy? Louisa Eugenie Sil—— is that your name, my dear?"

The question, simple as it was, seemed to throw the governess into much confusion, even agitation. At last she drew herself up with the old repulsive gesture, which of late had been slowly wearing off.

"No—I will not deceive you any longer. My right name is Louise Eugénie d'Argent."

Mrs. Halifax started. "Are you a Frenchwoman?"

"On my father's side—yes."

"Why did you not tell me so?"

"Because, if you remember, at our first interview, you said no Frenchwoman should educate your daughter. And I was homeless—friendless."

"Better starve than tell a falsehood," cried the mother indignantly.

"I told no falsehood. You never asked me of my parentage."

"Nay," said John, interfering, "you must not speak in that manner to Mrs. Halifax. Why did you renounce your father's name?"

"Because English people would have scouted my father's daughter. You knew him—everybody knew him—he was D'Argent the Jacobin—D'Argent the Bonnet Rouge."

She threw out these words defiantly, and quitted the room.

"This is a dreadful discovery. Edwin, you have seen most of her—did you ever imagine——"

"I knew it, mother," said Edwin, without lifting his eyes from his book. "After all, French or English, it makes no difference."

"I should think not, indeed!" cried Guy angrily. "Whatever her father is, if any one dared to think the worse of her——"

"Hush!—till another time," said the father, with a glance at Maud, who, with wide-open eyes, in which the tears were just springing, had been listening to all these revelations about her governess.

But Maud's tears were soon stopped, as well as this painful conversation, by the entrance of our daily, or rather nightly, visitor for these six weeks past, Lord Ravenel. His presence, always welcome, was a great relief now. We never discussed family affairs before people. The boys began to talk to Lord Ravenel; and Maud took her privileged place on a footstool beside him. From the first sight she had been his favourite, he said, because of her resemblance to Muriel. But I think, more than any fancied likeness to that sweet lost face, which he never spoke of without tenderness inexpressible, there was something in Maud's buoyant youth—just between childhood and girlhood, having the charms of one and the immunities of the other—which was especially attractive to this man, who, at three-and-thirty, found life a weariness and a burden—at least he said so.

Life was never either weary or burthensome in our house—not even to-night, though our friend found us less lively than usual—though John maintained more than his usual silence, and Mrs. Halifax fell into troubled reveries. Guy and Edwin, both considerably excited, argued and contradicted one another more warmly than even the Beechwood liberty of speech allowed. For Miss Silver, she did not appear again.

Lord Ravenel seemed to take these slight *désagréments* very calmly. He stayed his customary time, smiling languidly as ever at the boys' controversies, or listening with a half-pleased, half-melancholy laziness to Maud's gay prattle, his eye following her about the room with the privileged tenderness that twenty years' seniority allows a man to feel and show towards a child. At his wonted hour he rode away, sighingly contrasting pleasant Beechwood with dreary and solitary Luxmore.

After his departure we did not again close round the fire. Maud vanished; the younger boys also; Guy settled himself on his sofa, having first taken the pains to limp across the room and fetch the "Flora," which Edwin had carefully stowed away in the bookcase. Then, making himself comfortable, as the pleasure-loving lad liked well enough to do, he lay dreamily gazing at the title-page, where was written her name, and "From Guy Halifax, with——"

"What are you going to add, my son?"

He, glancing up at his mother, made her no answer, and hastily closed the book.

She looked hurt, but, saying nothing more, began moving about the room, putting things in order before retiring. John sat in the arm-chair—meditative. She asked him what he was thinking about.

"About that man, Jacques d'Argent."

"You have heard of him, then?"

"Few had not, twenty years ago. He was one of the most 'blatant beasts' of the Reign of Terror. A fellow without honesty, conscience, or even common decency."

"And that man's daughter we have had in our house, teaching our innocent child!"

Alarm and disgust were written on every feature of the mother's face. It was scarcely surprising. Now that the ferment which had convulsed society in our younger days was settling down—though still we were far from that ultimate calm which enables posterity to judge fully and fairly such a remarkable historical crisis as the French Revolution—most English people looked back with horror on the extreme opinions of that time. If Mrs. Halifax had a weak point, it was her prejudice against anything French or Jacobinical. Partly, from that tendency to moral conservatism which in most persons, especially women, strengthens as old age advances; partly, I believe, from the terrible warning given by the fate of one—of whom for years we had never heard—whose very name was either unknown to, or forgotten by, our children.

"John, can't you speak? Don't you see the frightful danger?"

"Love, try and be calmer."

"How can I? Remember—remember Caroline."

"Nay, we are not talking of her, but of a girl whom we know, and have had good opportunity of knowing. A girl who, whatever may have been her antecedents, has lived for six months blamelessly in our house."

"Would to Heaven she had never entered it! But it is not too late. She may leave—she shall leave, immediately."

"Mother!" burst out Guy. Never since she bore him had his mother heard her name uttered in such a tone.

She stood petrified.

"Mother, you are unjust, heartless, cruel. She shall *not* leave; she shall *not*, I say!"

"Guy, how dare you speak to your mother in that way?"

"Yes, father, I dare. I'll dare anything rather than——"

"Stop. Mind what you are saying—or you may repent it."

And Mr. Halifax, speaking in that low tone to which his voice fell in serious displeasure, laid a heavy hand on the lad's shoulder. Father and son exchanged fiery glances. The mother, terrified, rushed between them.

"Don't, John! Don't be angry with him. He could not help it—my poor boy!"

At her piteous look Guy and his father both drew back. John put his arm round his wife, and made her sit down. She was trembling exceedingly.

"You see, Guy, how wrong you have been. How could you wound your mother so?"

"I did not mean to wound her," the lad answered. "I only wished to prevent her from being unjust and unkind to one to whom she must show all justice and kindness, one whom I respect, esteem—whom I *love*."

"Love!"

"Yes, mother! Yes, father! I love her. I intend to marry her."

Guy said this with an air of quiet determination, very different from the usual impetuosity of his character. It was easy to perceive that a great change had come over him, that in this passion, the silent growth of which no one had suspected, he was most thoroughly in earnest. From the boy he had suddenly started up into the man; and his parents saw it.

They looked at him, and then mournfully at one another. The father was the first to speak.

"All this is very sudden. You should have told us of it before."

"I did not know it myself till—till very lately," the youth answered more softly, lowering his head and blushing.

"Is Miss Silver—is the lady aware of it?"

"No."

"That is well," said the father, after a pause. "In this silence you have acted as an honourable lover should towards her, as a dutiful son should act towards his parents."

Guy looked pleased. He stole his hand nearer his mother's, but she neither took it nor repelled it; she seemed quite stunned.

At this point I noticed that Maud had crept into the room; I sent her out again as quickly as I could. Alas!

this was the first secret that needed to be kept from her, the first painful mystery in our happy, happy home!

In any such home the "first falling in love," whether of son or daughter, necessarily makes a great change—greater if the former than the latter. There is often a pitiful truth—I know not why it should be so, but so it is—in the foolish rhyme which the mother had laughingly said over to me this morning!—

"My son's my son till he gets him a wife,
My daughter's my daughter all her life."

And when, as in this case, the son wishes to marry one whom his father may not wholly approve, whom his mother does not heartily love, surely the pain is deepened tenfold.

Those who, in the dazzled vision of youth, see only the beauty and splendour of love—first love, who deem it comprises the whole of life—beginning, aim, and end—may marvel that I, who have been young and now am old, see as I saw that night, not only the lover's but the parents' side of the question. I felt overwhelmed with sadness as, viewing the three, I counted up in all its bearings and consequences, near and remote, this attachment of poor Guy's.

"Well, father," he said at last, guessing by intuition that the father's heart would best understand his own.

"Well, my son," John answered sadly.

"*You* were young once."

"So I was," with a tender glance upon the lad's heated and excited countenance. "Do not suppose I cannot feel with you. Still, I wish you had been less precipitate."

"You were little older than I am when you married?"

"But my marriage was rather different from this projected one of yours. I knew your mother well, and she knew me. Both of us had been tried—by trouble which we shared together, by absence, by many and various cares. We chose one another, not hastily or blindly, but with free will and open eyes. No, Guy," he added, speaking earnestly and softly, "mine was no sudden fancy, no frantic passion. I honoured your mother above all women. I loved her as my own soul."

"So do I love Louise. I would die for her any day."

At the son's impetuosity the father smiled, not incredulously, only sadly.

All this while the mother had sat motionless, never uttering a sound. Suddenly, hearing a footstep and a light knock at the door, she darted forward and locked it, crying, in a voice that one could hardly have recognized as hers,—

"No admittance! Go away."

A note was pushed in under the door. Mrs. Halifax picked it up, opened it, read it mechanically, and sat down again, taking no notice, even when Guy, catching sight of the handwriting, eagerly seized the paper.

It was merely a line, stating Miss Silver's wish to leave Beechwood immediately, signed with her full name—her right name—"Louise Eugénie d'Argent."

A postscript added: "Your silence I shall take as permission to depart, and shall be gone early to-morrow."

"To-morrow! Gone to-morrow! And she does not even know that—that I love her. Mother, you have ruined my happiness. I will never forgive you—never!"

Never forgive his mother! His mother, who had borne him, nursed him, reared him; who had loved him with that love—like none other in the world—the love of a woman for her first-born son, all these twenty-one years!

It was hard. I think the most passionate lover, in reasonable moments, would allow that it was hard. No marvel that even her husband's clasp could not remove the look of heartbroken, speechless suffering which settled stonily down in Ursula's face, as she watched her boy—storming about, furious with uncontrollable passion and pain.

At last, mother-like, she forgot the passion in pity of the pain.

"He is not strong yet; he will do himself harm. Let me go to him! John, let me!" Her husband released her.

Faintly, with a weak, uncertain walk, she went up to Guy and touched his arm.

"You must keep quiet, or you will be ill. I cannot have my son ill—not for any girl. Come, sit down—here, beside your mother."

She was obeyed. Looking into her eyes, and seeing no anger there, nothing but grief and love, the young man's right spirit came into him again.

"O mother, mother, forgive me! I am so miserable—so miserable."

He laid his head on her shoulder. She kissed and clasped him close—her boy who never could be wholly hers again, who had learned to love some one else dearer than his mother.

After a while she said, "Father, shake hands with Guy. Tell him that we forgive his being angry with us, that perhaps, some day——"

She stopped, uncertain as to the father's mind, or seeking strength for her own.

"Some day," John continued, "Guy will find out that we can have nothing in the world—except our children's good—so dear to us as their happiness."

Guy looked up, beaming with hope and joy. "O father! O mother! will you, indeed——"

"We will indeed say nothing," the father answered, smiling—"nothing, until to-morrow. Then we will all three talk the matter quietly over, and see what can be done."

Of course I knew to a certainty the conclusion they would come to.

CHAPTER XXXIII.

LATE that night, as I sat up pondering over all that had happened, Mrs. Halifax came into my room.

She looked round, asked me, according to her wont, if

there was anything I wanted before she retired for the night (Ursula was as good to me as any sister), then stood by my easy-chair. I would not meet her eyes, but I saw her hands fluttering in their restless way.

I pointed to her accustomed chair.

"No, I can't sit down. I must say good-night." Then, coming at once to the point, "Phineas, you are always up first in the morning. Will you—John thinks it had better be you—will you give a message from us to —Maud's governess?"

"Yes. What shall I say?"

"Merely, that we request she will not leave Beechwood until we have seen her."

If Miss Silver had overheard the manner and tone of that "request," I doubt if it would not have hastened rather than delayed her departure. But, God help the poor mother! her wounds were still fresh.

"Would it not be better," I suggested, "if you were to write to her?"

"I can't; no, I can't"—spoken with the sharpness of exceeding pain. Soon after, as in faint apology, she added, "I am so tired; we are very late to-night."

"Yes; it is almost morning. I thought you were both in bed."

"No; we have been sitting talking in Guy's room. His father thought it would be better."

"And is all settled?"

"Yes."

Having told me this, and having, as it were, by such a conclusion confessed it was right the question should be thus "settled," Guy's mother seemed more herself.

"Yes," she repeated, "John thinks it ought to be. At least, that she should know Guy's—the feeling with which Guy regards her. If, after the probation of a year, it still remains, and he is content to begin life on a small income, we have given our consent to our son's marriage."

It struck me how the mother's mind entirely dwelt on the one party in this matter—"Guy's feelings," "Our son's marriage," and so on. The other side of the question, or the possibility of any hindrance there, never seemed to enter her imagination. Perhaps it would not, even into mine, for I shared the family faith in its best-beloved Guy, but for Mrs. Halifax's so entirely ignoring the idea that any consent except her son's and his parents' was necessary to this marriage.

"It will not part him from us so very much, you see, Phineas," she said, evidently trying to view the bright side, "and she has no relatives living—not one. For income, Guy will have the entire profit of the Norton Bury mills; and they might begin, as we did, in the old Norton Bury house—the dear old house."

The thought of her own young days seemed to come, soothingly and sweet, taking the sting out of her pain, showing her how it was but right and justice that Nature's holy law should be fulfilled—that children, in their turn, should love, and marry, and be happy, like their parents.

"Yes," she answered, as I gently hinted this, "I know you are right; all is quite right, and as it should be, though it was a shock at first. No matter. John esteems her—John likes her. For me—oh, I shall make a capital—what is it?—a capital *mother-in-law*—in time!"

With that smile, which was almost cheerful, she bade me good-night—rather hastily, perhaps, as if she wished to leave me while her cheerfulness lasted. Then I heard her step along the passage, pausing once—most likely at Guy's room door; her own closed, and the house was in silence.

I rose early in the morning—not one whit too early, for I met Miss Silver in the hall, bonneted and shawled, carrying down with her own hands a portion of her chattels. She evidently contemplated an immediate departure. It was with the greatest difficulty that, without betraying my reasons, which, of course, was impossible, I could persuade her to change her determination.

Poor girl! last night's events had apparently shaken her from that indifference which she seemed to think the best armour of a helpless, proud governess against the world. She would scarcely listen to a word. She was in extreme agitation ; half a dozen times she insisted on leaving, and then sat down again.

I had not given her credit for so much wholesome irresolution—so much genuine feeling. Her manner almost convinced me of a fact which every one else seemed to hold as certain, but which I myself should have liked to see proved—namely, that Guy, in asking her love, would have—what in every right and happy marriage a man ought to have—the knowledge that the love was his before he asked for it.

Seeing this, my heart warmed to the girl. I respected her brave departure—I rejoiced that it was needless. Willingly I would have quieted her distress with some hopeful, ambiguous word, but that would have been trenching, as no one ever ought to trench, on the lover's sole right. So I held my tongue, watching with an amused pleasure the colour hovering to and fro over that usually impassive face. At last, at the opening of the study door —we stood in the hall still—those blushes rose up to her forehead in one involuntary tide.

But it was only Edwin, who had lately taken to a habit of getting up very early to study mathematics. He looked surprised at seeing me with Miss Silver.

"What is that box ? She is not going ?"

"No ; I have been entreating her not. Add your persuasions, Edwin."

For Edwin, with all his quietness, was a lad of much wisdom, great influence, and no little penetration. I felt inclined to believe that though as yet he had not been let into the secret of last night, he guessed it pretty well already.

He might have done, by the peculiar manner in which he went up to the governess and took her hand.

"Pray stay, I beg of you."

She made no more ado, but stayed.

I left her with Edwin, and took my usual morning walk up and down the garden till breakfast-time.

A strange and painful breakfast it was, even though the most important element in its painfulness, Guy, was happily absent. The rest of us kept up a fragmentary, awkward conversation, every one round the table looking as indeed one might have expected they would look—with one exception.

Miss Silver, who, from her behaviour last night, and her demeanour to me this morning, I had supposed would now have gathered up all her haughtiness to resist Guy's parents—as, ignorant both of his feelings and their intentions towards her, a young lady of her proud spirit might well resist—was, to my astonishment, as mild and meek as this soft spring morning. Nay, like it, seemed often on the very verge of the melting mood. More than once her drooping eyelashes were gemmed with tears. And when, the breakfast-table being quickly deserted—Edwin, indeed, had left it almost immediately—she, sitting absently in her place, was gently touched by Mrs. Halifax, she started up, with the same vivid rush of colour that I had before noticed. It completely altered the expression of her face—made her look ten years younger, ten years happier, and, being happier, ten times more amiable.

This expression—I was not the only one to notice it—was, by some intuition, reflected on the mother's. It made softer than any speech of hers to Miss Silver the few words,—

"My dear, will you come with me into the study?"

"To lessons? Yes. I beg your pardon! Maud—where is Maud?"

"Never mind lessons just yet. We will have a little chat with my son.—Uncle Phineas, you'll come?—Will you come too, my dear?"

"If you wish it." And with an air of unwonted obedience she followed Mrs. Halifax.

Poor Guy!—confused young lover!—meeting for the first time after his confession the acknowledged object of his preference—I really felt sorry for him! And except that women have generally twice as much self-control in such cases as men—and Miss Silver proved it—I might even have been sorry for her. But then her uncertainties would soon be over. She had not to make —all her family being aware she was then and there making it—that terrible " offer of marriage," which, I am given to understand, is, even under the most favourable circumstances, as formidable as going up to the cannon's mouth.

I speak of it jestingly, as we all jested uneasily that morning, save Mrs. Halifax, who scarcely spoke a word. At length, when Miss Silver, growing painfully restless, again referred to " lessons," she said,—

" Not yet. I want Maud for half an hour. Will you be so kind as to take my place, and sit with my son the while ? "

" Oh, certainly ! "

I was vexed with her—really vexed—for that ready assent ; but then, who knows the ins and outs of women's ways ? At any rate, for Guy's sake this must be got over—the quicker the better. His mother rose.

" My son, my dear boy ! " She leant over him, whispering—I think she kissed him—then slowly, quietly, she walked out of the study. I followed. Outside the door we parted, and I heard her go upstairs to her own room.

It might have been half an hour afterwards, when Maud and I, coming in from the garden, met her standing in the hall. No one was with her, and she was doing nothing—two very remarkable facts in the daily life of the mother of the family.

Maud ran up to her with some primroses.

" Very pretty, very pretty, my child."

" But you don't look at them—you don't care for them—I'll go and show them to Miss Silver."

" No," was the hasty answer. " Come back, Maud ; Miss Silver is occupied."

Making some excuse, I sent the child away, for I saw that even Maud's presence was intolerable to her mother. That poor mother, whose suspense was growing into positive agony !

She waited—standing at the dining-room window—

listening—going in and out of the hall—for another ten minutes.

"It is very strange—very strange indeed. He promised to come to tell me. Surely, at least, he ought to come and tell me first—me, his mother——"

She stopped at the word, oppressed by exceeding pain.

"Hark! was that the study door?"

"I think so; one minute more and you will be quite certain."

Ay! one minute more, and we *were* quite certain. The young lover entered, his bitter tidings written on his face.

"She has refused me, mother. I never shall be happy more."

Poor Guy! I slipped out of his sight and left the lad alone with his mother.

Another hour passed of this strange, strange day. The house seemed painfully quiet. Maud, disconsolate and cross, had taken herself away to the beech wood with Walter; the father and Edwin were busy at the mills, and had sent word that neither would return to dinner. I wandered from room to room, always excepting that shut-up room where, as I took care, no one should disturb the mother and son.

At last I heard them both going upstairs—Guy was still too lame to walk without assistance. I heard the poor lad's fretful tones, and the soothing, cheerful voice that answered them. "Verily," thought I, "if, since he must fall in love, Guy had only fixed his ideal standard of womanhood a little nearer home—if he had only chosen for his wife a woman a little more like his mother!" But I suppose that would have been expecting impossibilities.

Well, he had been refused!—our Guy, whom we all would have imagined irresistible—our Guy, "whom to look on was to love." Some harsh folk might say this might be a good lesson for the lad—nay, for most lads—but I deny it. I doubt if any young man, meeting at the outset of life a rejection like this, which either ignorance or heedlessness on the woman's part had made totally unexpected, ever is the better for it: perhaps, for many years, cruelly the worse. For, most women being quick-sighted about love, and most men—especially young men—blind enough in its betrayal, any woman who wilfully allows an offer only to refuse it, lowers not only herself but her whole sex, for a long, long time after, in the lover's eyes. At least I think so; as I was thinking, in the way old bachelors are prone to moralize over such things, when, coming out of Guy's room, I met Mrs. Halifax.

She crossed the passage, hastily but noiselessly, to a small anteroom which Miss Silver had for her own private study, out of which half a dozen stairs led to the chamber where she and her pupil slept. The anteroom was open, the bedchamber door closed.

"She is in there?"

"I believe she is."

Guy's mother stood irresolute. Her knit brow and nervous manner betrayed some determination she had come to which had cost her hard. Suddenly she turned to me.

"Keep the children out of the way, will you, Phineas? Don't let them know—don't let anybody know—about Guy."

"Of course not."

"There is some mistake—there *must* be some mistake. Perhaps she is not sure of our consent—his father's and mine. Very right of her—very right! I honour her for her indecision. But she must be assured to the contrary—my boy's peace must not be sacrificed. You understand, Phineas?"

Ay, perhaps better than she did herself, poor mother!

Yet when, in answer to the hasty knock, I caught a glimpse of Miss Silver opening the door—Miss Silver, with hair all falling down dishevelled, and features swollen with crying—I went away completely at fault, as the standers-by seemed doomed to be in all love affairs. I began to hope that this would settle itself somehow—in all parties understanding one another after the good old romantic fashion, and "living very happy to the end of their lives."

I saw nothing more of any one until tea-time, when Mrs. Halifax and the governess came in together. Something in their manner struck me—one being subdued and gentle, the other tender and kind. Both, however, were exceedingly grave—nay, sad; but it appeared to be that sadness which is received as inevitable, and is quite distinct from either anger or resentment.

Neither Guy nor Edwin nor the father were present. When John's voice was heard in the hall, Miss Silver had just risen to retire with Maud.

"Good-night, for I shall not come downstairs again," she said hastily.

"Good-night," the mother answered in the same whisper—rose, kissed her kindly, and let her go.

When Edwin and his father appeared, they too looked remarkably grave—as grave as if they had known by intuition all the trouble in the house. Of course, no one referred to it. The mother merely noticed how late they were, and how tired they both looked. Supper passed in silence, and then Edwin took up his candle to go to bed.

His father called him back. "Edwin, you will remember?"

"I will, father."

"Something is amiss with Edwin," said his mother, when the two younger boys had closed the door behind them. "What did you wish him to remember?"

Her husband's sole reply was to draw her to him with that peculiarly tender gaze, which she knew well to be the forewarning of trouble—trouble he could not save her from, could only help her to bear. Ursula laid her head on his shoulder with one deep sob of long-smothered pain.

"I suppose you know all. I thought you would soon guess. O John, our happy days are over! Our children are children no more."

"But ours still, love—always will be ours."

"What of that, when we can no longer make them happy? when they look for happiness to others, and not to us? My own poor boy! To think that his mother can neither give him comfort, nor save him pain, any more."

She wept bitterly.

When she was somewhat soothed, John, making her sit down by him, but turning a little from her, bade her tell him all that had happened to-day. A few words explained the history of Guy's rejection and its cause.

"She loves some one else. When I—as his mother—went and asked her the question, she confessed this."

"And what did you say?"

"What could I say? I could not blame her. I was even sorry for her. She cried so bitterly, and begged me to forgive her. I said I did freely, and hoped she would be happy."

"That was right. I am glad you said so. Did she tell you who he—this lover—was?"

"No. She said she could not, until he gave her permission. That whether they would ever be married she did not know. She knew nothing, save that he was good and kind, and the only creature in the world who had ever cared for her."

"Poor girl!"

"John"—startled by his manner—"you have something to tell me? You know who this is—this man who has stood between my son and his happiness?"

"Yes, I do know."

I cannot say how far the mother saw—what, as if by a flash of lightning, *I* did; but she looked up in her husband's face with a sudden speechless dread.

"Love, it is a great misfortune, but it is no one's blame—neither ours nor theirs—they never thought of Guy's loving her. He says so—Edwin himself."

"Is it Edwin?"—in a cry as if her heart was breaking. "His own brother—his very own brother! Oh, my poor Guy!"

Well might the mother mourn! Well might the

father look as if years of care had been added to his life that day! For a disaster like this happening in any household—especially a household where love is recognized as a tangible truth, neither to be laughed at, passed carelessly over, nor lectured down—makes the family cease to be a family in many things from henceforward. The two strongest feelings of life clash; the bond of brotherly unity in its perfectness is broken for ever.

For some minutes we sat, bewildered, as it were, thinking of the tale as if it had been told of some other family than ours. Mechanically the mother raised her eyes; the first object they chanced to meet was a rude water-colour drawing, kept, coarse daub as it was, because it was the only reminder we had of what never could be recalled—one red-cheeked child with a hoop staring at another red-cheeked child with a nosegay—supposed to represent little Edwin and little Guy.

"Guy taught Edwin to walk. Edwin made Guy learn his letters. How fond they were of one another—those two boys. Now—brother will be set against brother! They will never feel like brothers—never again."

"Love——"

"Don't, John! don't speak to me just yet. It is so terrible to think of. Both my boys—both my two noble boys! to be made miserable for that girl's sake. Oh! that she had never darkened our doors. Oh! that she had never been born."

"Nay, you must not speak thus. Remember—Edwin loves her—she will be Edwin's wife"

"Never!" cried the mother desperately. "I will not allow it. Guy is the eldest. His brother has acted meanly. So has she. No, John, I will *not* allow it."

"You will not allow what has already happened—what Providence has permitted to happen? Ursula, you forget—they love one another."

This one fact—this solemn upholding of the pre-eminent right and law of love, which law John believed in, they both believed in, so sacred and firmly—appeared to force itself upon Mrs. Halifax's mind. Her passion subsided.

"I cannot judge clearly. You can—always. Husband, help me!"

"Poor wife!—poor mother!" he muttered, caressing her, and in that caress himself all but giving way. "Alas! that I should have brought thee into such a sea of trouble."

Perhaps he referred to the circumstance of his bringing Miss Silver into our house, perhaps to his own blindness, or want of parental caution, in throwing the young people continually together. However, John was not one to lament over things inevitable, or by overweening blame of his own want of foresight to imply a doubt of the foreseeing of Providence.

"Love," he said, "I fear we have been too anxious to play *Deus ex machinâ* with our children, forgetting in whose hands are marrying and giving in marriage—life's crosses and life's crowns. Trouble has come when we looked not for it. We can but try to see the right course, and seeing it, to act upon it."

Ursula assented—with a bursting heart it seemed—but still she assented, believing, even as in her young days, that her husband's will was wisest, best.

He told her, in few words, all that Edwin had that day confessed to his father; how these two, being much together, had become attached to one another, as young folks will—couples whom no one would ever think suited each for each—except Nature, and the instinct of their own hearts. Absorbed in this love—which, Edwin solemnly declared, was never openly declared till this morning—they neither of them thought of Guy. And thus things had befallen—things which no earthly power could remove or obliterate—things in which, whatever way we looked, all seemed darkness. We could but walk blindly on, a step at a time, trusting to that faith, of which all our lives past had borne confirmation—the firm faith that evil itself is to the simple and God-fearing but the disguised messenger of good.

Something like this John said, talking as his wife loved to hear him talk—every quiet, low word dropping like balm upon her grieved heart; not trying to deceive her into the notion that pain is not pain, but showing her how best to bear it. At length she looked up, as if with God's help—and her husband's comforting—she could bear it.

"Only one thing—Guy does not know. He need not know just yet—not till he is stronger. Surely Edwin will not tell him?"

"No; he promised me he would not. Do not start so. Indeed, there is no fear."

But that very assurance seemed to rouse it. She began straining her ears to catch the least noise in the rooms overhead—the boys' rooms. Guy and Walter shared one; Edwin had his to himself."

"They surely will not meet. Yet Guy sometimes likes sitting over Edwin's fire. Hark! was not that the creaking of Guy's room door."

"Love——" detaining her.

"I know, John. I am not thinking of going. Guy might suspect something. No, indeed I am not afraid. They were always fond of one another—my boys."

She sat down, violently forcing herself not to listen, not to fear. But the truth was too strong for her.

"Hark! I am sure they are talking. John, you said Edwin promised?"

"Faithfully promised."

"But if, by some accident, Guy found out the truth? Hark! they are talking very loud. That is a chair fallen. O John, don't keep me! My boys—my boys." And she ran upstairs in an agony.

What a sight for a mother's eyes! Two brothers—of whom it had been our boast that from babyhood they had never been known to lift a hand against each other—now struggling together like Cain and Abel. And from the fury in their faces the quarrel might have had a similar ending.

"Guy!—Edwin!" But the mother might as well have shrieked to the winds.

The father came and parted them. "Boys, are you gone mad, fighting like brutes in this way?—Shame, Guy!—Edwin, I trusted you."

"I could not help it, father. He had no right to steal into my room, no right to snatch her letter from me."

"It was her letter, then?" cried Guy furiously. "She writes to you? You were writing back to her?"

Edwin made no answer, but held out his hand for the letter, with that look of white passion in him so rarely seen—perhaps not thrice since his infancy. Guy took no heed.

"Give it me back, Guy. I warn you."

"Not till I have read it. I have a right."

"You have none. She is mine."

"Yours?" Guy laughed in his face.

"Yes, mine. Ask my father—ask my mother. They know."

"Mother!" The letter fell from the poor lad's hand. "Mother, *you* would not deceive me. He only says it to vex me. I was in a passion, I know. Mother, it isn't true?"

His piteous tone—the almost childish way in which he caught at her sleeve, as she turned from him—ah, poor Guy!

"Edwin, is it my brother Edwin? Who would have thought it?" Half-bewildered, he looked from one to the other of us all; but no one spoke, no one contradicted him.

Edwin, his passion quite gone, stooped in a sorrowful and humble way to pick up his betrothed's letter. Then Guy flew at him, and caught him by the collar.

"You coward! How dared you? No, I won't hurt him; she is fond of him. Go away, every one of you. O mother, mother, mother!"

He fell on her neck, sobbing. She gathered him in her arms, as she had used to do in his childhood; and so we left them.

"*As one whom his mother comforteth.*"

Ay, prophet of Israel, thou wert wise.

CHAPTER XXXIV.

JOHN and I sat over the study fire till long after midnight.

Many an anxious watch I had kept with him, but none sadder than this. Because now, for the first time, our house was divided against itself. A sorrow had entered it, not from without but from within—a sorrow which we could not meet and bear as a family. Alas! darker and darker had the bitter truth forced itself upon us, that neither joy nor affliction would ever find us as a family again.

I think all parents must feel cruelly a pang like this—the first trouble in which they cannot help their children—the first time when those children must learn to stand alone, each for himself, compelled to carry his own burthen and work out, well or ill, his individual life; when the utmost the wisest or tenderest father can do is to keep near with outstretched hand that the child may cling to, assured of finding sympathy, counsel, and love.

If this father had stood aloof all his life on some pinnacle of paternal "pride," paternal "dignity"—if he had not made himself his boys' companion, counsellor, and friend, how great would have been his terrors now!

For, as we both knew well—too well to trust ourselves to say it—if there was one thing in the world that ruins a lad, drives him to desperation, shuts the door of home upon him, and opens many another door, of which the entrance is the very gate of hell—it is such a disappointment as this which had happened to our Guy.

His father saw it all. Saw it clearer, crueller, than even his mother could see. Yet when, very late, almost at dawn, she came in, with the tidings that Guy was himself again now—sleeping as quietly as a child—her husband was able to join in her deep thankfulness, and give her hope for the days to come.

"But what is to be done with Guy?"

"God knows," John answered. But his tone expressed a meaning different from that generally conveyed in the words, a meaning which the mother caught at once, and rested on.

"Ay—you are right. He knows!" And so they went away together, almost content.

Next morning I woke late; the sunshine falling across my bed, and the sparrows chattering loud in the ivy. I had been dreaming, with a curious pertinacity, of the old days at Rose Cottage, the days when John first fell in love with Ursula.

"Uncle Phineas." I heard myself called.

It was John's son, who at opposite, with wan, wild eyes, and a settled anguish on his mouth—that merry, handsome mouth—the only really handsome mouth in the family.

"You are up early, my boy."

"What was the good of lying in bed? I am not ill. Besides, I wish to go about as usual. I don't wish anybody to think that—that I care."

He stopped—evidently fighting hard against himself. A new lesson, alas! for our Guy.

"Was I too violent last night? I did not mean it. I mean to be a man. Not the first man whom a lady has refused—eh?" And braving it out, he began to whistle; but the lips fell—the frank brow grew knotted with pain. The lad broke into a passion of misery.

The chief bitterness was that he had been deceived. Unwittingly, we well believed—but still deceived. Many little things he told me—Guy's was a nature that at once spent and soothed itself by talking—of Miss Silver's extreme gentleness and kindness towards him; a kindness which seemed so like, so cruelly like love.

"Love! Oh, she loved me. She told me so. Of course! I was Edwin's brother."

Ay, there was the sting, which never could be removed; which might rankle in the boy's heart for life. He had not only lost his love, but what is more precious than love—faith in womankind. He began to make light of his losings—to think the prize was not so great after all. He sat on my bed, singing—Guy had a fine voice and ear—singing out of mockery songs which I had an especial aversion to—light songs written by an Irishman, Mr. Thomas Moore, about girls and wine, and being "far from the lips we love," but always ready enough "to make love to the lips we are near." Then, laughing at me, he threw up the window and looked out.

I think it was wrong of those two, wrong and selfish, as all lovers are—young lovers in the flush of their happiness; I think it was cruel of Edwin and Louise to walk up and down there, in the elder brother's very eyes.

For a moment he struggled against his passion.

"Uncle Phineas, just look here. How charming! Ha, ha! Did you ever see such a couple of fools?"

Fools, maybe, but happy—happy to the very core—thoroughly engrossed in their happiness. The elder brother was almost maddened by it.

"He must mind what he does—tell him so, Uncle Phineas—it would be safer. He *must* mind, or I will not answer for myself. I was fond of Edwin—I was indeed—but now it seems sometimes as if I *hated* him."

"Guy!"

"Oh, if it had been a stranger, and not he! If it had been any one in the world except my brother!"

And in that bitter cry the lad's heart melted again; it was such a tender heart—his mother's heart.

After a time he recovered himself, and came down with me to breakfast, as he had insisted upon doing; met them all, even Miss Silver—and Edwin, who had placed himself by her side with an air of right. These lovers, however deeply grieved they looked—and, to do them justice, it was really so—needed not to be grieved over by any of us.

Nor, looking at the father and mother, would we have

dared to grieve over *them*. In the silent watches of the night, heart to heart, husband and wife had taken counsel together; together had carried their sorrow to the only Lightener of burthens. It seemed that theirs was lightened; that even in this strange entanglement of fate they were able to wait patiently—trusting unto the Almighty mercy not only themselves but the children He had given them.

When, breakfast being over, John, according to his custom, read the chapter and the prayer—no one rose up or went out; no one refused, even in this anguish of strife, jealousy, and disunion—to repeat after him the "Our Father" of their childhood.

I believe every one of us remembered for years, with an awe that was not altogether pain, this morning's chapter and prayer.

When it was ended, worldly troubles closed round us again.

Nothing seemed natural. We hung about in twos and threes, uncertain what to do. Guy walked up and down alone. His mother asked him if, seeing his foot was so well, he would like to go down to the mills as usual; but he declined. Miss Silver made some suggestion about "lessons," which Edwin jealously negatived immediately, and proposed that she and Maud should take a drive somewhere.

Mrs. Halifax eagerly assented. "Lady Oldtower has been wanting them both for some time. You would like to go, would you not, for a day or two?" said she, addressing the governess.

Guy caught at this. "Going away, are you? When?"

He put the question to Miss Silver direct—his eyes blazing right into her own. She made some confused reply about "leaving immediately."

"In the carriage, of course? Shall I have the honour of driving you?"

"No," said Edwin decisively.

A fierce, vindictive look passed between the brothers—a look terrible in itself—more terrible in its warning of days to come. No wonder the mother shuddered—no wonder the young betrothed, pale and alarmed, slipped out of the room. Edwin followed her. Then Guy, snatching up his sister, lifted her roughly on his knee.

"Come along, Maud. You'll be my girl now. Nobody else wants you. Kiss me, child."

But the little lady drew back.

"So, you hate me too? Edwin has been teaching you? Very well. Get away, you cheat!"

He pushed her violently aside. Maud began to cry.

Her father looked up from his book—the book he had not been reading—though he had seemingly thought it best to take no notice of what was passing around him.

"Come here, Maud, my child. Guy, you should not be unkind to your little sister. Try and command yourself, my dear boy!"

The words, though spoken gently, almost in a whisper, were more than the lad's chafed spirit could brook.

"Father, you insult me. I will not bear it. I will quit the room."

He went out, shutting the door passionately after him. His mother rose up to follow him—then sat down again. The eyes that she lifted to her husband were deprecating, beseeching, heavy with a speechless pain.

For John—he said nothing. Not though, as was plain to see, this, the first angry or disrespectful word he had ever received from any one of his children, struck him like an arrow; for a moment stirred him even to wrath—holy wrath—the just displeasure of a father who feels that the least portion of his child's sin is the sin against him. Perhaps this very feeling, distinct from, and far beyond, all personal indignation, all sense of offended dignity, made the anger strangely brief—so brief, that when the other children, awed and startled, looked for some ebullition of it—lo! it was all gone. In its stead was something at which the children, more awed still, crept out of the room.

Ursula even, alarmed, looked in his face as if for the first time she could not comprehend her husband.

"John, you should forgive poor Guy; he did not intend any harm."

"No—no."

"And he is so very miserable. Never before did he fail in his duty to you."

"But what if I have failed in mine to him? What if—you used to say I could not understand Guy—what if I have come short towards him? I, that am accountable to God for every one of my children."

"John—John"—she knelt down and put her arms round his neck. "Husband, do not look unhappy. I did not mean to blame you—we may be wrong, both of us—all of us. But we will not be afraid. We know who pities us, even as we pity our children."

Thus she spoke, and more to the same purport; but it was a long time before her words brought any consolation. Then the parents talked together, trying to arrange some plan whereby Guy's mind might be occupied and soothed, or else Edwin removed out of his sight for a little while. Once I hinted at the advantage of Guy's leaving home; but Mrs. Halifax seemed to shrink from this project as though it were a foreboding of perpetual exile.

"No, no; anything but that. Beside, Guy would not wish it. He has never left me in his life. His going would seem like the general breaking up of the family."

Alas! she did not, would not see that the family was already "broken." Broken, more than either absence, marriage, or death itself could have effected.

One thing more we had to consider—a thing at once natural and right in any family, namely, how to hide its wounds from the chattering, scandalous world. And so, when by a happy chance there came over that morning our good friend Lady Oldtower and her carriage full of daughters, Mrs. Halifax communicated, with a simple dignity that quelled all comment, the fact of "my son Edwin's engagement," and accepted the invitation for Maud and Miss Silver, which was willingly repeated and pressed.

One thing I noticed, that in speaking of or to the girl who in a single day from merely the governess had become, and was sedulously treated as, our own, Mrs. Halifax invariably called her as heretofore, "Miss Silver," or "my dear;" never by any chance "Louise," or "Mademoiselle D'Argent."

Before she left Beechwood, Edwin came in and hurriedly spoke to his mother. What he said was evidently painful to both.

"I am not aware of it, Edwin; I had not the slightest intention of offending her. Is she already made your judge and referee as to the actions of your mother?"

Edwin was a good lad, though perhaps a little less loving than the rest of the boys. His self-restraint, his exceeding patience, lulled the threatened storm.

"But you will be kind to her, mother?—I know you will."

"Did I not say so?"

"And may I bring her to you here?"

"If you choose."

It was the first open recognition between the mother and her son's betrothed. Their other meeting had been in public, when, with a sedulous dread, both had behaved exactly as usual, and no word or manner had betrayed their altered relations. Now, when for the first time it was needful for Miss Silver to be received as a daughter-elect, with all the natural sympathy due from one woman to another under similar circumstances, all the warmth of kindness due from a mother to her son's chosen wife—then the want, the mournful want, made itself felt.

Mrs. Halifax stood at the dining-room window, trying vainly to regain self-control.

"If I could only love her! If only she had made me love her!" she muttered, over and over again.

I hoped, from the bottom of my soul, that Edwin had not heard her—had not seen her involuntarily recoil, as he led to his mother his handsome girl that he seemed so proud of, his happy, affianced wife. Happiness melts some natures, like spring and sunshine. Louise looked up with swimming eyes.

"Oh, be kind to me! Nobody was ever kind to me till I came here!"

The good heart gave way: Mrs. Halifax opened her arms.

"Be true to Edwin—love Edwin, and I shall love you—I am sure I shall."

Kissing her once or twice, the mother let fall a few tears; then sat down, still keeping the girl's hand, and busying herself with various little kindnesses about her.

"Are you sure you are well wrapped up?—Edwin, see that she has my fur cloak in the carriage.—What cold fingers! Have some wine before you start, my dear."

Miss Silver altogether melted; sobbing, she murmured something about forgiveness.

"Nay, did I say a word about forgiveness? Then, do not you. Let us be patient—we shall all be happy in time."

"And—Guy?"

"Guy will be himself soon," returned the mother, rather proudly. "We will not mention him, if you please, my dear."

At this moment Guy must have heard the carriage wheels, and guessed Miss Silver was going, for he appeared at the parlour door. He found his mother toying with Miss Silver's hand—Edwin standing by, proud and glad, with his arm clasped round Louise.

He did not remove it. In his brother's very face—perhaps because of the expression of that face—the lover held fast his own.

Mrs. Halifax rose up alarmed. "She is just going, Guy. Shake hands, and bid her good-bye."

The girl's hand, which was sorrowfully and kindly extended, Guy snatched and held fast.

"Let her pass," cried Edwin angrily.

"Most certainly. I have not the least wish to detain her. Good-bye! A pleasant journey!" And, still keeping her hand, he gazed with burning eyes on the features he had so loved—as boys do love—with a wild imaginative passion, kindled by beauty alone. "I shall claim my right—just for once—may I, sister Louise?"

With a glance of defiance at Edwin, Guy caught his brother's betrothed round the waist and kissed her—once—twice—savagely.

It was done so suddenly and under such an ingenious disguise of "right," that open vengeance was impossible. But as Edwin hurried Louise away, the look that passed between the two young men was enough to blot out henceforward all friendship, all brotherhood. That insult would never be forgotten.

She was gone—the house was free of her and Edwin too. Guy was left alone with me and his mother.

Mrs. Halifax sat sewing. She seemed to take no note of his comings and goings—his restless starts—his fits of dark musing, when his face grew like the face of some stranger, some one whom he would have shrunk from—any one but our own merry Guy.

"Mother"—the voice startled me—such irritable, intolerable bitterness marred its once pleasant tones—"when do they come back?"

"Do you mean——"

"I mean those people."

"In a week or so. Your brother returns to-night, of course."

"My *brother*, eh? Better not say it—it's an ugly word."

Mrs. Halifax attempted no reproof; she knew that it would have been useless—worse than useless—then.

"Mother," Guy said at last, coming up and leaning against her chair, "you must let me go."

"Where, my son?"

"Anywhere—out of their sight—those two. You see, I cannot bear it. It maddens me—makes me wicked—makes me not myself. Or rather makes me truly *myself*, which is altogether wicked."

"No, Guy—no, my own boy. Have patience—all this will pass away."

"It might, if I had anything to do. Mother," kneeling down by her with a piteous gaze—"mother, you need not look so wretched. I wouldn't harm Edwin—would not take from him his happiness; but to live in sight of it day after day, hour after hour—I can't do it! Do not ask me—let me get away."

"But where?"

"Anywhere, as I said; only let me go far away from them, where no possible news of them can reach me. In some place, O mother darling! where I can trouble no one and make no one miserable."

The mother feebly shook her head. As if such a spot could be found on earth, while *she* lived!

But she saw that Guy was right. To expect him to remain at home was cruelty. As he had said, he could not bear it—few could. Few even among women—of men much fewer. One great renunciation is possible, sometimes easy, as death may be; but to "die daily"? In youth, too, with all the passions vehement, the self-knowledge and self-control small? No; Nature herself, in that universal desire to escape, which comes with such a trial, hints at the unnaturalness of the ordeal; in which, soon or late, the weak become paralyzed or callous; the strong—God help them!—are apt to turn wicked.

Guy's instinct of flight was, his mother felt, wisest, safest, best.

"My boy, you shall have your desire; you shall go."

I had not expected it of her—at least, not so immediately. I had thought, bound up in him as she was, accustomed to his daily sight, his daily fondness—for he was more with her, and "petted" her more than any other of the children—I had thought to have seen some reluctance, some grieved entreaty—but no! Not even when, gaining her consent, the boy looked up as if her allowing him to quit her was the greatest kindness she had ever in his life bestowed.

"And when shall I go?"

"Whenever you choose."

"To-day; perhaps I might get away to-day?"

"You can, if you wish, my dear boy."

But no sooner had she said it than the full force and meaning of the renunciation seemed to burst upon her. Her fingers, which had been smoothing Guy's hand as it lay on her lap, tightly closed round it; with the other hand she put back his hair, gazing—gazing, as if it were impossible to part with him.

"Guy—O Guy, my heart is breaking! Promise that you will try to be yourself again—that you will never be anything other than my own good boy, if I agree to let you go?" What he answered, or what further passed between them, was not for me either to hear or to know. I left the room immediately.

When, some time after John's hour for returning from the mills, I also returned to the house, I found that everything was settled for Guy's immediate departure.

There was some business in Spain—something about Andalusian wool—which his father made the ostensible reason for the journey. It would occupy him and distract his mind, besides giving him constant necessity of change. And, they say, travel is the best cure for the heartache. We hoped it might prove so.

Perhaps the sorest point, and one that had been left undecided till both parents saw that in Guy's present mood any opposition was hurtful, even dangerous, was the lad's obstinate determination to depart alone. He refused his mother's companionship to London, even his father's across the country to the nearest point where one of those new and dangerous things called railways tempted travellers to their destruction. But Guy would go by it—the maddest and strangest way of locomotion pleased him best. So it was settled he should go, as he pleaded, this very day.

A strange day it seemed—long and yet how short! Mrs. Halifax was incessantly busy. I caught sight of her now and then, flitting from room to room, with Guy's books in her hand—Guy's linen thrown across her arm. Sometimes she stood a few minutes by the window, doing a few stitches of necessary work, which, when even Nurse Watkins offered to do—Jenny, who had been a rosy lass when Guy was born—she refused abruptly, and went stitching on.

There were no regular meals that day; better not, perhaps. I saw John come up to his wife as she stood sewing, and bring her a piece of bread and a glass of wine—but she could not touch either.

"Mother, try," whispered Guy mournfully. "What will become of me if I have made you ill?"

"Oh, no fear, no fear!" She smiled, took the wine and swallowed it—broke off a bit of the bread—and went on with her work.

The last hour or two passed so confusedly that I do not well remember them. I can only call to mind seeing Guy and his mother everywhere side by side, doing everything together, as if grudging each instant remaining till the final instant came. I have also a vivid impression of her astonishing composure, of her calm voice when talking to Guy about indefinite trifles, or, though that was seldom, to any other of us. It never faltered—never lost its rich, round cheerfulness of tone; as if she wished him to carry it as such, and no other—the familiar mother's voice—in his memory across the seas.

Once only it grew sharp, when Walter, who hovered about disconsolately, knelt down to fasten his brother's portmanteau.

"No! Let go! I can do everything myself."

And now the time was fast flying—her boy must depart.

All the household collected in the hall to bid Mr. Guy good-bye—Mr. Guy whom everybody was so fond of. They believed—which was all that any one, save ourselves, ever knew—that sudden business had called him away on a long and anxious journey. They lingered about him respectfully, with eager, honest blessings, such as it was good the lad should have—good that he should bear away with him from England and from home.

Finally, Guy, his father, and his mother went into the study by themselves. Soon even his father came out and shut the door, that there should be not a single witness to the last few words between mother and son. These being over, they both came into the hall together, brave and calm—which calmness was maintained even to the last good-bye.

Thus we sent our Guy away, cheerfully and with blessings—away into the wide, dangerous world; alone, with no guard or restraint, except (and in that *except* lay the whole mystery of our cheerfulness)—the fear of God, his father's counsels, and his mother's prayers.

CHAPTER XXXV.

Two years rolled over Beechwood—two uneventful years. The last of the children ceased to be a child; and we prepared for that great era in all household history, the first marriage in the family. It was to be celebrated very quietly, as Edwin and Louise both desired. Time had healed over many a pang, and taught many a soothing lesson; still it could not be supposed that this marriage was without its painfulness.

Guy still remained abroad; his going had produced the happy result intended. Month after month his letters came, each more hopeful than the last, each bringing balm to the mother's heart. Then he wrote to others beside his mother. Maud and Walter replied to him in long home histories; and began to talk without hesitation—nay, with great pride and pleasure—" of my brother who is abroad."

The family wound was closing, the family peace about to be restored; Maud even fancied Guy ought to come home to " our wedding; "—but then she had never been told the whole of past circumstances; and, besides, she was still too young to understand love matters. Yet so mercifully had time smoothed down all things, that it sometimes appeared even to us elders as if those three days of bitterness were a mere dream—as if the year we dreaded had passed as calmly as any other year.

Save that in this interval Ursula's hair had begun to turn from brown to gray; and John first mentioned, so cursorily that I cannot even now remember when or where, that slight pain, almost too slight to complain of, which he said warned him in climbing Enderley Hill that he could not climb so fast as when he was young. And I returned his smile, telling him we were evidently growing old men; and must soon set our faces to descend the hill of life. Easy enough I was in saying this, thinking, as I often did, with great content, that there was not the faintest doubt which of us would reach the bottom first.

Yet I was glad to have safely passed my half century of life—glad to have seen many of John's cares laid to rest, more especially those external troubles which I have not lately referred to—for, indeed, they were absorbed and forgotten in the home troubles that came after. He had lived down all slanders, as he said he would. Far and near travelled the story of the day when Jessop's bank was near breaking; far and near, though secretly—for we found it out chiefly by its results—poor people whispered the tale of a gentleman who had been attacked on the high roads, and whose only attempt at bringing the robbers to justice was to help the widow of one and send the others safe out of the country at his own expense, not Government's. None of these were notable or showy deeds—scarcely one of them got, even under the disguise of asterisks, into the newspaper; the *Norton Bury Mercury*, for its last dying sting, still complained (and very justly) that there was not a gentleman in the county whose name so seldom headed a charity subscription as that of John Halifax, Esquire, of Beechwood. But the right made its way, as, soon or late, the right always does; he believed his good name was able to defend itself, and it did defend itself; he had faith in the only victory worth having—the universal victory of Truth; and Truth conquered at last.

To drive with him across the country—he never carried pistols now—or to walk with him, as one day before

Edwin's wedding we walked, a goodly procession, through the familiar streets of Norton Bury, was a perpetual pleasure to the rest of the family. Everybody knew him, everybody greeted him, everybody smiled as he passed—as though his presence and his recognition were good things to have and to win. His wife often laughed, and said she doubted whether even Mr. O'Connell of Derrynane, who was just now making a commotion in Ireland, lighting the fire of religious and political discord from one end to the other of County Clare—she doubted if even Daniel O'Connell had more popularity among his own people than John Halifax had in the primitive neighbourhood where he had lived so long.

Mrs. Halifax herself was remarkably gay this morning. She had had letters from Guy; together with a lovely present, for which he said he had ransacked all the *magasins de modes* in Paris—a white embroidered China shawl. It had arrived this morning—Lord Ravenel being the bearer. This was not the first time by many that he had brought us news of our Guy, and thereby made himself welcome at Beechwood—more welcome than he might have been otherwise; for his manner of life was so different from ours. Not that Lord Ravenel could be accused of any likeness to his father; but blood is blood, and education and habits are not to be easily overcome. The boys laughed at him for his aristocratic, languid ways; Maud teased him for his mild cynicism and the little interest he seemed to take in anything; while the mother herself was somewhat restless about his coming, wondering what possible good his acquaintance could do to us, or ours to him, seeing we moved in totally different spheres. But John himself was invariably kind, nay, tender over him—we all guessed why. And perhaps even had not the young man had so many good points, while his faults were more negations than positive ill qualities, we likewise should have been tender over him—for Muriel's sake.

He had arrived at Beechwood this morning, and falling as usual into our family routine, had come with us to Norton Bury. He looked up with more interest than usual in his pensive eyes, as he crossed the threshold of our old house, and told Maud how he had come there many years ago with his father.

"That was the first time I ever met your father," I overheard him say to Maud—not without feeling; as if he thought he owed fate some gratitude for the meeting.

Mrs. Halifax, in the casual civil inquiry which was all the old earl ever won in our house, asked after the health of Lord Luxmore.

"He is still at Compiègne. Does not Guy mention him? Lord Luxmore takes the greatest pleasure in Guy's society."

By her start, this was evidently new and not welcome tidings to Guy's mother. No wonder. Any mother in England would have shrunk from the thought that her best-beloved son—especially a young man of Guy's temperament, and under Guy's present circumstances—was thrown into the society which now surrounded the debauched dotage of the too notorious Earl of Luxmore.

"My son did not mention it. He has been too much occupied in business matters to write home frequently, since he reached Paris. However, his stay there is limited;" and this seemed to relieve her. "I doubt if he will have much time left to visit Compiègne."

She said no more than this, of course, to Lord Luxmore's son; but her disquiet was sufficiently apparent.

"It was I who brought your son to Compiègne—where he is a universal favourite, from his wit and liveliness. I know no one who is a more pleasant companion than Guy."

Guy's mother bowed—but coldly.

"I think, Mrs. Halifax, you are aware that the earl's tastes and mine differ widely—have always differed. But he is an old man, and I am his only son. He likes to see me sometimes, and I go—though, I must confess, I take little pleasure in the circle he has around him."

"In which circle, as I understand, my son is constantly included?"

"Why not? It is a very brilliant circle. The whole court of Charles Dix can afford none more amusing. For the rest, what matters? One learns to take things as they seem, without peering below the surface. One wearies of impotent Quixotism against unconquerable evils."

"That is not our creed at Beechwood," said Mrs. Halifax abruptly, as she ceased the conversation. But ever and anon it seemed to recur to her mind—ay, through all the mirth of the young people—all the graver pleasure which the father took in the happiness of his son Edwin; his good son, who had never given him a single care. He declared this settling of Edwin had been to him almost like the days when he himself used to come of evenings, hammer in hand, to put up shelves in the house, or nail the currant bushes against the wall, doing everything *con amore*, and with the utmost care, knowing it would come under the quick, observant eyes of Ursula March.

"That is, of Ursula Halifax—for I don't think I let her see a single one of my wonderful doings until she was Ursula Halifax.—Do you remember, Phineas, when you came to visit us the first time, and found us gardening?"

"And she had on a white gown and a straw hat with blue ribbons. What a young thing she looked!—hardly older than Mistress Maud here."

John put his arm round his wife's waist—not so slender as it had been, but comely and graceful still, repeating—with something of the musical cadence of his boyish readings of poetry—a line or two from the sweet old English song,—

"And when with envy Time transported
Shall think to rob us of our joys,
You'll in your girls again be courted,
And I'll go wooing with my boys."

Ursula laughed, and for the time being the shadow passed from her countenance. Her husband had happily not noticed it; and apparently she did not wish to tell him her trouble. She let him spend a happy day, even grew happy herself in response to his care to make her so, by the resolute putting away of all painful present thoughts, and calling back of sweet and soothing memories belonging to this their old married home. John seemed determined that, if possible, the marriage that was to be should be as sacred and as hopeful as their own.

So full of it were we all, that not until the day after, when Lord Ravenel had left us—longing apparently to be asked to stay for the wedding, but John did not ask him—I remembered what he had said about Guy's association with Lord Luxmore's set. It was recalled to me by the mother's anxious face, as she gave me a foreign letter to post.

"Post it yourself, will you, Phineas? I would not have it miscarry, or be late in its arrival, on any account."

No, for I saw it was to her son at Paris.

"It will be the last letter I shall need to write," she added, again lingering over it, to be certain that all was correct—the address being somewhat illegible for that free, firm hand of hers. "My boy is coming home."

"Guy coming home! To the marriage?"

"No; but immediately after. He is quite himself now. He longs to come home."

"And his mother?"

His mother could not speak. Like light to her eyes, like life to her heart, was the thought of Guy's coming home. All that week she looked ten years younger. With a step buoyant as any girl's she went about the marriage preparations; together with other preparations, perhaps dearer still to the motherly heart, where, if any preference did lurk, it was for the one for whom—possibly from whom—she had suffered most of all her children.

John, too, though the father's joy was graver and not unmixed with some anxiety—anxiety which he always put aside in his wife's presence—seemed eager to have his son at home.

"He is the eldest son," he repeated more than once, when talking to me of his hope that Guy would now settle permanently at Beechwood. "After myself, the head of the family."

After John! It was almost ridiculous to peer so far into the future as that.

Of all the happy faces I saw the day before the marriage, I think the happiest was Mrs. Halifax's, as I met her coming out of Guy's room, which ever since he left had been locked up, unoccupied. Now his mother threw open the door with a cheerful air.

"You may go in if you like, Uncle Phineas. Does it not look nice?"

It did indeed, with the fresh white curtains; the bed laid all in order; the bookshelves arranged, and even the fowling-piece and fishing-rod put in their right places.

The room looked very neat, I said, with an amused doubt as to how long it was to remain so.

"That is true indeed. How he used to throw his things about! A sad untidy boy!" And his mother laughed; but I saw all her features were trembling with emotion.

"He will not be exactly a boy now. I wonder if we shall find him much changed."

"Very likely. Brown, with a great beard; he said so in one of his letters. I shall hardly know my boy again"—with a lighting-up of the eye that furnished a flat contradiction to the mother's statement.

"Here are some of Mrs. Tod's roses, I see."

"She made me take them. She said Master Guy always used to stop and pick a bunch as he rode past. She hopes she shall see him ride past on Sunday next. Guy must pay her one of his very first visits; the good old soul!"

I hinted that Guy would have to pay visits half over the country, to judge by the number of invitations I had heard of.

"Yes. Everybody wants to steal my boy. Everybody has a welcome for him. How bright old Watkins has polished that gun! Sir Herbert says, Guy must come over to the shooting next week. He used to be exceedingly fond of going to the manor house."

I smiled to see the innocent smile of this good mother, who would have recoiled at the accusation of matchmaking. Yet I knew she was thinking of her great favourite, pretty Grace Oldtower; who was Grace Oldtower still, and had refused, gossip said, half the brilliant matches in the county, to the amazement and strong disapprobation of all her friends—excepting Mrs. Halifax.

"Come away, Phineas!" slightly sighing, as if her joy weighed her down, or as if conscious that she was letting fancy carry her too far into the unknown future. "His room is quite ready now, whatever time the boy arrives. Come away."

She shut and locked the door. To be opened—when?

Morning broke, and none could have desired a brighter marriage morning. Sunshine out of doors—sunshine on all the faces within; only family faces—for no other guests had been invited, and we had kept the day as secret as we could; there was nothing John disliked more than a show wedding. Therefore it was with some surprise that while they were all upstairs adorning themselves for church, Maud and I, standing at the hall door, saw Lord Ravenel's travelling carriage drive up to it, and Lord Ravenel himself, with a quicker and more decided gesture than was natural to him, spring out.

Maud ran into the porch; startling him much apparently; for indeed she was a sweet vision of youth, happiness, and grace, in her pretty bridesmaid's dress.

"Is this the wedding morning? I did not know—I will come again to-morrow;" and he seemed eager to escape back to his carriage.

This action relieved me from a vague apprehension of ill-tidings, and made less painful the first question which rose to my lips, "Had he seen Guy?"

"No."

"We thought for the moment it might be Guy come home," Maud cried. "We are expecting him. Have you heard of him since we saw you? Is he quite well?"

"I believe so."

I thought the answer brief; but then he was looking intently upon Guy's sister, who held his hands in her childish, affectionate way; she had not yet relinquished her privilege of being Lord Ravenel's "pet." When, hesitatingly, he proposed returning to Luxmore, unwilling to intrude upon the marriage, the little lady would not hear of it for a moment. She took the unexpected guest to the study, left him there with her father, explained to her mother all about his arrival and his having missed seeing Guy—appearing entirely delighted.

I came into the drawing-room, and sat watching the sun shining on marriage garments and marriage faces, all as bright as bright could be, including the mother's. It had clouded over for a few moments when the postman's ring was heard; but she said at once that it was most unlikely Guy would write—she had told him there was no need to write. So she stood content, smoothing down the soft folds of her beautiful shawl, which Guy meant her to wear to-day. This, together with his fond remembrance of her, seemed almost as comfortable as the visible presence of her boy—her boy, who was sure to come to-morrow.

"John, is that you? How softly you came in! And Lord Ravenel! He knows we are glad to see him. Shall we make him one of our own family for the time being, and take him with us to see Edwin married?"

Lord Ravenel bowed.

"Maud tells us you have not seen Guy. I doubt if he will be able to arrive to-day; but we fully expect him to-morrow."

Lord Ravenel bowed again. Mrs. Halifax said something about this unexpected arrival of his.

"He came on business," John answered quickly, and Ursula made no more inquiries.

She stood, talking with Lord Ravenel—as I could see her stand now, playing with the deep fringe of her shawl;

the sun glancing on that rich silk dress of her favourite silver gray; a picture of matronly grace and calm content, as charming as even the handsome, happy bride.

I was still looking at her, when John called me aside. I followed him to the study.

"Shut the door."

By his tone and look I knew in a moment that something had happened.

"Yes. I'll tell you presently—if there's time."

While he was speaking some violent pain—physical or mental, or both—seemed to seize him. I had my hand on the door to call Ursula, but he held me fast with a kind of terror.

"Call no one. I am used to it. Water!"

He drank a glassful, which stood by, breathed once or twice heavily, and gradually recovered himself. The colour had scarcely come back into his face when he heard Maud run laughing through the hall.

"Father, where are you? We are waiting for you."

"I will come in two minutes, my child."

Having said this, in his own natural voice, he closed the door again, and spoke to me rapidly.

"Phineas, I want you to stay away from church; make some excuse, or I will for you. Write a letter for me to this address in Paris. Say—Guy Halifax's father will be there without fail, within a week, to answer all demands."

"All demands!" I echoed, bewildered.

He repeated the sentence word for word. "Can you remember it? Literally, mind! And post it at once, before we return from church."

Here the mother's call was heard. "John, are you coming?"

"In a moment, love," for her hand was on the door outside; but her husband held the other handle fast. He then went on breathlessly, "You understand, Phineas? And you will be careful—very careful? *She must not know*—not till to-night."

"One word. Guy is alive and well?"

"Yes—yes."

"Thank God!"

But Guy's father was gone while I spoke. Heavy as the news might be—this ill news which had struck me with apprehension the moment I saw Lord Ravenel—it was still endurable. I could not conjure up any grief so bitter as the boy's dying.

Therefore, with a quietness that came naturally under the compulsion of such a necessity as the present, I rejoined the rest, made my excuses, and answered all objections. I watched the marriage party leave the house. A simple procession—the mother first, leaning on Edwin; then Maud, Walter, and Lord Ravenel; John walked last, with Louise upon his arm. Thus I saw them move up the garden, and through the beech wood, to the little church on the hill.

I then wrote the letter and sent it off. That done, I went back into the study. Knowing nothing—able to guess nothing—a dull patience came over me, the patience with which we often wait for unknown, inevitable misfortunes. Sometimes I almost forgot Guy in my startled remembrance of his father's look as he called me away, and sat down—or rather dropped down—into his chair. Was it illness? yet he had not complained; he hardly ever complained, and scarcely had a day's sickness from year to year. And as I watched him and Louise up the garden, I had noticed his free, firm gait, without the least sign of unsteadiness or weakness. Besides, he was not one to keep any but a necessary secret from those who loved him. He could not be seriously ill, or we should have known it.

Thus I pondered, until I heard the church bells ring out merrily. The marriage was over.

I was just in time to meet them at the front gates, which they entered—our Edwin and his wife—through a living line of smiling faces, treading upon a carpet of strewn flowers. Enderley would not be defrauded of its welcome—all the village escorted the young couple in triumph home. I have a misty recollection of how happy everybody looked, how the sun was shining, and the bells ringing, and the people cheering—a mingled phantasmagoria of sights and sounds, in which I only saw one person distinctly—John.

He waited while the young folk passed in—stood on the hall steps—in a few words thanked his people, and bade them to the general rejoicing. They, uproarious, answered in loud hurrahs, and one energetic voice cried out,—

"One cheer more for Master Guy!"

Guy's mother turned delighted—her eyes shining with proud tears.

"John—thank them; tell them that Guy will thank them himself to-morrow."

The master thanked them, but either he did not explain, or the honest, rude voices drowned all mention of the latter fact—that Guy would be home to-morrow.

All this while, and at the marriage breakfast likewise, Mr. Halifax kept the same calm demeanour. Once only, when the rest were all gathered round the bride and bridegroom, he said to me,—

"Phineas, is it done?"

"What is done?" asked Ursula, suddenly passing.

"A letter I asked him to write for me this morning."

Now I had all my life been proud of John's face—that it was a safe face to trust in—that it could not, or if it could, it would not, boast that stony calm under which some men are so proud of disguising themselves and their emotions from those nearest and dearest to them. If he were sad, we knew it; if he were happy, we knew it too. It was his principle, that nothing but the strongest motive should make a man stoop to even the smallest hypocrisy.

Therefore, hearing him thus speak to his wife, I was struck with great alarm. Mrs. Halifax herself seemed uneasy.

"A business letter, I suppose?"

"Partly on business. I will tell you all about it this evening."

She looked reassured. "Just as you like; you know I am not curious." But passing on, she turned back. "John, if it was anything important to be done—anything that I ought to know at once, you would not keep me in ignorance?"

"No—my dearest! No!"

Then what had happened must be something in which no help availed; something altogether past and irremediable; something which he rightly wished to keep concealed, for a few hours at least, from his other children, so as not to mar the happiness of this day, of which there could be no second, this crowning day of their lives—this wedding day of Edwin and Louise.

So he sat at the marriage table; he drank the marriage health; he gave them both a marriage blessing. Finally, he sent them away, smiling and sorrowful—as is the bounden duty of young married couples to depart—Edwin pausing even on the carriage step to embrace his mother with especial tenderness, and whisper her to "give his love to Guy."

"It reminds one of Guy's leaving," said the mother, hastily brushing back the tears that would spring and roll down her smiling face. She had never, until this moment, reverted to that miserable day. "John, do you think it possible the boy can be at home tonight?"

John answered emphatically, but very softly, "No."

"Why not? My letter would reach him in full time. Lord Ravenel has been to Paris and back since then.—But"—turning full upon the young nobleman—"I think you said you had not seen Guy?"

"No."

"Did you hear anything of him?"

"I—Mrs. Halifax——"

Exceedingly distressed, almost beyond his power of self-restraint, the young man looked appealingly to John, who replied for him,—

"Lord Ravenel brought me a letter from Guy this morning."

"A letter from Guy—and you never told me. How very strange!"

Still she seemed only to think it "strange." Some difficulty or folly, perhaps—you could see by the sudden flushing of her cheek, and her quick, distrustful glance at Lord Ravenel, what she imagined it was—that the boy had confessed to his father. With an instinct of concealment—the mother's instinct—for the moment she asked no questions.

We were all still standing at the hall door. Unresisting, she suffered her husband to take her arm in his, and bring her into the study.

"Now—the letter, please! Children, go away; I want to speak to your father. The letter, John?"

Her hand, which she held out, shook much. She tried to unfold the paper—stopped, and looked up piteously.

"It is not to tell me he is not coming home? I can bear anything, you know—but he *must* come."

John only answered, "Read,"—and took firm hold of her hand while she read—as we hold the hand of one undergoing great torture—which must be undergone, and which no human love can either prepare for, or remove, or alleviate.

The letter, which I saw afterwards, was thus:—

"DEAR FATHER AND MOTHER,—I have disgraced you all. I have been drunk—in a gaming-house. A man insulted me—it was about my father—but you will hear—all the world will hear presently. I struck him—there was something in my hand, and—the man was hurt.

"He may be dead by this time. I don't know.

"I am away to America to-night. I shall never come home any more. God bless you all.

"GUY HALIFAX.

"*P.S.*—I got my mother's letter to-day. Mother—I was not in my right senses, or I should not have done it. Mother, darling, forget me. Don't let me have broken your heart."

Alas, he had broken it!

"Never come home any more! Never come home any more!"

She repeated this over and over again, vacantly, nothing but these five words.

Nature refused to bear it; or rather, Nature mercifully helped her to bear it. When John took his wife in his arms she was insensible; and remained so, with intervals, for hours.

This was the end of Edwin's wedding day.

CHAPTER XXXVI.

LORD RAVENEL knew—as all Paris did by this time—the whole story. Though, as he truly said, he had not seen Guy. The lad was hurried off immediately, for fear of justice; but he had written from shipboard to Lord Ravenel, begging him himself to take the letter and break the news to us at Beechwood.

The man he had struck was not one of Lord Luxmore's set—though it was through some of his "noble" friends Guy had fallen into his company. He was an Englishman, lately succeeded to a baronetcy and estate; his name—how we started to hear it, though by Lord Ravenel and by us, for his sake, it was both pronounced and listened to, as if none of us had ever heard it before—Sir Gerard Vermilye.

As soon as Ursula recovered, Mr. Halifax and Lord Ravenel went to Paris together. This was necessary, not only to meet justice, but to track the boy—to whose destination we had no clue but the wide word, America. Guy's mother hurried them away—his mother, who rose from her bed, and moved about the house like a ghost—upstairs and downstairs—everywhere—excepting in that room, which was now once more locked, and the outer blind drawn down, as if Death himself had taken possession there.

Alas! we learned now that there may be sorrows bitterer even than death.

Mr. Halifax went away. Then followed a long season of torpid gloom—days or weeks, I hardly remember—during which we, living shut up at Beechwood, knew that our name—John's stainless, honourable name—was in everybody's mouth—parroted abroad in every society—canvassed in every newspaper. We tried, Walter and I, to stop them at first, dreading lest the mother might read in some foul print or other scurrilous tales about her boy; or, as long remained doubtful, learn that he was proclaimed through France and England as a homicide—an assassin. But concealments were idle. She would read everything—hear everything—meet everything—even those neighbours who out of curiosity or sympathy called at Beechwood. Not many times, though; they said they could not understand Mrs. Halifax. So, after a while, they all left her alone, except good little Grace Oldtower.

"Come often," I heard her say to this girl, whom she was fond of; they had sat talking a whole morning—idly and pensively; of little things around them, never once referring to things outside. "Come often, though the house is dull. Does it not feel strange, with Mr. Halifax away?"

Ay, this was the change—stranger at first than what had befallen Guy—for that long seemed a thing we could not realize; like a story told of some other family than ours. The present tangible blank was the house with its head and master away.

Curiously enough, but from his domestic habits easily accountable, he had scarcely ever been more than a few days absent from home before. We missed him continually; in his place at the head of the table; in his chair by the fire; his quick ring at the hall bell, when he came up from the mills—his step—his voice—his laugh. The life and soul of the house seemed to have gone out of it from the hour the father went away.

I think in the wonderful workings of things—as we know all things do work together for good—this fact was good for Ursula. It taught her that, in losing Guy, she had not lost all her blessings. It showed her what in the passion of her mother-love she might have been tempted to forget—many mothers do—that beyond all maternal duty is the duty that a woman owes to her husband; beyond all loves is the love that was hers before any of them were born.

So, gradually, as every day John's letters came—and she used to watch for them and seize them as if they had been love letters; as every day she seemed to miss him more, and count more upon his return; referring all decisions, and all little pleasures planned for her, to the time "when your father comes home"—hope and comfort began to dawn in the heart of the mourning mother.

And when at last John fixed the day of his coming back, I saw Ursula tying up the small bundle of his letters—his letters, of which in all her happy life she had had so few—his tender, comforting, comfortable letters.

"I hope I shall never need to have any more," she said, half smiling—the faint smile which began to dawn in her poor face, as if she must accustom it to look bright again in time for her husband's coming.

And when the day arrived, she put all the house in trim order, dressed herself in her prettiest gown, sat patient while Maud brushed and curled her hair—how white it had turned of late!—and then waited, with a flush on her cheek—like that of a young girl waiting for her lover—for the sound of carriage wheels.

All that had to be told about Guy—and it was better news than any one of us had hoped for—John had already told in his letters. When he came back, therefore, he was burthened with no trouble undisclosed—greeted with no anguish of fear or bitter remembrance. As he sprang out of the post-chaise, it was to find his wife standing at the door, and his home smiling for him its brightest welcome. No blessing on earth could be like the blessing of the father's return.

John looked pale, but not paler than might have been

expected. Grave too—but it was a soft seriousness altogether free from the restlessness of keen anxiety. The first shock of this heavy misfortune was over. He had paid all his son's debts; he had, as far as was possible, saved his good name; he had made a safe home for the lad, and heard of his safely reaching it, in the New World. Nothing more was left but to cover over the inevitable grief, and hope that time would blot out the intolerable shame. That since Guy's hand was clear of blood—and, since his recovery, Sir Gerard Vermilye had risen into a positive hero of society—men's minds would gradually lose the impression of a deed committed in heat of youth, and repented of with such bitter atonement.

So the father took his old place, and looked round on the remnant of his children, grave indeed, but not weighed down by incurable suffering. Something, deeper even than the hard time he had recently passed through, seemed to have made his home more than ever dear to him. He sat in his arm-chair, never weary of noticing everything pleasant about him, of saying how pretty Beechwood looked, and how delicious it was to be at home. And perpetually, if any chance unlinked it, his hand would return to its clasp of Ursula's; the minute she left her place by his side, his restless "Love, where are you going?" would call her back again. And once, when the children were out of the room, and I, sitting in a dark corner, was probably thought absent likewise, I saw John take his wife's face between his two hands, and look in it—the fondest, most lingering, saddest look! —then fold her tightly to his breast.

"I must never be away from her again. Mine—for as long as I live, mine—*my* wife, *my* Ursula!"

She took it all naturally, as she had taken every expression of his love these nine-and-twenty years. I left them, standing eye to eye, heart to heart, as if nothing in this world could ever part them.

Next morning was as gay as any of our mornings used to be, for, before breakfast, came Edwin and Louise. And after breakfast, the father and mother and I walked up and down the garden for an hour, talking over the prospects of the young couple. Then the post came—but we had no need to watch for it now. It only brought a letter from Lord Ravenel.

John read it somewhat more seriously than he had been used to read these letters—which for the last year or so had come often enough—the boys usually quizzing, and Mistress Maud vehemently defending, the delicate small handwriting, the exquisite paper, the coroneted seal, and the frank in the corner. John liked to have them, and his wife also—she being not indifferent to the fact, confirmed by many other facts, that if there was one man in the world whom Lord Ravenel honoured and admired, it was John Halifax of Beechwood. But this time her pleasure was apparently damped; and when Maud, claiming the letter as usual, spread abroad, delightedly, the news that "her" Lord Ravenel was coming shortly, I imagined this visit was not so welcome as usual to the parents.

Yet still, as many a time before, when Mr. Halifax closed the letter, he sighed, looked sorrowful, saying only, "Poor Lord Ravenel!"

"John," asked his wife, speaking in a whisper, for by tacit consent all public allusion to his doings at Paris was avoided in the family, "did you, by any chance, hear anything of—you know whom I mean?"

"Not one syllable."

"You inquired?" He assented. "I knew you would. She must be almost an old woman now, or perhaps she is dead. Poor Caroline!"

It was the first time for years and years that this name had been breathed in our household. Involuntarily it carried me back—perhaps others besides me—to the day at Longfield when little Guy had devoted himself to his "pretty lady;" when we first heard that other name which by a curious conjuncture of circumstances had since become so fatally familiar, and which would henceforward be like the sound of a dead-bell in our family—Gerard Vermilye.

On Lord Ravenel's reappearance at Beechwood—and he seemed eager and glad to come—I was tempted to wish him away. He never crossed the threshold but his presence brought a shadow over the parents' looks—and no wonder. The young people were gay and friendly as ever; made him always welcome with us; and he rode over daily from desolate, long-uninhabited Luxmore, where, in all its desolation, he appeared so fond of abiding.

He wanted to take Maud and Walter over there one day, to see some magnificent firs that were being cut down in a wholesale massacre, leaving the grand old Hall as bare as a workhouse front. But the father objected; he was clearly determined that all the hospitalities between Luxmore and Beechwood should be on the Beechwood side.

Lord Ravenel apparently perceived this. "Luxmore is not Compiègne," he said to me, with his dreary smile, half sad, half cynical. "Mr. Halifax might indulge me with the society of his children."

And as he lay on the grass—it was full summer now—watching Maud's white dress flit about under the trees, I saw, or fancied I saw, something different to any former expression that had ever lighted up the soft languid mien of William, Lord Ravenel.

"How tall that child has grown lately! She is about nineteen, I think?"

"Not seventeen till December."

"Ah, so young! Well, it is pleasant to be young! Dear little Maud!"

He turned on one side, hiding the sun from his eyes with those delicate ringed hands—which many a time our boys had laughed at, saying they were mere lady's hands, fit for no work at all.

Perhaps Lord Ravenel felt the cloud that had come over our intercourse with him; a cloud which, considering late events, was scarcely unnatural; for when evening came, his leave-taking, always a regret, seemed now as painful as his *blasé* indifference to all emotions, pleasant or unpleasant, could allow. He lingered—he hesitated—he repeated many times how glad he should be to see Beechwood again; how all the world was to him "flat, stale, and unprofitable," except Beechwood.

John made no special answer; except that frank smile, not without a certain kindly satire, under which the young nobleman's Byronic affectations generally melted away like mists in the morning. He kindled up into warmth and manliness.

"I thank you, Mr. Halifax—I thank you heartily for all you and your household have been to me. I trust I shall enjoy your friendship for many years. And if, in any way, I might offer mine, or any small influence in the world——"

"Your influence is not small," John returned earnestly. "I have often told you so. I know no man who has wider opportunities than you have."

"But I have let them slip—for ever."

"No, not for ever. You are young still; you have half a lifetime before you."

"Have I?" And for the moment one would hardly have recognized the sallow, spiritless face that, with all the delicacy of boyhood still, at times looked so exceedingly old. "No, no, Mr. Halifax, who ever heard of a man beginning life at seven-and-thirty?"

"Are you really seven-and-thirty?" asked Maud.

"Yes—yes, my girl. Is it so very old?"

He patted her on the shoulder, took her hand, gazed at it—the round, rosy, girlish hand—with a melancholy tenderness, then bade "Good-bye" to us all generally, and rode off.

It struck me then, though I hurried the thought away—it struck me afterwards, and does now with renewed surprise—how strange it was that the mother never noticed or took into account certain possibilities that would have occurred naturally to any worldly mother. I can only explain it by remembering the unworldliness of our lives at Beechwood, the heavy cares which now pressed upon us from without, and the notable fact—

which our own family experience ought to have taught us, yet did not—that in cases like this, often those whom one would have expected to be most quick-sighted, are the most strangely, irretrievably, mournfully blind.

When, the very next day, Lord Ravenel, not on horseback, but in his rarely-used luxurious coroneted carriage, drove up to Beechwood, every one in the house except myself was inconceivably astonished to see him back again.

He said that he had delayed his journey to Paris, and gave no explanation of that delay. He joined as usual in our midday dinner; and after dinner, still as usual, took a walk with me and Maud. It happened to be through the beech wood, almost the identical path that I remembered taking, years and years ago, with John and Ursula. I was surprised to hear Lord Ravenel allude to the fact, a well-known fact in our family; for I think all fathers and mothers like to relate, and all children to hear, the slightest incidents of the parents' courting days.

"You did not know father and mother when they were young?" said Maud, catching our conversation, and flashing back her innocent, merry face upon us.

"No, scarcely likely." And he smiled. "Oh yes—it might have been—I forget, I am not a young man now. How old were Mr. and Mrs. Halifax when they married?"

"Father was twenty-one and mother was eighteen—only a year older than I." And Maud, half ashamed of this suggestive remark, ran away. Her gay candour proved to me—perhaps to others besides me—the girl's entire free-heartedness. The frank innocence of childhood was still hers.

Lord Ravenel looked after her and sighed. "It is good to marry early; do you not think so, Mr. Fletcher?"

I told him (I was rather sorry after I had said it, if one ought to be sorry for having, when questioned, given one's honest opinion)—I told him that I thought those happiest who found their happiness early, but that I did not see why happiness should be rejected because it was the will of Providence that it should not be found till late.

"I wonder," he said dreamily—"I wonder whether I shall ever find it.'

I asked him—it was by an impulse irresistible—why he had never married?

"Because I never found any woman either to love or to believe in. Worse," he added bitterly, "I did not think there lived the woman who could be believed in."

We had come out of the beech wood and were standing by the low churchyard wall; the sun glittered on the white marble headstone on which was inscribed, "Muriel Joy Halifax."

Lord Ravenel leaned over the wall, his eyes fixed upon that little grave. After a while he said, sighing,—

"Do you know, I have thought sometimes that, had she lived, I could have loved—I might have married—that child!"

Here Maud sprang towards us. In her playful tyranny, which she loved to exercise and he to submit to, she insisted on knowing what Lord Ravenel was talking about.

"I was saying," he answered, taking both her hands and looking down into her bright, unshrinking eyes—"I was saying how dearly I loved your sister Muriel."

"I know that," and Maud became grave at once. "I know you care for me because I am like my sister Muriel."

"If it were so, would you be sorry or glad?"

"Glad, and proud too. But you said, or you were going to say, something more. What was it?"

He hesitated long, then answered,—

"I will tell you another time."

Maud went away rather cross and dissatisfied, but evidently suspecting nothing. For me, I began to be seriously uneasy about her and Lord Ravenel.

Of all kinds of love, there is one which common sense

and romance have often combined to hold obnoxious, improbable, or ridiculous, but which has always seemed to me the most real and pathetic form that the passion ever takes—I mean love in spite of great disparity of age. Even when this is on the woman's side, I can imagine circumstances that would make it far less ludicrous and pitiful; and there are few things to me more touching, more full of sad earnest, than to see an old man in love with a young girl.

Lord Ravenel's case would hardly come under this category; yet the difference between seventeen and thirty-seven was sufficient to warrant in him a trembling uncertainty, an eager catching at the skirts of that vanishing youth whose preciousness he never seemed to have recognized till now. It was with a mournful interest that all day I watched him follow the child about, gather her posies, help her to water her flowers, and accommodate himself to those whims and fancies, of which, as the pet and the youngest, Mistress Maud had her full share.

When, at her usual hour of half-past nine, the little lady was summoned away to bed, "to keep up her roses," he looked half resentful of the mother's interference.

"Maud is not a child now, and this may be my last night——" He stopped, sensitively, at the involuntary foreboding.

"Your last night? Nonsense! you will come back soon again. You must—you shall!" said Maud decisively.

"I hope I may—I trust in Heaven I may!"

He spoke low, holding her hand distantly and reverently, not attempting to kiss it, as in all his former farewells he had invariably done.

"Maud, remember me! However or whenever I come back, dearest child, be faithful, and remember me!"

Maud fled away with a sob of childish pain—partly anger, the mother thought, and slightly apologized to the guest for her daughter's "naughtiness."

Lord Ravenel sat silent for a long, long time.

Just when we thought he purposed leaving, he said abruptly, " Mr. Halifax, may I have five minutes' speech with you in the study ? "

The five minutes extended to half an hour. Mrs. Halifax wondered what on earth they were talking about. I held my peace. At last the father came in alone.

" John, is Lord Ravenel gone ? "

" Not yet."

" What could he have wanted to say to you ? "

John sat down by his wife, picked up the ball of her knitting, rolled and unrolled it. She saw at once that something had grieved and perplexed him exceedingly. Her heart shrank back—that still sore heart !—recoiled with a not unnatural fear.

" O husband, is it any new misfortune ? "

" No, love," cheering her with a smile, " nothing that fathers and mothers in general would consider as such. He has asked me for our Maud."

" What for ? " was the mother's first exceedingly simple question—and then she guessed its answer. " Impossible ! Ridiculous—absolutely ridiculous ! She is only a child."

" Nevertheless, Lord Ravenel wishes to marry our little Maud."

" Lord Ravenel wishes to marry our Maud ! "

Mrs. Halifax repeated this to herself more than once before she was able to entertain it as a reality. When she did, the first impression it made upon her mind was altogether pain.

" O John ! I hoped we had done with these sort of things ; I thought we should have been left in peace with the rest of our children."

John smiled again ; for, indeed, there was a comical side to her view of the subject. But its serious phase soon returned—doubly so, when, looking up, they both saw Lord Ravenel standing before them. Firm his attitude was, firmer than usual ; and it was with something of his father's stately air, mingled with a more chivalric and sincerer grace, that he stooped forward and kissed the hand of Maud's mother.

"Mr. Halifax has told you all, I believe?"

"He has."

"May I, then, with entire trust in you both, await my answer?"

He waited it, patiently enough, with little apparent doubt as to what it would be. Besides, it was only the prior question of parental consent, not the vital point of Maud's preference. And, with all his natural humility, Lord Ravenel might be forgiven if, brought up in the world, he was aware of his position therein; nor quite unconscious that it was not merely William Ravenel, but the only son and heir of the Earl of Luxmore, who came a-wooing.

Not till after a long pause, and even a whispered word or two between the husband and wife, who knew each other's minds so well that no more consultation was needed, did the suitor again, with a more formal air, ask for an answer.

"It is difficult to give. I find that my wife, like myself, had no idea of your feelings. The extreme suddenness——"

"Pardon me; my intention has not been sudden It is the growth of many months—years, I might almost say."

"We are the more grieved."

"Grieved?"

Lord Ravenel's extreme surprise startled him from the mere suitor into the lover; he glanced from one to the other in undisguised alarm. John hesitated; the mother said something about the "great difference between them."

"In age, do you mean? I am aware of that," he answered, with some sadness. "But twenty years is not an insuperable bar in marriage."

"No," said Mrs. Halifax thoughtfully.

"And for any other disparity—in fortune or rank——"

"I think, Lord Ravenel"—and the mother spoke with her "dignified" air—"you know enough of my husband's character and opinions to be assured how lightly he would hold such a disparity—if you allude to that supposed to exist between the son of the Earl of Luxmore and the daughter of John Halifax."

The young nobleman coloured, as if with ingenuous shame at what he had been implying. "I am glad of it. Let me assure you there will be no impediments on the side of my family. The earl has long wished me to marry. He knows well enough that I can marry whom I please—and shall marry for love only. Give me your leave to win your little Maud."

A dead silence.

"Again pardon me," Lord Ravenel said with some *hauteur;* "I cannot have clearly explained myself. Let me repeat, Mr. Halifax, that I ask your permission to win your daughter's affection, and, in due time, her hand."

"I would that you had asked of me anything that it could be less impossible to give you."

"Impossible! What do you mean?—Mrs. Halifax——" He turned instinctively to the woman—the mother.

Ursula's eyes were full of a sad kindness—the kindness any mother must feel towards one who worthily woos her daughter—but she replied distinctly,—

"I feel, with my husband, that such a marriage would be impossible."

Lord Ravenel grew scarlet, sat down, rose again, and stood facing them, pale and haughty.

"If I may ask—your reasons?"

"Since you ask—certainly," John replied. "Though, believe me, I give them with the deepest pain. Lord Ravenel, do you not yourself see that our Maud——"

"Wait one moment," he interrupted. "There is not, there cannot be, any previous attachment?"

The supposition made the parents smile. "Indeed, nothing of the kind. She is a mere child."

"You think her too young for marriage, then?" was the eager answer. "Be it so. I will wait, though my youth, alas! is slipping from me; but I will wait—two years, three—any time you choose to name."

John needed not to reply. The very sorrow of his decision showed how inevitable and irrevocable it was.

Lord Ravenel's pride rose against it.

"I fear in this my novel position I am somewhat slow of comprehension. Would it be so great a misfortune to your daughter if I made her Viscountess Ravenel, and in course of time Countess of Luxmore?"

"I believe it would. Her mother and I would rather see our little Maud lying beside her sister Muriel than see her Countess of Luxmore."

These words, hard as they were, John uttered so softly, and with such infinite grief and pain, that they struck the young man, not with anger, but with an indefinite awe, as if a ghost from his youth—his wasted youth—had risen up to point out that truth, and show him that what seemed insult or vengeance was only a bitter necessity.

All he did was to repeat, in a subdued manner, "Your reasons?"

"Ah, Lord Ravenel," John answered sadly, "do you not see yourself that the distance between us and you is wide as the poles? Not in worldly things, but in things far deeper—personal things, which strike at the root of love, home—nay, honour."

Lord Ravenel started. "Would you imply that anything in my past life, aimless and useless as it may have been, is unworthy of my honour—the honour of our house?"

Saying this, he stopped—recoiled—as if suddenly made aware, by the very words himself had uttered, what—contrasted with the unsullied dignity of the tradesman's life, the spotless innocence of the tradesman's daughter—what a foul, tattered rag, fit to be torn down by an honest gust, was that flaunting emblazonment, the so-called "honour" of Luxmore!

"I understand you now. 'The sins of the fathers shall be visited upon the children,' as your Bible says—your Bible, that I had half begun to believe in. Be it so. Mr. Halifax, I will detain you no longer."

John intercepted the young man's departure.

"No, you do *not* understand me. I hold no man accountable for any errors, any shortcomings, except his own."

"I am to conclude, then, that it is to myself you refuse your daughter?"

"It is."

Lord Ravenel once more bowed, with sarcastic emphasis.

"I entreat you not to mistake me," John continued, most earnestly. "I know nothing of you that the world would condemn, much that it would even admire; but your world is not our world, nor your aims our aims. If I gave you my little Maud, it would confer on you no lasting happiness, and it would be thrusting my child, my own flesh and blood, to the brink of that whirlpool where, soon or late, every miserable life must go down."

Lord Ravenel made no answer. His new-born energy, his pride, his sarcasm, had successively vanished; dead, passive melancholy resumed its empire over him. Mr. Halifax regarded him with mournful compassion.

"Oh that I had foreseen this! I would have placed the breadth of all England between you and my child."

"Would you?"

"Understand me. Not because you do not possess our warm interest, our friendship: both will always be yours. But these are external ties, which may exist through many differences. In marriage there must be perfect unity—one aim, one faith, one love—or the marriage is incomplete, unholy—a mere civil contract and no more."

Lord Ravenel looked up amazed at this doctrine, then sat a while, pondering drearily.

"Yes, you may be right," at last he said. "Your Maud is not for me, nor those like me. Between us and you is that 'great gulf fixed.' What did the old fable say? I forget. *Che sarà sarà!* I am but as others; I am but what I was born to be."

"Do you recognize what you were born to be? Not

only a nobleman, but a gentleman; not only a gentleman, but a man—man, made in the image of God. How can you, how dare you, give the lie to your Creator?"

"What has He given me? What have I to thank Him for?"

"First, manhood—the manhood His Son disdained not to wear; worldly gifts, such as rank, riches, influence, things which others have to spend half an existence in earning; life in its best prime, with much of youth yet remaining—with grief endured, wisdom learnt, experience won. Would to Heaven that by any poor word of mine I could make you feel all that you are—all that you might be!"

A gleam, bright as a boy's hope, wild as a boy's daring, flashed from those listless eyes—then faded.

"You mean, Mr. Halifax, what I might have been. Now it is too late."

"There is no such word as 'too late' in the wide world—nay, not in the universe. What! shall we, whose atom of time is but a fragment out of an ever-present eternity—shall we, so long as we live, or even at our life's ending, dare to cry out to the Eternal One, 'It is too late!'"

As John spoke, in much more excitement than was usual to him, a sudden flush, or rather spasm, of colour flushed his face, then faded away, leaving him pallid to the very lips. He sat down hastily, in his frequent attitude, with the left arm passed across his breast.

"Lord Ravenel." His voice was faint, as though speech was painful to him.

The other looked up, the old look of reverent attention, which I remembered in the boy-lord who came to see us at Norton Bury; in the young "Anselmo" whose enthusiastic hero-worship had fixed itself, with an almost unreasoning trust, on Muriel's father.

"Lord Ravenel, forgive anything I have said that may have hurt you. It would grieve me inexpressibly if we did not part as friends."

"Part?"

"For a time, we must. I dare not risk further either your happiness or my child's."

"No, not hers. Guard it. I blame you not. The lovely, innocent child! God forbid she should ever have a life like mine!"

He sat silent, his clasped hands listlessly dropping, his countenance dreamy, yet, it seemed to me, less hopelessly sad; then with a sudden effort he rose.

"I must go now."

Crossing over to Mrs. Halifax, he thanked her, with much emotion, for all her kindness.

"For your husband, I owe him more than kindness, as perhaps I may prove some day. If not, try to believe the best of me you can. Good-bye."

They both said good-bye, and bade God bless him, with scarcely less tenderness than if things had ended as he desired, and, instead of this farewell, sad and indefinite beyond most farewells, they were giving the parental welcome to a newly-chosen son.

Ere finally quitting us, Lord Ravenel turned back to speak to John once more, hesitatingly and mournfully.

"If she—if the child should ask or wonder about my absence—she likes me in her innocent way, you know—you will tell her—— What shall you tell her?"

"Nothing. It is best not."

"Ay, it is, it is."

He shook hands with us all three, without saying anything else; then the carriage rolled away, and we saw his face—that pale, gentle, melancholy face—no more.

It was years and years before any one beyond ourselves knew what a near escape our little Maud had had of becoming Viscountess Ravenel—future Countess of Luxmore.

CHAPTER XXXVII.

It was not many weeks after this departure of Lord Ravenel's—the pain of which was almost forgotten in the comfort of Guy's first long home letter, which came about this time—that John one morning, suddenly dropping his newspaper, exclaimed,—

"Lord Luxmore is dead."

Yes, he had returned to his dust, this old bad man—so old that people had begun to think he would never die. He was gone, the man who, if we owned an enemy in the world, had certainly proved himself that enemy. Something peculiar is there in a decease like this—of one whom, living, we have almost felt ourselves justified in condemning, avoiding—perhaps hating. Until Death, stepping in between, removes him to another tribunal than this petty justice of ours, and laying a solemn finger on our mouths, forbids us either to think or utter a word of hatred against that which is now—what ?—a disembodied spirit—a handful of corrupting clay.

Lord Luxmore was dead. He had gone to his account; it was not ours to judge him. We never knew—I believe no one except his son ever fully knew—the history of his death-bed.

John sat in silence, the paper before him, long after we had passed the news and discussed it, not without awe, all round the breakfast-table.

Maud stole up hesitatingly, and asked to see the announcement of the earl's decease.

"No, my child; but you shall hear it read aloud, if you choose."

I guessed the reason of his refusal, when, looking over him as he read, I saw, after the long list of titles owned by the new Earl of Luxmore, one bitter line. How it must have cut to the heart of him whom we first heard of as "poor William"!

"*Had likewise issue, Caroline, married in 17— to Richard Brithwood, Esquire, afterwards divorced.*"

And by a curious coincidence, about twenty lines further down I read, among the fashionable marriages :—

"*At the British Embassy, Paris, Sir Gerard Vermilye, Bart., to the youthful and beautiful daughter of——*"

I forget who. I only saw that the name was not her name, of whom the "youthful and beautiful" bride had most likely never heard. He had not married Lady Caroline.

This morning's intelligence brought the Luxmore family so much to our thoughts that, driving out after breakfast, John and I involuntarily recurred to the subject. Nay, talking on, in the solitude of our front seat—for Mrs. Halifax, Miss Halifax, and Mrs. Edwin Halifax, in the carriage behind, were deep in some other subject—we fell upon a topic which by tacit consent had been laid aside, as in our household we held it good to lay aside any inevitable regret.

"Poor Maud! how eager she was to hear the news to-day! She little thinks how vitally it might have concerned her."

"No," John answered thoughtfully; then asked me with some abruptness, "Why did you say 'poor Maud?'"

I really could not tell; it was a mere accident, the unwitting indication of some crotchets of mine, which had often come into my mind lately—crotchets, perhaps, peculiar to one who, never having known a certain possession, found himself rather prone to overrate its value. But it sometimes struck me as hard, considering how little honest and sincere love there is in the world, that Maud should never have known of Lord Ravenel's.

Possibly, against my will, my answer implied something of this, for John was a long time silent. Then he began to talk of various matters, telling me of many improvements he was planning and executing on his property and among his people. In all his plans, and in the carrying out of them, I noticed one peculiarity, strong in him throughout his life, but latterly grown stronger than ever—namely, that whatever he found to do, he did immediately. Procrastination had never been one of his faults; now he seemed to have a horror of putting anything off even for a single hour. Nothing that could be done did he lay aside until it was done; his business affairs were kept in perfect order, each day's work being completed with the day. And in the thousand and one little things that were constantly arising, from his position as magistrate and landowner, and his general interest in the movements of the time, the same system was invariably pursued. In his relations with the world outside, as in his own little valley, he seemed determined to "work while it was day." If he could possibly avoid it, no application was ever unattended to; no duty left unfinished; no good unacknowledged; no evil unremedied, or at least unforgiven.

"John," I said, as to-day this peculiarity of his struck me more than usual, "thou art certainly one of the faithful servants whom the Master when He cometh will find watching."

"I hope so. It ought to be thus with all men—but especially with me."

I imagined, from his tone, that he was thinking of his responsibility as father, master, owner of large wealth. How could I know—how could I guess—beyond this!

"Do you think she looks pale, Phineas?" he asked suddenly.

"Who? Your wife?"

"No; Maud. My little Maud."

It was but lately that he called her "his" little Maud, since, with that extreme tenacity of attachment which was a part of his nature—refusing to put any one love in another love's place—his second daughter had never been to him like the first. Now, however, I had noticed that he took Maud nearer to his heart, made her more often his companion, watching her with a sedulous tenderness—it was easy to guess why.

"She may have looked a little paler of late, a little more thoughtful, but I am sure she is not unhappy."

"I believe not—thank God!"

"Surely," I said anxiously, "you have never repented what you did about Lord Ravenel?"

"No—not once. It cost me so much that I know it was right to be done."

"But if things had been otherwise—if you had not been so sure of Maud's feelings——"

He started painfully, then answered, "I think I should have done it still."

I was silent. The paramount right, the high prerogative of love, which he held as strongly as I did, seemed attacked in its liberty divine. For the moment it was as if he too had in his middle age gone over to the cold-blooded ranks of harsh parental prudence, despotic paternal rule; as if Ursula March's lover and Maud's father were two distinct beings. One finds it so, often enough, with men.

"John," I said, "could you have done it? Could you have broken the child's heart?"

"Yes, if it was to save her peace—perhaps her soul—I *could* have broken my child's heart."

He spoke solemnly, with an accent of inexpressible pain, as if this were not the first time by many that he had pondered over such a possibility.

"I wish, Phineas, to make clear to you, in case of—of any future misconceptions—my mind on this matter. One right alone I hold superior to the right of love—duty. It is a father's duty, at all risks, at all costs, to save his child from anything which he believes would peril her duty—so long as she is too young to understand fully how beyond the claim of any human being, be it father or lover, is God's claim to herself and her immortal soul. Anything which would endanger that should be cut off—though it be the right hand—the right eye. But, thank God, it was not thus with my little Maud."

"Nor with him either. He bore his disappointment well."

"Nobly. It may make a true nobleman of him yet. But being what he is, and for as long as he remains so, he must not be trusted with my little Maud. I must take care of her while I live; afterwards——"

His smile faded, or rather was transmuted into that grave thoughtfulness which I had lately noticed in him, when, as now, he fell into one of his long silences. There was nothing sad about it, rather a serenity which reminded me of that sweet look of his boyhood, which had vanished during the manifold cares of his middle life. The expression of the mouth, as I saw it in profile—close and calm—almost inclined me to go back to the fanciful follies of our youth, and call him "David."

We drove through Norton Bury, and left Mrs. Edwin there; then on, along the familiar road, towards the manor house; past the white gate, within sight of little Longfield.

"It looks just the same; the tenant takes good care of it." And John's eyes turned fondly to his old home.

"Ay, just the same. Do you know, your wife was saying to me this morning that, when Guy comes back, when all the young folk are married, and you retire from business and settle into the *otium cum dignitate*, the learned leisure you used to plan—she would like to give up Beechwood. She said she hopes you and she will end your days together at little Longfield."

"Did she? Yes, I know that has been always her dream."

"Scarcely a dream, or one that is not unlikely to be fulfilled. I like to fancy you both two old people, sitting on either side the fire—or on the same side, if you like it best—very cheerful. You will make such a merry old man, John, with all your children round you, and indefinite grandchildren about the house continually. Or else you two will sit alone together, just as in your early married days—you and your old wife—the dearest and handsomest old lady that ever was seen."

"Phineas—don't—don't." I was startled by the tone in which he answered the lightness of mine. "I mean—don't be planning out the future. It is foolish—it is almost wrong. God's will is not as our will, and He knows best."

I would have spoken, but just then we reached the manor-house gate, and plunged at once into present life, and into the hospitable circle of the Oldtowers.

They were all in the excitement of a wonderful piece of gossip—gossip so strange, sudden, and unprecedented, that it absorbed all lesser matters. It burst out before we had been in the house five minutes.

"Have you heard this extraordinary report about the Luxmore family?"

I could see Maud turn with eager attention—fixing her eyes wistfully on Lady Oldtower.

"About the earl's death. Yes, we saw it in the newspaper." And John passed on to some other point of conversation. In vain.

"This news relates to the present earl. I never heard of such a thing—never. In fact, if true, his conduct is something which, in its self-denial, approaches absolute insanity. Is it possible that, being so great a friend of your family, he has not informed you of the circumstances?"

These circumstances, with some patience, we extracted from the voluble Lady Oldtower. She had learnt them—I forget how; but ill news never wants a tongue to carry it.

It seemed that on the earl's death it was discovered, what had already been long suspected, that his liabilities, like his extravagances, were enormous. That he was obliged to live abroad to escape in some degree the clamorous haunting of the hundreds he had ruined—poor tradespeople, who knew that their only chance of payment was during the old man's lifetime, for his whole property was entailed on the son.

Whether Lord Ravenel had ever been acquainted with the state of things, or whether, being in ignorance of it, his own style of living had in degree imitated his father's, rumour did not say, nor indeed was it of much consequence. The facts subsequently becoming known immediately after Lord Luxmore's death made all former conjectures unnecessary.

Not a week before he died, the late earl and his son—chiefly, it was believed, on the latter's instigation—had cut off the entail, thereby making the whole property saleable, and available for the payment of creditors. Thus, by his own act, and—as some one had told somebody that somebody else had heard Lord Ravenel say—"for the honour of the family," the present earl had succeeded to an empty title, and—beggary.

"Or," Lady Oldtower added, "what to a man of rank will be the same as beggary—a paltry two hundred a year or so—which he has reserved, they say, just to keep him from destitution. Ah—here comes Mr. Jessop; I thought he would. He can tell us all about it."

Old Mr. Jessop was as much excited as any one present.

"Ay, it's all true—only too true, Mr. Halifax. He was at my house last night."

"Last night!" I do not think anybody caught the child's exclamation but me. I could not help watching little Maud, noticing what strong emotion, still perfectly childlike and unguarded in its demonstration, was shaking her innocent bosom, and overflowing at her eyes. However, as she sat still in the corner, nobody observed her.

"Yes, he slept at my house—Lord Ravenel, the Earl of Luxmore, I mean. Much good will his title do him! My head clerk is better off than he. He has stripped himself of every penny except—— Bless me, I forgot. Mr. Halifax, he gave me a letter for you."

John walked to the window to read it, but having read it, passed it openly round the circle, as indeed was best.

"My dear Friend,—You will have heard that my father is no more." ("He used always to say 'the earl,'" whispered Maud, as she looked over my shoulder.)

"I write this merely to say, what I feel sure you will already have believed—that anything which you may learn concerning his affairs, I was myself unaware of, except in a very slight degree, when I last visited Beechwood.

"Will you likewise believe that in all I have done, or intend doing, your interests as my tenant—which I hope you will remain—have been, and shall be, sedulously guarded?

"My grateful remembrance to all your household.—Faithfully yours and theirs, Luxmore."

"Give me back the letter, Maud, my child."

She had been taking possession of it, as in right of being his "pet" she generally did of all Lord Ravenel's letters. But now, without a word of objection, she surrendered it to her father.

"What does he mean, Mr. Jessop, about my interests as his tenant?"

"Bless me—I am so grieved about the matter that everything goes astray in my head. He wished me to explain to you that he has reserved one portion of the Luxmore property intact—Enderley Mills. The rent you pay will, he says, be a sufficient income for him; and then, while your lease lasts, no other landlord can injure you. Very thoughtful of him—very thoughtful indeed, Mr. Halifax."

John made no answer.

"I never saw a man so altered. He went over some matters with me—private charities, in which I have been his agent, you know—grave, clear-headed, business-like. My clerk himself could not have done better. Afterwards we sat and talked, and I tried—foolishly enough, when the thing was done!—to show him what a frantic act it was both towards himself and his heirs. But he could not see it. He said cutting off the entail would harm nobody—for that he did not intend ever to marry. Poor fellow!"

"Is he with you still?" John asked in a low tone.

"No; he left this morning for Paris; his father is to be buried there. Afterwards, he said, his movements were quite uncertain. He bade me good-bye. I—I didn't like it, I can assure you."

And the old man, blowing his nose with his yellow pocket-handkerchief, and twitching his features into all manner of shapes, seemed determined to put aside the melancholy subject, and dilated on the earl and his affairs no more.

Nor did any one. Something in this young nobleman's noble act—it has since been not without a parallel among our aristocracy—silenced the tongue of gossip itself.

The deed was so new—so unlike anything that had been conceived possible, especially in a man like Lord Ravenel, who had always borne the character of a harmless, idle, misanthropic nonentity—that society was really nonplussed concerning it. Of the many loquacious visitors who came that morning to pour upon Lady Oldtower all the curiosity of Coltham—fashionable Coltham, famous for all the scandal of *haut ton*—there was none who did not speak of Lord Luxmore and his affairs with an uncomfortable, wondering awe. Some suggested he was going mad; others, raking up stories current of his early youth, thought he had turned Catholic again, and was about to enter a monastery. One or two honest hearts protested that he was a noble fellow, and it was a pity he had determined to be the last of the Luxmores.

For ourselves—Mr. and Mrs. Halifax, Maud, and I—we never spoke to one another on the subject all morning. Not until after luncheon, when John and I had somehow stolen out of the way of the visitors, and were walking to and fro in the garden. The sunny fruit garden—ancient, Dutch, and square—with its barricade of a high hedge, a stone wall, and between it and the house a shining fence of great laurel trees.

Maud appeared suddenly before us from among these laurels, breathless.

"I got away after you, father. I—I wanted to find some strawberries, and—I wanted to speak to you."

"Speak on, little lady."

He linked her arm in his, and she paced between us up and down the broad walk, but without diverging to the strawberry-beds. She was grave, and paler than ordinary. Her father asked if she were tired?

"No, but my head aches. Those Coltham people do talk so. Father, I want you to explain to me, for I can't well understand all this that they have been saying about Lord Ravenel."

John explained as simply and briefly as he could.

"I understand. Then, though he is Earl of Luxmore, he is quite poor—poorer than any of us? And he has made himself poor in order to pay his own and his father's debts, and keep other people from suffering from any fault of his? Is it so?"

"Yes, my child."

"Is it not a very noble act, father?"

"Very noble."

"I think it is the noblest act I ever heard of. I should like to tell him so. When is he coming to Beechwood?"

Maud spoke quickly, with flushed cheeks, in the impetuous manner she inherited from her mother. Her question not being immediately answered, she repeated it still more eagerly.

Her father replied, "I do not know."

"How very strange! I thought he would come at once—to-night, probably."

I reminded her that Lord Ravenel had left for Paris, bidding good-bye to Mr. Jessop.

"He ought to have come to us instead of to Mr. Jessop. Write and tell him so, father. Tell him how glad we shall be to see him. And perhaps you can help him, you who help everybody. He always said you were his best friend."

"Did he?"

"Ah, now, do write, father dear. I am sure you will."

John looked down on the little maid who hung on his arm so persuasively, then looked sorrowfully away.

"My child—I cannot."

"What, not write to him? When he is poor and in trouble? That is not like you, father," and Maud half loosed her arm.

Her father quietly put the little rebellious hand back again to its place. He was evidently debating within himself whether he should tell her the whole truth, or how much of it. Not that the debate was new, for he must already have foreseen this possible, nay, certain, conjuncture. Especially as all his dealings with his family had hitherto been open as daylight. He held that to prevaricate, or wilfully to give the impression of a falsehood, is almost as mean as a direct lie. When anything occurred that he could not tell his children, he always said plainly, " I cannot tell you," and they asked no more.

I wondered exceedingly how he would deal with Maud. She walked with him, submissive yet not satisfied, glancing at him from time to time, waiting for him to speak. At last she could wait no longer.

" I am sure there is something wrong. You do not care for Lord Ravenel as much as you used to do."

" More, if possible."

" Then write to him. Say we want to see him—I want to see him. Ask him to come and stay a long while at Beechwood."

" I cannot, Maud. It would be impossible for him to come. I do not think he is likely to visit Beechwood for some time."

" How long ? Six months ? A year, perhaps ? "

" It may be several years."

" Then I was right. Something *has* happened; you are not friends with him any longer. And he is poor —in trouble—O father ! "

She snatched her hand away, and flashed upon him reproachful eyes. John took her gently by the arm, and made her sit down upon the wall of a little stone bridge, under which the moat slipped with a quiet murmur. Maud's tears dropped into it fast and free.

That very outburst, brief and thundery as a child's passion, gave consolation both to her father and me. When it lessened, John spoke.

" Now, has my little Maud ceased to be angry with her father ? "

" I did not mean to be angry—only I was so startled—so grieved. Tell me what has happened, please, father ? "

" I will tell you—so far as I can. Lord Ravenel and myself had some conversation, of a very painful kind, the last night he was with us. After it, we both considered it advisable he should not visit us again for the present."

"Why not? Had you quarrelled? Or if you had, I thought my father was always the first to forgive everybody."

"No, Maud, we had not quarrelled."

"Then what was it?"

"My child, you must not ask, for indeed I cannot tell you."

Maud sprang up, the rebellious spirit flashing out again. "Not tell me—me, his pet—me, that cared for him more than any of you did. I think you ought to tell me, father."

"You must allow me to decide that, if you please."

After this answer Maud paused, and said humbly, "Does any one else know?"

"Your mother, and your Uncle Phineas, who happened to be present at the time. No one else; and no one else shall know."

John spoke with that slight quivering and blueness of the lips which any mental excitement usually produced in him. He sat down by his daughter's side and took her hand.

"I knew this would grieve you, and I kept it from you as long as I could. Now, you must only be patient, and like a good child trust your father."

Something in his manner quieted her. She only sighed and said, "She could not understand it."

"Neither can I—oftentimes, my poor little Maud. There are so many sad things in life that we have to take upon trust, and bear, and be patient with—yet never understand. I suppose we shall some day."

His eyes wandered upward to the wide-arched blue sky, which in its calm beauty makes us fancy that Paradise is there, even though we know that "*the kingdom of Heaven is within us*," and that the kingdom of spirits may be around us and about us everywhere.

Maud looked at her father, and crept closer to him—into his arms.

"I did not mean to be naughty. I will try not to mind losing him. But I liked Lord Ravenel so much—and he was so fond of me."

"Child"—and her father himself could not help smiling at the simplicity of her speech—"it is often easiest to lose those we are fond of, and who are fond of us, because, in one sense, we never can really lose them. Nothing in this world, nor, I believe, in any other, can part those who truly and faithfully love."

I think he was hardly aware how much he was implying, at least not in its relation to her, else he would not have said it. And he would surely have noticed, as I did, that the word "love," which had not been mentioned before—it was "liking," "fond of," "care for," or some such roundabout, childish phrase—the word "love" made Maud start. She darted from one to the other of us a keen glance of inquiry, and then turned the colour of a July rose.

Her attitude, her blushes, the shy tremble about her mouth, reminded me vividly, too vividly, of her mother twenty-eight years ago.

Alarmed, I tried to hasten the end of our conversation, lest, voluntarily or involuntarily, it might produce the very results which, though they might not have altered John's determination, would almost have broken his heart.

So, begging her to "kiss and make friends," which Maud did timidly, and without attempting further questions, I hurried the father and daughter into the house, deferring for mature consideration the question whether or not I should trouble John with any too-anxious doubts of mine concerning her.

As we drove back through Norton Bury, I saw that while her mother and Lady Oldtower conversed, Maud sat opposite, rather more silent than her wont; but when the ladies dismounted for shopping, she was again the lively independent Miss Halifax,

> ——"Standing with reluctant feet
> Where womanhood and childhood meet,"

and assuming at once the prerogatives and immunities of both.

Her girlish ladyship at last got tired of silks and ribbons, and stood with me at the shop door, amusing herself with commenting on the passers-by.

These were not so plentiful as I once remembered; though still the old town wore its old face, appearing fairer than ever as I myself grew older. The same Coltham coach stopped at the Lamb Inn, and the same group of idle loungers took an interest in its disemboguing of its contents. But railways had done an ill turn to the coach and to poor Norton Bury. Where there used to be six inside passengers, to-day was turned out only one.

"What a queer-looking little woman! Uncle Phineas, people shouldn't dress so fine as that when they are old."

Maud's criticism was scarcely unjust. The light-coloured flimsy gown, shorter than even Coltham fashionables would have esteemed decent, the fluttering bonnet, the abundance of flaunting curls—no wonder that the stranger attracted considerable notice in quiet Norton Bury. As she tripped mincingly along, in her silk stockings and light shoes, a smothered jeer arose.

"People should not laugh at an old woman, however conceited she may be," said Maud indignantly.

"Is she old?"

"Just look."

And surely when, as she turned from side to side, I caught her full face—what a face it was!—withered, thin, sallow almost to deathliness, with a bright rouge spot on each cheek, a broad smile on the ghastly mouth.

"Is she crazy, Uncle Phineas?"

"Possibly. Do not look at her." For I was sure this must be the wreck of such a life as womanhood does sometimes sink to—a life, the mere knowledge of which had never yet entered our Maud's pure world.

She seemed surprised, but obeyed me and went in. I stood at the shop door, watching the increasing crowd, and pitying, with that pity mixed with shame that every honest man must feel towards a degraded woman, the wretched object of their jeers. Half frightened, she still kept up that set smile, skipping daintily from side to side of the pavement, darting at and peering into every carriage that passed. Miserable creature as she looked, there was a certain grace and ease in her movements, as if she had fallen from some far higher estate.

At that moment the Mythe carriage, with Mr. Brithwood in it, dozing his daily drive away, his gouty foot propped up before him, slowly lumbered up the street. The woman made a dart at it, but was held back.

"Canaille! I always hated your Norton Bury! Call my carriage. I will go home."

Through its coarse discordance, its insane rage, I thought I knew the voice, especially when, assuming a tone of command, she addressed the old coachman,—

"Draw up, Peter; you are very late. People, give way! Don't you see my carriage?"

There was a roar of laughter, so loud that even Mr. Brithwood opened his dull, drunken eyes and stared about him.

"Canaille!"—and the scream was more of terror than anger, as she almost flung herself under the horses' heads in her eagerness to escape from the mob. "Let me go! My carriage is waiting. I am Lady Caroline Brithwood!"

The squire heard her. For a single instant they gazed at one another—besotted husband, dishonoured, divorced wife—gazed with horror and fear, as two sinners who had been each other's undoing might meet in the poetic torments of Dante's "Inferno," or the tangible fire and brimstone of many a blind but honest Christian's hell. One single instant—and then Richard Brithwood made up his mind.

"Coachman, drive on!"

But the man—he was an old man—seemed to hesitate at urging his horses right over "my lady." He even looked down on her with a sort of compassion—I remembered having heard say that she was always kind and affable to her servants.

"Drive on, you fool! Here"—and Mr. Brithwood threw some coin amongst the mob—"fetch the constable—some of you. Take the woman to the watch-house!"

And the carriage rolled on, leaving her there, crouched on the kerbstone, gazing after it with something between a laugh and a moan.

Nobody touched her. Perhaps some had heard of her; a few might even have seen her—driving through Norton Bury in her pristine state, as the young squire's handsome wife—the charming Lady Caroline.

I was so absorbed in the sickening sight that I did not perceive how John and Ursula, standing behind me, had seen it likewise—evidently seen and understood it all.

"What is to be done?" she whispered to him.

"What ought we to do?"

Here Maud came running out to see what was amiss in the street.

"Go in, child," said Mrs. Halifax sharply. "Stay till I fetch you."

Lady Oldtower also advanced to the door, but catching some notion of what the disturbance was, shocked and scandalized, retired into the shop again.

John looked earnestly at his wife, but for once she did not or would not understand his meaning. She drew back uneasily.

"What must be done? I mean, what do you want me to do?"

"What only a woman can do—a woman like you, and in your position."

"Yes, if it were only myself. But think of the household—think of Maud. People will talk so. It is hard to know how to act."

"Nay; how did One act—how would He act now, if He stood in the street this day? If we take care of aught of His, will He not take care of us and of our children?"

Mrs. Halifax paused, thought a moment, hesitated—yielded.

"John, you are right; you are always right. I will do anything you please."

And then I saw, through the astonished crowd, in face of scores of window-gazers, all of whom knew them, and a great number of whom they also knew, Mr. Halifax and his wife walk up to where the miserable woman lay.

John touched her lightly on the shoulder. She screamed and cowered down.

"Are you the constable? He said he would send the constable."

"Hush! do not be afraid. Cousin—Cousin Caroline."

God knows how long it was since any woman had spoken to her in that tone. It seemed to startle back her shattered wits. She rose to her feet, smiling airily.

"Madam, you are very kind. I believe I have had the pleasure of seeing you somewhere. Your name is——"

"Ursula Halifax. Do you remember?"—speaking gently, as she would have done to a child.

Lady Caroline bowed—a ghastly mockery of her former sprightly grace. "Not exactly; but I dare say I shall presently. *Au revoir*, madam!"

She was going away, kissing her hand—that yellow, wrinkled, old woman's hand—but John stopped her.

"My wife wants to speak to you, Lady Caroline. She wishes you to come home with us."

"*Plaît-il?* Oh yes, I understand. I shall be happy—most happy."

John offered her his arm with an air of grave deference; Mrs. Halifax supported her on the other side. Without more ado they put her in the carriage and drove home, leaving Maud in my charge, and leaving astounded Norton Bury to think and say—exactly what it pleased.

CHAPTER XXXVIII.

For nearly three years Lady Caroline lived in our house—if that miserable existence of hers could be called living—bedridden, fallen into second childhood;

"Pleased with a rattle, tickled with a straw;"

oblivious to both past and present, recognizing none of us, and taking no notice of anybody, except now and then of Edwin's little daughter, baby Louise.

We knew that all our neighbours talked us over, making far more than a nine days' wonder of the "very extraordinary conduct" of Mr. and Mrs. Halifax. That even good Lady Oldtower hesitated a little before she suffered her tribe of fair daughters to visit under the same roof where lay, quite out of the way, that poor wreck of womanhood, which would hardly have tainted any woman now. But in process of time the gossip ceased of itself; and when, one summer day, a small, decent funeral moved out of our garden gate to Enderley churchyard, all the comment was,—

"Oh! is she dead? What a relief it must be! How very kind of Mr. and Mrs. Halifax!"

Yes, she was dead, and had "made no sign," either of repentance, grief, or gratitude. Unless one could consider as such a moment's lightening before death, which Maud declared she saw in her—Maud, who had tended her with a devotedness which neither father nor mother forbade, believing that a woman cannot too soon learn womanhood's best "mission"—usefulness, tenderness, and charity. Miss Halifax was certain that, a few minutes before the last minute, she saw a gleam of sense in the filmy eyes, and stooping down, had caught some feeble murmur about "William—poor William!"

She did not tell me this; she spoke of it to no one but her mother, and to her briefly. So the wretched life, once beautiful and loveful, was now ended, or perhaps born in some new sphere to begin again its struggle after the highest beauty, the only perfect love. What are we that we should place limits to the infinite mercy of the Lord and Giver of life, unto whom all life returns?

We buried her and left her—poor Lady Caroline!

No one interfered with us, and we appealed to no one. In truth, there was no one unto whom we could appeal. Lord Luxmore, immediately after his father's funeral, had disappeared, whither no one knew except his solicitor, who treated with and entirely satisfied the host of creditors, and into whose hands the sole debtor, John Halifax, paid his yearly rent. Therewith he wrote several times to Lord Luxmore; but the letters were simply acknowledged through the lawyer, never answered. Whether in any of them John alluded to Lady Caroline I do not know; but I rather think not, as it would have served no purpose and only inflicted pain. No doubt her brother had long since believed her dead, as we and the world had done.

In that same world one man, even a nobleman, is of little account. Lord Ravenel sank in its wide waste of waters, and they closed over him. Whether he were drowned or saved was of small moment to any one. He was soon forgotten—everywhere except at Beechwood; and sometimes it seemed as if he were even forgotten there. Save that in our family we found it hard to learn this easy, convenient habit—to forget.

Hard, though seven years had passed since we saw Guy's merry face, to avoid missing it keenly still. The mother, as her years crept on, oftentimes wearied for him with a yearning that could not be told. The father, as Edwin became engrossed in his own affairs, and Walter's undecided temperament kept him a boy long after boyhood, often seemed to look round vaguely for an eldest son's young strength to lean upon, often said anxiously, "I wish Guy were at home."

Yet still there was no hint of his coming; better he never came at all than came against his will, or came to meet the least pain, the shadow of disgrace. And he was contented and prosperous in the western world, leading an active and useful life, earning an honourable name. He had taken a partner, he told us. There was real friendship between them, and they were doing well; perhaps might make, in a few years, one of those rapid fortunes which clever men of business do make in America, and did especially at that time.

He was also eager and earnest upon other and higher cares than mere business, entered warmly into his father's sympathy about many political measures now occupying men's minds. A great number of comparative facts concerning the factory children in England and America; a mass of evidence used by Mr. Fowell Buxton in his arguments for the abolition of slavery, and many other things, originated in the impulsive activity, now settled into mature manly energy, of Mr. Guy Halifax of Boston, U.S.—"our Guy."

"The lad is making a stir in the world," said his father one day, when we had read his last letter. "I shall not wonder if, when he comes home, a deputation from his native Norton Bury were to appear, requesting him to accept the honour of representing them in Parliament. He would suit them—at least, as regards the canvassing and the ladies—a great deal better than his old father—eh, love?"

Mrs. Halifax smiled, rather unwillingly, for her husband referred to a subject which had cost her some pain at the time. After the Reform Bill passed, many of our neighbours, who had long desired that one of John's high character, practical knowledge, and influence in the town, should be its M.P., and were aware that his sole objection to entering the House was the said question of Reform, urged him very earnestly to stand for Norton Bury.

To everybody's surprise, and none more than our own, he refused.

Publicly he assigned no reason for this except his conviction that he could not discharge as he ought, and as he would once have done, duties which he held so sacred and indispensable. His letter, brief and simple, thanking his "good neighbours," and wishing them "a younger and worthier" member, might be found in some old file of the *Norton Bury Herald* still. Even the *Norton Bury Mercury*, in reprinting it, commented on its touching honesty and brevity, and—concluding his political career was ended with it—condescended to bestow on Mr. Halifax the usual obituary line—

"We could have better spared a better man."

When his family, and even his wife, reasoned with him, knowing that to enter Parliament had long been his thought—nay, his desire—and perhaps herself taking a natural pride in the idea of seeing M.P.—M.P. of a new and unbribed House of Commons—after his well-beloved name—to us and to her he gave no clearer motive for his refusal than to the electors of Norton Bury.

"But you are not old, John," I argued with him one day. "You possess to the full the *mens sana in corpore sano*. No man can be more fitted than yourself to serve his country, as you used to say it might be served, and you yourself might serve it, after Reform was gained."

He smiled, and jocularly thanked me for my good opinion.

"Nay, such service is almost your duty; you yourself once thought so too. Why have you changed your mind?"

"I have not changed my mind, but circumstances have changed my actions. As for duty—duty begins at home. Believe me, I have thought well over the subject. Brother, we will not refer to it again."

I saw that something in the matter pained him, and obeyed his wish; even when, a few days after, perhaps as some compensation for the mother's disappointment, he gave this hint of Guy's taking his place and entering Parliament in his room.

For any one—nay, his own son—to take John's place, to stand in John's room, was not a pleasant thought, even in jest. We let it pass by unanswered, and John himself did not recur to it.

Thus time went on placidly enough; the father and mother changed into grandfather and grandmother, and little Maud into Auntie Maud. She bore her new honours and fulfilled her new duties with great delight and success. She had altered much of late years. At twenty was as old as many a woman of thirty—in all the advantages of age. She was sensible, active, resolute, and wise; sometimes thoughtful, or troubled with fits of what in any less wholesome temperament would have been melancholy; but as it was, her humours only betrayed themselves in some slight restlessness or irritability, easily soothed by a few tender words or a rush out to Edwin's, and a peaceful coming back to that happy home, whose principal happiness she knew that she, the only daughter, made.

She more than once had unexceptionable chances of quitting it; for Miss Halifax possessed plenty of attractions, both outwardly and inwardly, to say nothing of her not inconsiderable fortune. But she refused all offers, and to the best of our knowledge was a free-hearted damsel still. Her father and mother seemed rather glad of this than otherwise. They would not have denied her any happiness she wished for; still it was evidently a relief to them that she was slow in choosing it, slow in quitting their arms of love to risk a love untried. Sometimes, such is the weakness of parental humanity, I verily believe they looked forward with complacency to the possibility of her remaining always Miss Halifax. I remember one day, when Lady Oldtower was suggesting—half jest, half earnest—"better any marriage than no marriage at all," Maud's father replied very seriously,—

"Better no marriage than any marriage that is less than the best."

"How do you mean?"

"I believe," he said, smiling, "that somewhere in the world every man has his right wife, every woman her right husband. If my Maud's come, he shall have her. If not, I shall be well content to see her a happy old maid."

Thus, after many storms, came this lull in our lives; a season of busy yet monotonous calm. I have heard say that peace itself, to be perfect, ought to be monotonous. We had enough of it to satisfy our daily need; we looked forward to more of it in time to come, when Guy should be at home, when we should see safely secured the futures of all the children, and for ourselves a green old age,

"Journeying in long serenity away."

A time of heavenly calm, which, as I look back upon it, grows heavenlier still! Soft summer days and autumn afternoons, spent under the beech wood or on the Flat. Quiet winter evenings, all to ourselves—Maud and her mother working; Walter drawing; the father sitting with his back to the lamp—its light making a radiance over his brow and white bald crown, and as it thrilled through the curls behind, restoring somewhat of the youthful colour to his fading hair. Nay, the old youthful ring of his voice I caught at times, when he found something funny in his book and read it out loud to us; or laying it down, sat talking as he liked to talk about things speculative, philosophical, or poetical—things which he had necessarily let slip in the hurry and press of his business life, in the burthen and heat of the day; but which now, as the cool shadows of evening were drawing on, assumed a beauty and a nearness, and were again caught up by him—precious as the dreams of his youth.

Happy, happy time—sunshiny summer, peaceful winter—we marked neither as they passed; but now we hold both—in a sacredness inexpressible—a foretaste of that land where there is neither summer nor winter, neither days nor years.

The first break in our repose came early in the new year. There had been no Christmas letter from Guy, and he never once in all his wanderings had missed writing home at Christmas-time. When the usual monthly mail came in, and no word from him—a second month, and yet nothing—we began to wonder about his omission less openly, to cease scolding him for his carelessness. Though over and over again we still eagerly brought up instances of the latter—"Guy is such a thoughtless boy about his correspondence."

Gradually, as his mother's cheek grew paler, and his father more anxious-eyed, more compulsorily cheerful, we gave up discussing publicly the many excellent reasons why no letters should come from Guy. We had written, as usual, by every mail. By the last—by the

March mail—I saw that, in addition to the usual packet for Mr. Guy Halifax, his father, taking another precautionary measure, had written in business form to "Messrs. Guy Halifax and Co." Guy had always, "just like his carelessness!" omitted to give the name of his partner; but addressed thus, in case of any sudden journey or illness of Guy's, the partner, whoever he was, would be sure to write.

In May—nay, it was on May Day, I remember, for we were down in the mill meadows with Louise and her little ones going a-maying—there came in the American mail.

It brought a large packet—all our letters of this year sent back again, directed in a strange hand, to "John Halifax, Esquire, Beechwood," with the annotation, "By Mr. Guy Halifax's desire."

Among the rest—though the sickening sight of them had blinded even his mother at first, so that her eye did not catch it—was one that explained—most satisfactorily explained, we said—the reason they were thus returned. It was a few lines from Guy himself, stating that unexpected good fortune had made him determine to come home at once. If circumstances thwarted this intention, he would write without fail; otherwise he should most likely sail by an American merchantman—the *Stars-and-Stripes*.

"Then he is coming home. On his way home!"

And the mother, as with one shaking hand she held fast the letter, with the other steadied herself by the rail of John's desk—I guessed now why he had ordered all the letters to be brought first to his counting-house. "When do you think we shall see—Guy?"

At thought of that happy sight her bravery broke down. She wept heartily and long.

John sat still, leaning over the front of his desk. By his sigh, deep and glad, one could tell what a load was lifted off the father's heart at prospect of his son's return.

"The liners are only a month in sailing; but this is a barque, most likely, which takes longer time. Love, show me the date of the boy's letter."

She looked for it herself. It was in *January!*

The sudden fall from certainty to uncertainty, the wild clutch at that which hardly seemed a real joy until seen fading down to a mere hope, a chance, a possibility—who has not known all this ?

I remember how we all stood, mute and panic-struck, in the dark little counting-house. I remember seeing Louise, with her children in the doorway, trying to hush their laughing, and whispering to them something about "poor Uncle Guy."

John was the first to grasp the unspoken dread and show that it was less than at first appeared.

"We ought to have had this letter two months ago. This shows how often delays occur ; we ought not to be surprised or uneasy at anything. Guy does not say when the ship was to sail ; she may be on her voyage still. If he had but given the name of her owners! But I can write to Lloyd's and find out everything. Cheer up, mother. Please God, you shall have that wandering, heedless boy of yours back before long."

He replaced the letters in their enclosure, held a general consultation, into which he threw a passing gleam of faint gaiety, as to whether, being ours, we had a right to burn them, or whether, having passed through the post-office, they were not the writer's but the owner's property, and Guy could claim them, with all their useless news, on his arrival in England. This was finally decided, and the mother, with a faint smile, declared that nobody should touch them ; she would put them under lock and key "till Guy came home."

Then she took her husband's arm, and the rest of us followed them, as they walked slowly up the hill to Beechwood.

But after that day Mrs. Halifax's strength decayed. Not suddenly, scarcely perceptibly ; not with any outward complaint, except what she jested over as "the natural weakness of old age ;" but there was an evident change. Week by week her long walks shortened ; she gave up her village school to me ; and though she went about the house still, and insisted on keeping the keys, gradually, " just for the sake of practice," the domestic surveillance fell into the hands of Maud.

An answer arrived from Lloyd's : the *Stars-and-Stripes* was an American vessel, probably of small tonnage and importance, for the underwriters knew nothing of it.

More delay—more suspense. The summer days came, but not Guy. No news of him—not a word—not a line.

His father wrote to America, pursuing inquiries in all directions. At last some tangible clue was caught. The *Stars-and-Stripes* had sailed, had been spoken with about the Windward Isles, and never heard of afterwards.

Still, there was a hope. John told the hope first, before he ventured to speak of the missing ship, and even then had to break the news gently, for the mother had grown frail and weak, and could not bear things as she used to do. She clung, as if they had been words of life or death, to the shipowner's postscript—" that they had no recollection of the name of Halifax. There might have been such a gentleman on board ; they could not say. But it was not probable ; for the *Stars-and-Stripes* was a trading vessel, and had not good accommodation for passengers."

Then came week after week—I knew not how they went by—one never does, afterwards. At the time they were frightfully vivid, hour by hour. We rose each morning, sure that some hope would come in the course of the day ; we went to bed at night heavily, as if there were no such thing as hope in the world. Gradually, and I think that was the worst consciousness of all, our life of suspense became perfectly natural ; and everything in and about the house went on as usual, just as though we knew quite well—what the Almighty Father alone knew !—where our poor lad was, and what had become of him. Or rather, as if we had settled in the certainty, which perhaps the end of our own lives alone would bring us, that he had slipped out of life altogether, and there was no such being as Guy Halifax under this pitiless sun.

The mother's heart was breaking. She made no moan, but we saw it in her face. One morning—it was the morning after John's birthday, which we had made a feint of keeping, with Grace Oldtower, the two little grandchildren, Edwin, and Louise—she was absent at breakfast and dinner; she had not slept well, and was too tired to rise. Many days following it happened the same, with the same faint excuse, or with no excuse at all. How we missed her about the house!—ay, changed as she had been. How her husband wandered about, ghostlike, from room to room!—could not rest anywhere, or do anything. Finally he left our company altogether, and during the hours that he was at home rarely quitted for more than a few minutes the quiet bed-chamber, where, every time his foot entered it, the poor pale face looked up and smiled.

Ay, smiled; for I noticed, as many another may have done in similar cases, that when her physical health definitely gave way, her mental health returned. The heavy burthen was lighter; she grew more cheerful, more patient; seemed to submit herself to the Almighty will, whatever it might be. As she lay on her sofa in the study, where one or two evenings John carried her down, almost as easily as he used to carry little Muriel, his wife would rest content with her hand in his, listening to his reading, or quietly looking at him, as though her lost son's face, which a few weeks since she said haunted her continually, were now forgotten in his father's. Perhaps she thought the one she should soon see—while the other——

"Phineas," she whispered one day, when I was putting a shawl over her feet, or doing some other trifle that she thanked me for—"Phineas, if anything happens to me, you will comfort John!"

Then first I began seriously to contemplate a possibility, hitherto as impossible and undreamed of as that the moon should drop out of the height of heaven—What would the house be without the mother?

Her children never suspected this, I saw; but they were young. For her husband——

I could not understand John. He, so quick-sighted; he who, meeting any sorrow, looked steadily up at the Hand that smote him, knowing neither the coward's dread nor the unbeliever's disguise of pain—surely he must see what was impending. Yet he was as calm as if he saw it not. Calm, as no man could be contemplating the supreme parting between two who nearly all their lives had been not two, but one flesh.

Yet I had once heard him say that a great love, and only that, makes parting easy. Could it be that this love of his, which had clasped his wife so firmly, faithfully, and long, fearlessly clasped her still, by its own perfectness assured of its immortality?

But all the while his human love clung about her, showing itself in a thousand forms of watchful tenderness. And hers clung to him, closely, dependently; she let herself be taken care of, ruled and guided, as if with him she found helplessness restful and submission sweet. Many a little outward fondness, that when people have been long married naturally drops into disuse, was revived again; he would bring her flowers out of the garden, or new books from the town; and many a time, when no one noticed, I have seen him stoop and press his lips upon the faded hand, where the wedding ring hung so loosely—his own for so many years, his own till the dust claimed it, that well-beloved hand!

Ay, he was right. Loss, affliction, death itself are powerless in the presence of such a love as theirs.

It was already the middle of July. From January to July—six months! Our neighbours without—and there were many who felt for us—never asked now, "Is there any news of Mr. Guy?" Even pretty Grace Oldtower—pretty still, but youthful no longer—only lifted her eyes inquiringly as she crossed our doorway, and dropped them again with a hopeless sigh. She had loved us all, faithfully and well, for a great many years.

One night, when Miss Oldtower had just gone home

after staying with us the whole day, Maud and I sat in the study by ourselves, where we generally sat now. The father spent all his evenings upstairs. We could hear his step overhead as he crossed the room or opened the window, then drew his chair back to its constant place by his wife's bedside. Sometimes there was a faint murmur of reading or talk, then long silence.

Maud and I sat in silence too. She had her own thoughts—I mine. Perhaps they were often one and the same; perhaps—for youth is youth after all—they may have diverged widely. Hers were deep, absorbed thoughts, at any rate, travelling fast—fast as her needle travelled; for she had imperceptibly fallen into her mother's ways and her mother's work.

We had the lamp lit, but the windows were wide open, and through the sultry summer night we could hear the trickle of the stream and the rustle of the leaves in the beech wood. We sat very still, waiting for nothing, expecting nothing; in the dull patience which always fell upon us about this hour—the hour before bedtime, when nothing more was to be looked for but how best to meet another dreary day.

"Maud, was that the click of the front gate swinging?"

"No. I told Walter to lock it before he went to bed. Last night it disturbed my mother."

Again silence, so deep that the maid's opening the door made us both start.

"Miss Halifax—there's a gentleman wanting to see Miss Halifax."

Maud sprang up in her chair, breathless.

"Any one you know, is it?"

"No, miss."

"Show the gentleman in."

He stood already in the doorway—tall, brown, bearded. Maud just glanced at him, then rose, bending stiffly, after the manner of Miss Halifax of Beechwood.

"Will you be seated? My father——"

"Maud, don't you know me? Where's my mother? I am Guy."

CHAPTER XXXIX.

GUY and his mother were together. She lay on a sofa in her dressing-room; he sat on a stool beside her, so that her arm could rest on his neck and she could now and then turn his face towards her and look at it—oh, what a look!

She had had him with her for two whole days—two days to be set against eight years! Yet the eight years seemed already to have collapsed into a span of time, and the two days to have risen up a great mountain of happiness, making a barrier complete against the woeful past, as happiness can do—thanks to the All-merciful for His mercies. Most especially for that mercy—true as His truth to the experience of all pure hearts—that one bright, brief season of joy can outweigh, in reality and even in remembrance, whole years of apparently interminable pain.

Two days only since the night Guy came home, and yet it seemed months ago! Already we had grown familiar to the tall, bearded figure, the strange step and voice about the house; all except Maud, who was rather shy and reserved still. We had ceased to endeavour to reconcile this our Guy—this tall, grave man of nearly thirty, looking thirty-five and more—with Guy, the boy that left us, the boy that in all our lives we never should find again. Nevertheless we took him, just as he was, to our hearts, rejoicing in him one and all with inexpressible joy.

He was much altered, certainly. It was natural—nay, right—that he should be. He had suffered much, a great deal more than he ever told us—at least, not till long after—had gone through poverty, labour, sickness, shipwreck. He had written home by the *Stars-and-Stripes*—sailed a fortnight later by another vessel—been cast away—picked up by an outward-bound ship—and finally landed in England, he and his partner, as penniless as they left it.

"Was your partner an Englishman, then?" said Maud, who sat at the foot of the sofa, listening. "You have not told us anything about him yet."

Guy half smiled. "I will by-and-by. It's a long story. Just now I don't want to think of anybody or anything except my mother."

He turned, as he did twenty times a day, to press his rough cheek upon her hand and look up into her thin face, his eyes overflowing with love.

"You must get well now, mother. Promise!"

Her smile promised—and even began the fulfilment of the same.

"I think she looks stronger already—does she, Maud? You know her looks better than I. I don't ever remember her being ill in old times. O mother, I will never leave you again—never!"

"No, my boy."

"No, Guy, no." John came in, and stood watching them both contentedly. "No, my son, you must never leave your mother."

"I will not leave either of you, father," said Guy, with a reverent affection that must have gladdened the mother's heart to the very core. Resigning his place by her, Guy took Maud's, facing them; and father and son began to talk of various matters concerning their home and business arrangements; taking counsel together, as father and son ought to do. These eight years of separation seemed to have brought them nearer together; the difference between them—in age, far less than between most fathers and sons—had narrowed into a meeting-point. Never in all his life had Guy been so deferent, so loving, to his father. And with a peculiar trust and tenderness, John's heart turned to his eldest son, the heir of his name, his successor at Enderley Mills. For, in order that Guy might at once take his natural place, and feel no longer a waif and stray upon the world, already a plan had been started, that the firm of Halifax and Sons should become Halifax Brothers. Perhaps, ere very long—only the mother said privately, rather anxiously too, that she did not wish this part of the scheme to be mentioned to Guy just now—perhaps, ere long, it would be "Guy Halifax, Esquire of Beechwood," and "the old people" at happy little Longfield.

As yet Guy had seen nobody but ourselves, and nobody had seen Guy. Though his mother gave various good reasons why he should not make his public appearance as a "shipwrecked mariner," costume and all, yet it was easy to perceive that she looked forward not without apprehension to some meetings which must necessarily soon occur, but to which Guy made not the smallest allusion. He had asked, cursorily and generally, after "all my brothers and sisters," and been answered in the same tone; but neither he nor we had as yet mentioned the names of Edwin or Louise.

They knew he was come home; but how and where the first momentous meeting should take place we left entirely to chance, or, more rightly speaking, to Providence.

So it happened thus. Guy was sitting quietly on the sofa at his mother's feet, and his father and he were planning together in what way could best be celebrated, by our school-children, tenants, and workpeople, an event which we took a great interest in, though not greater than in this year was taken by all classes throughout the kingdom—the day fixed for the abolition of negro slavery in our colonies, the first of August 1834. He sat in an attitude that reminded me of his boyish lounging ways, the picture of content, though a stream of sunshine pouring in upon his head, through the closed Venetian blind, showed many a deep line of care on his forehead, and more than one silver thread among his brown hair.

In a pause—during which no one exactly liked to ask what we were all thinking about—there came a little tap at the door, and a little voice outside.

"Please, me want to come in."

Maud jumped up to refuse admission; but Mr. Halifax forbade her, and himself went and opened the door. A little child stood there—a little girl of three years old.

Apparently guessing who she was, Guy rose up hastily, and sat down in his place again.

"Come in, little maid," said the father; "come in, and tell us what you want."

"Me want to see grannie and Uncle Guy."

Guy started, but still he kept his seat. The mother took her grandchild in her feeble arms, and kissed her, saying softly,—

"There—that is Uncle Guy. Go and speak to him."

And then, touching his knees, Guy felt the tiny, fearless hand. He turned round, and looked at the little thing reluctantly, inquisitively. Still he did not speak to or touch her.

"Are you Uncle Guy?"

"Yes."

"Why don't you kiss me? Everybody kisses me," said everybody's pet, neither frightened nor shy, never dreaming of a repulse.

Nor did she find it. Her little fingers were suffered to cling round the tightly-closed hand.

"What is your name, my dear?"

"Louise—mamma's little Louise."

Guy put back the curls, and gazed long and wistfully into the childish face, where the inherited beauty was repeated line for line. But softened, spiritualized, as, years after its burial, some ghost of a man's old sorrows may rise up and meet him, the very spirit of peace shining out of its celestial eyes.

"Little Louise, you are very like——"

He stopped, and bending down, kissed her. In that kiss vanished for ever the last shadow of his boyhood's love. Not that he forgot it—God forbid that any good man should ever either forget or be ashamed of his first love! But it and all its pain fled far away, back into the sacred eternities of dreamland.

When, looking up at last, he saw a large, fair, matronly lady sitting by his mother's sofa, Guy neither started nor turned pale. It was another, and not his lost Louise. He rose and offered her his hand.

"You see, your little daughter has made friends with me already. She is very like you, only she has Edwin's hair. Where is my brother Edwin?"

"Here, old fellow. Welcome home."

The two brothers met warmly—nay, affectionately. Edwin was not given to demonstration; but I saw how his features twitched, and how he busied himself over the knots in his little girl's pinafore for a minute or more. When he spoke again, it was as if nothing had happened, and Guy had never been away.

For the mother, she lay with her arms folded, looking from one to the other mutely, or closing her eyes with a faint stirring of the lips, like prayer. It seemed as if she dared only *thus* to meet her exceeding joy.

Soon Edwin and Louise left us for an hour or two, and Guy went on with the history of his life in America and his partner who had come home with him, and, like himself, had lost his all.

"Harder for him than for me; he is older than I am. He knew nothing whatever of business when he offered himself as my clerk; since then he has worked like a slave. In a fever I had he nursed me; he has been to me these three years the best, truest friend. He is the noblest fellow. Father, if you only knew——"

"Well, my son, let me know him. Invite the gentleman to Beechwood; or shall I write and ask him?—Maud, fetch me your mother's desk.—Now then, Guy—you are a very forgetful fellow still; you have never yet told us your friend's name."

Guy looked steadily at his father, in his own straightforward way, hesitated—then apparently made up his mind.

"I did not tell you because he wished me not—not till you understood him as well as I do. You knew him yourself once; but he has wisely dropped his title. Since he came over to me in America he has been only Mr. William Ravenel."

This discovery, natural enough when one began to think over it, but incredible at first, astounded us all.

For Maud—well was it that the little Louise seated in her lap hid and controlled in some measure the violent agitation of poor Auntie Maud.

Ay—Maud loved him. Perhaps she had guessed the secret cause of his departure, and love creates love oftentimes. Then his brave renunciation of rank, fortune, even of herself—women glory in a moral hero—one who has strength to lose even love, and bear its loss, for the sake of duty or of honour. His absence, too, might have done much—absence which smothers into decay a rootless fancy, but often nourishes the least seed of a true affection into full-flowering love. Ay—Maud loved him. How, or why, or when at first no one could tell—perhaps not even herself; but so it was, and her parents saw it.

Both were deeply moved—her brother likewise.

"Father," he whispered, "have I done wrong? I did not know. How could I guess?"

"No, no—my son. It is very strange—all things just now seem so strange.—Maud, my child"—and John roused himself out of a long silence into which he was falling—"go, and take Louise to her mother."

The girl rose, eager to get away. As she crossed the room—the little creature clinging round her neck, and she clasping it close, in the sweet motherliness of character which had come to her so early—I thought—I hoped——

"Maud!" said John, catching her hand as she passed him by—"Maud is not afraid of her father?"

"No"—in troubled uncertainty; then with a passionate decision, as if ashamed of herself, "No!"

She leaned over her chair back and kissed him, then went out.

"Now—Guy."

Guy told, in his own frank way, all the history of himself and William Ravenel; how the latter had come to America, determined to throw his lot for good or ill, to sink or swim, with Maud's brother—chiefly, as Guy had slowly discovered, because he was Maud's brother. At last—in the open boat, on the Atlantic, with death the great revealer of all things staring them in the face—the whole secret came out. It made them better than friends—brothers.

This was Guy's story, told with a certain spice of determination too—as if, let his father's will be what it might, his own, which had now also settled into the strong "family" will, was resolute on his friend's behalf. Yet when he saw how grave—nay, sad—the father sat, he became humble again, and ended his tale even as he had begun, with the entreaty, "Father, if you only knew——"

"My knowing and my judging seem to have been of little value, my son. Be it so. There is One wiser than I—One in whose hands are the issues of all things."

The sort of contrition with which he spoke—thus retracting, as it costs most men much to retract, a decision given, however justly at the time, but which fate has afterwards pronounced unjust, affected his son deeply.

"Father, your decision was right; William says it was. He says also that it could not have been otherwise; that whatever he has become since, he owes it all to you, and to what passed that day. Though he loves her still, will never love any one else, yet he declares his loss of her has proved his salvation."

"He is right," said Mrs. Halifax. "Love is worth nothing that will not stand trial—a fiery trial, if needs be. And as I have heard John say many and many a time—as he said that very night—in this world there is not, ought not to be, any such words as 'too late.'"

John made no answer. He sat, his chin propped on his right hand, the other pressed against his bosom—his favourite attitude. Once or twice, with a deep-drawn, painful breath, he sighed.

Guy's eagerness could not rest. "Father, I told him I would either write to or see him to-day."

"Where is he?"

"At Norton Bury. Nothing would induce him to come here, unless certain that you desired it."

"I do desire it."

Guy started up with great joy. "Shall I write, then?"

"I will write myself."

But John's hand shook so much, that instead of his customary free, bold writing, he left only blots upon the page. He leant back in his chair, and said faintly,—

"I am getting an old man, I see. Guy, it was high time you came home."

Mrs. Halifax thought he was tired, and made a place for his head on her pillow, where he rested some minutes, "just to please her," he said. Then he rose, and declared he would himself drive over to Norton Bury for our old friend.

"Nay, let me write, father. To-morrow will do just as well."

The father shook his head. "No—it must be to-day."

Bidding good-bye to his wife—he never by any chance quitted her for an hour without a special tender leave-taking—John went away.

Guy was, he avouched, "as happy as a king." His old liveliness returned; he declared that in this matter, which had long weighed heavily on his mind, he had acted like a great diplomatist, or like the gods themselves, whom some unexacting, humble youth calls upon to

> "Annihilate both time and space,
> And make two lovers happy!"

"And I'm sure I shall be happy too in seeing them. They shall be married immediately. And we'll take William into partnership—that was a whim of his, mother—we call one another 'Guy' and 'William,' just like brothers. Heigho! I'm very glad. Are not you?"

The mother smiled. "You will soon have nobody left but me. No matter. I shall have you all to myself, and be at once a spoiled child and an uncommonly merry old bachelor."

Again the mother smiled, without reply. She, too, doubtless thought herself a great diplomatist.

William Ravenel—he was henceforward never anything

to us but William—came home with Mr. Halifax. First, the mother saw him; then I heard the father go to the maiden bower where Maud had shut herself up all day —poor child!—and fetch his daughter down. Lastly, I watched the two—Mr. Ravenel and Miss Halifax—walk together down the garden and into the beech wood, where the leaves were whispering and the stock-doves cooing, and where, I suppose, they told and listened to the old tale—old as Adam—yet for ever beautiful and new.

That day was a wonderful day. That night we gathered, as we never thought we should gather again in this world, round the family table—Guy, Edwin, Walter, Maud, Louise, and William Ravenel—all changed, yet not one lost. A true love-feast it was, a renewed celebration of the family bond, which had lasted through so much sorrow, now knitted up once more, never to be broken.

When we came quietly to examine one another and fall into one another's old ways, there was less than one might have expected even of outward change. The table appeared the same; all took instinctively their old places, except that the mother lay on her sofa and Maud presided at the urn.

It did one's heart good to look at Maud, as she busied herself about, in her capacity as *vice-reine* of the household; perhaps, with a natural feeling, liking to show some one present how mature and sedate she was—not so very young after all. You could see she felt deeply how much he loved her—how her love was to him like the restoring of his youth. The responsibility, sweet as it was, made her womanly, made her grave. She would be to him at once wife and child, plaything and comforter, sustainer and sustained. Ay, love levels all things. They were not ill-matched, in spite of those twenty years.

And so I left them, and went and sat with John and Ursula—we, the generation passing away, or ready to pass, in Heaven's good time, to make room for these.

We talked but little, our hearts were too full. Early, before anybody thought of moving, John carried his wife upstairs again, saying that, well as she looked, she must be compelled to economize both her good looks and her happiness.

When he came down again he stood talking for some time with Mr. Ravenel. While he talked I thought he looked wearied—pallid even to exhaustion; a minute or two afterwards he silently left the room.

I followed him, and found him leaning against the chimneypiece in his study.

"Who's that?" He spoke feebly; he looked—ghastly!

I called him by his name.

"Come in. Fetch no one. Shut the door."

The words were hoarse and abrupt, but I obeyed.

"Phineas," he said, again holding out a hand, as if he thought he had grieved me, "don't mind. I shall be better presently. I know quite well what it is—oh, my God—my God!"

Sharp, horrible pain—such as human nature shrinks from—such as makes poor mortal flesh cry out in its agony to its Maker, as if, for the time being, life itself were worthless at such a price. I know now what it must have been; I know now what he must have endured.

He held me fast, half unconscious as he was, lest I should summon help; and when a step was heard in the passage, as once before—the day Edwin was married—how, on a sudden, I remembered all!—he tottered forward and locked, double-locked, the door.

After a few minutes the worst suffering abated, and he sat down again in his chair. I got some water. He drank, and let me bathe his face with it—his face, gray and deathlike—John's face!

But I am telling the bare facts—nothing more.

A few heavy sighs, gasped as it were for life, and he was himself again.

"Thank God, it is over now! Phineas, you must try

and forget all you have seen. I wish you had not come to the door."

He said this, not in any tone that could wound me, but tenderly, as if he were very sorry for me.

"What is it ?"

"There is no need for alarm—no more than that day—you recollect ?—in this room. I had an attack once before then—a few times since. It is horrible pain while it lasts, you see ; I can hardly bear it. But it goes away again, as you also see. It would be a pity to tell my wife, or anybody ; in fact, I had rather not. You understand ?"

He spoke thus in a matter-of-fact way, as if he thought the explanation would satisfy me and prevent my asking further. He was mistaken.

"John, what is it ?"

"What is it ? Why, something like what I had then ; but it comes rarely, and I am well again directly. I had much rather not talk about it. Pray forget it."

But I could not ; nor, I thought, could he. He took up a book and sat still ; though oftentimes I caught his eyes fixed on my face with a peculiar earnestness, as if he would fain test my strength—fain find out how much I loved him, anu loving, how much I could bear.

"You are not reading, John ; you are thinking—what about ?"

He paused a little, as if undetermined whether or not to tell me, then said, "About your father. Do you remember him ?"

I looked surprised at the question.

"I mean, do you remember how he died ?"

Somehow—though, God knows, not at that dear and sacred remembrance—I shuddered. "Yes ; but why should we talk of it now ?"

"Why not ? I have often thought what a happy death it was—painless, instantaneous, without any wasting sickness beforehand—his sudden passing from life present to life eternal. Phineas, your father's was the happiest death I ever knew."

"It may be—I am not sure. John," for again something in his look and manner struck me, "why do you say this to me?"

"I scarcely know. Yes, I do know."

"Tell me, then."

He looked at me across the table—steadily, eye to eye, as if he would fain impart to my spirit the calmness that was in his own. "I believe, Phineas, that when I die my death will be not unlike your father's."

Something came wildly to my lips about "impossibility," the utter impossibility, of any man's thus settling the manner of his death, or the time.

"I know that. I know that I may live ten or twenty years, and die of another disease after all."

"Disease!"

"Nay—it is nothing to be afraid of. You see I am not afraid. I have guessed it for many years. I have known it for a certainty ever since I was in Paris."

"Were you ill in Paris? You never said so."

"No; because—— Phineas, do you think you could bear the truth? You know it makes no real difference. I shall not die an hour sooner for being aware of it."

"Aware of—what? Say quickly."

"Dr. K—— told me—I was determined to be told—that I had the disease I suspected, beyond medical power to cure. It is not immediately fatal. He said I might live many years, even to old age; and I might die suddenly, at any moment, just as your father died."

He said this gently and quietly—more quietly than I am writing the words down now; and I listened—I listened.

"Phineas!"

I felt the pressure of his warm hand on my shoulder—the hand which had led me like a brother's all my life.

"Phineas, we have known one another these forty years. Is our love, our faith, so small, that either of us, for himself or his brother, need be afraid of death?"

"Phineas!"—and the second time he spoke there was some faint reproach in the tone—"no one knows this but you. I see I was right to hesitate; I almost wish I had not told you at all."

Then—I rose.

* * * * * *

At my urgent request he explained to me fully and clearly the whole truth. It was, as most truths are, less terrible when wholly known. It had involved little suffering as yet, the paroxysms being few and rare. They had always occurred when he was alone, or when feeling them coming on he could go away and bear them in solitude.

"I have always been able to do so until to-night. She has not the least idea—my wife, I mean."

His voice failed.

"It has been terrible to me at times, the thought of my wife. Perhaps I ought to have told her. Often I resolved I would, and then changed my mind. Latterly, since she has been ill, I have believed, almost hoped, that she would not need to be told at all."

"Would you rather, then, that she——"

John calmly took up the word I shrank from uttering. "Yes, I would rather of the two that she went away first. She would suffer less, and it would be such a short parting."

He spoke as one would speak of a new abode, an impending journey. To him the great change, the last terror of humanity, was a thought—solemn, indeed, but long familiar and altogether without fear. And as we sat there, something of his spirit passed into mine: I felt how narrow is the span between the life mortal and the life immortal—how, in truth, both are one with God.

"Ay," he said, "that is exactly what I mean. To me there is always something impious in the 'preparing for death' that people talk about; as if we were not continually, whether in the flesh or out of it, living in the Father's presence; as if, come when He will, the Master should not find all of us watching? Do you remember saying so to me one day?"

Ah, that day!

"Does it pain you, my talking thus? Because, if so, we will cease."

"No—go on."

"That is right. I thought, this attack having been somewhat worse than my last, some one ought to be told. It has been a comfort to me to tell you—a great comfort, Phineas. Always remember that."

I have remembered it.

"Now, one thing more, and my mind is at ease. You see, though I may have years of life—I hope I shall—many busy years—I am never sure of a day, and I have to take many precautions. At home I shall be quite safe now." He smiled again, with evident relief. "And I rarely go anywhere without having one of my boys with me. Still, for fear—look here."

He showed me his pocket-book; on a card bearing his name and address was written in his own legible hand, "*Home, and tell my wife carefully.*"

I returned the book. As I did so, there dropped out a little note—all yellow and faded—his wife's only "love-letter"—signed, "Yours sincerely, Ursula March."

John picked it up, looked at it, and put it back in its place.

"Poor darling! poor darling!" He sighed, and was silent for a while. "I am glad Guy has come home; very glad that my little Maud is so happily settled. Hark! how those children are laughing!"

For the moment a natural shade of regret crossed the father's face, the father to whom all the delights of home had been so dear. But it soon vanished.

"How merry they are! How strangely things have come about for us and ours! As Ursula was saying to-night, at this moment we have not a single care."

I grasped at that, for Dr. K—— had declared that if John had a quiet life—a life without many anxieties—he might, humanly speaking, attain a good old age.

"Ay, your father did. Who knows? we may both be old men yet, Phineas."

And as he rose he looked strong in body and mind,

full of health and cheer—scarcely even on the verge of that old age of which he spoke. And I was older than he.

"Now, will you come with me to say good-night to the children?"

At first I thought I could not—then, I could. After the rest had merrily dispersed, John and I stood for a long time in the empty parlour, his hand on my shoulder, as he used to stand when we were boys, talking.

What we said I shall not write, but I remember it, every word. And he—I *know* he remembers it still.

Then we clasped hands.

"Good-night, Phineas."

"Good-night, John."

CHAPTER XL.

FRIDAY, the first of August 1834.

Many may remember that day. What a soft, gray, summer morning it was, and how it broke out into brightness; how everywhere bells were ringing, club fraternities walking with bands and banners, school-children having feasts and workpeople holidays; how, in town and country, there was spread abroad a general sense of benevolent rejoicing—because honest old England had lifted up her generous voice, nay, had paid down cheerfully her twenty millions, and in all her colonies the negro was free.

Many may still find, in some forgotten drawer, the medal—bought by thousands and tens of thousands, of all classes, in copper, silver, or gold—distributed in charity schools, and given by old people to their grand-children. I saw Mrs. Halifax tying one with a piece of blue ribbon round little Louise's neck, in remembrance of this day. The pretty medal, with the slave standing upright, stretching out to Heaven free hands, from which the fetters are dropping—as I overheard John say to his wife, he could fancy the freeman Paul would stand in the Roman prison, when he answered to those that loved him, "*I have fought the good fight. I have finished my course. I have kept the faith.*"

Now, with my quickened ears, I often heard John talking quietly to his wife in this wise.

He remained by her side the whole forenoon, wheeling her about in her garden-chair, taking her to see her school-children in their glory on our lawn—to hear the shouts rising up from the people at the mill yard below. For all Enderley, following the master's example, took an interest, hearty even among hearty hard-working England, in the Emancipation of the Slaves.

We had our own young people round us, and the day was a glorious day, they declared one and all.

John was happy too—infinitely happy. After dinner he carried his wife to her chair beside the weeping ash, where she could smell the late hay in the meadow, and hear the ripple of the stream in the beech wood—faint, for it was almost dried up now, but pleasant still. Her husband sat on the grass, making her laugh with his quaint sayings—admiring her in her new bonnet, and in the lovely white shawl—Guy's shawl—which Mr. Guy himself had really no time for admiring. He had gone off to the school tea-drinking, escorting his sister and sister-in-law, and another lady, whose eyes brightened with most "sisterly" joy whenever she glanced at her old playfellow. Guy's "sister" she nevertheless was not, nor was ever likely to be; and I questioned whether, in his secret heart, he had not begun already to feel particularly thankful for that circumstance.

"Ah, mother," cried the father, smiling, "you'll see how it will end: all our young birds will soon be flown; there will be nobody left but you and me."

"Never mind, John;" and stooping over him, she gave him one of her quiet, soft kisses, precious now she was an old woman as they had been in the days of her bloom. "Never mind. Once there were only our two selves—now there will be only our two selves again. We shall be very happy. We only need one another."

"Only one another, my darling."

This last word, and the manner of his saying it, I can hear if I listen in silence, clear as if yet I heard its sound. This last sight—of them sitting under the ash tree, the sun making still whiter Ursula's white shawl, brightening the marriage ring on her bare hand, and throwing, instead of silver, some of their boyish gold-colour into the edges of John's curls—this picture I see with my shut eyes, vivid as yesterday.

I sat for some time in my room; then John came to fetch me for our customary walk along his favourite "terrace" on the Flat. He rarely liked to miss it. He said the day hardly seemed complete or perfect unless one had seen the sun set. Thus, almost every evening, we used to spend an hour or more pacing up and down, or sitting in that little hollow under the brow of the Flat, where, as from the topmost seat of a natural amphitheatre, one could see Rose Cottage and the old well-head where the cattle drank; our own green garden gate, the dark mass of the beech wood, and far away beyond that Nunneley Hill, where the sun went down.

There, having walked somewhat less time than usual, for the evening was warm and it had been a fatiguing day, John and I sat down together. We talked a little, ramblingly—chiefly of Longfield: how I was to have my old room again, and how a new nursery was to be planned for the grandchildren.

"We can't get out of the way of children, I see clearly," he said, laughing. "We shall have Longfield just as full as ever it was all summer-time. But in winter we'll be quiet, and sit by the chimney-corner, and plunge into my dusty desert of books—eh, Phineas? You shall help me to make notes for those lectures I have intended giving at Norton Bury these ten years past. And we'll rub up our old Latin, and dip into modern poetry—great rubbish, I fear! Nobody like our old friend Will of Avon, or even your namesake, worthy Phineas Fletcher."

I reminded him of the "Shepherd's life and fate," which he always liked so much, and used to say was his ideal of peaceful happiness.

"Well, and I think so still. 'Keep true to the dreams of thy youth,' saith the old German. I have not been false to mine. I have had a happy life, thank God—ay, and what few men can say, it has been the very sort of happiness I myself would have chosen. I think most lives, if, while faithfully doing our little best, day by day, we were content to leave their thread in wiser hands than ours, would thus weave themselves out, until, looked back upon as a whole, they would seem as bright a web as mine."

He sat, talking thus, resting his chin on his hands, his eyes, calm and sweet, looking out westward, where the sun was about an hour from the horizon.

"Do you remember how we used to lie on the grass in your father's garden, and how we never could catch the sunset except in fragments between the Abbey trees? I wonder if they keep the yew hedge clipped as round as ever."

I told him Edwin had said to-day that some strange tenants were going to make an inn of the old house, and turn the lawn into a bowling-green.

"What a shame! I wish I could prevent it. And yet, perhaps not," he added, after a silence. "Ought we not rather to recognize and submit to the universal law of change? how each in his place is fulfilling his day, and passing away, just as that sun is passing. Only we know not whither he passes; while whither we go we know, and the Way we know—the same yesterday, to-day, and for ever."

Almost before he had done speaking (God grant that in the Kingdom I may hear that voice, not a tone altered —I would not wish it altered even there) a whole troop of our young people came out of Mrs. Tod's cottage, and nodded to us from below.

There was Mrs. Edwin, standing talking to the good old soul, who admired her baby boy very much, but wouldn't allow there could be any children like Mrs. Halifax's children.

There was Edwin, deep in converse with his brother

Guy, while beside them—prettier and younger-looking than ever—Grace Oldtower was making a posy for little Louise.

Further down the slope, walking slowly, side by side, evidently seeing nobody but one another, were another couple.

"I think sometimes, John, that those two, William and Maud, will be the happiest of all the children."

He smiled, looked after them for a minute, and then laid himself quietly down on his back along the slope, his eyes still directed towards the sunset. When, brightening as it descended, the sun shone level upon the place where we were sitting, I saw John pull his broad straw hat over his face, and compose himself, with both hands clasped upon his breast, in the attitude of sleep.

I knew he was very tired, so I spoke no more, but threw my cloak over him. He looked up, thanked me silently, with his old familiar smile. One day—one day I shall know him by that smile! I sat half an hour or more watching the sun, which sank steadily, slowly, round, and red, without a single cloud. Beautiful as I had never before seen it; so clear that one could note the very instant its disc touched the horizon's gray.

Maud and Mr. Ravenel were coming up the slope. I beckoned them to come softly, not to disturb the father. They and I sat in silence, facing the west. The sun journeyed down to his setting—lower—lower; there was a crescent, a line, a dim sparkle of light; then—he was gone. And still we sat—grave, but not sad—looking into the brightness he had left behind, believing—yea, knowing—we should see his glorious face again to-morrow.

"How cold it has grown!" said Maud. "I think we ought to wake my father."

She went up to him, laid her hand upon his, that were folded together over the cloak—drew back startled—alarmed.

"Father!"

I put the child aside. It was I who moved the hat from John's face—*the* face—for John himself was far, far away, gone from us unto Him whose faithful servant he was. While he was sleeping thus the Master had called him.

His two sons carried him down the slope. They laid him in the upper room in Mrs. Tod's cottage. Then I went home to tell his wife.

* * * * * *

She was at last composed, as we thought, lying on her bed, deathlike almost, but calm. It was ten o'clock at night. I left her with all her children watching round her.

I went out, up to Rose Cottage, to sit an hour by myself alone, looking at him whom I should not see again for—as he had said—" a little while."

" A little while—a little while." I comforted myself with those words. I fancied I could almost hear John saying them, standing near me, with his hand on my shoulder—John himself, quite distinct from that which lay so still before me, beautiful as nothing but death can be, younger much than he had looked this very morning—younger by twenty years.

Farewell, John! Farewell, my more than brother! It is but for a little while.

As I sat, thinking how peacefully the hands lay, clasped together still, how sweet was the expression of the close mouth, and what a strange shadowy likeness the whole face bore to Muriel's little face, which I had seen resting in the same deep rest on the same pillow, some one touched me. It was Mrs. Halifax.

How she came I do not know; nor how she had managed to steal out from among her children; nor how she who had not walked for weeks had found her way up hither, in the dark, all alone; nor what strength, almost more than mortal, helped her to stand there, as she did stand, upright and calm, gazing—gazing as I had done.

" It is very like him; don't you think so, Phineas?" The voice low and soft, unbroken by any sob. " He once told me, in case of—this, he would rather I did not come and look at him; but I can, you see."

I gave her my place, and she sat down by the bed. It might have been ten minutes or more that she and I remained thus, without exchanging a word.

"I think I hear some one at the door. Brother, will you call in the children?"

Guy, altogether overcome, knelt down beside his mother, and besought her to let him take her home.

"Presently—presently, my son. You are very good to me; but—your father. Children, come in and look at your father."

They all gathered round her—weeping; but she spoke without a single tear.

"I was a girl, younger than any of you, when first I met your father. Next month we shall have been married thirty-three years. Thirty-three years."

Her eyes grew dreamy, as if fancy had led her back all that space of time. Her fingers moved to and fro mechanically over her wedding-ring.

"Children, we were so happy, you cannot tell. He was so good; he loved me so. Better than that, he made me good; that was why I loved him. Oh, what his love was to me from the first!—strength, hope, peace; comfort and help in trouble, sweetness in prosperity. How my life became happy and complete! how I grew worthier to myself because he had taken me for his own! And what *he* was—— Children, no one but me ever knew all his goodness, no one but himself ever knew how dearly I loved your father. We were more precious each to each than anything on earth; except His service, who gave us to one another."

Her voice dropped all but inaudible; but she roused herself, and made it once more clear and firm, the mother's natural voice.

"Guy, Edwin, all of you, must never forget your father. You must do as he wishes, and live as he lived—in all ways. You must love him, and love one another. Children, you will never do anything that need make you ashamed to meet your father."

As they hung round her she kissed them all—her three

sons and her daughter, one by one; then, her mind being perhaps led astray by the room we were in, looked feebly round for one more child—remembered—smiled.

"How glad her father will be to have her again—his own little Muriel."

"Mother! mother darling! come home," whispered Guy, almost in a sob.

His mother stooped over him, gave him one kiss more—him her favourite of all her children—and repeated the old phrase,—

"Presently, presently! Now go away, all of you; I want to be left for a little, alone with my husband."

As we went out, I saw her turn toward the bed. "John, John!" The same tone, almost the same words, with which she had crept up to him years before, the day they were betrothed. Just a low, low murmur, like a tired child creeping to fond, protecting arms. "John, John!"

We closed the door. We all sat on the stairs outside; it might have been for minutes, it might have been for hours. Within or without—no one spoke—nothing stirred.

At last Guy softly went in.

She was still in the same place by the bedside, but half lying on the bed, as I had seen her turn when I was shutting the door. Her arm was round her husband's neck; her face, pressed inwards to the pillow, was nestled close to his hair. They might have been asleep—both of them.

One of her children called her, but she neither answered nor stirred.

Guy lifted her up very tenderly; his mother, who had no stay left but him—his mother—a widow——

No, thank God! she was not a widow now.

THE END.